Blink of an Eye

Blink of an Eye

John H. K. Fisher

Winchester, UK
Washington, USA

JOHN HUNT PUBLISHING

First published by Cosmic Egg Books, 2019
Cosmic Egg Books is an imprint of John Hunt Publishing Ltd., 3 East St., Alresford,
Hampshire SO24 9EE, UK
office@jhpbooks.com
www.johnhuntpublishing.com

For distributor details and how to order please visit the 'Ordering' section on our website.

ISBN: 978 1 78535 205 8
978 1 78535 206 5 (ebook)
Library of Congress Control Number: 2015943110

A CIP catalogue record for this book is available from the British Library.

Design: Stuart Davies

UK: Printed and bound by CPI Group (UK) Ltd, Croydon, CR0 4YY
US: Printed and bound by Thomson-Shore, 7300 West Joy Road, Dexter, MI 48130

Chapter 1

The Interrogation

"The martyr cannot be dishonored. Every lash inflicted is a tongue of fame; every prison a more illustrious abode."
Ralph Waldo Emerson

'What doesn't kill ya', makes ya' stronger', or so the saying goes, but Hamasa weakened by the minute. On the second day of interrogation, Hamasa was not yet an open book, but interrogators have their methods. The captive begins by thinking they would rather die in agony than reveal their secrets. Some start talking when they are given a reason to live, or on the promise of a mother or brother protected and allowed to live out their lives in peace. Others sell their soul for the promise of vast sums of money to enable them to escape all the madness in a faraway haven.

For Hamasa, the key was not the money nor the pain, but the woman he had fallen in love with, Nayanna. He assumed they had taken her, too, and he knew his captors would not hesitate to destroy her in order to get what they wanted from him.

"Pay attention would ya'!" snarled Mike.

"You keep blanking out on us! Don't close your eyes when we're talking to you!" snapped agent Harlan.

Mike and Harlan never had a good reputation with Hamasa. He knew they were in it for the power and money. What else could they do: stock shelves at the local grocery store? Who would want to hire the local bullies? Now he was at their mercy. Israeli Intelligence officers interrogating him in America, how could he be surprised?

He forced himself to a show of calmness. "Hey, guys, you don't have to yell. I've told you everything, believe me! Nayanna means the world to me. I'd sacrifice my life to save hers. You've got to realize, right now we also have the responsibility of protecting the whole planet."

"Ha ha." The two agents laughed so hard the coffee Mike had just swallowed began to cough up, washing over his tongue and dribbling out the corners of his mouth, splattering all over Hamasa.

"You keep talkin' crap 'bout savin' the world and we'll just have to put a bullet in your head – save us the misery of having to hear this bullshit talk. You got that?" Mike yelled, drowning out the obscenities spewing from Hamasa as he tried to shake off the coffee spilled on him.

Mike looked over at Harlan, who was bashing his palm on his forehead. "Imagine, a gun for hire is suddenly Earth's greatest humanitarian," he scoffed. "Harlan, what the hell are we doing here?"

"I don't know." Harlan shook his head, his expression morose. "But we had more fun yesterday, beating the crap out of him." He turned to Hamasa. "Remember, nobody even knows you're missing, or where you are, no colleagues, no governments, and no family. Where are friends and family when you need them, huh? Do you know how easy it would be to make you disappear, or your loved ones for that matter? You should be pissin' your pants by now, telling us everything we need to know."

Old snake eyes, as Hamasa privately thought of Agent Harlan, flicked an icy gaze over him. He was playing into Hamasa's fears and vulnerabilities.

"Tell me, Hamasa, why aren't you screaming for mercy? You got a special place in your head you go to or something? Is that your secret? Is that all you have to save you?"

Harlan made a derogatory sound in his throat. "I mean – you keep talking rubbish about some mystical experiences and 'saving the world' crap, closing your eyes on us as if you're trying to tell us you have something going on in there. We're not going to fall for that." He grabbed Hamasa by the throat, shaking him like a terrier with a rat.

"I don't see the usual fear I aught'a be seein' from you, but we're gettin' there." Harlan barred his teeth in something vaguely resembling a smile and finally let go of Hamasa with a slap to his face.

"We need to step things up a notch, so you start to realize what we're capable of doing to you to make you talk."

He treated Hamasa to another flat, chilling stare. "It's beyond fear," he persisted. "I want to see the terror in your eyes, like a little fawn that's being torn apart by a pack of hungry wolves."

He glanced at his partner, and this time his smile had real warmth behind it, as if to egg Mike on.

Mike took another sip of his coffee and intentionally splattered it over Hamasa. "I think we should bring out a few tools of the trade," he crowed, "show this guy how we're going to 'save the world' from these kinds of..."

"OK, boys, we'll call it a wrap for now," commanded a tall, slim figure who entered the room with a quiet purpose, like a vulture circling its prey.

The two agents looked up at the striking man who moved with a fluid, feline grace. He had appeared in the large subterraneous room from a side door, over by the mirrored wall, which gave everyone ample time to size him up.

Hamasa thought it strange his footsteps didn't echo throughout the place as the others did. He also looked way up to stare at the clean-shaven, black-haired man, meticulously attired in an authoritative blue suit. His slicked back hair and the shine on his hand-made, leather shoes looked out of place in the gray, mildewed cave. The place was carved out of the rock, deep underground as though it had been an abandoned mine. "Hey, you saw that, right? Spittin' on me like I'm an animal. Wait 'til my lawyer hears about all this abuse," Hamasa threatened. His nostrils, filled with the scent of fresh brew, kept him in the moment.

"Guys, we got to show some respect. He's one of ours," contested Harold.

The two agents started to leave, grumbling amongst themselves... "He's gotta show us respect, too, Harold!"

"By confessing!" shouted Mike as he glared at Hamasa.

"Yeah!" echoed Harlan.

"And by stop going into those weird trances," Mike bellowed as he ran back and shook Hamasa's head.

"Yeah!"

As they exited, mocking their prisoner, Harold sat himself right in front of Hamasa, whose once cropped hair overgrew his ears; a bleeding chest exposed through a ripped t-shirt. Although Hamasa's hands were painfully tied behind his back, sweat pouring off his nose, he managed a wry smile, knowing he would finally have a break from the two goons beating him. He wondered who this Harold fellow thought he was and why he had not seen him until now.

"That smile for me?" inquired Harold. "Caged animals aren't usually happy to see their captor, but then, this is our first encounter."

Hamasa was being held inside a not so typical interrogation chamber, with a large table, a mirrored wall he knew they observed him from the other side of, and a wall consisting of a locked, huge, iron gate. He could peer through the bars to see an enormous, expansive hall carved out from the rocks with water running down one rock wall. There were four corridors, or shafts running into darkness from it, and only one way in and out: the elevator. He could envision the miners from a distant past gathering in such a place before they made the journey up the shaft to the light. Now the place held even deeper secrets as not a scream could make it out of a place like this. A mysterious natural light seeped into the room, but he could not see where the light came from. He would often hear the sounds of a large orchestra, with a choir performing an ethereal, angelic symphony, with sounds that seemed to have originated from all the countries of the world. It gave him a sense of calm and hope, and a feeling of being watched over. There were other strange sounds, too, that tugged at his heart strings by bringing back memories of better, freer times: sounds of humongous, swooshing kites fighting for their freedom. During a bathroom break, he hit the ground, as the sound of an approaching kite forced him to take cover. He knew those noises well, from the many times in his youth he had dealt with wind swells that could change a kite's direction and have it crashing to the earth, or turning on its puppeteer, who would have little time to run from its fury. He couldn't see the kites though, only hear them. But where did these wind swells originate, he wondered? He had a hunch though, and it gave him great comfort and strength to persevere. Oddly, no one else heard them, not the cleaning staff who came by once in a while, or the guards or even the agents, whom he wasn't afraid to ask. They couldn't see the lights either, or hear the ethereal music that he did. By now, though, strange and mysterious were almost commonplace after all the events of the past few months. However, he was constantly forced from this inner bliss by the two knuckle-cracking agents and the putrid smell of bleach washed floors, mixed in with the musky scent of stubborn mold that must be growing somewhere in spite of all the sanitization.

Alone, he faced the greatest challenges of his life. The cement and steel around him imprisoned the damp and cold. An eerie sound resonated repeatedly from down the corridor: steel scraping on steel: large iron gates creaking open and shut. Like a caged tiger, he usually paced, unable to sleep. Now, imprisoned again in his chair, he felt like a mouse in the mouth of a purring cat, sometimes being tossed from one paw to the other.

Looking straight into his eyes, Harold hissed, "Listen, Hamasa, we've been at this for two days now, and unlike the others I've been giving your statements serious consideration.

Actually, I have a team of agents seeing if anything you've been telling us checks out. I must say you even surprised me. Nevertheless, you're still avoiding answering our questions about your involvement or any knowledge you might have of Sky's murder. We need to know the whole truth, everything you know. Some things just don't add up here. You talk about Nayanna as if she's your wife. So, do you still want to say you don't know who Sky is? You deny this completely, but I'll say it again, Nayanna married Sky, and you must have known about it!"

Hamasa twisted in his chair. "Hey, is it necessary to have my hands bound so tight? Where the hell are we anyway? When can I get my people here, my lawyer?"

Harold delved into his inside coat pocket and took out a switchblade. Getting lightly to his feet he cut the wet, leather straps that were drawing blood around Hamasa's wrists.

Hamasa showed his appreciation by staying calm; he folded his hands on his lap, expecting to be re-tied.

"No, no, no!" he insisted earnestly. "You've got it all wrong! Nayanna is my girl, she always was, and she always will be. I've no idea what you're talking about. When do I get to see a lawyer? I demand to see a lawyer! I've got rights! We're not in Israel. I'm the eagle! I've flown to freedom! You know what I'm saying! This is America!"

Pulling up a chair to a desk loaded with surgical tools and other weird looking contraptions, Harold sat down and carefully wrapped each one in cloth, placing them in a large, leather, doctor's bag. Looking from the corner of his eyes, he made sure Hamasa watched as he opened a small drawer, pulled out a syringe, and inserted a large needle.

"This is most effective after a good amount of torture like you've received," Harold casually commented as he thrust the needle into Hamasa's toned arm. "So, whether you like it or not, we will get the information we need. I call this stuff 'liquid truth.' It'll get you focused on answering our questions, so we can get to the bottom of this mess. What goes on here is strictly off the radar. I figure you know that by now. Sorry, but no lawyers allowed. This place doesn't even exist in the real world. It would be like asking the government what they know about UFOs: absolutely nothing would be the answer.

"You're in serious trouble here, with some significant charges leveled against you – the murder of an innocent civilian! Come on now, you should have known better than that. Every agent knows they're on their own once that happens. If you want to see Nayanna, you'd better tell us everything. We want a full confession. You do that for us and we can work out an arrangement that will be a lot better for you. You might as well accept the fact you've been caught. We're gathering up all the evidence against you as we speak. So with or without your cooperation, we will get to the bottom of this murder. You're lucky to be alive. After 9/11, nobody's putting up with terrorists."

Hamasa knew he couldn't give up. He had to keep fighting. 'I'm the eagle!' Where the hell did that come from, he thought? That person, when he talked like that, shocked him. How could he have done those things, said those things: murdered? He knew he had to answer to himself before he would ever allow himself to answer to another. Where were these demons hiding? Where was Hamasa, the man he loved, the man Nayanna loved? Hamasa was outraged at himself when he thought about his jealousy and all the things he had done to try to win Nayanna back: he knew it would be his death to show it now.

Harold spoke again as he paced the floor. "I can't understand how you've been able to go undetected for so long. You certainly went off on your own. Maybe you acted as a double agent for the Russians? Maybe you're a lady's man? That how you did it, hiding behind a few skirts? You look like you've walked out of a Harlequin romance novel, as the hero, saving damsels in distress. Who would suspect such a pretty boy, right? Nevertheless, your education and degrees leave me wondering how you ever had the time to put so many notches on your belt. You know I'm not talking about your girls this time? I don't know of anybody else who's got away with so many unauthorized killings. We know what you've been up to. You just have to fill us in on a few of the details, isn't that right, Hamasa? So far, your information is turning out to be true, so let's keep it that way. Wasting our time wouldn't be a smart move."

Hamasa wasn't reacting to anything Harold said but became overjoyed with his new freedom of arm movement and it didn't faze Harold in the least when he bounced his leg bound chair closer to the table and poured himself a drink of water.

"By the way, we already checked out your story about your grandfather. The Americans had no idea he had gone back to Afghanistan from his hiding place in Pakistan. We cased that out. You got that? Yes, the Israelis! Remember us, Hamasa? Do you remember for whom you're supposed to be working? Do you remember the oath you took with your mom and dad to honor and serve the Israeli Government? Isn't it a tell-all the FBI tracked you down but it's me that's doing the interrogating?"

Hamasa, getting engrossed in the magical, mysterious music emitting from the Mausoleum could swear he even heard his favorite song playing, "Imagine," by John Lennon. It somehow made Harold's words clearer and even more pronounced, as if they were coming from within his own mind and were being amplified by the chamber.

"Hey, come on, we've more important things to take care of. Can't you hear the music? Man, I tell you it's a sign. We've been chosen! We've been chosen, man!" Hamasa disappeared inside himself, caught up in the haunting melody and in the driving need for unity expressed by the song.

Harold could see he wasn't getting through. He slowly rolled up his sleeves, revealing a tattoo of a fist holding the 'Torch of Truth' symbol and words inked on his forearm. A sure sign he was a New Yorker even if he didn't resonate as American. He grabbed a bucket of ice water and drenched Hamasa with it.

Finally, Harold got a reaction; Hamasa tried to jump out of the way but with his legs still bound to the chair, he fell over. Harold decided to cuff him and left him tied to the chair as he put it back up using all the strength he had. Hamasa was not a small man.

"Why the hell did you do that?" Hamasa screamed.

"Calm down, Hamasa. If you do, I'll gladly un-cuff you," Harold said in his usual understated manner. He waited for the tide of anger to wash from Hamasa's face before removing the handcuffs.

"OK, Hamasa, you focused enough for me to continue now?"

Pulling in a ragged breath, Hamasa gave a jerky nod in reply. "I thought it was the torch of freedom? Your tatoo...the statue of liberty...right? Didn't it represent freedom from slavery?" Hamasa asked.

"My journey is for truth, I don't give a damn what it means to you," Harold replied.

"Truth! What the hell would you know about looking for truth? Maybe you mean justice or 'the torch of revenge' for your pathetic life," Hamasa countered. "So we're in New York then, right?"

Harold saw the diversion tactics, ignored him, and continued. "So was it for the sake of the Afghans, who worshiped your grandfather as their leader and as someone who so bravely fought off the Russians, he went back there?" Harold's voice dripped sarcasm. "He secured free clearance to live in the USA or anywhere he wanted, with you, your father and mother. I'm sure he took all the opium money he made, never mind what the Americans had given him to fight the Russians. He had absolutely no reason to be back there," he added flatly. He poured himself a glass of water and took a breath of musky air deep into his lungs.

He studied Hamasa dispassionately. "So what drove him back?" he asked. "We were able to find out the bombing that rocked your village many years ago killed him, and he never did make it to Canada with you." Harold chuckled drily. "I'm sure he died in style, with naked, virgin nymphs dancing around in an opium-smoke filled den. The reason his name finally surfaced is he's classified as a terrorist by our Government – for good reasons, that you've now verified. What blows me away is how and why your father kept your activities and your grandfather's activities a secret from us. So let's continue from there. And I don't want more of your delusions and grand schemes to save the world." Letting a long, calming breath out through his nose, he said, "Your dad moved the family to Canada when you were around ten or twelve, right?"

Harold knew there was a line that couldn't be crossed. If they pushed a prisoner too hard they could suddenly die, or their minds could snap and they would become delusional. Finding that line was anyone's guess. Hamasa's odd responses were already making Harold nervous. He could only push ahead and watch for clues, but he decided it best just to let him unravel at his own pace for now.

He never enjoyed this part of his job, even though he had done it for many years. The meticulous gathering of evidence and a fine eye for detail was his forte. He had spent innumerable hours piecing together the clues that finally led to Hamasa's arrest. He preferred to let others do the torturing, but since 9/11, torture was the first line of defense and a lot more of it happened. It made him downright irritable. Previously, he could return home to his wife and kids without carrying this burden with him. A person in this line of work couldn't count on weekends off or even regular holidays. However, he somehow managed to keep up a good game of tennis, mostly because of a court right where he worked and someone always being around to challenge to a game.

As his contemptuous gaze locked with Hamasa's dark eyes, he found himself unable to pull his stare away. Something in those endless dark pits made it impossible to consciously yank himself away. Turning his back on Hamasa for a moment, he strolled over and sat down on the couch at the opposite end of the room to wait for the drugs he had injected into Hamasa to kick in and for the truth to start pouring out.

Chapter 2

Interrogation–Recollections

"The abuse of greatness is when it disjoins remorse from power."
William Shakespeare

"First of all, they wouldn't have been virgins, nor were they necessarily girls, but naked for sure," Hamasa mumbled, feeling as if he was tunneling his way out of a coma. "How can you be holding me like this? I always did your dirty work. Now this is how I'm rewarded?" he rambled. "You should know what it's like out there on the front lines. To get things done an agent has to use the power and freedom he's been given. We have to make quick decisions and we can't always make reports and wait for feedback. Just work with me on this and you'll realize I did everything in our country's best interest. Stand by me on this one, and let the Americans know I'm one of yours. We can go on doing great things."

He still was not accustomed to the bright lights he saw every time he closed his eyes. Pain kept him focused on the present, his heart pounding kept him focused on what he had to do to protect Nayanna, but his out of control mind wandered over his past and became afraid of the emotions that were conjured up. He kept looking for clues to answer the urgent question of how he ended up in this mess, and more importantly, how to get out of it. It was the first time he had ever been caught and interrogated. He swore it would be his last.

Hamasa thought it must have been his upbringing that got him into trouble. He could have done well, putting his education to better use, he reflected, which Nayanna, too, always encouraged him to do.

They knew each other from school, but they really discovered one another when their grade 10 science teacher paired them up for a project. That science class produced more than just test tube chemical reactions. Those were his formative years, but Hamasa had to look much further back to understand the deep, dark forces that had propelled him into captivity…

…He remembered the time his grandfather gave him a machine gun to fire. The year: 1989. Grandfather explained the irony that the mujahedeen had used that particular weapon, made by the Russians, to chase the Russians out of Afghanistan.

The day had started much the same as every other day he could remember; up at the crack of dawn to the sound of roosters and the bustling noise of people and dogs interacting. He would always stand on his bed, draw the curtains, or if it had been rainy or windy unlatch the shutters and look out on the compound below. He could always count on having someone to shout at or someone giving him a wink or a friendly good morning wave.

He rushed down the stairs in his bare feet and pajamas to be warmly greeted by the person he loved most in the whole world, his mother. She would have to coax him from her charming, loving presence back up those long, cold, stone stairs to the bathroom. She would never allow him to the breakfast table without a morning wash up and without being fully clothed, with house shoes on. On this day, Grandfather surprised them by being there all geared up for battle.

"Grandfather, why do you wear that cape even on these hot sunny days?" Hamasa enquired.

"People always have to be reminded who their leader is," was his quick reply. "I've told you many times, my father passed this down to me and someday your father will pass it to you to wear, for you to show your power." Grandfather threw open his robe revealing his weapons belt loaded with bullets and grenades.

"I know, I know, but I just love it when you tell me your

stories, Grandad. Wow! What's happening today?"

Hamasa ran to his grandfather to touch the grenades, but Grandfather scolded, "Hamasa, these are not toys! Show your respect."

Hamasa moved back and bowed his head. "Sorry, Grandfather, but I am a man now and I deserve to know what is going on today. Let me know! Let me know! It's about time I protect my mother at the house here. I should have a gun. When am I getting that gun you promised?" Hamasa couldn't contain his excitement.

"Well today is your special day. It's just you and me going to get you that gun. How's that Hamasa?"

Hamasa's mom gave Grandfather a stern look. "Don't be teasing Hamasa like this before he's even had his breakfast. You sit down right now, Hamasa, you know how long I've been preparing this for you. Yes, you're my big protector but you don't need a gun in this house to do that. Even with Dad and Granddad away all the time, we still have the neighbors, too, remember."

Hamasa and his grandfather had gone out of the compound to the far side of the rocky hills, where the war games and training for war would occur. The area was a forbidden zone for kids. Not only were the secret escape tunnels nearby, but here, all the explosives were tested and hidden. Whenever Hamasa had to come to this place, he had to repress the terrifying nightmare memories of when the family had to seek refuge from invaders. He would focus on the good fortune of his family coming out alive and he would try to picture the area as a safe haven, a place to escape danger.

The area was a kid's 'dream come true playground' of burnt out vehicles, collapsed buildings riddled with bullet wounds and of course the caves and tunnels. Hamasa and the other kids were never allowed to play there, though. But that didn't stop

Hamasa from begging his grandfather to let him bring his friends there so they, too, could play their war games. His grandfather had other intentions for the day, however.

When they arrived, a mysterious lady greeted them. Her whole body and face were covered, but Hamasa knew he had never seen her before. Grandfather handed him the machine gun and disappeared with the cryptic veiled lady into one of the caves. Hamasa took a deep breath of dusty, gunpowder air and began firing his weapon while chanting, 'Allah O Akbar, Allah O Akbar'. The morning sun turned to afternoon fire.

"Hamasa, I'm so proud of you. You've been hitting all the targets," Grandfather yelled as he emerged from the shadows with his exposed enigmatic guest. They were drinking – laughing hysterically. The lady's burqa was flying in the wind, revealing her transformation to belly dancer. Her near naked body glistened in the sun, beads of sweat arose on Hamasa's face as she seduced him with her eyes and her curvaceous, heaving hips.

"You're becoming a man now, Hamasa! I'll show you how to be a man!" Grandfather said, beaming with pride. Right there, in broad daylight, his grandfather held him so tight the machine gun slipped from Hamasa's tiny hands. Chanting over and over, 'You're my little mujahedeen, my little mujahedeen,' his grandfather lifted up their perahons, and pulled down their tunbans, entering and thrusting against Hamasa's yielding flesh to the rhythms of the nympho's dance and her hyena howls.

"I thought it was my job to make him a man" she moaned, her libidinous claws tore at her raw naked flesh parading on virtuous eyes.

The ancient robes, with their official colors and markings of a hero his grandfather loved to wear, even when the sun pounded down, camouflaged the pair. Hamasa gritted his teeth and trusted this had to be just another necessary experience on the road to being a man and warrior. With machine gun fire still echoing in his ears, he wondered if his dad had also been so brave when he must have gone through the same rituals, perhaps from his own grandfather.

They never spoke about that day and Hamasa never knew if it was just lack of opportunity, luck or otherwise that kept Grandfather from taking him again. The femme fatale had danced back into the wild night of the cave with the brute in tow, leaving trust obliterated. Hamasa couldn't quite accept the old man's way of showing love and admiration, even if he was allowed to drive the guarded Mercedes home alone, with his new gun on his lap. He could never feel at ease again around the old man, or most anyone for that matter. He was now a man but at what price? He would never see the world through innocent eyes again. He would never forget the sound of Grandfather's breath, so hard and so close, like a vampire descending on its prey; or how the sky had grown suddenly dark and overcast as the sun turned its gaze away in shame.

Chapter 3

Growing up in Afghanistan

"The childhood shows the man, as morning shows the day."
John Milton

"Hamasa! Hamasa! The big clouds are coming! The big clouds are coming!"

"I heard you the first time, Salman, my little charkha gir," Hamasa echoed back. "How many times have I told you not to climb up here, especially with that kite in your hands? Are you trying to kill yourself? Look how far down that is!

"So are you trying to tell me there's enough wind for the gudiparan today, or what?"

"I'm not your charkha gir anymore, so stop calling me that. You always win the kite fights because I'm there to help you, but from now on, I'll be your fiercest opponent. You'll have to get another charkha gir boy to hold the spool of wire."

"After becoming Sharti, the champion kite flyer, teaching you everything I know about flying and making the best gudiparans in all of Afghanistan, this is how you want to thank me?"

"Later! Come to the roof and see for yourself, there must be more than one car coming to make that cloud of dust." Salman took in Hamasa's surroundings. "Wow, look at this mess! Your books are everywhere. With visitors coming, you'll get the day to show off and recite all your high learning again, while I'll be on garbage duty as usual."

Hamasa, who was used to being woken up by the dawn roosters yapping, noticed they were eerily silent. Climbing out his bedroom window and up to the roof, he couldn't see a single rooster in the yard below. Turning to his friend, who had followed him, he said, "They must have driven all night to get here this early. This can't be a friendly visit to hear me recite poetry."

The boys scrambled back inside as they saw their protectors, rifles slung over their shoulders, running towards the gated entrance. They were getting into firing positions all around the compound. Hamasa started to get the shakes as he remembered the last time they had come under attack. He had been seven years old when his mother saved his life. They never found out who it was, a rival tribe, the Russians or maybe the Americans. The women had to bring the children to safety by climbing to the far side of the hill, above the compound. There, a hidden, deep cave they had fortified with tunnels and supplies would protect them. The most dangerous part came as they began their escape, only to be immediately met with a barrage of gunfire. Hamasa's palsy increased as he felt his mother thrusting him behind her, shielding him from the bullet that would have ended his life. Gravely injured, she forced herself to carry on and bring him safely to the tunnels. Once there, she hung on grimly as they waited out the attack until she received the medical attention that saved her. Hamasa would never forget her courageous deed. It created a bonding that felt as deep and eternal as the night sky into which they had escaped. Were they about to be attacked again? Hamasa ran to his closet to get the gun his grandfather had given him when he was nine.

"Hey, hold on Hamasa, you don't have to take it personally! Of course I'll still be your charkha gir and I'll even be your kite runner and fetch your kites, come on now, relax, put that gun away." Salman put his hands in the air in mock surrender.

Just then they heard Hamasa's mom calling, "Hamasa, who are you talking to? You're not one to talk in your sleep, so it's good to know you're up. Please come down right away and get your breakfast. I need to see you right now."

Life in Afghanistan was not only about wars and initiation rites. Hamasa had an insatiable zest for knowledge. He spent much of his time poring over all the books he could find and committing them to memory. Being the leader's grandson gave him countless chances to recite, from memory, all his research, to the amazement of their many visitors. Having striking, handsome features and a rare intelligence kept him in their company and away from all the arduous daily chores which most of the other village children had to endure. He had a way about him that would draw forth the best from the guests and they would share their life stories and wisdom. He could always count on the fact the main advice from visitors would be to study the Koran and surrender to the will of Allah. 'The Koran is the only book that anyone ever needs to read. This book will give you all the knowledge and wisdom you will ever want,' they told him. However, Hamasa had devoured its content and craved to read whatever else he could get his hands on. Centuries ago, his people had led the age of enlightenment and made many of the discoveries that shaped the modern world. Hamasa hoped to bring back that glory again to his people.

Standing in the midst of all his strewn about books, with machine gun in hand, Hamasa yelled to his friend. "Get the hell out of here – you heard my mom, I gotta go! We'll see you later. I bet we'll have to go to the tunnels again." Hamasa managed to put on a smile, turned to see his friend for what could be the last time, and gave him a hug. "I'll see you later for sure, hey? Now go back out the window, the way you came, and don't fall. I'll throw your kite to you when you're safely down."

"Mom, I'm coming." Hamasa dressed for war and rushed down for breakfast with gun still in hand. Even at ten years old, he could convince anyone of his readiness to defend and kill to protect his mom.

"What's up, Mom? Who's visiting this early? Is it another attack, you think?" Where's Dad? I'm going with him."

"No you're not, Sharti! Look at you, my little, big hero. Where's my morning kiss and hug? Come on, don't give me that face."

Hamasa put the gun down, hugged his mom, and sat at the table that was usually laid out with fruit baskets and poppy flowers: but not today. Today, the usual smell of sweet bread, onions, and eggs frying were absent. They sat for tea and porridge.

"There's an attack where the crops are. Reinforcements are coming and your father is going with them. They're trying to take over the fields."

"You mean the poppy fields?" Hamasa stated, trying to hide his revulsion by putting his hands up over his eyes as they rolled upwards in his head.

He knew where their money came from: harvesting the poppy to make drugs. Hamasa also knew he had a lot to be grateful for. Because of the poppy fields his family had riches others could only dream of, bringing him great advantages and privileges, like all the books he read, the materials to build his kites, heck, his three-story house was of stone while others lived in rooms made from mud. Because of the poppy flowers, he lived in a huge compound, protected by a great stone wall. His family had plenty of trucks and motorcycles and his grandfather even had a black, German, Mercedes-Benz they drove on special occasions to the big city of Kabul. Grandfather himself would keep the car washed and polished; usually the nasty jobs were always done by someone else: tending to the animals and their mess, garbage duty and cleaning the toilets, houses and vehicles. He was 'Prince Hamasa' to most of the other kids whose parents toiled at the compound. Their house even had lights and heat, from the electricity created by the newly introduced big generators. Before electricity, they had to gather wood and produce oil to burn in the lamps: a huge chore.

His family also ran the school. The girls stayed home with their mothers, who educated them. Their language was Pashto, but his mom and dad made certain he learned English.

Poppy flowers decorated inside and outside the houses. He would help to dry them and make all kinds of decorations. His mom made him a poppy seed paste when he had a tummy ache. Poppy seeds were made into oil for cooking and into breads and spicy pastes. The only color in Afghanistan came from the kites and the earthy smelling poppy flowers. When the poppies bloomed, everyone would be in a celebratory mood. When the kites came out everyone would be in a cheering, fighting mood. They both brought out the best that people still had left inside of them and could be happy about in this dreary, dusty land of destitution and dispute.

His grandfather inherited the big fortress, as well as his high rank, along with the poppy business.

Hamasa was warned about all the bad things caused by opium and cocaine and once met some crazies in the village that were messed up by drugs. When the older boys tempted him, he knew to stay away. He was much too focused on developing his mind to start taking stuff that would destroy it. His grandfather would not allow the drugs to be used within the compound. However, Hamasa once spied on the neighbors and caught them sitting around smoking the hookah pipe filled with opium. Hamasa could not stand cigarette smoke, never mind what came out from the hookah pipe and his hiding place was compromised when he started madly coughing from the smoke. He ran for his life and wasn't caught for spying.

His family grew the crops, but they manufactured the drugs in a very secret location Grandfather controlled: even Hamasa didn't know its location.

Ameera continued gently talking to Hamasa like a purring cat. "Yes...well...you'll have the place to yourselves: you, and your friends. You'll be able to sneak into the TV room again and watch another movie or go down to the river and ride your secret rafts."

"Hey, you've been spying on me! How do you know about

all that? " Hamasa was genuinely surprised. His mouth turned down. "I just want to fly my kite but with all the Taliban officials around, they won't allow it."

"Well, you can do that down by the river, too, no one will be watching the canals today. Take the walkie-talkies and I'll call you when Dad comes back." Ameera kept her composure and didn't let on her crippling fear of what was really going on.

Hamasa consumed his porridge in under a minute and ran out the door to get his friend, Salman. Ameera was left alone in the house with the sound of her thumping heart. She had to make a plan, she thought. A few minutes later, Hamasa and his friend were off to find adventure and to fly their kites.

Hamasa, a champion kite flyer and fighter, would always win contests because of his many flying and fighting skills, his own unique kite making designs and especially for his bold style of flying. He could make his kite fly like an eagle, swooping down on its prey or like a jet fighter, streaking through the sky. By the pull of the strings his kite could go wild, showing off his aerial skills: flips, spins, somersaults and backward flips were a few of the moves he could get his kite to do. Hamasa could perform a dance routine or do gymnastic maneuvers such as cartwheels or flips while he flew the kite: an amazing spectacle to behold.

The kites, or gudiparan, (literally meaning flying doll in Afghan) came in different sizes, but only one size for fighting. Two kites had to be airborne simultaneously and at a close proximity. As soon as the wires of these two kites connected, the fight had begun. The tournament would last from a split second up to a half hour. Generally, the handler with the most experience and patience would win, given the same quality of the tar, kite, and charkha gir.

Kite flying for the Afghans would be like hockey to the Canadians or baseball to the Americans if the government sponsored it; the Afghan people had that much passion and commitment to the sport. Competitions were always fierce and a person had to develop strength and athletic abilities, along with hours and hours spent in actual training with the kite itself. Although kite flying was not an official sport and the government didn't support the competitions, local communities, parents and businesses did their best to give as much recognition and support as they could to the kite fliers for all their effort and talent.

Actually, kite flying was thought to be far too dangerous to be officially recognized. First of all, the wires would often cut to the bone, even when wearing a kilkak, a special leather cover for the index finger. Then there were the falls. The boys would get so involved in the fight or flight they would forget to watch where they were running. Many would fall off roofs, a favorite place to catch wind, fall off cliffs or trip on rocks or holes in the ground.

Jaabir got the latest updates about the situation when the trucks pulled into the compound to pick up the village fighters. "Ameera," he called, "I'm going now. I'll take our truck. Where's Hamasa? Keep him at home 'til I get back. It doesn't look good," he told her, face clouded with worry. "There could even be bombing. Paratroopers have been flown in to take over the fields. It must be the CIA, who else would fund such a campaign."

Ameera turned a bloodless white, whispering, almost to herself, "What will we do?"

Clutching onto her husband she pleaded, "Can you stay? We'll pack now, we have to make a break for it, that's all there is to it. We don't have a choice. They'll never stop now that they've found this place. We'll go to Canada as we planned."

Jaabir broke free from Ameera and started frantically gathering up the family weapons and ammunition. "OK, OK, we'll go to Canada. We'll leave tonight...when I get back. You can start packing but stay close to home. Where's Hamasa? Make sure he stays here with you. Make sure no one sees you.

Grandfather will be away, but we can't take any chances of him or anyone finding out we're leaving. I'll be back after midnight and we'll leave shortly after that. We'll contact our people once we get to Kabul." Drawing Ameera into his arms, he kissed her upturned face. "I love you," he said gruffly, "be safe."

He gently touched her cheek, wiping away the tear trembling on her lower lashes before it could fall. This time when he spoke, he couldn't keep a tremor out of his voice. "If you hear helicopters or planes, go to the tunnel immediately. We never know when they'll start bombing. Don't take any chances." He smiled crookedly. "We'll get through this," he reassured, adding, as if it were some protective talisman, "I love you."

Ameera remembered she had sent Hamasa off to play with his friends, but she dared not tell her husband and give him more things to worry about. She knew her son was a call away and in a safe place and she wanted his last memories of Afghanistan to be as good as possible. She would only cause him grief if he were here to see her in her state of terror, madly packing for their getaway. Besides, he might not be able to keep it secret if he were here feeling all the pressure.

It was later than usual when Hamasa, with his mother's permission, arrived home after playing with his friends by the canals. He'd had a glorious day flying his kite. What he didn't know was it would be his last.

His mother had dinner waiting when he arrived. When she told him the news that they would be moving to Canada, she said it was a secret, and not to be shared with anyone. Hamasa's dark eyes shone with excitement. Now he would be able to advance his quest for knowledge without limits. He would have a chance to go to a university: a dream he held close to his heart. He knew he would never be able to experience it if he stayed in the village. He grinned widely; he would grow up to be a wise, old, big horned, Marco Polo Sheep. But that was if they could get out of this alive, he fretted, after being told of the dangers ahead.

His mom told him he could think of a new name to call himself in Canada. That wiped the grin off his face. Abdul Hamasa Baghrani, the courageous one, was his birth name. Because of his kite flying talents, the locals called him Sharti Abdul Hamasa Baghrani and he could not imagine changing it. They lived in the Afghan Province of Helmand, district of Baghran, and they lived near the village of Baghran. To change his name would mean erasing any reference to his birthplace. That might be a good thing, he realized, since it was the major poppy growing area. His grandfather, as the village leader, was named Mir Abdul Naqeeb Baghrani. His father, the only teacher, was named, Quri Abdul Jaabir Baghrani, and his mother, because she was the village princess, was named, Ameera Baghrani. Now they were going to a place where none of that would matter. In their new country, there would be no family history, no family home, and no friends. A new start, maybe with a new name; something he would have to think about long and hard.

Although Hamasa felt a freedom and sense of adventure he imagined only his best and biggest kite would ever have known at the thought of going to Canada and being allowed to study, a part of him knew he would always yearn to be back in Afghanistan. He loved all the people dearly and he allowed himself to dream of coming back to help re-build and modernize his country. He longed to make life better for all. The first thing he promised himself he would do was pave all the roads so everyone could travel in style. The kids would have cool roads for the bikes and skateboards he would buy them. Of course, everyone would have a kite and a nice park to fly them in; then they, too, would know the exuberance and complete freedom he had enjoyed. For now, kites were the only way for any of the villagers to experience freedom, and indeed, for most ordinary people beyond the village, who weren't into drugs, as well. For Hamasa it kept the hope alive; one day there would be freedom in all things, for all Afghanis and no more wars. Hamasa had long been told he had special talents, and he strongly believed they were bestowed on him in order to help others.

After eating, he helped his mother clean up and pack but he started to wander why his dad was not home yet. His mom kept saying it was early and not to worry but Hamasa kept rushing up to the roof to see if he could spot him returning. Staring out into the clear, warm night, he chewed at his lower lip. Something was not right; it was now past midnight and his father still wasn't back but his mother, busy with the packing, had failed to notice or if she had realized, she refused to say anything about it.

Suddenly he became aware of a strange sound, a rhythmic wop-wop noise. Staring frantically around himself, he tried to pinpoint where it came from. By the time he saw its source, it was too late. The helicopter swooped down from over the mountaintop, like a dragon spewing fire. Bullets chewed up the compound and screaming erupted from every corner and every house.

"Hamasa, get off the roof!" Ameera screamed. It's chasing after the trucks that are coming back from the fields. Your dad's on his way, but we have to be ready to leave quickly. Everyone will be going to the caves, but you have to stay with me to help. Stay calm and bring these boxes to the front of the house. Hamasa are you listening to me?"

Hamasa burst into the room, staring wildly at his mother. "Mom," he blurted. "It's Dad! He's driving up but that sky monster followed him. It's shooting at him! It's shooting at Dad!"

"Hamasa, stay in the house! Where are you going?" Ameera yelled. Seeing him run towards the door, she scooped him up safely in her arms. They both stared in horror as the truck, careering recklessly as it took a direct hit, burst into flame, lighting up the night sky. Hidden from view by the flames erupting from the gas tank, Jaabir had jumped from the passenger side moments before the vehicle exploded. Hamasa wrestled free from his mother's iron grip and ran to the blazing truck. Ameera, right behind him, saw Jaabir emerge from behind the burning wreck.

"Go back! Stay inside!" Jaabir yelled. "I'll get the Mercedes and meet you at the front of the house."

Inside, the two of them stood huddled together, silent and unmoving, waiting as long seconds ticked by. The Mercedes was quiet but the night filled with a cacophony of screams, gunfire, and the noise of the helicopter. Abruptly, the door crashed open. Hamasa's heart, already pounding, seemed to constrict as he saw his mother press her hand to her mouth to choke off a scream. Their relief was palpable as they saw the familiar figure slip swiftly into the room. His father crushed them to his chest for an instant before setting them loose.

"Quickly!" he said, grabbing several bags from the pile of things by the door.

Hamasa and his mother hurried to help. Among all the chaos they managed to pack the car and head out for safety.

"They won't be so quick to shoot at a civilian car, I hope, but our boys will soon bring that flying ship down."

Hamasa glanced at his father. He had never seen him so edgy, but talking seemed to calm him down so Hamasa stayed silent and listened, biting back his terror and his questions.

"It came out of nowhere," his father mumbled. "We were capturing the soldiers that parachuted in from the plane. We should've known there'd be backup for them – Americans for sure."

His mother laid her head on his father's shoulder, stroking his hair the way she often did with Hamasa. Rolling down his window, Hamasa searched the sky for signs of the warbird. This was it for Afghanistan: no looking back, and no saying goodbye to friends and family. Hamasa wondered when he would be able to return to fulfill all his dreams.

Suddenly, Hamasa screamed out, in blind loyalty and learned

obedience, "But where is Grandad? Why are we leaving without Grandad? Didn't you tell him we were leaving? Why didn't you tell him we were leaving?"

Chapter 4

Hamasa's Parents

"Either war is obsolete or men are."
R. Buckminster Fuller

Hamasa's parents would never have met if it were not for the threat of nuclear war, government interventions and espionage. It was a clandestine operation with an unlimited budget and cunning imagination. The goal of the Israelis was to find out as much as possible about Pakistan's nuclear program, and who else in the region was developing one. The goal of the Russians was very similar, with a slightly sinister twist. They already had nuclear weapons. They just needed them stationed in the Afghan region so they could control the Middle East's oil industry. Power was money; money was power.

A little romance to heat up the cold war chills was completely unexpected.

Jaabir was a third generation spy in Afghanistan. Starting with his grandfather, and then parents, they were all Israeli plants. Jaabir had been brought up as an Afghan. His family worked for the Afghan Government as Directors of Education and Jaabir worked his way into that position as well. That was how he met Ameera.

Ameera was exceedingly bright and ambitious. Before the Taliban had taken over, women were succeeding in pushing through some rights and responsibilities for themselves within government and society. Her father was consumed with empire building, tribal conflicts and eventually, war against Russia. Ameera pointed out there was nobody left to teach the children as the men were being killed off or were needed elsewhere. Her father ultimately conceded and allowed Ameera to help with the education of the village children. For that purpose, Ameera was permitted to further her studies in Kabul, where she met Jaabir.

Ameera sat on the tiled floor, hugging her knees to her chest. She gave Jaabir a long, searching look and, eliciting no response, she finally spoke, "So, here we are, hiding out in the city where we first met." She tugged at her hair, as she always did when anxious. "Do you think they spotted us coming here?" She shook her head quickly, before Jaabir could answer, knowing it was a useless question. She knew Jaabir would have already spoken if he had seen anyone and also understood the fact he hadn't didn't mean they hadn't been marked. She fiddled with her hair again. "Anyway, we can't stay here long. Every moment we're here we put these good people's lives at risk."

"They took care of ditching the car, so hopefully it's safe to wait for our connections." Jaabir avoided meeting her eyes. "Once we have all our papers in order and we've been given more money, we can wait at the hotel near the airport. We should be safe here for now. Who's going to check the bathroom for a hidden door to this place? Besides, there's a tunnel out of here," Jaabir said, reaching for the tin container of clean water standing close by and splashing his face.

"It seems ridiculous, we're next door to a bathroom and we have to use these buckets," Ameera complained, gesturing at two metal buckets in the farthest corner of the room. "Good thing there's a lid on them," she added.

Silence filled the room for several minutes, then. "It doesn't feel right being separated from Hamasa," Ameera fretted. "If something goes wrong—" She dry washed her face. Burying her head against his neck, she sighed. "But you're right, it's better that he's allowed to mix with the other kids and sleep in their room. The less he sees and knows, the better for him and everyone." She sighed again. "Tomorrow we can do all the banking and hopefully, by then, all the documents will have arrived. Everything can be done from here without Hamasa knowing any of it."

The harrowing events of the past day caught up to Ameera. Tears flooded her dark eyes and slipped silently down her cheeks. She hid her head in Jaabir's shoulder and gave herself up to her fear.

"There, there, let it out, dear," Jaabir comforted her. "When I first met you, you were never afraid to speak your mind or let your emotions show. But all these years you've had to bottle them up and keep silent. Soon you'll be able to express yourself freely and bravely. For a daughter of the Taliban, you had some pretty radical ideas on how things needed changing back then."

For a few moments, his thoughts ranged inward as he replayed how their love had developed. First, he was her professor, then her confidant, subsequently her lover and then husband. No one had ever questioned his authenticity as an Afghan or his commitment to the Taliban. That was until Ameera saw through him. She had told him she felt he was just too sympathetic to her rebel ideas to be a true Taliban. Of course, the fact he didn't turn her in helped, and in time they grew to trust each other completely. Together they were going to help create a new Afghanistan.

It went against protocol, but with the amazingly quick advances in technology, spies had to make many adaptations; having a husband and wife team was one of them. They were allowed to marry and have a family. Before they were married, Ameera was sworn in by the Israeli Government to serve and obey. It was a new era. It was the nuclear arms race. They were as close to the enemy's epicenter as it was possible to get.

Ameera sniffed, lifting her head and managing a strained smile. "We've come this far against all odds. We've avoided certain death if caught, so it definitely isn't ending here. Dance with me, Jaabir, like we used to do. Remember how exciting and incredibly romantic it was when we first started traveling the world, undercover?"

They had so many excuses and reasons to be out of the country, researching the latest educational innovations or checking out and purchasing the latest technologies for the government. Their extra pay as spies gave them the ability to soak up the sun and the good life as well, even if it was for a short time.

"Yeah, that was before budget cuts, babies and arthritis kicked in, ha-ha," Jaabir responded.

They were risking their lives, not for the money, but in the hopes they could build a new, fairer, less troubled future for all Afghans, and for the rest of the world. Israel was aligned with America and America had democracy and human rights. They were taking the world into a bright future. Whereas the Taliban were taking the Afghans and the world, if they had the chance, back into the dark ages.

As they cranked up the music in their heads, Jaabir and Ameera were dancing on the shores of the Pacific Ocean. The tune playing in Ameera's head, a Viennese Waltz didn't quite jive with the tune that played in Jaabir's head, a Beatles classic, but they managed to avoid each other's bare toes. As the dance wound to a close, they curled up in each other's arms on the floor.

There they stayed, asleep, until a noise woke Jaabir. Beside him, Ameera stirred and blinked sleepily.

"Shush, Shush! Someone's in the bathroom! They'll hear us!" Jaabir whispered. "We can't risk any more of our friends to the cause."

There were many in Afghanistan who risked and sacrificed their lives for the same reasons and causes, but Israeli spies could not openly support them. Ameera and Jaabir were considered Taliban first and then Pashtun – which was the largest tribe and the most spoken language – to the Afghans. The greater good would be done if they kept their cover, no matter how hard it was to stand by helplessly watching their fellow idealists perish.

"It's just the kids," Ameera whispered back, aware that even the children hearing them could lead to their deaths.

"It's bad enough that so many would want us dead for spying for the Israelis, but think how many more would want us dead for spying for the Russians." Jaabir shook his head. "Until Massoud is safe, we have to keep up the charade."

They had to live their lives around so many secrets and lies that at times they forgot who they really were and which mask they needed when. The hardest part, though, was lying to Hamasa.

They had told the Israelis that their son, Massoud had died. If the Israelis knew the Russians had him, they would have pulled them out of Afghanistan. They would know they were too vulnerable to keep working as spies. Now they were double agents, danger surrounded them on all sides. Even an elephant would have a hard time out maneuvering a pack of hungry lions, and it was merely a matter of time before someone pounced on them.

The secret door to their hidden chamber flew open suddenly.

"Sorry, I forgot to give the coded knock. I'm lucky you didn't shoot me," said an elderly woman. Dressed in a white, stained sweater, long, black, wool skirt and with a scarf covering her hair, her arm trembling, she handed them a parcel.

Jaabir clasped the package gratefully to his chest. "Thank you so much, Pakiza."

"Is – is everything OK?" Ameera asked.

Pakiza hesitated. "I'll go get Hamasa, you have to leave immediately," she told them. "You'll have to take the tunnel," she added, turning her back on them.

"Wait, what's going on? Pakiza you have to tell us!" Jaabir begged.

Pakiza swung back to them. "Tell Hamasa the Americans came looking for you…but I think it's the Russians. The Afghanistan National Police came to the door asking about you," she hurried on. "There's a car parked across the street, with a couple of male foreigners in it who look to be watching the place. If it were the Taliban or the Americans, we'd have been raided by now and we'd all be in jail or dead." She shook her head. "No, it has to be the Russians. The ANP can be bought by anyone. They'll keep Russian secrets for a price. They must have put up a lot of money for you to be tracked here," Pakiza stated, trying to hide the fear her eyes betrayed.

Ameera gave a small cry. "This is the worst nightmare – to put you and your family in danger like this!" She stared wildly from one to the other. "Maybe we should surrender, keep you all out of it?"

"Nonsense! Don't think like that! The Russians can't risk making any waves. They'll just wait it out, nothing more to worry about," Pakiza said firmly, lying to herself.

"Behind this wall there's a hidden door that opens to another room. In there, under the carpet, is a trapdoor with stairs leading down to a tunnel. No one's been through in a while but it should be dry, but I've no idea what else could be in there, so be careful. There are some gloves and blankets next door, as well as burqas," she told them. "Use the gloves and blankets to cover yourselves with. It's crawling space only for part of the way and there might be rats, deadly snakes, scorpions or camel spiders," she said frankly.

"Oh great, just what I needed to hear," Ameera responded as she quickly put on the gloves.

"The tunnel leads to a crematorium at the end of the block, but there shouldn't be anyone there, it hasn't been used in years. The tunnel comes out in a cement and steel room covered with ashes, but a steel ladder will take you to another trap door that opens on a secret room." Pakiza shot them a worried glance. "There shouldn't be a risk of anyone being there either. Unbolt the door on the right and you'll see the food market workers' 'women's bathroom'. It's not for public use, but just be careful, make sure no one's there when you enter. The washrooms are behind a tent, so Ameera can go first to see if the coast is clear, so you might not need the burqas.

"From the market, you can get a taxi to the airport hotel. The documents will get you safely to where you need to go." For a second or two, fear flashed across her face again, but then she collected herself and giving Ameera a warm hug, and a smile to Jaabir, she hurried away. "I'll go get Hamasa," she told them over her shoulder, "and then you must hurry and go."

Hamasa was still half-asleep and accepted his father's explanation without question, following him into the tunnel uncomplainingly. Ameera bringing up the rear.

"Ha-ha, I'm so glad it's men first in these situations," she joked as they made their way through the tunnel.

"Ah, but what if we're being chased – then you'll be the first eaten," Jaabir joked back. Hamasa, wide-awake now, plodded along silently.

The tunnel was thick with dust, a myriad of cobwebs and droppings announcing the presence of other tunnel dwellers. Thankfully, they made it to the end without encountering anything deadly.

Dropping down into the concrete and steel room, Hamasa tried his best not to dwell on the origin of the ashes lying ankle deep as they traversed the floor. Nevertheless, he breathed a sigh of relief once that part of their journey was behind them and they stepped into the relative cleanliness of the women's washroom facilities.

"It's almost over now, Hamasa," his mother comforted, forcing a smile.

Hamasa said nothing. His throat was dry and parched and it seemed to demand more energy than he had to speak.

"You and your father wait here, darling. I'm just going to check if the coast is clear. I'll be straight back."

His mother faked another smile, but Hamasa could see her nervousness and it filled him with dread.

True to her word, she was gone only minutes. "Come, hurry!" she called softly.

Clinging to the shadows, they quickly made their way to where a taxi waited, and a short time later Hamasa was drinking white herb tea before being tucked into bed safely at the Heetai Hotel. He lay, physically and mentally drained and listened to the quiet murmur of his parent's voices. Finally, he slept.

"Now we can relax," Jaabir commented, "and reflect on what the hell we just went through."

"Look at you in your comfy chair," Ameera said. "I bet you'll find the remote and I won't hear another peep from you. But hold those thoughts and we'll talk as soon as I come back. I'm going to pop downstairs for a moment to get some supplies and put stuff in the safety deposit."

Jaabir didn't even notice her leaving as he surfed through the TV channels with the remote. He couldn't ignore her when she came back though.

"Jaabir, you won't believe what just happened." Ameera's dark-brown eyes danced, her face flushed from running up the stairs, unable to wait for the elevator. "Our son's alive! Massoud, he survived! He escaped and survived! There are pictures, a letter, it's incredible!" Ameera, pushed a parcel at Jaabir. They had a two-bedroom suite at the Hotel and Ameera dragged Jaabir out of his comfortable love seat, where he had been glued to the TV, pulling him into their private bedroom.

Jaabir's jaw had dropped. "What? Please...slow down. Keep your voice low. I don't know if Hamasa's sleeping yet. What are you telling me?"

"I went downstairs to put things in the safety deposit box—"

"Like that? To the front desk? Dressed like that, with no head scarf!" Jaabir interrupted. "Everyone will remember you now. Anyway, go on, and then...what happened?"

"Well, they told me I'd just received a package from a gentleman who was waiting at the bar to see me. They were about to phone us when I showed up. He saw me and asked me to join him. I explained I'd have to wait for you to come down. But he insisted, he was in a hurry and preferred to talk right away."

"That's just a little too coincidental," Jaabir muttered, anxiously pacing the carpeted room. "If this is a setup, or if he was followed, we could be sitting ducks. We better transfer out of this hotel, quick."

"Oh, Jaabir!" Ameera's excitement had all but evaporated. "This is the news we've been waiting for all these years."

Pressing his hands to his temples, Jaabir hissed, "Don't you understand? If he could find us so easily, then so can the Russians. Since Massoud escaped, they've only one option, and that's to be rid of us. They've nothing to hold over us anymore and that makes us useless to them...and dangerous."

"That war's over! Why would they stick their necks out to get rid of us?"

"Why wouldn't they?" Jaabir shot back at her. "You should've called me down as soon as the guy approached you and gave you this?" Frustrated and afraid, Jaabir threw the parcel on the bed.

"I told you, he was in a hurry. Sticking around was not on his agenda." She paused, before adding, "He...he seemed very nervous."

"What did he tell you? What's going on?"

Despite her own tension, Ameera couldn't hold back a smile. "Well, it turns out Massoud got himself married to a British lady, from a fairly well-to-do family. She hired a detective, the man I spoke with. Oh, Jaabir! We get to see our son again," Ameera said softly. "He – the detective, said Massoud was doing great. He told me Massoud can't wait to be reunited and to find out whether he has a brother or sister." She paused, a scowl crossing her features. "I can't believe the Russians didn't tell him a thing.

They promised us he'd get special treatment."

"Well, at least he's safe," Jaabir said, a little calmer now. "When do you think he'll be able to visit?"

"The man at the bar told me to read the letter. Massoud has all our contact information now. I told the detective to tell him he has a brother."

"The letter," Jaabir muttered, picking up the parcel from the bed and opening it. He unfolded the single sheet of paper inside.

Dear Mom and Dad,

I hope this letter finds you in good health and happy. There is so much to say, to express. The dream of being reunited with you, my family, has kept me alive all these years. Mom, I'm still your little boy! But I am now married and have two children of my own, a boy and a girl and we are expecting another one soon. I promised to stay here for at least five years to repay my debt. That deadline has come and gone so it shouldn't be long. Soon I will make my way to your door. Hopefully, we will be able to communicate more freely one day. For now, it is too dangerous. Once I know this letter has found you, we can then continue to communicate through these channels. My wife goes to America fairly often. I will write more next time. For security reasons I left out names. Please, do not put your lives in jeopardy trying to find or help me. I will locate you when it is safe to do so. I hope I am not bringing danger to you. Keep safe.

Love

Your son

Ameera squealed as she spun around letting her dress flare out, "We're grandparents! How does that make you feel?" she asked.

Jaabir shook his head, smiling widely. "Life in Afghanistan makes me old and weary, but being a grandpa…I'm excited! I want to play with my grandchildren. I'll still be young enough to out run them, I hope. Every time we leave Afghanistan, I look back and realize we are like fish swimming upstream against a current so strong we're constantly pushed backwards. To leave for good is finally to break free, to be able to swim with the current and to fly over waterfalls and overcome all our obstacles. As Hamasa would say, we could be 'free as a kite.' I'm so glad we're making a break for it before it's too late. Massoud can find us in Canada or the USA…I don't know…how does it make you feel?"

"Well, if you're talking play time then I think I can handle that. I'm not changing diapers anymore or yelling at them. I'm done with the yelling. Kids just don't listen unless you show anger and yell at them. Who's conditioning them to be like that? It's too stressful for me now. But there's just too much work to be done, isn't there, I mean, for us to get away from it all?" Ameera sighed. "You know, I feel guilty about leaving, giving up the fight, but we have no other choice."

Jaabir stroked her cheek. "No, we no longer have any choice, my dear. We escaped the Americans who thought we were the Taliban. Now the Russians will want to eliminate us because they no longer need us, or because they think we'll betray them now that Moussad is free. The Taliban could find out at any moment that we did betray them and come after us. We also face the threat of our government. It's just a matter of time. Not even your father could protect us then."

"I've been hearing that the Americans have been warning the Israeli government our lives are in serious danger." He gave a humorless laugh. "Probably because they knew they were going to bomb us, but also because maybe they know the Taliban are on to us. We're sitting ducks now unless they pull us out of here soon." He put his arm around Ameera, drawing her to him. "After today, it can't happen soon enough."

"Can we settle in Canada, do you think?" Ameera asked. "Maybe the West Coast, close to the USA, so if you have to go there it would be less hassle. Hamasa would love it. There would be so many things for him to do."

"Well, that's what we'll do then. We'll check out a few areas, check out the real estate situation, and find a place to settle down and maybe we can finally retire and get away from all this madness. Maybe life will throw us a little joy after all this and we can celebrate our eventual reunion with Massoud."

Jabir wasn't able to sleep or calm his fears until he finally made contact with Mossad, the Israeli spy agency, and they assured him they could safely fly out of Kabul in two days and not have to escape to Pakistan first. They were to stay put at the Hotel to receive all the necessary travel documents. A Mossad agent assured them they had their backs covered; they were as safe as could be for now.

Chapter 5

Massoud Escapes

"I shall be released."
Bob Dylan

His hands bleeding, face covered in mud, Hamasa's brother, Massoud, finally lifted himself out of the grip of hell. Even though a deep breath of frozen Siberian air burned his nostrils and seared his lungs, it was the sweetest breath of freedom he had ever tasted and he promised himself never to forget. As arranged, the 'Jesus Followers' were there, waiting to snatch them to safety. Everyone involved knew their lives were at risk and escaping took total focus from everyone. Greetings and celebrations were saved for later. They had all practiced their parts mentally for years. Not a word was spoken as each of them placed total trust in the other.

It was not until he was safe, next to a fire, eating steaming potato stew, that he acknowledged those around him and reflected on his life.

Jesus! He was ten when the Russians rolled into Kabul with their tanks on December 27th, 1979. He remembered it as clearly as if it had just been yesterday. He could still hear the screams as everyone at the market abandoned their goods and ran for their lives as the mujahedeen did their utmost to stop them. He had held tight to his pregnant mother's hand as the pressure of the crowd stampeding, jostling and pushing, drew them along. And...suddenly...his mother was gone!

Massoud squeezed his eyes closed as the terror and anguish washed over him, as sharp and fresh as if it had only just happened. "They took my life," he said aloud.

No one gave any sign of having heard him as they tore at their food and devoured their meals. Eyes – barely peering out from mud covered faces and scraggy hair – didn't even see he was there as they gazed into the abyss of their disappearing food.

Massoud stared into his bowl, a beetle had fallen out of his hair onto his potatoes: years of habit, without a second thought, it too was devoured.

He had been picked up by one scumbag Russian soldier after the other, sometimes thrown through the air like a football. Finally, tiring of their game, they threw him up onto a tank and shoved him down into the belly of the beast. Weeks passed before he saw the light of day again, when he was transferred to the back of a covered truck full of other prisoners.

"Tahir," he shouted, "you were there with me from the beginning. We survived!"

This time his shout elicited a reaction, but Massoud wasn't sure if the strange grunts and groans were in response to what he had said or the sounds of crazed zombies enjoying a good feast.

He looked over to Tahir, a ghost of a man. He had long white hair and a long white beard that shone in memory only as months of mud and dirt covered the wisdom that use to flame from his mane. Tahir was thin, frail and near death, as so many of the others. From the start, he was always at Massoud's side, protecting him as best as he could. Now, Massoud silently promised to see his friend back to life.

"They threw us into a train that took us to hell, and we might have been the first to escape from a secret Siberian Gulag."

Massoud started to sing a familiar song they had made up. The singing often bonded them together, "Oh, the Gulag's got us grumpy, got us gruffy-n-grizzly, cause we guzzle Gulag grub, 'til Gulag geezer's gizzards get gobbing gobs of gout. Oh, the Gulag's… "

No response! Not even from their saviors, who also seemed captured by the zombie mood as they helped serve food and drink in silence.

As if trolls had gathered all emotions and sucked them into a deep pit as payment for liberation, the morose group kept on staring into their empty bowls as if there they would find something more than food to fill them up and return their souls: some reticent, ethereal wraith.

For the past ten years they had witnessed one prisoner after another die from forced labor, disease and abuse. AK-47s guarded them 24 hours a day. They were sent to nearby logging camps with the North Koreans or to the mining pits with some of Russia's worst criminals.

Often their lives were in the hands of murderers and rapists as they labored together for the coal many feet under the Earth.

Defying the odds – they also dug for their freedom. They worked well together, tunneling themselves out – their future depended on it.

The sole thing that had kept Massoud going was he knew his mother was out there, waiting for him with a sibling he had promised to help raise. He did not wish his mother to worry herself to death and had planned to escape from the moment they incarcerated him. Now that he was finally free, he wondered if the Jesus Followers would do as they had promised: help reunite him with his family. He often wondered whether his mother had given birth to a boy or a girl.

He and the others had promised them five years of their labor to pay the debt for their freedom. Each were taken to different locations to serve out their time. Following that, they expected to be granted safe passage to their homes. Massoud was taken to one of their secret forest hideaways. He could see all the work that had to be done and he wondered if he had simply exchanged one prison labor camp for another; as in the Bob Dylan song, he was about to be introduced to, 'Gotta Serve Somebody'.

Chapter 6

Massoud

"The worst prisons were not constructed of warped steel and stone. They were carved out of expectations and lies, judgment and corruption."
Kelsey Leigh Rebert

He never stood a chance. The moment he laid eyes on her, he was smitten, as was she. That was years ago. Before that moment, he had demanded an end to his servitude and safe passage home to see his mother. Now, two kids later, and a third on the way, his dream and resolve to reach home was still not shattered and he was more determined than ever. However, the Jesus followers had told him he must stay and surrender to the will of his wife and their leader.

"So, Betty, do you still really think the same as your 'Jesus', or are you just playing at being a follower?" Massoud tore into her. The evasiveness stressed him out. "You're just playing a game. It's all in your mind that you're sacrificing your life, living in the wild to herald this new Messiah to the world. It's all a fraud, the guy's a sex crazed egomaniac. He conquered you and now he's going after our daughter. Can't you see that by now?"

"How can you talk like that in this house, on these sacred grounds? After all I've done for you and the kids, don't you dare talk to me that way. You're just jealous, that's all it is," Betty stated as she wrapped her shawl tighter around her slender form. Then, coldly, "Would you mind putting some more logs in the stove? I'll make lunch soon."

She came from a reputable family of English decent who had immigrated to the east coast, Boston area. Her parents were third generation Catholics who came to help build the church with their banking business means and knowledge. They had left England because of the lingering effects of the proclamation of the Church of England, along with the betrayal of the Pope and the Catholic Church by King Henry the Eighth. For three generations the family business had grown as strong and rich as the Catholic Church.

Coming in with some wood for the stove, Massoud continued his attack. "It's only a matter of time till you completely return to your life of comfort; you're hardly here anymore, flying out every chance you can get. It must be dreadful for you to have to come back here?"

"Massoud, you know we've been over this. You know my fear of flying since my brother's plane crash, and the work I'm entrusted to do is becoming so legally complicated, these things are torturing me – forcing me to be away from my family. Can't you see that?" Betty challenged.

"Are you tortured to be away from family or only your 'Jesus' friend, that's what I really want to know?" Massoud shot back.

"I could be gone twice as long if I did the journey by land and sea, at least I get up the courage to fly to make the trips shorter. You don't appreciate anything about me anymore." Betty's eyes flashed fire. She was a striking woman who carried herself with dignity at all times. Sighing, she undid her carefully placed bun and took off the apron she wore and prepared herself for the long fight. She re-directed her anger at a heap of clean laundry, throwing it into the 'to be washed' basket by mistake. She knew better than to prepare food with the rage she was feeling.

"I do appreciate our potential as a family but I sure as hell do not appreciate the things that are going on around here, I can tell you that much." Massoud had as much as he could take for one day, but he could see Betty was not going to budge and would keep defending her position, declining to listen to reason. He was at his wits end, not knowing what to do.

Realizing her mistake, Betty had started to fold the clothes that were ready to be put away.

"Listen, my dear," Massoud said, his voice tightly controlled, "I'd honestly be so happy for you if you reconnected to your family and their financial businesses. You and your brother were the first to stray away from getting involved and look what happened to your brother, and we're headed towards the same fate if things don't change around here soon. The Russians are closing in and could strike at any moment or this lunatic 'Jesus' is going to continue doing stupid things that'll get us killed by the Russian Mafia – or even the police if they raid the place. I'm worried sick about the kids, don't you see that? I know your 'Master' isn't allowing them to leave with you, but you could sneak them out with you the next time and allow them to have a chance in life. What kind of a life can we give them here?"

Betty drew in a long breath and held it before letting it go again. Why couldn't Massoud see how important this was, she fumed.

Her parents had worried she would become a nun. But she had felt stifled in the church with all their pompous rituals and their constant craving for expansion and fund raising. She had felt that her talents were overlooked and underappreciated. The priests gave all their attention to the young boys in order to cultivate the next generation of leaders, and to gratify whatever else priests wanted with young boys. Meanwhile, she had longed for a Jesus that would touch her deeply and personally. The Catholic Church never gave her that earth shattering, soul gripping purpose that she hungered for. For a while she had wavered, like a blade of grass in a high wind but she had never stopped searching for that sense of purpose she needed so badly and, after completing a degree in fine arts, she shocked everybody by becoming a nurse. After a while, that, too, was not enough. So she had volunteered to go overseas to help Third World countries in their life and death struggles. That was how she met followers of a real 'living Jesus'. She had often wondered what it would have been like to sit at the feet of Jesus when he walked the Earth and why it was people two thousand years ago were allowed a visit from God's very own Son, while now people had to be content with visits from bishops in their funny hats. To her mind, the Popes had shamed the cross many times in the past and the idea of a visit to see one did not stir her soul in the least. Finally, though, her faith and courage had been blessed by a personal relationship with God's new living Son that did stir the depths of her soul. Not only that, but He would seek her out to perform high-level duties and sought her opinion and her expertise on many matters. She now knew what it felt like to give one's life completely to another, to God, and to a great cause. She would die for her teacher. If he needed her body, that was a small honor and sacrifice in comparison to being a martyr.

Massoud was still watching her, waiting. Betty dug her fingers into her heavy hair. "You think I don't constantly worry about the kids and what's best for them? Have you forgotten your values and what we used to agree on was best for them? This life is temporary, but the hereafter is forever and that's what they're being prepared for."

Massoud shifted his weight. "I know, I know! You're doing the best that you can, but for Christ's sake, I will not sit idly by while my daughter's being groomed for your teacher's harem!"

There was a deadening silence and Massoud headed out the door to cool off.

Outside, Massoud prowled the grounds restlessly. At first, he had stayed silent when the leader had many legal duties for Betty to tend to in the West, as well as promotions to carry out to attract more followers. She always came back with a renewed vigor for life as a Jesus follower. Massoud usually found it hard to complain, as it was on these trips that she was able to do the research that eventually led to making contact with his family. She let them know he was still alive and eager to meet. She had hired a private detective who found out he had a younger brother. Despite his joy at these developments, he was deeply worried that war still surrounded them and it was very difficult to keep in touch or to talk freely with them.

His wife also brought the outside world with her when she came home to him. She would smuggle in books and music from the West and Massoud's dreams of freedom grew bigger and bigger. His favorite music became the songs of Bob Dylan; he, too, seemed to be searching for truth and freedom.

The challenge for Massoud to overcome was Betty did not have as much to gain as Massoud, and nothing to lose she had not already given up on, which included Massoud, and he knew it. He knew he had lost her to the leader years ago. Now she was pregnant with their third child, and he found himself wondering if it was even his. He had heard the rumors, that even though the leader was married, he could not resist the temptations of having control over the other women who threw themselves at him. Now the rumors were swirling that the leader took a special interest in the younger girls, too. He had warned his wife that he did not want his own daughter, Elizabeth, to become a victim. But Betty stoically ignored his worries, along with his pleas. As much though as Massoud despised the leader's need to control every aspect of all their lives, he was forever indebted to the group and knew if it wasn't for them he wouldn't be planning to meet his brother in Afghanistan, and soon after, his mother and father in Canada. Still, there was only so much a man could take and he had made his decision.

Going back inside, Massoud announced, "Betty, I'm leaving. I feel it's our only hope." His eyes slid away from his wife's stunned face. "I'm doing this for all our sakes. But if I leave first, they might never allow you or the kids out of here again. I want you all to leave while I'm still here. You can think of some reason, your pregnancy, the kid's teeth, some education experience, something, but you have to all leave now. We can start over in Canada or in America, and you can always come back here to your heart's content, but without risking our children's lives. Either way, I'm out of here within the week."

Betty's eyes blazed with agony. "This is how it ends! This is it!" she screamed. "You coward, after all we've been through, after all we've sacrificed. You'll leave your kids?"

"You know I can't take them with me or I would, and this is the only way I can come back and save them, since you intend to stay put with them. If I stay here, I'm only going to be a witness to their destruction, without being able to do anything about it!

"You know the Jesus followers are expanding and meddling with local politics. Well, the government is sure as hell not going to let them have influence at the federal level." He paused, sadness written on the planes of his face. "KGB will follow me," he added quietly. "They'll want to know what I'm up to and why I'm leaving. I'll be in touch when I know it's safe to do so. If they find out who I am, they'll lay a trap for my parents, too. Their best insurance policy is not to need an insurance policy. They'll get rid of their liabilities and honor their oath – 'no one leaves and lives to tell'."

Chapter 7

Growing up in Canada

> "Freedom is never voluntarily given by the oppressor; it must be demanded by the oppressed."
> *Martin Luther King*

Hamasa knew his parents were glad to get him away from the influence of guns, drugs and wars: the very things his grandfather used to secure and expand his empire. He was smart enough to know that being the warlord's grandson had many benefits, of which one was that it kept him from being trained as a suicide bomber, a fate most of the little boys in the village did not escape. Not that being blown to pieces seemed to bother any of them. As soon as they were old enough to understand, they were taught to believe that dying a martyr was the greatest honor they could know and would secure them immortal life. For those who survived into adolescence, the fact they had 72 virgins waiting for them was also an undeniably powerful motivator; they couldn't wait for all the attention they would receive, but first they had to martyr themselves.

Hamasa shook his head sadly, his eyes cloudy with memories: Faraj's dark eyes, open, staring, filled with blood and him running, running away from what was left of his friend's body. Three years older than him, Faraj had been a favorite of his parents. The two of them shared a thirst for knowledge and out of that had grown a friendship that drew them together more surely than a bee to honey. The day Faraj stood up before the council and volunteered to strap bombs to his body and go amongst the approaching American soldiers, Hamasa had listened with horror in his heart and a terrible fear gnawing at his insides. As soon as the meeting finished, he had grabbed hold of his friend, dragging him aside. "Faraj! Please – don't do this!" he begged.

Faraj laughed. "Would you deny me my chance for eternal life? Come, my friend, don't be jealous. Your opportunity will come."

His body came back two days later and the village erupted in a victory celebration. Hamasa retreated to his room. His eyes ached from unshed tears. He missed his friend; anger burned in him for the waste of not only Faraj's life but also the countless other innocents spurred into the arms of 72 cold-hearted virgins.

The noise of the feasting hunted him out even in his bed, pillow covering his ears. "Islam," the villagers' chant rose on the still air. Hamasa gritted his teeth as they continued their rhetoric, snatches finding their way into his unwilling hearing –"The greatest and only true religion, we will dominate the world!"

All the glory would go to Allah and His Prophet, Muhammad. Everyone on Earth would submit to the will of Allah or die. According to the teachings, that was the law of Allah as written in the Koran. A true Muslim, it was told, could never rest until they converted the whole world.

His mother and father had tried their best to shelter him, providing him with proper schooling and encouraging him to question and think for himself, but the outside influences were insurmountable. Now, much to their relief, they had a chance to start fresh, but Hamasa remembered he had heard them talking, worrying, just before they had left Afghanistan.

One bitterly cold night, fifteen minutes after curfew, Hamasa stole silently into the house. His parents were in the kitchen, and his plan was to creep past the door and upstairs to his room. As he carefully placed his foot on the first stair, his mother's voice drifted out to him.

"Is it already too late, Jaabir? Is our son already a rebel warrior

– a terrorist in training, like all the other boys of the village?"

Hamasa stood stock still, momentarily paralyzed by his bafflement; he was the last person who would want to end up being a terrorist. He put his mother's worries down to growing up forced to hide his true thoughts and feelings. His grandfather had dominated the household and he had always, on some level, known it would be nothing short of murder if what he really thought was revealed.

Hamasa, now in Canada, still hung on to the words he had overheard his dad telling Ameera when they were still in Afghanistan.

"Listen, Ameera, soon we will be in Canada and this will all seem like a fading dream." Hamasa waited for the bad dreams to dissolve.

In Canada, Hamasa was grateful he didn't have any chance to be a forced warrior in training. The family moved to South Surrey, Grandview area, on acreage near White Rock, British Columbia.

"Dad, this is amazing, I can't believe we get to live here," Hamasa belted out as they were touring around Vancouver, planning future activities.

"Look, Hamasa, there's the road to go up to the ski hill," his dad yelled back over the roar of wind and traffic coming in through the open windows of their car. "We'll come back on a clear day. Apparently a person can see all of Vancouver from the top of that hill. I hear there is a trolley or chair lift that takes people to the top – sounds cool."

"Yeah, that's so cool," Hamasa said. "We can golf or play at the beach during the day and go skiing at night up there. Remember all the lights we saw on that mountain there – it's so people can ski at night. It's so cool. I can't wait 'til I can try that. Can I, Mom? Can I, Dad, please?"

"Well, son, there's so much to do here. We'll have to see. Maybe you'll meet a few friends and you'll be able to tag along with them if they go. I mean, look, there's water sports, summer activities like riding bikes, winter sports and so many team sports you will hopefully do through school."

"Wow, you are one lucky boy," his mom offered. "I am so happy for you."

"Yeah, but I still worry about what happened back home. Have you heard from Grandad, and how are my friends, the ones who aren't martyrs? I feel we deserted them when they needed us the most." Hamasa sulked. "I'll do the best I can here so I can go back and help. I was a man there, Grandad said I was a man, but here I feel like a helpless little boy again. I fired machine guns and protected the village and you, Mom. Here, I am just a helpless little boy expected to play all day."

"Hey, that's not true, you have your studies," Ameera pleaded. "You have to focus on your studies and you will be protecting us with your brains and the new skills you will develop. Maybe you will save us and help our people by becoming a doctor, or maybe you will invent new ways computers will save the world. Here in Canada, the gifts you were born with can be fully developed. You'll see, you'll understand someday. Just give it some time. It's so different here and the things you excelled at are not recognized here, like your kite flying, so it will take time to adjust. At least you can speak English and you love learning. Soon you will be on top of the world here."

As they drove over the Lions Gate Bridge from North Vancouver, Hamasa cried out to visit Stanley Park.

"It's so clean here, look at the huge trees. There's no dust, it's clean, clean, clean. Even the salty air smells so clean. Park the car, Dad, we'll go explore! Yes, we'll make the best of it here. I am so ready for new experiences, and we're going to live the American dream, right?" He chuckled.

"But this is Canada," his dad bellowed as they all laughed.

Hamasa slowly started to adjust to his new life in Canada and twelve turned into thirteen and into those difficult teenage years of trying to fit in and be cool.

"Hey, Mas," Billy called from across the ballpark. Billy was the kind of boy nobody gave bad attitude to or ignored. Sixteen, and he was already at least six feet, shaggy blond hair, blue eyed and a chiseled chin, plus a grin girls could not abstain from, even though they knew it only promised a moment's ecstasy until the heartache and slut labelling took them to a dark place where his blue eyed leer couldn't penetrate.

Billy waited until Hamasa came to him before continuing. "Not too many get this privilege, but you wanna' cruise in my car after practice? There's this bitch I gotta' get off my back. You kiss 'em once and they think they can own you. Anyway, she keeps askin' about you – says it's for a friend but I'm sure it's her, if you know what I mean. I think you'll hit it off with her. Just wait by the road there. You're about to have your mind blown. How old are you anyway? I'm guessing you must be at least sixteen, like me, right? You would have to be, to be that good at soccer and ball. Thank God you're not one of those weird religious types, Muslim or whatever, that wear weird things on their heads. You seem pretty cool and you sure drive the girls crazy. I just don't have time for any of those religious nuts that keep movin' to these parts."

"Right, but hey, man, you're not even eighteen yet – I don't know – how is it you can drive a car?" Hamasa countered.

"Sixteen is legal here, man. Where the hell are you from? And eff off, you be there or you're a chicken shit. Guys'd kill to be in your shoes, cruisin' with the man – don't be talking shit like that. You be there, and hey, Mas, take a shower, the girls like it clean. Gotta keep it cleeeen, you know what I meeean."

Hamasa had heard all the rumors about Billy and the boys stealing cars and joy riding, flying cars off ramps and hills, squealing around until there was not much car left and then using them for shagging in the woods. By now, Hamasa was too busy with his studies and all the school sporting activities to remember his homeland and his humanitarian goals. He found that his energy was through the roof and he always had to keep moving. Wild sensations and thoughts were trying to take over his usual caring, reflective vibes. Did Billy mention girls?

"What, this isn't a fancy cruise! How're we gonna' pick up chicks in this?" Hamasa screamed as Billy rolled up in a beat-up old station wagon. It was hard to tell dark blue was its color. Black paint was splashed over the dents and there were bare rusty scrapes.

"This is the cleanest place on Earth, and yet you managed to get this thing so dirty I can't see the rims never mind the car. Is this some kinda' joke you puttin' on me?"

"OK, OK, first we'll go to your house and you can introduce me to your parents and I'll let them know you're with me for the weekend. Just let me do all the talkin', I'm good at this. Here, you can give 'em this note with my parent's phone numbers. That'll shut 'em up from asking too many questions. You just tell 'em we got ball practice and games out in the Chilliwack area. Don't worry, my Pa'll cover for us. He keeps tellin' me he was young once, too. He keeps tellin' me it's all a numbers game for us boys. I'm talkin' girls now, that's what this is all about, right? Can you believe it, that's my old man talkin' here. You'll have to meet him – blow your mind. When I was nine, he taught me how to scare the livin' daylights out of the old neighbors across the street. Yeah, we'd tie up nuts and bolts and with fishin' line stretched out to the nearest hiding spot, we'd yank on it, causin' the bolts to hit against the door. At night they wouldn't see the line and they would come to the door wonderin' who was knockin' and sometimes they would be greeted with splattered eggs all over 'em if our aim was good. Can you believe it, that's my old man tellin' me to do that. He'd be the one watchin' and laughin' the hardest. Anyway, man, it's all about freedom.

You're gonna' experience more freedom than you've ever felt in your life, man."

It seemed as if Billy would and could go on and on forever.

"Yeah the freedom to get yourself killed or put in jail, maybe that's the freedom you're talkin' 'bout," Hamasa managed to squeak. "So where's the girls you keep talkin' 'bout?"

"Leanne, the one I told ya' 'bout can't come. I think she's on the rag, but don't worry, I got that shit covered. Remember it's all a numbers game. When a guy's old n dyin' he'll wish he banged a lot more girls than he did. When a girl's old n dyin' she'll still be wishin' she never kissed so many frogs and had only met that one perfect prince who stayed with her forever. Man, can it get any more eff'd up than that? The complete opposite! So you gotta' just ignore what everyone's tellin' ya' and just go with what your biology is screamin' at ya'. When you're old n' dyin' you'll be thankin' me for tellin' ya'. You gotta' hit that shit when you're young, man. Don't be regrettin' nothin'. Yeah freedom! Crank up the tunes, man, let's get this show on the road."

"This thing even have tunes?" Hamasa snarked.

"Hey eff-off." Billy slammed on the brakes and let Hamasa hit his head on the dash. "Of course this ain't my wheels. You think I'm gonna' let a little shit like you cruise in my wheels? Wait 'til you see how the back seat folds down – gives lots of shaggin' room, you know what I mean. Besides, I might just teach you to drive, and that would never happen in my car. You smash this up n' you'll be our little hero. It'll get you laid faster than a twenty dollar bribe. And you'll be one of the gang; yeah you'll be in on all our secrets."

"So you stole this son of a bitchin' car? I can't believe what I'm gettin' myself into. Let's get the effin' out a' here." Hamasa knew there was no turning back, no copping out.

By the end of the weekend, Hamasa had lifted those four wheels off the ground, soaring over steep inclines on the lakeside roads near Chilliwack. He smoked his first cigarette, drank, and got into a rock fight with the local boys. It happened when their out of town group hit on the local lake girls: they just couldn't take the competition. But they couldn't stop the hook-ups and later, Hamasa watched one of the girls getting laid – well, at least he saw the sleeping bags going crazy – by none other than Billy, in the back of the station wagon, while he pretended to be asleep in the front seat.

Yes, Hamasa had met all of Billy's male friends who were hanging out at beautiful Cultus Lake near Chilliwack B.C. He let go of all his inhibitions and just went with the flow. There were no limits for these delusional, convinced of their own immortality and invincibility, thrill seekers. He felt free, flying to new horizons. He yearned for his friends back home to see him free as a kite, and for them to be flying free, too. He wanted to get the most out of it before the dream ended and he was uprooted once more and dragged back to Afghanistan: confined to a life hidden behind four, high, gloomy, stone walls.

The only thing required from him was to let his parents know what he was up to and who he hung out with, and to keep getting good marks at school. He had a curfew but he was allowed to sleep over at friends and his freedom seemed to double when his friend's parents were in charge, especially Billy's.

His mom, Ameera, still carried with her many of the fears and nightmares of war torn Afghanistan. Hamasa's dad, Jaabir, would keep telling her not to worry because they were now in Canada.

"Here in Canada, Hamasa can have a normal upbringing and be like the other boys his age," his dad would say.

So almost every weekend and holidays, Hamasa took off on other adventures. He was determined to make the most of his good fortune of being in Canada, but he had no idea of the consequences that would soon follow his newfound freedoms.

One weekend, on Sunday, the boys rode their bikes to Kits Beach, where kites were popular and Hamasa finally showed off his flying feats. At first, he was shy and thought the boys would laugh at him. However, even Billy was amazed.

"Hey, Mas, you gotta teach me how to do that. Look at all the chicks comin' to watch you. I never knew you did gymnastics, and how do you do that while you're flying that thing? Here, let me take a hold of it," Billy ordered as he took control of the string, trying to keep the kite in the air.

"Hold it tight, it's a gloriously sunny day but that wind is extremely strong," Hamasa ordered back. Just then, a mighty wind tore the string from Billy, leaving him yelling in pain as blood rushed out of his cut up hands.

"Sorry, I couldn't hold it, come on we'll catch it when it crashes."

Billy and Hamasa ran and ran, hoping to catch a hold of the magnificent kite that teased them with its freedom flight. They ran past the old army cannon towers, all the way to a distant secluded area where it had crashed into the ocean and washed up on the shores of Wreck Beach. This beach was segregated from the rest of the area; Hamasa knew the reason for that, of course. Wreck Beach was home to a colony of nudists. However, knowing and seeing were different ball games. Like a two-legged giraffe, his neck stretched as far as possible to see the nudes all the way to the end of the beach, and his tongue hung out like a sun bear's. If his tongue had hung out any more, he could have licked the place clean as well as retrieving his kite. Billy had forgotten all about the kite and joined the nudists in their birthday suits. He had honed in on a group of university girls who weren't too serious about their studies.

Hamasa grabbed his kite and headed over to a group of musicians who were jamming with guitars and bongos and singing up a storm. Naked bodies were twisting and jiving to the strange wild rhythms. He was surprised no one made out in this sensual, hot, almost tropical paradise. He soon realized why when he saw a self-motivated group of vigilantes chase after sexual deviants with sticks and the wrath of their screams. He saw one poor fellow who couldn't contain his erection chased off into the forest. He also saw the police patrolling the area. Even so, Hamasa knew this would have to become his new hangout, a place he knew his parents would never venture. Wreck Beach added a completely new dimension to the word 'freedom'.

"Hey, Billy, we better get back to the boys, we have a long ride ahead of us," Hamasa stated.

"Forget that, I've arranged a truck to pick us up with our bikes, so relax. The boys aren't going anywhere without us. Come on, I'll introduce you to some girls I met, but you look mighty weird with all your clothes on. The girls will strip you down though, which might be a good strategy. How's the kite? Did it survive?"

"Yeah, it survived. Maybe the girls would like to fly it?" Hamasa speculated.

Walking back to school after lunch the next day while thinking about the lithe, naked, female bodies he had seen that weekend, Hamasa's attention focused on a noisy huddle of boys. As he drew closer, he realized what was happening; the lads had ganged up on a girl. Hamasa started running. The hornet's nest was three or four hornets deep as they swarmed around the terrified girl, and to his shame, he saw they had ripped the clothes from her body. "Stop!" he yelled.

Immediately, one of the boys ran out from the center of the frenzied mob, almost falling onto Hamasa. Hamasa half caught him; the boy's face was red, his eyes shining. "I think I touched her boob!" he crowed.

Hamasa didn't have a sister, but his mother had raised him to have respect. Yes, he got excited seeing the girls on Wreck Beach, but that was their choice; no one tore their clothes off them or grabbed at them. No one humiliated them, as these boys were doing to this poor girl! Somehow, he had to stop them before things went too far and they raped her. He swooped in and started dragging the boys away. "Let her go, you idiots! Leave her alone!" But as soon as he pulled one away, another rushed back into the melee.

"Let her go, you guys!" he yelled frantically. "What the hell do you think you're doing! Just let her go!"

At that moment, Louise Holden, an older, taller and surprisingly muscular girl hove into view. Sizing up the situation in one glance, she sprang into action.

"Hamasa, get out of my way!" she barked. Picking up the nearest boy by his collar, she sent him flying with a punch. Her enraged screams would have been enough to intimidate an elephant. Charging forward, she clawed through the group until she reached the naked girl, who lay sobbing, curled up into the fetal position.

"Are you OK, Anita?" Louise asked, recognizing the girl as she gently stroked Anita's shoulder length, sandy-brown hair. "These guys are monster rabbits! I let them have a screw every Friday. I don't know why they couldn't wait for me to get here! Here...here's your panties. You'd better put this sweater round you 'til I find all your clothes." She glared at the boys, her eyes flashing daggers. "You guys are horny monsters!" she growled. "Get me her clothes, quick! You'll never get another Friday 'piece day' from me, I can swear to that!"

Glancing back at Anita, the fire in her gaze gave way to compassion. "You're the only girl they've seen with big tits," she whispered. "I think that's why they went after you. I hope you're OK. Try not to get too upset, in their own twisted way, these fools think they were giving you the highest of compliments. It's not your fault, hon, you did nothing wrong."

"Yeah, I'm OK." Anita had stopped crying. She sniffed. "I don't want to tell the school about this. They didn't really hurt me or do much." She giggled breathily. "It's the first time I ever saw a boy's hard snake though."

Louise frowned, she finished helping Anita get back into her clothes and wrapping her up in her sweater started to walk her back to school.

"You have to tell," she said, "or they'll just keep doing it. Next time you'll end up pregnant and you won't even know who the daddy is, because so many of them lizards would be spittin' it at you." Louise stopped, spinning Anita around to face her. "You're a beautiful lady. You don't deserve to be treated like that. You have to tell on them. If you don't, I will!" she said flatly. "It's all a game of power and money. They took your power and didn't pay a thing. When I screw those rabbits I make sure they give me whatever I want. It's me who has the power and they know it. Don't sell yourself short; the poor things need it so bad they'll give whatever you desire, it's just nature. Use whatever you got to seduce 'em, after the dirty pigs have gone in for the kill, you 'n the kids can blackmail 'em for the rest of their lives."

"There were four of them that started it," Anita said, a catch in her voice. "I took the short cut back to school, through the woods here. Bobby came out of nowhere and begged me to let him feel my boobies." She bit her lip. "It's OK at school, I feel safe flirting with the boys there, and even the male teachers, showing them my cleavage, it's kinda' nice to get all the attention, but out here, in the woods – freakin' scary! All of a sudden, there were four of them groping me. They were pushing at me and I fell. I guess that's when the rest of the boys joined in. She glanced away from Louise, her eyes shiny with unshed tears. "I'll give you the names of the four boys, but other than that..." She shook her head, "I don't know who did what. "Hamasa..." she gave a jerky nod to where he was following a few steps behind, "tried to stop it before you came along, so don't get him involved in this," she pleaded.

They did tell, and Hamasa found out later the attitude of the heads of school was 'boys will be boys.' They did, however, call the four lads involved into the principal's office and whatever was said stopped the attacks from happening again.

His parents must have sensed he was going through some heavy changes that were crushing down on him, like being smothered by a hippopotamus. They tried to introduce him to Christianity in a big way, hoping Jesus would influence him to have forgiveness and peace in his heart, instead of following in the old ways of war. In Afghanistan, his parents had never let it be known they believed in Jesus, now, they, too, were free of many restrictions and were exploring different ways of being.

"Islam has betrayed the Afghani people and brought more bad than good to our country," his father told him as his mother silently nodded in agreement. "Before the Muslims took over, only a few decades ago, there were many religions, beliefs and even great scientific discoveries in Afghanistan – Buddhists, Zoroastrians and others, too," he went on. "Islam is not the religion of peace it proclaims itself to be," his father said, voice rising. "Politicians took it over and used it to build their empires. Their agenda is for Islam to dominate the world, kill everyone who opposes it! And all that violence, just so they can have money, power and the right to an eternal after-life with their God."

His parent's words fell largely on deaf ears, however. The timing was just not right. An outgoing, handsome boy of fourteen, introduced to a completely new world of western culture and going through adolescence, already questioning the validity of his own religion, was not suddenly going to absorb and embrace this new Christian religion and accept Jesus as his new savior.

Hamasa became obsessed with girls, with meeting girls, thinking about girls and the love he longed to express and feel that only a girl could unlock. He drew the Canadian girls to him as easily as breathing, and they were not shy, usually making the first move to break through any language or cultural barriers. They made sure they invited him along with them wherever they were going and kept him informed of any cool events.

Even when school events died down, the parties dried up or the weather was too cold, there was always television and movies to keep the magic thoughts and fantasies going. For the first time he saw movies on a big screen, too. Music that gave feelings of magic powers, freedom and rebellion went with every minute of the day. He could not believe he was free to openly dance with girls. He went wild for dancing; twisting his body around and shaking his head about sent him into blissful trances. Of course, boys and girls secretly flirted in Afghanistan, but there was hell to pay if you were ever caught. Here, the two sexes openly touched and even kissed. This new culture seemed to pump his body with hormones and urges. He was not sure, however, how or if he should control them. He grew desperate with desire to touch a girl and fantasized about kissing the girls he met. Seeing them and being so close at school every day became insufferable. Often, his manhood would get hard and ache as it pulsated with blood. He would unconsciously start rubbing it against his desk or try to push it, using his pocketed hand, back into its sheathed shell where it could hide and pretend to be a harmless slug. Unlike a turtle's head, he couldn't scare it back into hiding. The girls would look at him and giggle, never understanding, he hoped, why he squirmed around in his desk. He was no longer the Hamasa that he knew and understood. How does one deal with urges they can't control?

To make it worse, they even taught sex education at school, telling the boys it would be better to 'spank the monkey' than to get girls pregnant. There was so much information out there on everything about sex.

Barry Thomas, one of the boys who girls always rejected, found out about a sexual high created by asphyxiation during masturbation. His mother found him hanging by a rope with his hands still wrapped around his oiled up banana. Sex and love, the greatest purpose and pleasure of life, yet so elusive and hard to come by and hold on to.

Hamasa tried masturbation, too, but could not get anything to come out like the other boys, who all insisted they could. At school, one cool, fall day, Hamasa asked his friends about it.

"Hey, I'll come over to your place tonight and help you with that little problem of yours," Terry teased.

"Really," Hamasa replied. I saw you with Peggy at the party the other night. You done the nasty yet? Why don't you bring her with you?"

"Hey, no problem, I'll see you later then."

"But it'll be better to sleep over at your place, my parents won't go for something like that," Hamasa whined.

Terry had the door open almost before Hamasa had knocked. To Hamasa's relief, the house seemed empty and quiet except for the low sound of the TV coming from the living room. He followed Terry up the narrow, dark stairs to his room, which seemed like a converted attic. You could only stand in the middle corridor as the ceiling quickly slanted to the four-foot walls. A hurried glance around showed him Peggy had decided not to join them. Terry wasted no time in shucking off his clothes and sliding into bed. Hamasa, more reluctantly, took off his own clothes and slipped under the covers next to Terry, who had started without him.

Hamasa, too, began masturbating, after some time he was moved to speak. "See," he said, sounding a little out of breath, "I pull and pull and milk it for all I'm worth and nothing happens."

"Here." Terry reached over to his bedside table, scooping up a tin. "You gotta' try this cream. It makes all the difference. I'll put it on for you."

Hamasa tensed, feeling awkward as Terry smothered his penis in cream and started milking it for what seemed like forever. Hamasa grew more and more uncomfortable with the situation, with Terry touching him. When he agreed to come here, he'd hoped there would be a manual or magazines with pictures. He hoped Peggy would offer some solution or point out his bad technique. Instead, he was lying naked in bed with another guy, who obviously enjoyed playing with a new toy, one that happened to be attached to Hamasa and affecting him in the most peculiar way. Suddenly he started to feel a weird, burning sensation he wasn't sure was painful or pleasurable. Before he had time to analyze it more, a volcano erupted, and there it was, finally, white gobs of semen spewing out everywhere. Hamasa lay in the aftermath, overcome with mixed emotions, images flashed across his mind: the dancing naked nymph his grandfather thrust on him, then horror, Grandfather's smelly breath on his skin, probing, pushing: pain and fear tumbling together, suffocating him…and rage exploded in his head. He turned his face into the pillow. "Get out!" he hissed. He screwed his eyes closed and kept them shut until he heard the bedroom door open and close. Throwing himself out of bed, Hamasa wiped himself clean with the sheets, dressed, and silently let himself out. As he made his way home, he realized what an idiot he had been. What if Terry had tried to kiss him or penetrate him like his grandfather had? Why had his grandfather done that to him? He understood men could be born homosexual, it was natural, but he quivered at the thought there were forces greater than love and respect that forced their way onto humanity. Hamasa, shaken up by the whole experience, felt a mix of a rage of hate and revulsion, along with his continued devotion to his grandfather. When he reached home, he ignored everyone and only calmed down after taking it out on a punching bag.

A few weeks later, still fourteen, recovered, he stole his first kiss. He was determined to explore his sexuality through love only, but it was frustratingly hard to come by. A year later, he touched a girl intimately for the first time. They were outside the school, leaning up against the wall in the dark, waiting for the doors to open and for the school dance to begin. Hamasa, shy and awkward, not helped by an owl that stared intently at them from a nearby tree, turned to her. She was two years older and her name was Shelley. Her boyfriend had driven them there and left since he couldn't get in to the dance as he was a drop out and too old, anyway, at twenty. He assured them he would pick them all up later. Hamasa reached out for her hand and she responded in kind.

"So, have you ever touched a girl's private parts?" Shelley whispered, staring into his eyes. "You're so cute; I bet all the girls show their private parts to you."

"No, not…not really," Hamasa admitted sheepishly, embarrassed. "I believe it'll happen when I fall in love."

Taking hold of Hamasa's right hand, she slowly and coyly rubbed it over her flat, smooth belly. Suddenly she grabbed his wrist and forced his hand under her blue-jeans and onto the elusive soft, moist prize. The sensation could never be repeated. This once in a lifetime event of gigantic significance had Hamasa's brain flooded with dopamine and the bliss that followed. Shelley allowed his fingers to penetrate her and to explore her sex. Hamasa twisted his arm around so he could face her. She was the most beautiful Canadian girl he had ever seen. She had long, blondish hair, stirred by a light breeze into wispy trails that fell across her face: her eyes peering through the silky strands, an image so sexy he was convinced it would stay ingrained in his mind forever. He wanted her to touch him, too, so, so badly. He could not control the urge to rub against her. He melted away by the second in a burning blaze that engulfed his whole mind and body. Almost without volition, Hamasa found himself grinding madly up against her leg like a dog in heat. His left hand searched blindly for her soon to be woman's breast. Somewhere in the back of his brain, luscious thoughts burst into being; this would be his first girlfriend, his first love, and their love would explode into a rapturous joy that would fill the world and the Universe. Her full lips beckoned him to a life of exquisite fulfillment and he leaned in ready to experience a passionate kiss. Puckering up, he waited for the ecstasy of contact.

"Hey, what are you doing, lover boy?" Shelley asked as she excommunicated his hand from the 'Garden of Eden.' Turning into an ice queen, she exiled all bananas, peaches and coconuts from the lost frozen paradise. "I've got a boyfriend, remember? Come on, the dancing's started. Let's find the gang inside."

"Why did you let me do that?" Hamasa whimpered.

"Hey, today's Friday, 'Peace Day.' Remember? Boys get a piece, but just a piece – not the whole apple pie, besides, you're payin' now." She snickered.

Hamasa got lost in another world the whole night. He had never danced so wildly, showing off his moves. In his heart, he was still convinced she loved him and that there was a chance they could be together again.

He joined his friends who were going outside to do some hashish and marijuana. It was Hamasa's first encounter with hashish. By the time he went back inside, his head was in a whirl. Throwing himself down into a comfortable chair, he closed his eyes in the hope the lights streaking across the room would stop. Everyone was acting strange, as if drawn into a dream world.

"Hamasa, how are you? Are you having fun tonight?"

Squinting, Hamasa vaguely recognized shy, insecure Alice. She was a pretty, popular girl, a year younger and a grade below and for a moment he toyed with the idea that she could remedy his current dejection, although he'd always been drawn to the older girls.

"Hey, how's it going, Alice?" he slurred, then he tittered. "Hey, lo-oo-ok at Mr. Smith, our science teacher, he's dancing with, with, ha-ha, I don't know. Everything's blurry. Ish it blurry for you? Hey, have you seen Alice? He chuckled. I was just thinking she should be dancing with Mr. Smith, she loves science." Hamasa began giggling again.

"Wow!" Alice shook her head, "I don't know what you're on, but you are so weird tonight. I love the way you dance though.

By the way, you are talking to Alice." She leaned towards him, tapping her finger on his forehead. "Hamasa are you in there?"

"Oh my God! Did you just barf on me? Alice just barfed on me, you guys. Hey, guys, Alice just barfed on me!"

"Hamasa! How rude! Of course I didn't barf on you! Why would you say such a thing?"

"Look, it's all over me. Guys, what should I do?"

His friends finally wandered over.

"Hamasa, stop being weird man," Billy said, "just get on with it. Alice wants you, man – she wants to dance. Isn't that right, Alice? Go dance!"

"Oh my God," he cried, in the grip of his hallucination, "she barfed on me!"

He turned on Alice. "Why did you barf on me? Why did you barf on me?"

His friends had begun to move away but hearing him yelling they returned to see what the matter was.

"Help me," he pleaded. "Help me get cleaned up!"

Tom slapped his own forehead. "You're crazy, man," he growled. "There's no vomit."

Hamasa couldn't believe his friends would desert him like this. He ran to the washroom, only to reappear some time later, soaking wet from head to toe.

"Look at Hamasa!" Alice gasped. "He must have really believed I barfed on him." She shot the group a worried look. "What kinda' drugs did he take? You guys better stay with him and help him – he obviously gets really affected. It's making him go crazy! I've never seen anybody go that insane from smokin' weed!" she exclaimed.

After, the girls kept their distance and Hamasa sank into a stupor dreaming about Shelley. Soon it was him running outside to puke. As he did his best to clean off his shoes, he swore he would never smoke anything again. He hated regular cigarettes anyway.

After the dance, Jimmy arrived to pick up his girl, Shelley, and give the rest of them a ride down the road to their friend's place. Shelley jumped in the cab and was all over Jimmy, like a lost, hungry puppy just reunited with its owner. They were kissing passionately, seemingly oblivious to everyone else.

Hamasa and his friends jumped in the back of the pickup for a quick ride down the road. When the truck slowed down, they all jumped off the back. Hamasa was so heavy hearted he didn't clear the rear truck bed properly. As Jimmy burned rubber, squealing his tires on the pavement, the truck swerved, and Hamasa fell under it. The back tire rolled over his leg. Hamasa screamed while the boys dragged him to safety onto the sidewalk. The truck sped off into the night without Shelley so much as giving him a single glance. Hamasa knew she must have heard the screaming; the truck windows were rolled down.

"OK, OK, Hamasa, you can stop the screaming," Tom teased.

"She ain't comin' to save you; she didn't even notice you getting hurt." Harry snorted.

As he dragged himself to his feet, Hamasa finally accepted the ice queen would not be his first love. He never told anyone about their encounter. He didn't think Shelley did either, as no one ever brought it up. It was a non-event that lingered in his mind indelibly. As he limped around waiting for his leg to heal, his fingers burned with the memory.

As soon as he was back to normal, he went back to exploring what his new country had to offer, filled with hope and awe at what the future might hold. There were bikes with more than one gear that could go up hills. He had never seen so much pavement to skateboard on: the ocean, the boats, surfing, it was all too much. The seasons were amazing and there was always a new activity to make each one special. He had never skied before moving here; of course, how could hockey not become a favorite sport? Chewing gum, coke-a-cola, and snickers bars were to die for. He could have camp-outs where boys and girls could actually meet up in the girl's tents and play spin the bottle, until all the glorious mysteries about the birds and bees had been explored. Then there were the secret digs, to uncover buried treasure: magazines with real women in their true glory. They slid these glossy rites of passage under their jackets while shopping at the local magazine store; they refused to call it stealing because for some reason it was against the law for them to buy them. All they were doing was protesting their lawful right to a proper education. Someone had once said a picture told a thousand words; to Hamasa it was pure poetry. They had them buried all over the place, in back yards, alleyways, by the paths leading to school and places in the woods where they hung out.

Several weeks later, Hamasa and some school friends were out aimlessly wandering the streets and drinking, when Jerry Holms, a boy they sometimes hung with who played clarinet in the school band, drove by in his 'old tank', a 59 Bentley. He had spent many days, nights and weekends fixing up the old car, and Hamasa had to admit, done an excellent job. The paint job shone and the leather upholstery gleamed. From the sound of the engine, Hamasa was pretty sure things were just as sparkling clean under the hood.

"Hey," he called, pulling over. "You guys want a lift? She's a beauty, right?" he said, proudly running his hand over the polished wood dashboard.

"You're drinking and driving aren't you?" Hamasa asked. "I admit I did it, too, once, but I nearly killed myself racin' with Billy. I couldn't make a turn and I flew over a ditch into a gravel parking lot. It's a miracle there were no cars on the road that day or in the parking lot because I slammed on the brakes and the car spun around and around completely out of control. I'm so lucky to have survived that. But when my car stopped working I was stupid enough to jump in with Billy, who proceeded to crash into the first parked car he saw on the side of the road. Billy was too drunk to even know what happened, but I went through the windshield and when I woke up with blood everywhere, Billy just drove off in that stolen car, not givin' a damn and left me to walk myself to the hospital. You listening to me, Jerry? You should park that thing and walk with us, but we're not gettin' in that car with you all drunked up."

"What's it to ya'?" Jerry retorted sarcastically. "Nobody's gonna' tell me what to do." He laughed. "Come on, we'll pick up some chicks and show 'em how to have fun." He revved the engine, burning rubber all over the road. "I'll show you guys," he shouted. He floored it down a couple of blocks, spun around and raced towards Hamasa and the group, but just as suddenly lost control. The old Bentley slewed around, hit a telephone pole, and flipped onto the roof. Hamasa and his friends, frozen with shock, stared as Jerry hung upside down in front of them. A show for all the world, as if he was flying a plane upside down and having the time of his life – except for his unblinking brown eyes and the blood that spewed out from him; pouring through the open window and onto the dirty street.

Hamasa was the first to move, running over to the wreck. "Jerry," he said softly, frightened by that unblinking stare and the amount of blood everywhere. Receiving no reply, he gently shook him by the shoulder. "Jerry, are you OK? Sa...say something."

By now, the others had reached them, but no one knew what to do, how to help. Hamasa wondered if, like him, they already knew in their guts there was nothing they could do.

The crash had brought people out of their homes.

"Leave him be, boys," a burly man in a white string vest told them. "The police are coming."

Another couple of men were trying to talk to the young driver but getting no response. Time seemed to have stopped because Hamasa had no idea how long it was before he heard the wail of the black and white and the ambulance siren. The police asked them a bunch of questions, which they numbly did their best to answer, while the ambulance men slid the lifeless body into their vehicle and set off. Was this the cost of freedom, Hamasa had wondered, but life just kept on rolling on.

"Hey, what's up?" Hamasa asked, as Billy pulled up, in his souped up '87, black, Corvette, fire airbrushed on the sides and hood, early one Saturday morning. It had a super charger, a raised hood scoop and a tail wing.

"We found a new construction site and there's no guards, nothin'. We'll play your favorite game, runnin' from one end to the other without touching ground."

"So what's in it for me?" Hamasa asked.

"Well, Mas, how 'bout a night at the drive-in, just you 'n a babe in my hot, and I mean hot, roadster. There's not a babe this side of the moon that wouldn't go with you in this."

"Easy for you to say, you always win. So what's your prize this time?"

'I'm sure the boys will think of something. Let's go!"

As luck would have it, it was a rainy Saturday afternoon by the time the game got started. No matter what happened, the game couldn't end 'til there was a winner, even if the police came. It was a large, fresh site. Building materials were stacked up everywhere and only one of the three buildings was framed. The third building looked like it would be a tall, cement tower as the foundation was already poured and cement walls were already towering up from a deep pit. Plastic covered most everything, with one slip you'd be a bloody, muddy mess.

As Hamasa followed behind Billy's usual lead, they heard a terrified scream echo through the silent site, quickly followed by a muffled thump and a cry of pain. As Billy and Hamasa stopped to look at what had happened, another competitor, Harry, jumped off the first building, to take the lead. Not willing to lose the game, Billy quickened his pace and ran on the top of a ten-foot pile of plywood sheets, then jumped to a pile of loosely stacked pellets. They gave way and Billy tumbled to the ground, striking a pile of two by fours that crashed on top of him. Since he landed on a plywood sheet, he was technically still in the game, so he threw the wood off himself and climbed back up the mountain of pellets. It looked like he might lose this match to Harry, so he doubled his determination to win, not giving a thought to the accident Tom just had.

His heart pounding, Hamasa had run to see Tom huddled over, clutching his foot, sobbing. Hamasa thought he must have broken something, but when he made his way down to him, he saw the nail which had pierced the bottom of his foot, gone all the way through, narrowly missing bone, and stuck up through the top. Hamasa, repressing a shudder, mouthed words meant to comfort, and the gang helped Tom hobble back to Harry's truck. Hamasa ran to find Harry so they could drive Tom to the hospital. He was also desperate to stop any one else from being hurt and yelled for Billy and Harry to stop the game. He closed in on Billy.

"Stop the game! Stop the game! Tom's hurt real bad and we got to get Harry to drive him to the hospital. He jumped onto a board with a six inch rusted nail that crashed through his foot."

Hamasa kept running, together with Billy, to find Harry so they could drive Tom to the hospital.

It was too late; they heard another scream and then complete silence.

Billy said, "I last saw him jumping onto the third building there and running along those cement walls rising from the foundation."

They ran to the building at ground level and found Harry at the bottom of a deep, unfinished elevator shaft, blood spewing from his mouth and stomach. He was dead. He must have over jumped the wall and fallen headfirst, landing on the cement flooring, littered with tools, crowbars and shovels.

Hamasa had hoped Harry would take Tom to the hospital.

Then no one would get into trouble for being at the construction site, but now there was no way out and he had to phone the police and get an ambulance to the scene as quickly as possible.

"Don't even think about it, Billy, we've got to phone 911. We can't move the body, we can't even get to him down there to move him somewhere else." Hamasa's voice trembled as he held back tears, but he was sure he knew what Billy was thinking.

"You listen to me good now, Mas, you got that!" Billy screamed. "We're gonna' take Tom to the hospital on the other side of the city from here. We're gonna' leave this place like we were never here and we're gonna' never say a word about this to anyone, you got that, Mas? They'll find Harry soon enough and it'll be a stupid thing he did to himself. You got that, Mas? You got that? Now let's get the hell out of here!"

"We have to find a phone," Hamasa screamed back, emotions getting the better of him now. One more look down at his friend and Hamasa was puking all over himself.

By then the other boys had come and they knew they had to get going and take Tom to the hospital, but they had all agreed on the story they were going to tell everyone after they phoned 911. They agreed they were all supposed to meet at the Dairy Queen down the street but when Harry didn't show up they drove around to find him. They would then say they found his truck, parked in front of the construction site, but no sign of him anywhere. They were worried he may have strayed onto the site. They called out for him but no answer came. There was no one around. Tom said he would look around for Harry, but then he stepped on the nail and they had to rush him to the hospital with the piece of wood still mounted to his foot. That's when they called Harry's family and the police. Of course, they had one of the boys stay with Harry's truck, in case he came back, but he never did. That was the story, that's how it happened, that's what they all agreed to say.

The police came and it wasn't long before their tracking dog was barking at a corpse.

The cost of freedom was getting too much for Hamasa to bear.

The very next day Billy and a girl were found naked in the back of that old, beat up station wagon Billy had stolen. Billy's souped-up, lonely Corvette was patiently waiting nearby. The shag wagon was parked up against a dirt embankment, plugging up the exhaust. During the night, they had started up the engine to stay warm; they didn't stand a chance of surviving the odorless, poisonous gas fumes that stole their young lives while they slept holding on to each other's dreams of immortality.

Hamasa was once again spending more time with his parents than with the boys. It seemed as if family time was a chance to return to innocence and to hope. They were once more exploring the wonders of Stanley Park and many other beautiful destinations around Vancouver. They would watch the seaplanes land on the water or see the yachts docking while the elite disembarked. They would walk around the sea wall and watch for dolphins or whales to come up for air, staring at the seals and people in kayaks. Trees there were taller than the biggest buildings they had ever seen in their homeland. There were large cedars the three of them could not put their arms around.

His parents never found out about the secret places where the teenagers would hide out at Stanley Park: far from the snooping eyes of the grays. He had seized upon freedom but his heart was crushed by the consequences. He would see his friends hanging out but he kept his distance and soon the intoxication of being in their presence drifted away. He once again turned to his reflective ways and began reading again in earnest.

"So, Dad, do you know anything about these totem poles here? They are amazing. School hasn't given out much information about Canada's history yet, but these speak of a great civilization that was once here, I'm sure," Hamasa inquired, as he looked upon the biggest one in Stanley Park.

"Yes, son, I have to admit I don't know much either. It seems to be a history those in power would rather keep secret. From what I've read, it's a story of the victory of colonization and not much is said about those who were colonized. Apparently, the First Nation's peoples were here for thousands of years, the colonizers for only a few hundred.

"So what happened to them all, the First Nation's peoples?" asked Hamasa.

"Well, for the most part they are all around us. When treaties were signed, the tribes agreed to settle on reserve lands that are scattered throughout Canada in mostly isolated areas. That's why you might not run into many in the cities. Like the history of Afghanistan – invaders tried colonizing our lands, too. It's a sad, brutal history here also."

"I will make it a point to talk to someone soon, to hear their side of the story. Let's go to the library! I want to read about these totem carvers and learn of their history and culture."

"Yes, and then you can teach me, but I'm sure it will be a complicated task to uncover the truth of what really happened. Heroes might be the villains and villains might be the heroes when you read between the lines. Generals and explorers were following orders given by their Gods and Kings. Remember, the winners get to write the history of things, but if you find out how, who, or what stopped the genocide, let me know – now that's something I'm curious about. Everything's politicized and monetized these days, by both sides. These days, wars are fought by the pen and in the courts and the usual shaming. But just look at this magnificent carving. The people who carved these totems have many legends. They believed that certain people or spirits could transform from human to animal. Some believe in a great spirit, Xelas, who's a shapeshifter and turned monsters into rocks or animals."

Hamasa looked at his dad until he knew his dad felt his

admiration.

At fifteen now, it looked as if his forced introduction to Jesus was finally going to pay off; he had a real life changing spiritual experience of biblical proportions. By this time, he had gone through a few broken hearts as relationship after relationship failed. It was a mystery never to be figured out, and it was perfect timing for something supernatural or spiritual to take hold. He told everybody he could find, and who would listen, just what had happened.

"The boys and I had our drinks spiked with bad drugs: acid laced with strychnine. We all ended up with strychnine poisoning and had to be rushed to the nearest hospital to get our stomachs pumped. However, nobody could find me to take me to the hospital with the others. I had been running around Barry's, parents gone for the weekend, party house, chasing my childhood pet squirrel, Homer, come back from the dead. I swear I could see it. First I spied him running around in a nature picture hung on the living room wall. Then Homer jumped out of the frame and onto the couch. I tried but couldn't catch him. Eventually I had convinced everyone at the party to help me look for my pet squirrel and help catch him. I was sure I saw Homer jump up on a person's shoulder and then run into a dark bedroom. Everyone piled into the bedroom, scrambling around looking for the squirrel.

"Most of the kids there remembered playing with Homer when I brought him to the park. They had a chance to hold him in their hands and feed him from their fingers. Homer would climb up on people and ride around on their shoulders or in their pockets. It was a high for everyone who experienced it and they had no problem agreeing to help recapture the little creature.

"Eventually the bedroom was taken over by a hot to trot couple, who started making out on the bed, which had everyone hitting the exit."

Homer, who had been eaten by a cat a year earlier, apparently disappeared back into the picture he had jumped out of.

Hamasa wandered off alone after being mercilessly teased for thinking he had seen his long lost dead pet. That was when his hallucinations went from sweet and innocent to wild and murderous. Hamasa's home was near a park where all the wannabe hippies, bikers, revolutionists and all the teenage mall-rats hung out when they were kicked out of the mall. Wandering aimlessly along, Hamasa met up with more stoned school friends and it wasn't long before his drug clouded eyes began to perceive each of these friends turning into a creature resembling their true personalities, usually kept hidden behind the masks people put on. He watched one friend turn into a pig, while another became a fox. All of a sudden, he saw an angel playing in a kid's wading pond. Running over, he saw it was one of his good school buddies, Heather.

"Come on!" Heather yelled. "Come and join me! The water's lovely."

Hamasa had taken a step towards her when all of a sudden a bear with a huge knife, dripping blood, came out from behind a tree. The water that Heather was ankle deep in started to turn into a ferocious whirlpool. The bear jumped in and began stabbing Heather. Abruptly, they both disappeared: sucked down into the vortex. Hamasa wailed, distraught, his mouth opened wider than he could ever have imagined possible. He tore off through the main street, towards the mall, trying to yell for help with a pried open mouth he could not close.

Another good friend, Susan, spotted him and ran after him. "Stop! Hamasa! Wait!" she shouted.

Hamasa slowed fractionally, trying to explain, but he could see she didn't understand; he was screaming through a gaping, open mouth.

"Hamasa, I don't know what you're saying! Calm down!" Finally, she was able to drag him into a church where he calmed down a bit and his mouth finally shut. When he had stopped shaking enough to speak, he started to express the horror he had witnessed. "We have to get to the police!" he begged, his mouth almost dropping open with shock again as Susan started laughing hysterically like a freaked out monkey.

"Hamasa – the bear was Henry! He was just messing with you because he knew you were screwed up on drugs."

A noise from the back brought Hamasa's head around just as Heather and Henry entered the church.

"God, Hamasa, thank heavens you're all right!" Heather called, rushing over to him, closely followed by Henry.

"Man, I'm sorry," Henry apologized. "We never meant for this to happen. We were just kidding around."

Hamasa hardly heard what they were saying; they were alive, right there before his eyes! That, and the overwhelming relief he felt, was all that mattered.

"How did you know where we were?" Susan asked.

Henry shook his head. "Easy, we just followed the trail of bewildered looking people – we knew they must've seen him." Henry slapped him on the back. "Sorry again, man."

Hamasa nodded, staring at his clasped hands. He couldn't believe how real it had all been, creating deep emotions and even conjuring up smells. He needed time alone to figure things out.

He ended up hiding in a tree, hallucinating there were snakes all around him, ready to attack. The pain from drug poisoning and the fear of the snakes was so terrible he cried out to God. At that instant, a bolt of lightning struck him, filling him with joy, energy, sobriety and health that lasted for several weeks. No one knew where the lightning had come from as it was a clear, hot, summer night. Much as he wanted to talk about his life changing experience, everyone he told only teased him for being a stoned-out freak. But from that day on, Hamasa never again touched a drink or any drug.

A few weeks later, while camping on his own, he had an out

of body experience that took him up into a sky of stars and light, filling his every cell with an undeniable rapture of love.

He was sitting under a tree, playing his guitar and singing John Lennon's song 'Imagine,' when his thoughts turned to God and a prayer came to his lips. All of a sudden, he was out of his body, flying in the sky and experiencing an exquisite feeling of love like nothing he had ever known before. At first, this love reached out only to his close family and friends but soon he felt love for all the souls of every country. This wondrous feeling kept expanding until he felt oneness and love with the whole Universe. Soon he wondered where he was and where he was going, and looking around, he realized he was flying towards the stars. A moment of fear entered his mind and he looked down, only to see himself still sitting under the tree with his guitar. He was convinced God had just given him a glimpse of his very soul. For the first time, Hamasa really understood we are not just the body and the mind but also a soul that is capable of knowing the greatest love that could ever be imagined. He felt God would soon give him the complete experience of merging with Him and knowing the whole truth about everything: all the answers to the mysteries of why we are here, of who created us and for what purpose. He would finally know why there is evil, death and suffering. God would introduce him to all His saints, Jesus, Abraham, Buddha and Mohammad. Now, more than ever, Hamasa was convinced. All he wanted to do was to meditate and let it take him to the Divine and truth. In that instant, he vowed to be a vegetarian.

When he returned home, he took to reading the Bible, as well as whatever else he could get his hands on about spirituality. He was consumed by the need to find the answers to life's many mysteries. It was time to pursue a more meaningful life, a life with more purpose. Ever since he was born, the people around him had been driven, even if it was not always for the right causes. They were full of passion to fulfill their goals. Now he wanted to be just like that. For now, he was not sure what his mission would be, but to his parent's delight, he was certain and determined he would find out soon.

Chapter 8

Interrogation Continued

"When plunder becomes a way of life for a group of men in society, over the course of time they create for themselves a legal system that authorizes it and a moral code that glorifies it!"
Frederic Bastiat

The drugs Hamasa had been given were having a profound effect on him, and from the depths of his despair he spewed forth his rapture.

"Many times I've been told they killed Grandfather but he always resurfaces. The two most hated people on the planet are the pedophile and the terrorist, so what chance did I have, brought up by someone who was both," Hamasa reflected. "I think many people are terrorists or pedophiles to some degree, especially some of the rich and the governments that cater to their every desire. Everyone's exploiting someone for their own gain. Governments that work for the rich say they'll protect their poor working class slaves from pedophiles and terrorists, but in truth, they do things of equal terror and sometimes far worse than the crimes these people commit. Nobody sees their deadly sins because they brainwash everybody. They call it the free market or capitalism, colonization to spread democracy, the recession, the cold war, collateral damage or progress, or they'll tell you it's in the nation's interest. They put the blame on cancer, suicide, acts of God or accidental death." He laughed bitterly. "They never once identify society's ills and crime as the effects of greed, selfishness, narcissism, indifference, elitism, corruption, corporations, dictatorships, consumerism, commercialism, domination, exploitation, colonization, pollution, war or slavery."

Hamasa foamed at the mouth, working himself into a frenzy of anger, violently twisting about in his chair, trying to break out of his restraints.

Harold pounced on the moment. "Did you kill Sky? You're only angry with yourself, that's obvious. But do you want peace? You want this madness to end? Confess!"

Hamasa ignored him and carried on, spurred on by the presence of spectators and fueled with the serum of truth. With Harold, and whoever was behind the glass wall, listening to his ideas, he finally had an audience. He wasn't about to let the opportunity slip through his bound up fingers.

"If they care so much, then why do they let millions of kids die every year from starvation? Why do they bomb innocent civilians? Why do they create societies where everyone has to live in a constant state of competition, fear of being shamed and excommunicated, and fear of losing their jobs, their health, their pensions and their lives? Why do they allow millions of people to die because they couldn't afford health insurance? Their only concern is power, money, keeping it, and protecting themselves from the worry the common person would revolt if they thought they weren't being protected from pedophiles and terrorists. They'll do anything to hang on to their power and money.

"If the masses knew what the rich and powerful thought of them and how they're farming them for every drop of blood they can get, then, yes, there would be a revolution. But as long as the masses aspire to be like them, and most are as greedy as them, then things will never change."

Harold started pacing. "Stop with the rant," he muttered. Then more loudly, "Stick to the questions. Answer the damn questions or I'll plug your mouth with my fist. So far, we've been at this for what, forty minutes, and all the torture has been on me!"

Harold's words were only encouragement to Hamasa and he

continued, hoping to get more reaction.

"Some people have kids just to experience the power they can have over another, and to ease their own loneliness or to give their lost lives temporary meaning and to have a slave in old age who will look after them."

Harold sighed, his stomach growled noisily, protesting its hunger as he glanced toward the exit doors.

"What society doesn't force children to do what's best for that society, instead of trying to do what's best for the child? What religion, government, or business doesn't brainwash children for their own sake. Children should be brought up to be critical, fearless and independent thinkers, so they can eventually decide for themselves what's in their best interests and the best interest of the world they have to live in. If they are to be brainwashed, it should be to make the world a better place for everyone." Hamasa's burning gaze turned on Harold. "Instead, everyone's brainwashed to compete, to exploit, to be consumers, to have big egos, to be elitists, and to work, work, work, 'til they drop dead. They don't realize soon they'll be competing against robots and that the rich will exploit them even further. At the rate the rich pillage, they'll annihilate the Earth within a hundred years, and no one is doing a damn thing about it.

"The rich and powerful bully everyone they can get away with bullying and then they turn around and make rules that children and poor people shouldn't bully. They invented the idea of sin and say it's a sin to kill, but every dollar they have is from the blood of others. Every rule invented is for the benefit of the rich and powerful by the rich and powerful – but do they follow the rules?"

Harold looked at his watch. Trying to match the intensity of his prisoner, he yelled, "So what the hell does any of this gibberish have to do with the murder of a civilian? Tell me that, please, Hamasa!"

"It's our country, it's our world, don't you see? I had to do something to save us. The way people are – someone had to do something. Life's a bitch with death and diseases and everything else and then humans come along and make it a hundred times worse. I mean, who hasn't wished another dead or stabbed them in the back because they stood in the way of one of their desires, or for revenge, or money, or need for power? Societies and governments are hypocritical! They allow politicians to lie and let the lies of religions exist. They throw individuals in jail for far less than they themselves do. They allow the raping of the land, gambling, drugs and alcohol. They allow additives and plastics that kill to be put in everything and they pollute the air, water and land. Thousands of people die in car accidents every year – but does government or society do anything to prevent this? Of course not, this would affect the economy! They allow the economy to be run by debt and for it to enslave billions who have to do mundane, dead end jobs to keep from starving to death. They allow the corruption of Wall Street, with the rich getting richer just by pushing money around. They allow the collapsing of markets and economies so trillions can be stolen from hard working slaves. After they've taken everything, all the money and pensions, they have no mercy and create inflation to make hard working people even more penniless. The common man is completely disposable to the rich, who send them to die in wars or jobs that kill them or create rules that stifle them to death.

"Don't you think it's time some rich people were put in jail for their crimes against humanity? Most of the rich do nothing to help the starving, the poor or the abused, except when it's a tax write-off or they are spending to promote and support the system that favored them. When the poor die of hunger, their blood is on the hands of the rich, because only they can prevent it from happening. Most people are narcissistic but the rich take it to the outer limits. They're elitists who think they're entitled. With their gigantic egos, they think they're better than everyone else, that they're entitled to plunder the Earth and create a hell, not only for most of the people, but for all life. Are they put in jail? No! Instead, societies and governments worship the rich, and of course, most people want to be just like them and have the power to do just like them. Everybody wants to have a slave to do all their nasty work. Most rich are predators and they've cunningly created a world where everybody desires to be a predator and worships the predator without realizing they're being devoured by them and will never get to swim in the same waters with these sharks. Unfortunately, most people are ignorant, delusional and think they're invincible and they don't realize their ignorance and greed are killing them – along with the rest of the world. I would rather live in a world where power and money are given equally to everyone with some oversight, then, not one single person or group will have enough money or power to destroy the world the way that a few rich are doing today. Sure, there will always be those who are lazy, incompetent, handicapped by disabilities or corrupt, but at least they would not be able to ruin the Universe.

"Moreover, ironically, all this evil happens under the loving, watchful eye of an omniscient, omnipotent, benevolent God. Give me a break! If it wasn't for the Master taking me to His Kingdom, and allowing me to warn you I might have—"

"OK, OK!" Harold snapped. "You're in no position to philosophize on such matters and there you go, blabbing on about your hallucinations again. Don't you dare be threatening here! You – puttin' rich people in jail! If it wasn't for the rich we wouldn't have an economy! You got that? Let's just get back to the story, shall we! I'm so glad you were able to get all that crap off your chest, but now we have to get down to business. We have to make sure those drugs don't carry your twisted brain completely over the edge to insanity. You keep going on and on, trying to justify your actions, but what we need to know is what the hell you did or what the hell you know about Sky's murder. Look at you! You're no better than the ones you're so eager to condemn. Why did Sky have to die? What sin did he commit, other than getting in your way? All your grand speeches sound like nothing more than hypocrisy to me! Maybe if you just get the confession over with and accept responsibility you will feel a whole lot better about yourself and the world you love to put down.

"Listen, people have always been locked into their bubbles and their delusions and nothing you say or do is going to change that. It's the only way they can get through the day because they won't face up to the hard, cold facts of life. If you're trying to bring some kind of enlightenment to the people, then just let them be, let them stay in their bubbles. It's the only way to find happiness, and that's the best enlightenment. But you, Hamasa, you'll be dragged out of your bubble, and you will tell us the truth. I'll drag you out myself if I have to, you got that!"

Abruptly, he fell silent, drawn into Hamasa's eyes.

"Yes," Hamasa whispered, "let it in!"

Harold suddenly turned away, dropping heavily into his chair. "What the hell? What are you trying...some kind of mind trick? You've got me hearing shit, too!"

Hamasa smiled.

Harold dry washed his face. "Must be some kind of vertigo," he mumbled, his mind retreating from the serenity of a peace beyond description and the harmony of symphonies. Harold remembered where he was and pulled himself together. "How were you involved with your parent's death?" he asked, trying to steer the interrogation in a new direction.

Hamasa took a deep breath. "How can you be so sure my parents are dead? That's very disturbing, but I assure you I had nothing to do with it if it's true. If it's just a ploy to get my tongue wagging, like I keep saying, I'm here to tell you everything I know."

Grinding his teeth, Harold motioned with his hands for Hamasa to get back to the story, but interjected instead. "After listening to all your opinions and biases I am sure you can appreciate I have a few of my own. Maybe I'm not in the church business or look 'churchy', but I can assure you, that is exactly where my heart is and where my wife and kids are every Sunday. I've resisted many a temptation that has come my way but I'm not sure how much longer I can resist bashing your face in. You see, Hamasa, you've got a sick, delusional mind as far as I'm concerned and the only reason I'm letting you blab on is to see if you will talk yourself into a confession. Maybe it will be the catalyst which puts an end to all this business so you can get some rest. How's that stomach of yours? I bet it could use some goodies. This can all be over and you can eat if you just let us know what happened."

Hamasa was determined to tell his story his way. "All right, I spit on your tattoo, your fiery 'torch of truth'. What do you know of truth? I am the Owl. I fly to your temple, to your statue of liberty, your witch of freedom. I created the fire. I gave the flint and iron but now I carry the torch and I will burn her. What do you know of truth? OK, I'll tell you. I will tell you. Oh, but do you have the ears? We'll see whose truth will set who free. Truth is above all else. You're looking for the truth, Harold? Then why aren't you listening to me?"

Settling himself down, Hamasa remembered his youth with longing and started to tell his story. He wanted to get it over with and get on with saving the world. He tired of waiting for the appointed hour: for the Power to arrive.

"Just after my eighteenth birthday, 1998, my parents told me I would be going back to Afghanistan during my summer holidays, to visit relatives and to help rebuild the village school…

"Hamasa, can we talk?" Jaabir asked as he stopped the mower, having completed only half the lawn. He was still adjusting to having to do all the household chores himself, rather than having servants to do the menial, everyday tasks. Although he did manage to put a rake in Hamasa's hands, his son was not the most willing gardener. "We'll finish this later," he said, glancing at their efforts. "Come, sit with me."

"Yeah, so what's up?" Hamasa sank gratefully onto the bench next to his father. "Look," he complained sulkily, "I've got blisters and it's only been ten minutes. I don't think I'll ever own a house, Dad. You're always in a mess up to here." Hamasa put his arms up over his head as far as they could reach. "I want my weekends to be free."

His father chuckled. "I guess it's my way of meditating. Besides, you had your taste of freedom and where did that get you? Listen, son, your mom and I know you might not be ready to accept Jesus as your Savior, but we just want you to know we support you in all you have to go through. We know it hasn't been easy for you lately. But you're a truth seeker. We can see that, and we just want you to know we believe in you. I mean, one minute we're worried you're getting too wild with those boys and the next minute we're worried you're going to be some kind of monk or recluse. But hey, with Nayanna in the picture now, we don't have to worry about that, do we?"

"You hard working men, you look like you need a beer," Ameera said, emerging from the house to serve Jaabir a cold one. "I heard Nayanna mentioned." She raised an inquisitive eyebrow. "It seems as if that's getting to be pretty serious, and yet we haven't seen much of her lately. I hope you plan to rectify that soon, but give us a heads-up, so I can prepare something special for the special lady. Can I get you something cold?" she asked Hamasa, laying her hands on his shoulders from behind and leaning over to kiss his cheek.

"No thanks, Mom."

"Listen, son, an opportunity's come up for you to go back and help our people, those in the village and those at the compound who have stayed loyal to us," Jaabir continued as Ameera sat beside them. "We want to rebuild the school and there's other things that have come up, too, but we can't say much about those yet, until we've had them confirmed. It's your dream to give back and here's your chance. What d'ya say to that?"

"I thought there was a civil war going on? Is it safe? Won't they be mad that we ran out on them? What if they want revenge?" Hamasa asked, surprised.

"Well, that's sort of true," Ameera answered. "But we told them we had to leave so that we could be strong and safe, and so we could one day go back to help them. This is the time to prove to them that we meant what we said. The Taliban has full control of Kabul now and promises safe travel there."

"Are you coming with me?" Hamasa asked, confirming that he agreed to go.

Ameera shook her head. "Not at this time, but Uncle Rahim will be coming to travel with you."

After the family escaped to Canada, their grandfather had supposedly fought the Americans to his death: at least that is what they told Hamasa. The compound had been demolished, but as the years passed, the poppy fields had once again flourished, and the money to rebuild was abundant. Their friends in the village had rebuilt the huge protective walls and several buildings. Now it was time for the school, and for the people to rejuvenate and heal.

Hamasa didn't delay getting the news of their pending separation to Nayanna.

"I was so looking forward to having our summer together. Now I'll be miserable, missing you every day." Nayanna's big, almond shaped, dark-brown eyes filled with tears. "I know! I'll find an excuse to go back to India, and I'll fly over to Afghanistan and hunt you down with my eagle eyes. I won't let you desert me."

Hamasa loved the way she looked at him with her longing for

oneness eyes. He loved the way she constantly reached out for him to draw him close, her lips always within striking distance, but always a moving target. Round and round they would intertwine, like a cat chasing its tail, until finally, exhausted by rejection, their lips would melt together.

Nayanna brought a romantic style to everything she did. She exuded femininity and had a passion and enthusiasm that was contagious. She dedicated herself to family, society and religion. Those within her sphere were engulfed by her zealousness. In her presence it was easy to forget the world was a dark place of disease, rape, murder and death.

Part of Hamasa longed for nothing more than to spend every moment of the rest of his life by her side, yet he had a yearning in his soul that was insatiable. His spiritual experiences had awakened an urgency for God to deliver him from his confusion, ignorance and spiritual blindness and to bless him with the experience, once and for all, of the bliss of eternal oneness with the Creator.

"Yes, Nayanna," he told her softly, "you'll join with me in the eternal dance of love that Rumi taught the mysterious whirling dervishes, the Sufis. We'll search together, as one soul, for truth and for God's love."

Right there in the school library, amongst the shelves of books, they held each other and swayed to some mystical rhythm that poured from their hearts. Passers-by felt the sacredness of the occasion and kept a silent, respectful distance, careful not to interrupt the worshippers.

"But if you go to India, your father will have an arranged marriage waiting for you." Hamasa pouted. "He's a powerful spiritual leader in the community – no one will question his wishes. High caste, rich families would feel blessed if he chose one of their sons to be your groom. But here I am, stealing their beautiful princess right from under their noses. I think I'm a dead man walking."

"No, Hamasa," Nayanna's voice was grave. "I'm the dead one if my father finds out. Which reminds me, I better get a move on before he comes home and finds I'm not there."

Thinking of Nayanna jolted Hamasa back to his incarceration and the endless glares from Harold.

"Why are you holding Nayanna?" he asked, avoiding Harold's eyes. "You've got to let me see her! At least give her the message that I love her. You must believe me, she has nothing to do with any of this. She never had a clue about any of the things I've been telling you. If you told her I'm the terrorist you accuse me of being, she would never believe you. Anyway, have you read the documents you took from me? That's only half of what's out there. You've got to let me go! There really isn't much time left. I've got to reach the Successor. You know what I'm talking about! You've read the documents, right? Listen, you didn't need to give me the drugs, I want to tell you everything. We've got to go! I hope these drugs aren't going to screw me up, or keep the Power from visiting me."

Chapter 9

Nayanna

> "Equality is the soul of liberty; there is, in fact, no liberty without it."
> *Frances Wright*

Nayanna got off the bus two stops down from where she usually got off. Her hair was a mess and her eighteen-year-old face was a mess, too, so she had to zip into the neighborhood's Caribbean restaurant to change her clothes and fix herself before going home, in case her dad was already there. Most days she could change at school or in the bus and be able to get off at the stop just a few doors down from where she lived: not today though. Today was one of those dreamy, special days when she was able to hide out and make out with Hamasa. He was her first kiss, her first boyfriend and the first male friend she could relate to. They had both come from other worlds around the same time and had sports, academic interests and a whole lot of other things in common. It was exciting, thrilling and so rebellious to be expressing her sexuality and she loved being in love and having someone special there for her, someone who deserved her beauty. He was persistent and didn't give up until he'd won her kisses and they'd been making out ever since. She was still a virgin, so making out was just kissing, until they got married. She knew they'd have awesome kids and an exquisite marriage. She was willing to wait for the appropriate time but she wasn't sure if Hamasa thought the same. He didn't seem to be worried by the consequences of getting carried away by passion. For now, they both worked hard to achieve their goals, and had obtained the highest standing in their academics. What could go wrong? They'd seized the moment. Now they must continue making the most of opportunities that would hopefully come to them. Unfortunately, her dad would never understand any of it, she worried.

"Hello, may I use the washroom while I wait for a friend who is meeting me here?" Nayanna asked the cheerful, middle-aged hostess who also seemed to be the only waitress on at the moment. Nayanna hated to lie to such a sincere, hard working person who seemed genuinely interested in the lives of her customers. She would call them by name and ask about their families as if she was a regular at their tables. Besides, a black permanent marker had penned out, on bright yellow, thick, stock paper, 'ONLY PATRONS CAN PEE HERE!!!' Nayanna would have put up a typed note in a wood or bamboo frame with seashells covered by glass and right below the 'PLEASE WAIT TO BE SEATED' sign. It would read, 'For the people coming to use the washrooms only, please respect the privacy, safety and protection of our cherished guests; please use the public washrooms at the gas station across the street. Thanks! We hope to see you here soon, as a guest!'

"I'm so glad you stopped by. Yes, by all means, use the washroom," the waitress gushed as if Nayanna were a regular.

She made a beeline for the washroom and didn't care who saw her. She knew the chances of her dad catching her here or of her dad ever talking to someone from this restaurant were as slim as aliens beaming her to another planet. Looking in the mirror, she morphed from a typical, slutty looking, Canadian teenager to the quiet, respectful daughter she loved presenting to her dad, who would demand it anyway. Sure it was fun to play 'survival of the fittest' against teen girls with their psychological warfare or play the edgy, sexy submissive to school boy predators, but when it came to family, that's when she knew how to act sweet, humble and honor her dad. By doing so, it drew her closer to her own soul and to God.

Nayanna put a long skirt over her firm butt revealing, black, legging tights and put a high-necked sweater over her almost nipple exposing, pink halter-top. She reluctantly removed her sexy, black, push-up bra that gave her ample breasts just a bit too much prominence. Most importantly, she had to put her hair up in a bun. Her beautiful, long, black hair, let loose to linger in the wind and attract the wrong kind of attention, would land her in big trouble with her dad. She sighed at the girl in the mirror; she hated all the deceit but had no other choice if she wanted to have anything like the sort of life enjoyed by the other girls at school.

Her father definitely would not allow her to think of, never mind have a boyfriend. She did not know what he would do if he found out that she was going out with Hamasa, who was not even a Sikh. She had good reason to worry; she could be the next victim of an honor killing. Everyone had heard about the appalling, unspeakable acts of honor killings happening in India and now they were even happening in Canada. Families, so they could save face with the community, would track down and murder daughters who ran off with lovers. Some families killed them just for not agreeing with or for losing respect for their elders. The girl in the mirror now stared at the fear in her eyes.

Scrubbing hard, she washed off the eye shadow. With a few wipes her luscious red lips, which had been ravished by Hamasa earlier, were all over the Kleenex being flushed down the toilet. If anyone noticed her going into the washroom, she doubted they would have known it was the same girl leaving.

She hurried along the busy streets towards home until she could see the grand, pillared entrance. Her father had said, if they had to live in the smallest house on the block it did not have to look like the smallest, and modified the entrance himself. Against her will, her steps slowed – was he there already, sitting in his favorite chair, impatiently awaiting her arrival? Screwing up the courage, she quickened her steps and let herself in. The lounge door was open, her heart sank; he was home. Fixing a smile, she entered.

"Dad, you're home!" Are you back for a quick bite before tearing up the city again?" she joked.

Her father, Bhajan, sighed. "Nayanna, Nayanna, how you test me – worse than my Gurus. It's all I live for, to come home to see my sweet daughter behaving and doing her school work. I would die if you had to work as hard as I do for so little. Come, sit with me in sweet remembrance of the great Masters."

Obediently, she sat. "Yes, I always have their sweet remembrance. I've been thinking, for the coming summer holiday I could join you every day. You can teach me how to drive and I can give you a rest occasionally. We should spend more time together, before you know it, I'll be off to university, and you are not getting any younger."

"You are so much like your mother. Shanti was always so concerned to keep the family together, just as you are," her dad replied as he unraveled his turban and let his gray hair, just a bit longer than his beard, flow down his back.

"So I guess this means you're staying home and not driving again tonight?" Nayanna inquired.

"I need some hot water on my aching joints and I haven't bathed in a week. I'm so glad you're here to look after me and to see to it that I am eating. Without your mother here, I would have faded away if not for you."

"But, Dad, we hardly talk anymore, or have time to talk or maybe you are pushing me away because I remind you of Mom and it is too painful for you? If only I hadn't leaned over the boat to see the fishes and fallen in, then Mom wouldn't have had to die rescuing me."

"That day, on the river Beas in India, God and the Gurus were crying out for death, for the repayment of Karma and for souls to make the journey to our eternal home. You were their little, innocent angel of opportunity. We were already there in complete surrender to spread your grandmother's ashes. Death was accepted and death was remembered and glorified for being the angel that brings us to our true home. It was God's perfect timing, but alas not ours. Your mom was the first to notice and the first to jump in to save you, but after struggling against the currents to get you to safety she succumbed. That's the story you tell, Nayanna, but if I had learned to swim and had overcome my fear of water, I would have been able to save her. Don't ever blame yourself my sweet princess, you can blame me. The Guru says to thank God that His will was done, we are humbled and surrendered."

"I love you, Dad, and I know you love me," she answered, hoping to steer the conversation away from memories of her mother before she broke down in tears and ran to her bedroom as she usually did. "I'll always be here for you, you know that, right – as you have been here for me. I'm just worried I won't be able to live up to all the expectations you have for me. You brought me to this new world and it's having a huge impact on me. This world shows women can be equal human beings, follow their own dreams, and be independent."

"Yes, we are all equal, but God has ordained the duties we must perform. We must surrender to God. When you obey your father's wishes you are obeying God, and He will bless you with eternal peace. Stay in the protective arms of the family and the comforting ways of God and everything will work out. You have nothing to fear."

"How will I ever make you understand how important it is for me to be true to myself, to follow my own heart, to do the things I feel I am being called to do? I'm afraid you will never accept the real me. I can't ever imagine having to have an arranged marriage."

"So this is what this is all about? Dear child, what are you talking about? Your true self is your soul, a drop of God. You just have to listen carefully to hear what it says to you and not to follow your mind, which is the negative power. It will lead you to death and destruction. We have been through this so many times and now is not the time to be concerned with anything to do with boys or marriage. God wants you to finish your studies. Many years from now, we will talk of these things, right? Now let me have my bath." As Bhajan made his way to the upstairs washroom there was a knock on the door.

"Dad, there's a knock at the door! Did you want me to get it?"

"Yes please," her father replied, before closing the bathroom door to bathe.

Opening the door, Nayanna found herself face to face with a refined black gentleman in a fedora, suit and tie and polished shoes to boot. "Hello, Ms. Singh? The waitress at the Caribbean restaurant said you dropped these earlier. She asked if I would return them to you as I was headed this way."

"Oh my God, there are aliens on other planets! I must be more careful," she muttered through the hand she quickly covered her mouth with. She then let out a muffled shriek.

"Pardon Miss?" A bit bewildered, the gentleman handed over a student card, a bus pass, some condoms and a thin, silver make-up case that was open, revealing a picture of a naked, from the waist up, handsome boy where the mirror should have been.

"I...it must've fallen out of my knapsack, but some of these things are just not mine. Will you keep them? Thank you very much – this is so embarrassing – thank you so much," she gushed as she managed a tight smile. She grabbed some of the items, shoved them under her sweater and then directed the other things, along with the stranger's hand, into his jacket pocket. Just then, her father opened the bathroom door. The handsome stranger tipped his hat to Nayanna, winked and was off with one hand still in his jacket pocket.

"Nayanna, did you know that gentleman?" Father asked as he raced down the stairs. "What's that about the Caribbean restaurant? Was he talking about the place a couple of blocks from here?" Father, curiosity etched onto his tired face, looked out the window and joined Nayanna watching the stranger float down the street. He transferred his gaze to her again. "I often go there to pick up a coffee, and one of the servers is a regular 'fare'. We've had some great talks, she enjoys sharing her family stories with me," he rambled on. "Of course, I enjoy bragging about my wonderful daughter to her. She likes to see all the pictures I carry around of you and of our homeland. She even invited us to visit her family. She wants to learn how to make chai tea and mango ice cream. She came here once for lunch, when your auntie was here, and we made her roti, paneer, chapatti, and chai. She was so curious to try the real home-cooked taste of it. Um…I forgot all about that, and didn't even mention it to you yet." Abruptly he stopped, a frown creasing his forehead. "What were you doing there at the restaurant?"

Nayanna started to wonder when the aliens were going to beam her up to their planet. "Dad, your bath water is running, you better hop in. I'll have chai waiting for you…" she pleaded, hoping to change the topic and give herself time to think.

"I'm not going anywhere until you explain to me what you were doing there!"

"Dad, please! It's a girl thing, OK! A monthly thing, OK! I couldn't just walk down the road without checking something first."

Dad was nodding his red face all the way to the bathroom and didn't bother coming down for chai after his bath. Some things the Singh family just did not discuss.

Chapter 10

Interrogation Continued

"All that we see and seem is but a dream within a dream."
Edgar Allan Poe

Harold looked at his watch, although it felt as if he had been interrogating Hamasa for hours, in fact, only a little over an hour had passed.

"Oh my God! Stop mouthing off! Maybe pumping you full of drugs wasn't the best idea." Harold pulled in a long, deep breath, shooting Hamasa a look of disgust. "Just answer the damn questions; simple questions just need some simple answers. Can you do that?"

They both had a bathroom break, but food was scarce and the sound of Harold's stomach could tell you to the minute the last meal it had.

"OK, OK!" Hamasa muttered. "Well…Dad gave me a carry-on bag, full of big, sealed envelopes. He told me I had to give them to a man who would be with my Uncle Rahim. He'd call me by my middle name as a kinda' code. It was all unusually secretive, but it was supposed to be a good surprise for me, and Dad said not to ruin it with a million questions." Hamasa grinned. "Didn't stop me asking." He shook his head mournfully. "Didn't get me any answers either. Anyways, I eventually got tired of asking about it and not getting anywhere, other than it was a surprise that would make me and the whole family happy. In the end, I just accepted it. I'd just have to wait to be approached on the plane or at the airport, either by this man or by my uncle. Then, after giving him all the envelopes, I would be free to enjoy the best holiday of my life. Oh, yeah, I had to promise not to mention any of this to anyone."

"Hey, Harold, when do you think they're going to bring some food? Maybe you need to remind them. I'd even settle for some prison food, smells good." He stopped and started considering. "Um, what is it today, corn soup I think, anyway, smells delicious."

"Well, you give the confession now that you will eventually give anyway, and I'll have the meal of your dreams here in twenty minutes," Harold countered.

Hamasa ignored Harold and thought it best to continue his story; it was just a matter of time before the Power appeared.

"Well, the guy never showed on the plane or at any of the stops along the way, but I hoped he'd meet me at the airport in Kabul.

"When I got off the plane, there was a lot of confusion and chaos. People were running in every direction and there was smoke and fire all around. I tried to keep up with the group of people from the plane. Someone was running towards me yelling, 'Run!' Men with machine guns were also running towards us yelling at everyone to move quickly into the terminal building and shooting anyone who tried to run away. There was a gigantic explosion. Everything went blank. I must have passed out. When I woke up, everything was quiet. I started panicking. Looking around, I could see people running, screaming, but I didn't hear a sound; my hearing was gone. I saw the men with machine guns pile into a van and drive off, shot at by security. I tried to get up but I couldn't move my legs. I began panicking even more, and then I realized there was a dead man sprawled over them. I lay back down, dazed, confused, more afraid than I'd ever been in my life, and closed my eyes. I was in the wind, flying my kite. I felt a strange longing for Mom and for home. It felt...as if Mom was there with me. I don't know how long I was out for, but when I opened my eyes, Grandfather was running towards me. I remember I was so surprised he was there; I'd been told he had been killed. No one ever suggested he might still be alive in Afghanistan, never mind greeting me! He dragged the bleeding corpse off me. I could see Grandfather's mouth moving but I was still completely deaf. When he realized I had lost my hearing, he checked me over from head to foot and helped me up on my feet. If it hadn't been for the soldiers, the security and police, he would have walked us right out of there. Instead, soldiers herded us through security to waiting doctors and nurses. I was one of the lucky ones. The bombs had gone off inside the terminal, targeting the waiting passengers." Hamasa shook his head, squeezing his eyes closed as if blocking the scene out. "I wish I could forget the sight – the smell of burnt flesh! The tattered, mutilated dead were being spread around for identification. Next to them, unidentifiable body parts were piling up.

"Waiting to be released, waiting for my bags, seemed to take forever. But it gave my utter shock some time to thaw a little and for my hearing to start to come back. It hurt like the devil, and I heard weird sounds; I thought the ringing would never cease. I had a bump on my head and I was told to check into a hospital to see if there was a concussion.

"Finally, I was able to follow Grandfather out of the airport and we let all the chaos disappear behind us."

As he spoke, Hamasa was pulled back through time.

"Looked like the man I pulled off of you took a bullet that had your name on it," his grandfather said, looking Hamasa over. He smiled. "Come, my little mujahedeen, but not so little any more, are you?" He clapped Hamasa on the shoulder.

Hamasa winced. His head pounded and, although his legs no longer shook, they still felt as weak as if he had run up a mountain without stopping.

"It's been much too long since I've seen you and we have a lot of catching up to do now, don't we?" His grandfather smiled again. "And we have important work for you to do; you won't have time to break any poor girl's heart. Ha-ha. Your father didn't send you here for an arranged marriage, yet! The villagers asked him to send you here so you can help them with their cause: rebuilding. But I figure my cause should have greater priority."

The smile had disappeared and a frown decorated his forehead. "We got rid of the Russians but now we have bigger enemies from within our own country, not to mention the Americans. Listen to me ramble on," he said without pausing. "How was your trip? Let's go feed you some dinner. You're now a day ahead and past your bedtime. Speak up, son! Don't let me chatter away like this."

Hamasa had been silently studying his grandfather. There was something obviously different about him, but try as he would, he couldn't figure out what it was.

"I never knew you were here," Hamasa said. "I was told that you might have been killed. But you look amazing!" he burst out. "You look so young; you're supposed to look like an old man, but you're wearing a young man's body! You look better than I remember the last time I saw you." Abruptly, it hit him. "That's it! Your beard's trimmed, and what happened to all your white hair?" Hamasa stopped, wondering if he had crossed the line. Maybe his grandad didn't want him mentioning it if he was using hair dye. "Sorry for blurting out about that," he added, contritely, "but I can't get over it. Anyway, do you know anything about the school I'm supposed to help build? And who do you think was responsible for that attack on the airport? Who were they targeting? It's a miracle I made it out alive."

"So you like my latest disguise do ya'? Grandfather chuckled. "The ladies like it too, ha-ha." He sobered suddenly. "The attack? It could have been a false flag operation so the Americans can get more power in the region." He shrugged. "They let me go, so they obviously don't think it was the Taliban. Could have been the Sunni or Islamic State."

He smoothed his beard. "Suicide bombings were unheard of

just a few years ago, now everyone's doing it." He sighed. "Well, we have a bit of a journey ahead. I'll fill you in as we drive. So many in the village are excited to meet the American who was once an Afghan."

"Grandfather, don't say that! You know I'll always be an Afghan. And it's Canadian, not American – I live in Canada!"

"Canadian, American, what's the difference? They're all over here now stealing our oil. Nevertheless, you'll never be one of them. You're gonna' keep being my little mujahedeen, right, Hamasa?"

It felt as if he had only been gone from Afghanistan for a short while. All the memories flooded back. They piled into an old pick-up truck driven by one of the villagers. As they drove through the city towards the southern village, the driver started repeatedly glancing nervously in the rear and side mirrors.

"We're being followed," he said, "a big, black Cadillac."

His grandfather grabbed a walkie-talkie from the glove compartment and spoke into it urgently. Within minutes a few men on motorcycles drew up alongside. In addition, a car pulled in front of them. Hamasa could hear the heated voice through the walkie-talkie.

"Stop, just pull over," the voice yelled.

"No, they might have weapons and shoot, I'll out-run them," Grandfather yelled back.

"We have you covered – by coincidence I've got my soldiers in the area, but you've got to stop, now!" the voice urged again.

Suddenly they pulled over and stopped. The black menace drove right past, but was forced to a stop as a number of cars quickly blocked the road.

As promised, around twenty men appeared from out of the shops, all armed with machine guns, and ran towards the Cadillac as more cars sped up and blocked any escape routes. Men piled out of their cars, joining the army of twenty, but before they opened fire Grandfather yelled out the window.

"Don't shoot! Take them alive! Don't shoot!" Hearing gunfire Grandfather yelled again. "I said don't shoot! We need them alive."

Hamasa saw his grandad open the door and get out and scrambled to follow as he ran across to where three men were pulling someone out of the Cadillac. Hamasa watched as they threw him to the ground.

Men were shouting, yelling, "The gunships are coming!"

The Americans were coming. Everything happened so fast, too fast for Hamasa to feel anything, but now, as Grandfather took out his pistol, smashing it over the man's head, demanding to know why he was following them, a surge of adrenaline blasted through him.

The man writhed on the ground, holding his head. Then he said something Hamasa couldn't understand.

Grandfather yelled, "Russians! Why the hell are the Russians here?"

One of Grandad's men trotted over. "There are two dead Afghans in there." He jerked his head at the Cadillac. "The driver and a passenger in the front seat. They must be spies, dirty traitors, working for the Russians."

"Shot with the Russian's gun I imagine, to keep them from talking to us," Grandfather said, shaking his head.

Everywhere people were yelling for everyone to leave as the Americans were very close. As some were hurriedly laying bombs in the road, Grandfather took the Russian's gun and handed it to Hamasa.

"Here," he said, "you will have the honor."

Hamasa stared at the weapon. This was how it was done. Traditions started long before the Russians came to take over Afghanistan when there were the tribal wars. The job of killing the captured had always been given to the regular villagers and their children in order to toughen everyone up for war. Later, in their war with Russia, they were expected to kill the traitors and informants or those taking water or food from the Russians.

The Russian wouldn't talk so it fell to Hamasa to kill him. He tried to swallow in a suddenly dry as dust throat. He wanted to throw the gun down, scream out he was no longer a mujahedeen, no longer a Muslim, no longer a Taliban, and, as a Christian, wouldn't be killing anyone. Instead, he stood frozen. The penalty for apostasy was death. He had no choice.

The feel of the gun in his hand once again flooded his body with adrenalin. Without ever looking at his face, he pointed the gun and fired. It hardly made a sound but the fellow fell over, blood spraying everywhere. Hamasa didn't move until someone pried the gun from his fingers.

"Get in the car," his grandfather ordered.

Shakily, Hamasa obeyed. His stomach heaved and his bowel threatened to let go. He was sweating and shivering and his mind could not come to terms with the fact his parents had sent him into this hell.

His luggage was already in the back seat of the Cadillac. Looking back as they drove off, he saw a car explode into flame. Almost everyone had disappeared, only a few cars that were trying to stop the American convoy from getting through to them remained. For a few moments, Hamasa thought the Americans would be able to break through the resistance and overtake them, but then the bombs in the road were triggered and the enemy were stopped dead in their tracks. Hamasa saw at least three of the armored vehicles explode.

As they roared down the highway to the village, his grandpa chatted to him as if they had just come from the market or from a friendly family gathering.

"So, now you've got yourself some pretty nice wheels for the months you'll be here. That's right, this is your new car! Don't look so shocked and don't think you can shag any of the girls here in the village in this car. A boy from America with a Cadillac will be irresistible to the pretty ones, who will say they are modern women now. Remember, around here, girls are still being killed if they marry without being virgins. So don't mess up their lives for them. You must keep them intact. The ones who are married, well that's a different story, they'll be all over you, too. There are no modern ways here, don't forget that. If you're smart, you'll stick to sodomy. But don't try to get permission, just say, 'oops sorry, I missed'. Ha-ha, works every time!"

Hamasa let him talk. He didn't have the strength to answer. His body was clamoring at him to sleep, and maybe he would awake at home, out of this nightmare. He knew his life would never be the same. There was no going back to the new Canadian Hamasa, it was back to fitting into the old reality of his grandfather's world. When he couldn't ignore his grandfather any longer he replied.

"Grandpa, I can't believe you're talking to me like this. What makes you think I don't already have a girl?"

"Girls, girls, you won't have time for girls anyway. I'm sending you to Pakistan for guerrilla warfare training. After what happened here today, you can see what we are in for."

"A camp?" Hamasa asked weakly. He was too shaken up and his body was still in pain, but he managed to protest. "But I crave all the delicacies I miss so much from your generous table. You always had the best kababs to die for and your chefs made the best qabli pulao. How else will I heal? Now I'll be eating dry rice for weeks, oh the sacrifices of a mujahedeen! And my new car, when will I be able to drive my new car?"

Abruptly his grandfather stopped the car and got out. Walking around to the back, he opened the door and started throwing Hamasa's luggage out.

"It must be something you have the Russians wanted," he said.

As he ransacked the suitcases, not finding what he was looking for, he noticed the carry-on bag still tucked under Hamasa's arm and lunged towards it.

"No!" Hamasa called out. "Papa said I'm not to tell anyone about this. No one's to see this but the man on the plane, who didn't show," he ended lamely.

By now, his grandfather had the bag, wrestled it open and scanned through the papers.

"No! No! No! This can't be! Not my own daughter…and your father…betraying our people!"

Hamasa stared at his grandpa. Never had he seen the old man cry: a monsoon flooding the desert. He would have doubted he could, and yet, tears coursed down his rough, craggy cheeks. He felt the fear roil in his belly.

"How could they put my little mujahedeen's life at risk?" The old man ranted. He turned to Hamasa. "You're not safe here! You must get out as soon as possible! I'm sending you straight to Pakistan for training, you'll have to prove which side you're on. If you're a true mujahedeen, as soon as the training is over you'll return home…" He paused, his eyes as cold and bitter as the Canadian winters. "Hamasa – you must be the one to kill your father and mother. Did you hear me? Do you understand? Look at me...OK. It infuriates me to no end that your parents deserted me at the moment the Americans attacked," his grandfather grated. "But it gave me the motivation to live, to get my revenge. I had a feeling something like this betrayal was behind their leaving."

They got back in the car and carried on with their journey home in silence. Grandfather showed his disgust when he stopped at the gate to the compound and kicked an approaching dog.

"Get out of my way you mutt. If I have to open this gate myself, with you in the way, it'll be over your dead, mutt body. Where is everybody? As soon as the money's gone, then everyone's gone!"

As they entered the compound, a bolt of fear struck Hamasa: the place looked deserted except for the two of them.

"I'll deal with your parents. Get some sleep!" Grandfather growled. "Tomorrow, early, you'll be on a truck to Kabul. There, you'll join a convoy going through Jalalabad to Pakistan."

Those words...'you must be the one to kill your father and mother' rang in Hamasa's ears as his mind prepared for war. What the truth about anything was, he no longer knew.

His grandpa had let him read all the documents, along with the many pictures that he had been carrying. They clearly proved that his parents were spying for the Russians.

Hamasa had never been so confused. His parents had lied to him about everything. The man he was supposed to meet, and who had lain dead across his legs at the airport, was amongst the pictures. The information declared he was his brother. But that must have been a cover story because his brother had been killed by the Russians years ago. Piecing the puzzle together as far as he could, it seemed he was meant to somehow smuggle this man out, maybe back to Canada with him.

There were all kinds of identification papers and passports, which must have been forged. Hamasa didn't know who or what he could believe or trust in anymore. He no longer even knew who he was. It was as if his whole identity had been ripped away from him. Sometimes he asked himself if he had ever lived in Canada at all, if his life with Nayanna was but a buried, secret dream. He was back under his grandfather's control and he couldn't leave even if he wanted to. The years growing up there, under his dominating rule, flooded his mind as he surrendered to the painful transition of going back to becoming a mujahedeen.

He knew he was born to always be loyal to Afghanistan and to fight for the cause, but now he was confused; did his grandfather represent the Afghan cause? For now, he had no choice but to enter his grandfather's world of war.

Leaving early the next day quickly turned to leaving in a few days and then finally they left after a week as Grandfather helped prepare Hamasa for his journey to Pakistan and to being a terrorist. First, safe passage out of Afghanistan had to be arranged and then they had to make it to the training camp undetected. Grandfather accompanied Hamasa to the border and then turned back home. Hamasa was blindfolded the moment they entered Pakistan. They arrived at the camp just as evening prayers were being performed. A group of heavily armed boy soldiers descended on the truck and rushed Hamasa into a barely lit room where he joined the prayer ritual. After, the elders came and told him about the initiation process that would convince them and Hamasa that he was ready to serve the cause. Later, he was introduced to a giant, bushy bearded man they called 'The Bomb'.

"Everyone here's got an agenda, a score to settle," The Bomb told him casually. "It doesn't matter to us if it's Kashmir, Israel, or the US you're going after. Or if your enemies are personal, political or religious. All that matters here, is you do what you're told, you give it one hundred percent, and you stay alive to become the best solder you can be. Training starts tomorrow. Osama Bin Laden will be here to welcome you into the brotherhood. Allah is great," he chanted.

"Allah is great," they all chanted back.

Hamasa's inward gaze returned to the present and he looked at Harold while continuing with the interrogation.

"Days turned into weeks, into long months and then years. I even became good friends with 'The Bomb'. By the end, I was prepared for life as a terrorist. There could be no turning back. My fate was sealed. Instead of finding a way to be one with God, I would become an instrument to deliver God's justice. Everything would now be the will of Allah."

Harold had sunk back into his comfortable chair as he listened to Hamasa's story. He nodded. "I know you want us to understand your motives. You don't want to be judged without a chance to explain yourself, and I can understand that.

Hopefully," he added, "you realize how important it is for you to confess everything now."

Hamasa was silent for a long moment, then... "Yes. I'll tell you everything," he said.

Chapter 11

Interrogation Continued

"Imagine"
John Lennon

Hamasa was sick of looking at his captor, as much as Harold was getting sick of the whole interrogation process. However, they both knew there could be hours still ahead for them.

Hamasa carried on with his story, it was all he had to pass the time, besides he quite enjoyed having a captive audience, even if he was the one tied to a chair.

"Precisely as Grandpa had anticipated, my parents were gone by the time I got home. They were delayed on holiday but would be back shortly, I was told. Grandpa told me the Russians would force them to hide or they would get rid of them completely. Their usefulness had come to an abrupt end and they only had themselves to blame, he said. Their mistake was to be so buried in ideology and power that they were willing to sacrifice their son.

Grandpa arranged to have the same gun I used to kill the Russian agent smuggled in for me."

"It's a 'Russian made PSS silent pistol," he said. "So you'll be able to do what you have to quietly."

"He explained that it had to be the only gun that made it to the West, as it was only issued to special Russian agents. It would seem I must have taken out a high-ranking Russian spy. All I had to do was to wait for my parents to show up. But all I got was a phone call, telling me they would make sure there was money for me in my account. They said they would be in touch. Everything else would be explained, they pleaded."

For a long moment, Hamasa stared silently at Harold, his

eyes burning with hatred. Then he said, "Can you imagine what was going on inside me? My mind exploded. I'd just talked to my mom, the woman who nurtured me, saved my life at her peril, the one person I would die to protect, and yet, I'd been given orders to kill her. But that was in the future, and right then I was busy surviving. I got on with my life."

Hamasa was talking faster and faster now as the drugs took effect.

"Nayanna and I got back together but the years apart while I was back in Afghanistan came at a huge cost. She was pissed I hadn't kept in touch. She wouldn't let me forget that I'd never contacted her while I was away. She insisted it had worked out for the best. She said that now, all the pieces of the puzzle that was her life were all coming together. She told me she realized she had to love herself first and that nobody else was going to look after her happiness." Hamasa shook his head, sighing. "I protested greatly, I wanted so much to be one with her. But she complained I'd changed somehow. She said I should be able to understand. Again, I protested." His drug glazed eyes fought to focus on Harold. "I had to have her, to be inside of her completely, and she in me. Finally, my persistence started to pay off. Even though it was winter, and we both had a backlog of studies to catch up on, we started talking again, and hanging out more. Time sped by, the months swallowed up the seconds of anticipation."

Hamasa smiled softly, his head drooping as his mind, free to travel, carried him to another place.

"I think I'll always remember the year we finally turned eighteen, I became a man, and you, an incredibly beautiful woman. Do you see me as a man, as your man, Nayanna?" he asked as he scooped her up into his arms.

"Yes, for you everything changed – you had the freedom to do the things you always wanted to," Nayanna protested, pushing Hamasa away from her. "But for me, nothing changed. I'll always be my family's little girl. I'll never have my own life." Nayanna busied herself putting her hair in a ponytail to hide her true motivation for expelling Hamasa from her bosom.

"Remember the first time I brought you home to meet my parents?" Hamasa countered. "We were fourteen, I think? You bonded with my mom in the kitchen, baking up a storm, and Dad, he was so happy to have your attentive ears, hanging onto his every word about himself. Remember how they'd vouch for you and tell your auntie or your dad you were busy with your girlfriends, my make-believe sisters, doing homework, so we could be making out in my room. By the time we were fifteen you were able to come here and hang out even when I wasn't here. Come here, don't push me away," he demanded. "Let me free your hair, I love to feel it on my face." Once again, he folded Nayanna into his arms, burying his face in her bosom, feeling the silky strands of her hair touch his skin.

"All I'm saying is you were always free to be yourself at my home and you always had a family that accepted you here, too. And I kissed you forever here, remember? Making love to you one day will be like going to Heaven for the first time. I want your naked body against mine more than the 72 virgins Allah promises."

"What are you saying? You better not be thinking of having 72 virgins," Nayanna protested as she slapped his shoulder. "You only get that if you're a martyr, right!"

"Sorry, Nayanna, I was only joking. Come here, I love you so much. You're so sweet and down to Earth. I wish I could tell the world. I hate all this sneaking around and keeping it all secret. No wonder everything is so intense with you. The things we're not allowed are always the things we crave the most. We desire the forbidden fruit and when we get it, we savor it intensely."

He closed his eyes, tasting her soft skin against his lips, the warm, clean smell of her in his nostrils. "Maybe it's best that I'm your forbidden fruit," he murmured, kissing her reverently. "I'll always be here for you, Nayanna, I'll always protect you."

Gradually, Nayanna relaxed into him, their kisses becoming deeper and more passionate.

Hamasa held his breath as she slowly removed her top and gave herself over to his urgent hands and hot, eager mouth. It was their first time: virgins in love.

Abruptly, Nayanna pulled away, scrabbling around in her purse, she pulled out a condom. "You won't believe how long I've been carrying this around with me." Her eyes met his uncertainly. "This better not hurt, Hamasa. I love you, baby. Take it slow, maybe next time you'll be able to give it to me hard," she said with a nervous laugh.

The birds were chirping, kids screaming in play, the neighbor's dog kept howling and it all blended with the primal sounds now emitting from his bedroom.

"Hamasa! God damn you! Hamasa!" Harold shouted, frustrated with being ignored.

Hamasa came back to the present with a jolt as Harold shook his arm. He blinked. "I didn't have time for team sports," he rambled, "but Nayanna joined woman's basketball and soccer. There were times when those activities kept us apart, especially when she had her sleepovers. That's when I focused on the terrorist activities I'd been trained to do, but, it was mostly administrative stuff."

"That's where your university law degree came in handy, then. So, what kind of activities? Can you explain that further?" Harold asked as he took out a note pad and poured himself water.

"Grandfather contracted me to do many jobs, mostly the laundering of money into legit businesses I had to help start and run until others managed them properly. Surveillance for Grandfather and the organizations he was involved with was another important assignment. For political and security reasons, and, of course, for power and money, he entered an alliance with Al-Qaeda, which Osama Bin Laden started and funded. They needed me to keep their opium trade routes open and prospering, and for corporate espionage of drug companies that were testing and using opium. In addition, they wanted me to communicate with their secret, sleeper terrorist cells. They needed to find and develop ways to accomplish their goals of freeing their lands from foreign influences. Grandfather's reach now extended internationally," Hamasa stated as he watched Harold take notes.

Harold nodded. "And I bet the money flowed generously at that time. So what kind of quantities are we talking about here, six figures?"

"Nothing less than two hundred thousand flowed through me," Hamasa told him.

"Grandfather was obsessed with finding out everything he could about my parents spying activities. He was also awfully suspicious they might have been spying for other countries as well. Bin Laden had all the papers grandfather had taken from me examined by top forensic technicians and they concluded they were forged out of Israel and not the US or Russia as he first suspected. It was hard not to believe my parents were somehow involved with the number one archenemy of all Muslims, the Israelis."

"Were you involved in any direct attacks on Israel at that time or did you know of any?" Harold asked.

"No, I had my hands full where I was, and as far as I know, there were no connections to anything happening against Israel directly. However, it's interesting how I found out about my parent's activities while they were in hiding. I was into my fourth year at university when Nayanna told me she had a sleepover coming up at her friend's, Helen Kaplan. I knew I would have to take advantage of our time apart and complete some missions. By the time I found out it would involve the family she was having the sleepover with, it was too late, all the listening devices and cameras had already been put in place.

I was told to spy on this Israeli family, Mr. and Mrs. Kaplan, and their business. They were involved with developing the scientific methods to extract the oil from Canada's northern tar sands. Finding ways to disrupt or impede an enemy's oil industry is always the quickest way to get attention."

In his line of work, Hamasa knew it was imperative not to mix business with anything that had even a remote chance of creating emotion or being personal. That kind of combination could distort a person's thinking and intent, and rapidly lead to mistakes which could summon death.

Now business was mixed up with the girl he loved. It was a dangerous combination, but, Hamasa reasoned, this was only a sleepover and he was only doing surveillance. What could go so wrong?

This time his attention was pulled back to the interrogation room by Harold slamming his hand down on the trolley holding the various instruments of a questioner's trade.

Hamasa looked at Harold, annoyed at his impatience and chuckled dryly. "I was shocked by what I overheard next."

The girls, who were camped out in the basement rumpus room, ironically had just finished watching a program on TV about terrorists.

Chapter 12

Surveillance

"People's egos are always feeding off the carcasses of those they slight."
John H. K. Fisher

Nayanna, getting agitated after watching the TV documentary on terrorists, exclaimed, "What's up with these terrorists anyways? I mean none of us would ever think of killing somebody, right?"

"Right, certainly not!" chorused the girls as if they had rehearsed their response. It was girl's 'night in' for Nayanna, Helen, Nancy and Noriko. They were off to a good start, filling up on their favorite homemade dishes while the smell of freshly popped corn hung deliciously in the air. They had promised each other that there would be activities – no TV or gossip. Somehow, the documentary had caught their attention as they were slipping into their PJs and preparing their mattresses and bedding in the rumpus room.

"Well, I guess I would have to admit I might have been tempted once. There was this one manager, 'the pit bull', which was the nicer reference people made," Nayanna growled as she put her hair up in a bun. "Oh my God, I could go on all day about that creepy lady. The adjectives to describe that monster are just too nasty for me to say in the company of you ladies. Her plan, to rule the world and have a thousand slaves, failed, so she thought she'd rule the family restaurant I worked at instead. Yes! We're talking family restaurant, not a Siberian prison work camp or dictator in charge of some remote military school, where she should have been. She would threaten our jobs just for smiling and greeting our fellow workers. She was always sarcastic, arrogant, egotistical, a bigot, greedy, selfish, manipulative, an abusive tyrant, a narcissistic perfectionist and a total Jekyll and Hyde. Her moods could change minute by minute, from being very charming when the owners were around, to her usual snarling. Everyone knew about her obsessive addiction to booze but I often wondered if her husband and kids knew about her addiction to gigolos. The boys and girls for hire were always hanging around the restaurant as she said it was good for business. She would have pimped us, too, given the chance. She said we had to show lots of leg and cleavage.

She would openly tell us we were not to encourage any ethnics to the restaurant and no ethnics would be hired, no blacks or orientals, only whites. You guys, this was in Canada! Can you believe it? I always had special white powder on my face and I guess she thought I was Italian. She ruined so many careers. People were always being fired if they stood up for their human rights or they were forced to quit from all the abuse or to save their sanity. She was power mad and she blamed her failures on everyone but herself. I think that to build up her ego and power in her own sick mind, she had to abuse and put down others as much as she was able to get away with. Like a cocaine fix, it boosted her dopamine to get her through the day I guess.

"To harass and prove her great power over everybody, she ordered the house entertainer to stop singing and to hire a tall, blond, blue-eyed, sexy female to sing. The perfect carrier of the perfect womb that would create the perfect, superior human race Hitler had raved about. Then she said, she didn't care if she couldn't sing, as long as she would show lots of leg, cleavage and act really sexy."

"Gross, no wonder I didn't get hired there, I don't have any cleavage and I'm Asian," Noriko shrieked.

"I know, hey," Nayanna continued, "she told the house entertainer who played guitar he would be fired if he allowed any ethnics to sing with him. The house musician had been there for many, many years but was fired when he complained about the racism and abuse. I'm not racist against any nationality, lord knows, the country's people may be the greatest humanitarians. Anybody from any tribe or country can be a Nazi type. I hope I'm getting that across here.

"But get this! She was friends with a biker gang and started inviting them to the restaurant. Diners would see them and leave. Everyone knew if the word got out that the bikers hung out there, no one else would come and the business would be ruined. We all complained the bikers were scaring off customers and intimidating us, but again she just said she was the boss and she liked the money they tipped her. We knew they were there because they shared the same white supremacy views."

"Oh my God, can I ever relate to how horrible that must have been to go through," hissed Helen, the evening's hostess, who already had her long blond hair in a bun and was dressed as if she had just come from a run. "Don't mind me, I can talk while I'm doing my stretches," she said. "My dad, my grandfather, three uncles and thousands upon thousands of Canadians died to protect us from Nazis types, to give us freedom, human rights and to end racism and abuse. Then they allow Nazis into our country, give them the top jobs where they again have influence to reintroduce their evil ways. What a joke, but on us! The government agencies set up to protect people are a joke – they do nothing. They're probably staffed by the same Nazis types! I can't believe we have to put up with these monsters here in Canada. It's such a weird country in the way that it doesn't know what the hell culture is. They promote multiculturalism and want to be so sensitive to everyone's culture that they allow anything. Give me a break! Ignorance is not culture. Mutilation is not culture. Jihad is not culture. Honor killing is not culture. Mental illness is not culture. Evil is not culture. Cannibalism is not culture. Culture is the way groups of people agree to express their joys, accomplishments, hardships they overcome and the knowledge they acquired: the things that have a positive effect on everyone and the way they pass it to the next generation. If out of ignorance the group is doing something that has negative effects in some way, then it has to be changed. It's so simple really. It's not racism to say that a certain belief or way of doing things is wrong if it has negative consequences or benefits a few at the expense of others. Hello, people, wake up! Anyway, so what happened next?" Helen asked as she continued doing her stretches.

"Whoa," Nayanna sighed. "I'm sorry to hear your family had to sacrifice so much and still we have to live with all this evil here. Thank God for popcorn to take the edge off things. Anyone else want more?" Nayanna asked as she loaded up her second bag.

"The reason for all the evil, all the wars and why nothing is done about it, all boils down to money, which buys power. You're crazy to think we went to war for freedom or democracy. It's all about the rich getting and keeping power so they can get more money to get more power, period!" insisted Helen. "Sorry to interrupt. So what happened next?"

"Hey, no problemo! Well, eventually the owners had to put an end to the nonsense of bikers at the restaurant before they went bankrupt," continued Nayanna. "I just wanted to blow the place up."

"My goodness, how did you win Miss Congeniality?" scoffed Nancy, I can't wait to tell my nightmare story and how it led me to want to kill someone. But," continued Nancy, nervously stroking her fingers through her hair, "that doesn't come close to justifying terrorism. I'm not into all that God fairytale stuff. But just because I'm an atheist doesn't mean I'm not into love, looking after yourself and your fellow man. You don't have to believe in God to meditate or do yoga as it's been scientifically proven to have health benefits. World cooperation would be great but let's be real! The way our brains are wired and how we're programmed genetically from millions of years existing as animals in an 'eat or be eaten world', you can't trust anyone. It's better to have science saving us, systems and some governance in place to deal with the fall out. No wonder we're all so screwed up and upset with life! Ever since we were born, we've been told nothing but lies about Santa Clause, the Easter Bunny and that there's a God of love that saves our soul. As we get older and our intellect grows, we find out there's absolutely no proof for the existence of any of it. It's all a pack of lies to benefit a few very manipulative assholes looking to cash in and have all the power. If we'd built a society based on the facts, we would have a fair and just world to live in. Let me tell you about the world I'd create if I ruled the Universe. He-he! First, it would be accepted that we're all animals and need protection from each other and ourselves, as well as from ignorance, violence, greed, death and all the other natural problems, until cures were found. Every child would be taught the truth, which is no one knows the truth. The one goal unifying everyone would be to find the truth about everything and to evolve together for the benefit of all as well as the planet. One goal for societies would be to have all lifelong necessities guaranteed for each new birth and eventually for each human being. This would create true equality.

I would create a world where the goal would be for each living organism to evolve towards love, respect and nonviolence towards each other and themselves. Even bugs, especially mosquitoes, fish, reptiles and mammals would all evolve to exist without killing and eating others. Everything would live in harmony to experience the greatest joy, happiness, love, health and longevity that can be created. This might take a long time, but with the help of science, computers, genetic modification and drugs, it could happen. If humans don't play God, then who will? There sure aren't any gods stepping up to the plate to help us. We should be protected from people who say they are God or in touch with a god, because that is the biggest insult of all, since there's nothing to prove their claims. It destroys life by creating false hope, it creates false ideals we're forced to live up to, separates people into fighting tribes and keeps us from helping ourselves to reach the true goals that would unite everyone and actually get results. Our belief in God keeps us from finding answers and solutions to all the mysteries and challenges."

"OK, OK, now we're getting way off topic, into politics, religion or non-religion, science and who knows what else. We'll be up all night," exclaimed Nayanna! "How about you, Noriko, did you ever want to kill somebody? By the way, I love how you did your hair, it's so traditional Japanese, with a touch of sexy grunge, right? You shaved the one side, kept a long braid, put a bun on the back and topped it off with a chopstick, brilliant; it has to be called a traditional sexy grunge punk cut, right?"

"OK, OK, I'll shut up. I can take the hint. I see the God-fearing far outnumber me here anyway," Nancy hollered as she interrupted the conversation while diving under the blankets. "I'd get creamed, right?"

"Right!" the girls shouted back as they threw their pillows at Nancy.

"Yes, I'm not afraid to experiment with my hair and look – traditional sexy grunge style is fine by me," replied Noriko. "But here's my terrorist story. It never ceases to amaze me how people can destroy another's life with a momentary impulse or by giving in to a desire or a temporary rage over some little thing," Noriko exclaimed. "This lady just didn't realize the total devastation her selfish, abusive actions had on others..."

"Wow!" interrupted Helen, "I'm sure we could go on all night bitching about all the abuses we all have to go through, but I hate to interrupt but isn't this supposed to be our fun night together, instead of coming up with reasons to be a terrorist. Anyway, one man's terrorist is another man's freedom fighter, right! But it sounds like we girls really need some heavy healing from all we've been through. I think we should do a healing circle and send out some prayers of forgiveness. You know what they say,

God punishes the victims more than the abusers if the victims seek revenge or don't forgive. We have a lot of work to do here tonight. What'd you say girls? Hey, can you imagine the people that were victims of rape or had a family member murdered or had to deal with the rape or murder of a child and were able to forgive? You've seen it on Oprah, I'm sure. So I'm certain we can do it!"

"Sounds like something witches would do." Nayanna laughed.

"Maybe we should be doing voodoo," squealed Nancy.

"OK, let's hold hands in a circle," Helen said, getting to her feet with palms out.

"It's all about breathing out the bad and breathing in the good, calmly," implored Noriko. "Maybe Nancy should teach us all how to meditate?"

"I should know all about meditation because my grandparents and even my parents were really into it. I know my dad still meditates when he has the time. They follow the Sikh religion," Nayanna said.

"So what distracted you from learning all about it then? Was it that tall, dark, handsome hunk, Hamasa, who we used to see you with? Oh, come on! You really don't believe we knew nothing about the two of you? We also know about Sky, the musician you've been seeing. We hear rumors he's going to teach you to play the flute. Wow, that could be the way to his heart. I think we should take a moment for Nayanna to tell us all about her exciting love life. Quite the balancing act!" Noriko exclaimed.

"Hey, you didn't mention the guy my dad's arranged for me to marry. You haven't even begun to do your homework. But, OK, OK! Later!" squealed Nayanna. "Let's do this forgiving circle thing first though. Wow, I can't believe you're bringing that up and you all knew everything all along! By the way, that Sky thing is totally unfounded. He doesn't even know I exist. But yeah, I did mention to someone about wanting flute lessons, still, let's get real here. You better have come prepared to help me figure out what the hell I'm supposed to be doing though."

Nayanna had no one to confide in. Even Hamasa's parents weren't around these days to talk with, and Hamasa had changed a great deal, though he was in denial and wouldn't talk. He was always gone or busy and yet he wanted to control her every move.

"Listen, ladies," Nayanna interjected, "if I end up dead in the next little while, you'll know either my father killed me for not doing what he wants me to do, or my arranged husband's family killed me for not doing what they want or Hamasa killed me for not doing what he wants me to do. Either way I'm screwed, oops, sorry, excuse my French!"

Hamasa remembered how taken aback he had been by Nayanna's confessions, only to quickly have them relegated by more pressing matters when he finally tore himself from spying on the girls and remembered why he was there in the first place. He had found out Mr. and Mrs. Kaplan were Israeli spies – and their main contact was with his parents, Jaabir and Ameera. Hamasa intercepted their communications, which led to him actually following the Kaplans to a rendezvous with his father.

Sitting at the interrogation table, Harold realized the pain and confusion Hamasa was reliving and decided to go easy on him and give him a chance to put those feelings into words.

Chapter 13

Interrogation Continued

"War is over…If you want it."
John Lennon

Hamasa was still tied to his unyielding chair, but, as Harold had moved back to his comfy spot, gazing at each other was no longer necessary. He relished his freedom of hand movement and continued to pour himself water, or whatever beverage the foreign operatives would leave for him. But no matter how he complained, food was still a mirage.

At the time of the surveillance of the girls and the house, Hamasa had thought it was he who wasn't doing his homework. Sky, who was this Sky dude Nayanna talked about and why hadn't she told him of the pending arranged marriage her father had secured in India? It was his new mission to find out.

It was also the first time he had heard the ideas held by atheists. He was so busy terrorizing people from other religions to honor Allah and his grandfather that he had never thought to terrorize atheists. He was disgusted at the thought that there were people who rejected the very foundation and beliefs for his life and purpose. Anger built up inside and he wanted to strike out and kill as the Koran instructed. But at the same time he had a repulsive urge and curiosity to learn more about them and their practices. He made a commitment that he would look into their ideas and study their organizations.

When he finally did find time to do some study and after careful discernment, he realized what the world without a god could be like. He realized if the documents were true and there were no God, then there could still be hope and purpose for humanity to carry on. It gave him even more zeal to do whatever he could to find the truth. But he had also got more and more confused with all the diverse opinions, religions, interpretations and contradicting organizations. His encounter with the Power left little room for doubt though, and he was back to being a believer.

But not only was he going through torture worrying about and trying to hold on to Nayanna, he now was worried about his parent's involvement with Israeli spies.

Hamasa shook himself free of the past and continued with his story to appease his captors.

He grinned ruefully. "The girls really gave the forgiveness thing a try." He paused. "Which, I suppose, is something I still need to learn how to do." He paused again, collecting his thoughts. "I guess I really glimpsed a different side of Nayanna. And it made me want her even more." He shook his head. "Some of the things those girls talked about, I mean, I thought guys were bad when they got together! Wow! Not even close! But hearing all the wonderful things she said about me to the other girls, I couldn't have been prouder." He laughed softly. "I tell you, it was difficult not to say something to her about it all. The things I heard! But, of course, I didn't." Hamasa ran his fingers through his hair and massaged his head and neck.

Harold picked that up as a signal he was hiding something.

"Are you sure she only mentioned the great things about you, Hamasa?" he probed. "Are you sure she didn't say anything about how you were screwing up the relationship?" He saw Hamasa tense. "Are you forgetting to mention something?" he pushed. "We know what happened to poor, innocent Sky. I'm sure he didn't know what hit him…or why." Harold suddenly rose to his feet and started heading for the iron gate. Someone was staring at Hamasa, moving in the shadows down one of the corridors.

"I've no idea what you're talking about, but for Nayanna's

sake, there might be some things that will go to the grave with me, *but* nothing about murder." Hamasa ploughed on. He had to keep talking to avoid answering the difficult questions.

"Who's there?" Harold called out to the person in the shadows. Whoever it was had gone. Harold made note of the time and continued to pace about for a while, until he found his way back to his comfy chair.

Hamasa was ready. "When my dad and I finally got together I'd even forgotten I still had the Russian gun, but of course, I didn't have it on me."

It was a beautiful spring morning and Hamasa was making the most of his time in Stanley Park. Already the enthusiasts were out: walking fast, jogging, playing tennis, biking, kayaking, playing lawn bowling, picture taking, skate boarding, roller blading, flying kites, feeding squirrels, flying helicopters and small planes, sailing, docking yachts, playing beach volleyball, playing guitars and bongos, while others were driving over the Lions Gate Bridge to North Vancouver. However, Hamasa had a lot on his mind and decided to find a quiet spot to relax amongst the colossal, costal cedars. He sat down and barely had time to collect his thoughts when his mobile phone started vibrating, buzzing, and tickling his chest.

"Hello, son, it's Dad."

"Oh really, I never would have guessed, especially since I hardly ever hear from you fugitives," Hamasa said, his voice loaded with sarcasm. "So how's retired life...or that's what you want me to believe. But you won't guess who I spied on recently that suggests old habits die hard."

His father laughed. "So you caught me in the act, did you? It must have been the get together with my old friends, the Kaplan's. Hey, that's easily explained. I know exactly where you are. I want you to stay put until I get there. Remember you learned spying from the best."

"Oh my God, was that an echo?" Hamasa whispered to himself. "How could you sneak up on me like that?" Hamasa yelled as he leapt forward to give his dad, who appeared from behind a big cedar, a hug.

Jaabir grinned widely as he rushed into his son's arms, catching his sunglasses as they fell from where they were perched on his cap.

"Oh my God, it's been too long! Listen, son…uh…we don't have much time. We both know how easy it is to be followed and it's only a matter of time before they trace the phone calls and find us here."

"Who are, 'they', Dad? How's Mom? Is everything OK?"

"Son, I'm not going to beat about the bush here. Let's sit down, this could take some time, and it's not going to be easy for me to explain everything, but I feel now's the time."

Hamasa knew he had to hold his tongue as his mind raced over all the worst scenarios his father might be about to disclose. Memories of being a child and at the mercy of the world, as well as some members of his family flooded his mind.

Abruptly his father blurted, "I know you know, that I know, that you're working with Grandfather and that he wants us dead and that you've been sent to do that. There, I got it out! Grandfather spilled the beans long ago. He couldn't contain the disappointment and anger he felt towards me and let it slip that as family betrayed him, so, too, would family betray your mom and me."

Jaabir grabbed Hamasa's arm as he flew off his seat, pulling him into his embrace.

Hamasa saw tears standing in his father's eyes and was conscious of his own wet cheeks. For the moment all that mattered was that he was here, held in his father's arms, the love between them tangible.

After a while, Jaabir sighed. "Son, you're on the wrong side of the war. You've got to see the big picture." He took off his cap and wiped the tears that ran down his cheeks. "The world's changing so quickly. It's no longer about saving the village, your friends, Grandfather, or the values with which you grew up." He glanced down before meeting Hamasa's gaze again. "It's entirely my fault you're caught up in all this. I take full responsibility for you becoming a terrorist and working with Grandfather. From your point of view, he's the king we all worshipped and obeyed. All you knew and saw was everyone following Grandfather's orders, so you naturally believed he must have the authority of truth. By obeying Grandfather, you felt you were obeying God and your family, am I right? You had no idea that your mom and I secretly fought against everything he stood for. The way you were raised and all the values that were instilled in you that we had to allow to keep our cover destroyed any chance for you to be anything but a terrorist. I'm so sorry, son. But it's not too late. We can turn this around. I'll do whatever I have to do to bring you out of it. I understand you were given no way out with Grandfather; you'd be dead, too, if you went against him. Like you, I was given no choices either, but my story's a bit more complicated. I wouldn't even be able to sit here telling you all that I'm going to say if the people I work for didn't allow it. They want you, Hamasa. They're going to offer you a job, a deal, a new way of life, a new worldview. You've got to say yes. Let me finish before you interrupt," he urged, holding up his hand. "I know you have a million questions.

"Yes, your mom and I were forced to spy for the Russians after they captured your brother, Massoud. If we hadn't, we would have all been killed. In addition, your grandfather was more useful to them alive and spied on, rather than dead. Massoud is the one who died at the airport, and the one you were supposed to give the documents to." He stopped, overcome with grief. Visibly gathering himself, he shook his head. "There's more, so much more. Hamasa, I'm also an Israeli spy. I'm a Jew, well; I converted to being a Christian Jew."

"What!" Hamasa stared at his father, open mouthed. "This – this can't be real! It can't be happening to me." Hamasa shot to his feet and stormed away from the bench they were sitting on.

Jaabir hurried after him. "I know it's a lot to take in, son, but just let me finish," he pleaded. "Like I said, the world's changing fast and something catastrophic is about to happen. I don't know what, but I'm picking up a lot of chatter about it. Who knows, maybe it's a natural disaster coming…a volcano or meteors, but I don't think so. All over the world, the elite are talking and preparing to create a New World Order. They don't want to wait to see what terrorist organization gets a nuclear bomb first or what special interest groups like anti-globalists will do to the world if they get some new technology. They know it would be naive to think the Chinese or Russians won't use their nuclear weapons to gain power.

"These elite have the power and money to change the world now. They want to see it done while they're still alive, to make sure they get to keep their power and money and that it passes to the right people, their people. Everyone will be monitored 24/7 and everyone will work and pay a global tax. Right now, they're arguing over who gets to be on top and make all the rules and decide what the one religion will be. Obviously, the Catholics have the most money and power. That's why you hear the Pope talking about a One World Government and a New World Order. They need the Catholics, but they also need America, and yes, even the Israelis, since there are enough Messianic or Christian Jews. If they can get the moderate Muslims on side then it'll be a go. It's going to happen soon and we have to be on the winning side of this war. Your grandfather, the Chinese, Russians, Iranians, Libyans, and a few others will put up the worst resistance, but nobody stands a chance opposing this new world order. They already monitor all lines of communication – phones, computers, emails, you name it. In addition, they have the latest technologies and weapons, things you wouldn't believe.

"I want you to take their offer and work for the Israelis. You have to think globally. Let go of your tribalism and boyhood concerns and look to see what the future holds for you in this 'New World Order'."

"So am I a Jew then, Dad? My brother... a Jew? Did he even know? Did my brother die saving me?" Hamasa asked as he still paced about madly. "How can a Jew be a Christian? I'm so messed up by all of this. You'll have to realize this is going to take a considerable amount of processing. I've always been searching for my truth and purpose, you know that, but this... this is just unbelievable." Suddenly, all the anger drained out of him and Hamasa sat down on the nearest bench, his face in his hands.

"To me, you're my Jewish son," Jaabir said softly. "But because your mother wasn't Jewish and we didn't raise you as a Jew, you would have to make an official conversion to Judaism. The same holds true of Judaea Christianity."

Hamasa sat silent and Jaabir rushed on. "We believe the same as Jews, only we believe Christ is the Messiah. Listen, son, my main concern is that you'll be safe in this crazy world, and if you're looking for truth and a higher purpose then you'd be doing yourself a favor by working with the Israelis to stay alive long enough to find it. I am getting too old for all this nonsense. Your mom and I just want to get away from it all…you know… retire. But they keep sucking us back in.

"There are some missions I keep telling them you'd be the perfect candidate for." He gave Hamasa a long look. "Think about it, will you. Right now, they're telling me about some secret documents that could destroy the church if they got in the wrong hands. They want them retrieved. You're the man who could do this. Son, there's so much more we should go over. All these years of secrets, but we always loved you, we were always there for you. Nothing ever changes that. You got that?"

Hamasa said nothing.

"Right now though, we're running out of time," Jaabir continued. "Great wars are upon us, and we have to be prepared and on the right side – on the winning side."

Hamasa thought about the way he had talked with his parents on the phone for most of that year. Hearing their side of the story repeatedly had made him sympathetic, to say the least. They had also talked about his older brother, and how horrible it had been for him as a Russian prisoner. Hamasa was losing trust in everything and everyone but he wanted so badly to hang on to family. He listened carefully to his father.

Once more, Hamasa made a determined bid to break away from his past and re-focused on the interrogation.

"So, yes, I was trained by and fought for Muslims. And all along I was their worst enemy, a Jew, how ironic."

Harold showed no reaction to Hamasa's statements, seeming preoccupied with his notes.

"I never heard any more news about Grandfather, other than when I was told he might have been killed in an American bombing campaign in the region. He'd always managed to survive before, so I assumed it was just a matter of time before we heard from him again.

"By the time I was twenty-five, I was ready for whatever the world threw my way, although I was more confused than ever about the world and myself.

"I grew up being told the greatest honor was to die a martyr and ascend into the waiting arms of seventy-two virgins. I had Nayanna telling me it had better not be true, my parents telling me it wasn't true, and all the while, I knew the blood of thousands of martyrs was on the line.

"Just before I kidnapped the Masters, I started to realize that the whole world was crazy. I realized there is not one thought, one idea or any one person or group of people and all they have created which is not corrupt. Everything exists to express survival at any cost, through any means available. Even the idea of perfection, truth or the ideals of compassion, unconditional love and God's love were all created for survival and are corrupt, along with the idea of who God is. For the sake of survival we have to pretend everything is OK and that we're happy, striving for perfection in all things. We have to believe there is a loving God and truth will prevail, that there's a reason for everything and everything will work out for the best. If we don't, then we can't be part of the group. We become outsiders and are perceived to be untrustworthy. A person outside the group or society has few choices for work and certainly can't become any kind of a leader or be elected president. Now, the world was on the brink of extinction and no one cared.

"That was how I started to see the world just before the kidnappings and before all this happened, and now I'm just finding out there seems to be a God, but He is also corrupt because He got bored. What a wild web of weirdness He's wielded on us. But listen, none of this is important now! If you read the documents then you'll know what I'm talking about. We've got to get a move on. Please, why the delay? I'm not crazy. What I told you earlier is really happening to me."

Hamasa heard the kite swooshing sound and this time knew exactly what that meant.

"Hey, the Master is here, right now, in this room. Can you see his presence as I can? He keeps insisting the time has come. He's showing me where they are hiding the Successor. We have to leave now, soon the world will start to disintegrate. You must believe me! Only the Successor can take on the Karma that keeps this from happening. Please, just read the documents. Bring the documents here so we can go over them and I'll be able to prove their authenticity."

"Hamasa," Harold said impatiently, "stop all this crazy talk, right now! Let's get this over with. Just answer these few more questions. We just need some of the missing pieces to the puzzle you've presented to us. If you keep talking like this, you'll be able to confess everything and blame it on a mental disorder. Even if you plead insanity, you'll still end up behind bars. Is that what this is about – all your crazy talk? Do you want a padded cell and visits from shrinks? Just keep to the story, Hamasa. Tell us what happened next."

Harold was out of patience and out of his comfortable chair, pacing around. When his eyes met with Hamasa's, everything changed immediately. There was no way to deny it anymore. It was so obvious. It wasn't vertigo attacks, or hypnosis, there was a real experience that took place when he looked in Hamasa's eyes. Harold knew Hamasa had the same effect on others, too. People who passed by were spellbound: deer caught in car headlights. They lingered in the shadows, hoping to get a glimpse of Hamasa's eyes and the strange power they emitted. He also had to admit, but only to himself, that he heard and felt the air shimmering without a knowable cause in the same way Hamasa described it.

Chapter 14

Nayanna

"Being born is like being kidnapped, and then sold into slavery."
Andy Warhol

Nayanna's father, Bhajan, would have nothing to do with her learning to drive or with helping him with his job as a taxi driver. She knew how difficult it was for him to keep the long hours to bring hope to the family, but he had told her it would be more difficult to know he was a burden. It was his honor and purpose to see to it that he took care of her, he had said. Then he went on and on how his greatest dream was to live long enough to be able to afford to pay for Nayanna's arranged marriage into a suitable family. He would find the right family that could bring her a life of status and security. He said it would help to make up for all the tragedies and hardships they had all faced. Day and night, whenever he could find the time, he prepared and planned for that big day. The word got out, all across the world, wherever Sikhs migrated, of his beautiful daughter's eligibility. Sikh temples were everywhere and he had a network of family, friends, and even Sikh priests who knew Nayanna was motherless and they eagerly volunteered to step in to perform what would have been her mother's duty in this sacred tradition. Friends would tease her dad and warn him to heed the warning of the 'Guru Granth Sahib', that followers of God should 'be like the Koel or Cuckoo and sing of the Beloved: not the vacant, virtuous virgin'.

Nayanna's only hope was that he would never be able to afford his lavish schemes. She felt like an elephant had chosen to sit on her so she might find spiritual enlightenment. However, she knew her father couldn't help the way he behaved, any more than she or anyone else could for that matter. We are all a product of our genes and upbringing, she felt. Living in this strange new world of Canada, where everyone was brought up differently made that very clear for her.

When Hamasa didn't come back from his travels, when he failed to even phone or write, she knew she had been left on her own to oppose thousands of years of tradition by standing up against an arranged marriage. She thought about phoning Hamasa's parents to let them know she didn't appreciate being forgotten, but she never got up the courage. Anyway, it would only have broken her heart to hear them telling her of all his adventures. It was another lonely summer holiday and she had no one to confide in with Hamasa always gone. She decided to call her best friend, Helen, who, fortunately, had the day off from work and happily agreed to meet her at 'Mary's Place'.

She hadn't been in a while, but she used to go there alone. It would be nice to share it with someone, Nayanna thought. It was a real homey place, with a fireplace for damp, cold, West Coast days like this one. The best thing was nobody else they knew went there, so they could talk freely.

"Thanks for meeting me here," Nayanna said, embracing Helen in a warm hug. "I'm so glad you came. It's so good to see you!" she said, beaming at her. "This is a cool place isn't it? Take a whiff, the fireplace with the scent of chocolate and mint, it's to die for. So come on," she urged, "tell me, how's your summer going so far?"

"Hey, girl," Helen said, smiling all over her face. "It's been a long while hasn't it – since our last sleep over with everyone? Right? We'll have to plan another one soon. Who needs to wait for school or sports to bring us back together? This time we should plan it around a cooking feast, where we all bring a favorite recipe instead of talking about terrorism." Helen paused, her eyes staring past her friend. "Ooh, look at the cute waiter who's too shy to get his tight buns over here." She brought her gaze back to Nayanna. "You know, he hasn't stopped looking at you since the moment we got here."

"Yeah, another girl's night together," Nayanna answered, getting into the idea of some female bonding and ignoring the waiter comments. "Or, we can plan a game night where everyone brings their best game ideas. Anything but watching a movie!"

"Yeah, I know what you mean, that's all I've been doin' lately. So how's that hunk of yours? I heard he's left you alone for the summer?"

"What! There you go again, teasing me about rumors that may or may not be true." Nayanna pulled on a fake frown. "Who do you hear all these rumors from? Who's your source? OK, tell me the truth. And anyway, where the hell did you see us together? I'm sure we were careful to keep our meetings secret. And what about you? But then you never seem to need a reason to keep your lovers a secret. I've seen you smooching with at least a couple of guys this past year," Nayanna teased.

Helen grinned. "Yeah, Yeah. Well you know how it is with us western folk. Things just get a bit too boring and dangerous the longer you let 'em stick around, if you know what I mean. I guess you would be absolutely killed if your family found out – it was the library by the way. Yeah, girl, right there behind the stack of biology books. I guess those diagrams of the reproductive system got the better of you," Helen teased back.

"Good afternoon, ladies, is there anything I can help you with today? My name is Sky, and I'm all yours 'til we get some more customers in here. Nice to see you here again," he said, looking at Nayanna.

"Hey, thanks, but I think we need a bit more time here," Helen responded. "We've gotten carried away with our gossiping I'm afraid and haven't even looked at the menu." She shot him a big, toothy smile. "Any suggestions?"

"I know what I want," Nayanna stated, her attention on Sky, as having taken their orders, he headed for the kitchen. Helen was right; she thought he was yummy, too: yes, one hot package, she daydreamed. Still, she knew Helen had it covered and that she would make sure she had first dibs. Besides, Nayanna was already driven over a cliff by the lover she had. But a little ego boost about now would be nice, she thought, along with the double chocolate latte topped with whipped cream and a strawberry cheese cake topped with more chocolate she'd ordered. She held back a sigh. None of it would fill the empty place Hamasa had left, but it sure as hell would make it easier to stay focused on the beauty of the moment, she fantasized. She lingered on her naughty thoughts for a little longer before forcibly bringing her attention back to the conversation with Helen.

"There's no way I'm going to get an arranged marriage, just no way. My dad says to surrender to God's will. But how is it God's will tore my family apart? I know from direct experience family isn't the be all and end all of life. I understand when people give their lives to God – that's an eternal reward, but I'm just not built that way. I question everything and I'm not even sure if I believe in God anymore and definitely not the God my dad believes in. Maybe, if I could have some direct experience, instead of God talking to me through my father all the time, a-ha." She laughed at her moment of epiphany.

"Whoa, whoa, girl, you've got some heavy shit weighing on you there. That's heavy stuff, and it's way over my head to be commenting about. I don't know a thing about what you're going through, but you keep going and I'll listen. I'm just a sweet, innocent, naive, non-practicing Jewish girl. But I'm here for you, you know that. But hey, back up a bit will ya'. So you know this guy? Why didn't you introduce me earlier? You're savin' him all for yourself, a-ha."

It's been a couple of years now, but I talked to him about flute lessons. Everyone made such a stink – I figured Hamasa would get upset so I just dropped it. But yeah, I keep runnin' into him here and other places." Nayanna felt some of her frustration ease. "Thanks, Helen, for your support. I didn't even know you were Jewish. I guess I should have guessed by your last name, Kaplan does sound kosher," she said laughing. "Do you ever wish you could be a genius at something you could dedicate yourself to?"

"Listen, girl." Helen fluttered her lashes. "It's enough for me that I'm a genius at getting what I want for myself. You can ask my dad to verify that." Helen giggled. "But seriously, you believe in yourself, right? You can do it. You can be true to yourself but you just have to take the consequences. I mean, what kind of love do people have for you if they can't accept who you really are or support what you believe in? Oh my God, here he comes, here he comes, and look at those goodies he's packin', and that long blond hair. I want to get my hands wrapped around that. He looks like one of those surfer boys from a movie, especially if he let his hair down. So that's the flute lessons guy?"

"Helen, you're shameless!"

"Is there anything else I can help you with today, ladies?" asked Sky, as he served drinks and delicacies.

"Sure, but it would be better served after you get off work." Helen winked.

"Helen, behave! You're making the poor boy turn all red!" Nayanna looked at Sky, who was doing his best to conceal his embarrassment. "You have to excuse my friend, Sky. She's trying to spice up her boring summer holidays at your expense."

"Well, I would like to mention our restaurant is hosting a meditation retreat here tonight. There'll be vegetarian dishes served, a speaker, some massage, music my friends and I'll be playing and even free door prizes, as you can see in the window display there," he said, pointing. "Thanks for coming in today and I hope to see you later," he said. Turning to Nayanna, he added, "and if you're still interested in flute lessons, we can talk about that, too, later."

Helen barely waited for Sky to leave before bursting out, "Nayanna! I swear, that guy can't keep his eyes off you. He didn't even notice I was on planet Earth. He just invited you on a date. Someone's playing matchmaker with the two of you, I know it. What are you going to do? I wonder what other instruments he plays?" she rushed on. "He can play on my bongos any day," she said, snorting with laughter.

"I brought you here to discuss how we're going to stop being sexually objectified by men and society," Nayanna joked. "How to stop inequality and getting less pay than men. How to stop honor killings, female mutilations and how to stop females from being marginalized." She gave a mock sigh. "But here you are, taking women back to the caveman days of being raped and loving it." She paused, drawing in a long breath. "And you know I'm just kidding. I love how you can be so free in your thoughts and in your actions and not have to worry what others say. For me, I'd be too worried about the consequences of that freedom. But I know I can't let myself be buried under the weight of traditions and superstitions. At the same time, I love my dad and I'm so grateful for all he's done for me. I'm in a jam or…how do you say it…'caught between a rock and a hard place'. Anyway, enough of my stuff, what's going on with you?"

They talked none stop for the next two hours and somewhere in that time, Nayanna made the decision to come back later, check out the meditation retreat and listen to Sky perform. She also needed to balance out her afternoon indulgence with something healthy, and although Sky looked wholly healthy, she meant food-wise. She was sure her dad would be working, so she knew she wouldn't be missed at home.

Chapter 15

Interrogation Continued

"I am sometimes a fox and sometimes a lion. The whole secret of government lies in knowing when to be the one or the other."
Napoleon Bonaparte

Hamasa knew he had to cooperate as best he could; there would be no lawyer coming to represent him in his current situation. He continued putting up with the interrogation, wondering when the Power would free him from this mess. The Power promised that if he didn't resist and just cooperated, help would be forthcoming. Where was that help? Was it all just a dream and his encounter with 'the Power' just a hallucination? His eyes blinked more than usual, he stroked his newly formed whiskers. Barely containing his impatience, Hamasa continued answering the questions Harold fired at him.

"OK, Hamasa, let's finish hearing your side of the story," Harold commanded.

Hamasa coughed, clearing his throat. "As I already mentioned, after I got my Master's degree, my parents came to me for help. Like I said, they were offered an extremely dangerous assignment with the promise of a substantial reward. This was to be their final mission before they retired to their safe haven.

Guiardo, an eccentric mafia boss, was dying of cancer and petitioned the Vatican to have his sins absolved. He'd suffered a lot of loss and hardship in his life, so he was determined to make up for it in the next. His wife had passed away from a heart attack while gorging on the good life. He had a daughter who drowned while diving off his yacht, and a son who was gunned down as a revenge killing for Guiardo's hit on a rival's son. His other daughter had packed up her family and gone into hiding in protest, and they hadn't spoken in decades. Family was all he'd lived for and now they had all gone. His hope was to meet up with them all in Heaven, if he could pull this swindle off."

Hamasa retreated into himself, eyes closed, head down. Inside himself was where his strength lay. "His larger-than-life ego demanded from the Pope a guaranteed safe entry to Heaven and ten million dollars. In return, he would relinquish the special documents that were in his possession. This was all accomplished through highly respected, crooked lawyers who worked both sides of the pearly gates, easily giving the slip to St. Peter as he stood on guard.

Israeli intelligence had discovered at around the time the Dead Sea scrolls were found, the documents in question had also been found but were sold off to the mafia. Evidently, they had been verified as authentic and were proven to have been written at the time of Jesus. Indeed, Jesus could actually have written some. One was the gospel of Judas, another was the gospel according to St. Thomas, the one Jesus wrote to his brother and a further one was the gospel of Mary Magdalene. These, everyone was already familiar with. The others, like the Gospel by Jesus and His wife Mary, had never been seen before. The scariest ones talked of aliens and atheists.

"The balding, decrepit, mafia boss knew these precious documents would never be revealed, nor garner any worth if he died with them still in his possession. Although, after they were interpreted, the Vatican wanted to have some of them destroyed because of their content. As a precaution, he apparently had copies made and threatened to release them to the world through various other channels if they did not buy them. The Vatican demanded guarantees all existing documents would be destroyed.

"Our government wanted the documents and was prepared to kill the mafia boss, Guiardo, to get them before he could transfer the documents to the Vatican. The Muslims equally desired the documents and were willing to pay more than ten million. Even the Russians and the Americans were interested in getting the documents before they were forever destroyed. Other mafia members wished Guiardo dead before he began confessing, in case he incriminated them, after all, as a member of the mafia family, he knew all about their crimes. The Israelis provided all the support my parents required to complete the task."

Hamasa recognized the sudden stillness that signaled Harold's interest in what he was saying. Of course, Harold would've heard the rumor secret documents were in the hands of the mafia, but this was probably the closest he had come to any real details.

Harold nodded slowly. "OK, Hamasa, I'm listening. Don't let me interrupt, just let me know if you need anything to drink."

"I need some food here – are the kitchen staff on strike? Or are you trying to starve me to death," Hamasa grumbled, his paranoia kicking in. "Anyway, my parents weren't prepared to go back to war – they handed the whole operation over to me. There were too many players and uncertainties, but they felt I would be able to handle the situation. That's how I was introduced to the Israeli secret service agents and managed to gain their trust. Eventually, I reclaimed my Jewish heritage, became an orthodox Jew, which was a job requirement, and your agency officially hired me. But you know all this. My conversion however, was not sincere. I love my mother and father and to show my honor and respect to them I secretly became a Christian Jew like them. I realized money and power corrupted Grandfather. I wanted nothing more to do with protecting his interests. I became an Israeli citizen and Nayanna didn't even know about it. But I was also a seeker of truth. I found deception and flaws in everything I had believed in, so I carefully nurtured my doubts and questioned everything. I was undercover, so I was ordered not to show my conversion, outwardly anyway. That was perfect for me as I groped my way through the darkness of human experience. The horrible things I had to do to survive, to serve my country, God, and to make a living the way Grandfather brought me up to do, were much better done in utter darkness. I was a lost soul in a lost world of lost hope.

"The Mafia boss, Guiardo, had utilized my services in the past for a few hits that needed done in Canada in such a way as not to be traced back to anyone in his organization. So it wasn't a problem to get hired as one of his personal bodyguards. Sometimes it paid off being undercover for all sides, a double agent."

The memory of that event flooded into Hamasa's brain.

"Hey, Boss, I hear you're in need of a little protection? It's Hamasa. Sorry for the noise, we're just off the highway at a phone booth, so the call can't be traced. Ricky's still here with me. You wanna' talk to him?"

"No, I talked enough with the little shit. He knows what he's gotta' do. Stop with the boss shit, you're just an associate. You can refer to me as Mr. Guiardo. You've been on the lam since our last meet up, but Ricky's cleared you, so get your ass down here. Tell that little button his mother's here scratching my itch, ha-ha. I'll make her my puttana if he doesn't stay clean. Those young Turks are messed up and most vanish. Effin' hell, I miss Montreal. You say hello to the family up there for me."

Hamasa was responding as he heard the phone call disconnect: so much for goodbyes. The next day he was face to face with the boss's German Shepherd.

"Nice place you have here, I'm glad I had these airport snacks to keep from being bitten in the ass. Have you ever thought to try a dog leash?" Hamasa yelled as he saw Guiardo come from around the corner of his house.

"Rodger, how many times have I tried to train you not to

accept gifts from a stranger?" Guiardo patted his dog. "He always meets my guests first. If they aren't torn apart, it's a good sign. Then they get to meet Ronnie." Guiardo pointed to a giant of a man coming out of the house, with a pimply-scarred face and a nose that was hard not to notice, as it must have been broken a number of times. "He still loves to get into fights, even after retiring from boxing. We're just heading out, but here's the key to the garage. You'll find everything you need to know and do – it's where you'll be staying."

After watching the videotaped messages, signing all the required documents, disposing of some as instructed and settling in to the job-routine for a couple of days, Hamasa decided it was time to prepare for his true purpose there. Although he hadn't seen anyone, the dog was getting let out at times and a second floor balcony door had been opened. Was there a mafia soldier inside, a family member or a house cleaner, and how many, Hamasa wondered? He had no idea when the Boss would be back. All he needed was to find the documents' hiding place and put in the surveillance devices: an hour at most. He knew if he stayed alive getting into the house, there was a good chance someone would be dead coming out.

After casing the house and finding the surveillance camera's blind spots, Hamasa realized he would have to enter from the roof and climb down to the balcony. He got started at 3:00 a.m. By 3:27 a.m., he was in the house. He had entered the Master bedroom. Immediately Hamasa covered his nose, the stench was unbearable. Did someone beat him to murder? He tripped over garbage, smelly, wet laundry and soon realized there could certainly be no housekeeper. He was in the most likely spot where a safe would be. Listening carefully at the bedroom door, he could hear a faint snore. He wasn't alone: confirmed. Checking out the closet, he found what he was looking for, a safe, tucked in one corner, behind a shoe rack. Hamasa gave himself a high-five and a closed fist victory elbow. He was just finishing hooking up the last of the surveillance devices when he heard a phone ringing. Running to the bedroom door he could hear the conversation.

"Hey, Boss. Yes, yes, everything's been quiet. No...no...no phone calls. Yeah, I'll alert Hamasa to check the perimeters. Yeah...yes, I'll check all the rooms."

The phone call died. Hamasa had only one option.

Pulling in a deep breath, heart racing, low to the carpet, he bolted out of the bedroom with his gun ready. He saw the surprised look of the guard and instinctively his gun started blazing. His bullets hit their mark, but he had no idea who else was in the house and if their bullets were now racing towards him. He flew down the stairs and rolled between a couch and a wall. The only thing racing towards him was Rodger. He had already passed the doggy test, so the attack from Rodger was only as serious as a slobbering tongue all over his face.

"Rodger, quiet! Come here! You're just a big friendly guy aren't you?" Hamasa whispered, stroking the ecstatic animal. "Who else is in the house, huh? OK, come on, let's go raid the fridge."

The refrigerator burst with the type of food that would keep a dog happy, and he left his new friend face down in what looked like around a kilo of ham as he got busy cleaning up the house. As he worked, his brain churned, desperately looking for a plan B, or any damn plan at all. The Boss would be there soon and he needed to be ready. Plan A was out the window. Aborting at this time was out of the question. What the hell was he going to do?

Hamasa knew he had been caught on camera as he moved around the property. He scoured the place until he found the monitors and recording devices and removed all the evidence.

So far, nothing had gone according to plan and Hamasa was pacing madly and hitting the walls.

Rodger started barking. Glancing through the window Hamasa saw Guiardo's car pulling into the driveway. Hamasa ran upstairs, frantically searching for somewhere to hide.

"Well look who's always happy to see me." Guiardo laughed, walking through the door. He leaned down to pat his dog. "Ronnie, you go round and find that prick Frank, he didn't respond to the signal. And get the other prick from Montreal here, too. I'll be right down. Jesus, didn't I just call a short while ago – agita."

Guiardo, with gun in hand, took his time lifting his weight on weak knees up the stairs. He entered his bedroom and headed straight to his safe. As he opened it, a bullet from Hamasa's silencer tore through his brain and he fell back on his blood stained, white, shag carpet.

Hamasa emerged from behind the line of hanging clothes in the darkest corner of the walk-in closet and put another bullet in the Don, this time his heart. Now he had to whack Ronnie before he would have a chance to call his crew. He flew out the window, hoping to sneak up on him from behind. He checked the garage and saw the open door. Ronnie was coming out yelling, "Hamasa's not here!" Before he had a chance to reach for his gun, Hamasa tackled him but he didn't budge. Instead, Hamasa emptied his gun on his body and he finally dropped to the ground. That left only one witness: Rodger. Hamasa made sure the dog couldn't get into the bedroom where he had spread out the corpses. He put a bullet between their eyes to make it look like an execution style hit. Then he meticulously wiped the place clean of any finger prints he might have left. Next, he ransacked the place to make it look like the killers were looking for something they could not find.

Hamasa was abruptly brought back from his nightmare thoughts by Harold's voice.

"Playing both sides against each other, eh?" Harold's voice dripped scorn. "But which two sides would that be? Sounds like the only thing that mattered to you was you. What happened to your principles, what did you stand for as a man, Hamasa? Sounds like you were on one big ego trip, fueled by easy money."

"Hey, it wasn't like that at all. You should know, it's war, man, it's just war." Hamasa shrugged, looking away from Harold and finding his hands abruptly riveting, he continued with a made-up version of the story.

"The man was in and out of New York's Memorial Sloan Cancer Institute, and my job was to guard his house, so it wasn't too hard to break into his safe when he was away. After securing all the documents, I believe someone did him a favor. His cancer was incurable and the treatment unbearable, so someone simply sped things up by killing him. Unfortunately for him, it was before he had time to have a priestly confession." Hamasa glared at Harold. "It was a hit ordered by your country, anyway. But they didn't hear about it from me.

"In all the confusion, with all the players after that fat egomaniac, it just looked like another mafia hit. However, I was still able to walk away with the documents before all that went down. So don't say I never confess anything here, Harold! I would have turned in the documents eventually, but they got the better of my curiosity and I held onto them for my own interests. And wasn't that a bright thing to do, because now, they might just be my ticket out of here." He bared his teeth in what vaguely resembled a smile. "Yes, I made copies, and you and your *superiors*," he spat the word, "have those. But the originals are in a place no one can get to unless I'm kept alive. The documents will be distributed to the press after a year if I'm not heard from. That's all I'm saying. The Israelis have a long reach and I need to protect the location.

"The Vatican, as I've said before, have verified the authenticity of the documents. And, as I'm sure you've seen, I've got proof of that as well – signed by the Pope himself. This went all the way to the top and you can bet they're dreadfully worried as to who has the documents and how they'll be used." Hamasa shook his head, stared straight into Harold's eyes. "I tell you, these documents have had a huge influence on my life, too. They would definitely be of interest to humanity and they're very controversial, to say the least. The leaders of most religions would not want them to get out to their followers."

Harold sighed. "OK, Hamasa, I can see there's no quick summary here. I gave you the drugs so I guess I have to live with you blabbing on and on. Listen, Mas, you know I'm recording everything with this handy little recorder." Harold patted a machine sitting on a corner of the desk, "so why don't you just blurt it all out, every little detail. Just keep talking the way you have been. Don't worry about taking too long or how crazy you might sound – and I gotta' tell you friend, some of the things you're saying do sound crazy. Just let it all out. I'm going to get me some grub. Isn't that how some of you Americans say it?"

Hamasa knew Harold was desperate to get him to talk, to reveal his motives, and would try anything, even this ridiculous recorder idea. He just had to stay focused on the long bullshit version of things and wait for the Power to take over. For now, he would get a break from Harold's negative reaction to all the things he said. Yes, let him leave, especially if he was getting food Hamasa thought.

As Harold got up to leave, a tantalizing aroma filled his nostrils and he saw that food had been brought for him by the people hiding in the shadows.

"You have no authorization to be here," Harold's voice was cold, hard and the kitchen staff scurried away without argument.

"I'm not American! Remember? I'm Canadian! Ah ha," Hamasa crowed, "you thought I would say Israeli. Shush, that's a secret, remember. Anyway, sounds like a good idea and bring me something, too. Soon, please, I'm starving!" Hamasa's stomach gurgled loudly, as if to support his plea. "Like a hungry hyena, I'll tear into whatever you bring me. I bet the people behind the glass wall have already been recording everything and they know how hungry I am – they just don't care. Isn't that right, Harold? And just when food's finally being brought to me, you chase it away. I smelled fresh baked bread, now I won't be able to stop drooling. Wait 'til my lawyer hears about this. Come on, Harold, let them give me the food at least," Hamasa yelled to Harold's retreating back.

As soon as Harold had left the area, the devotees came out from the shadows and started to gather outside the gates chanting Hamasa's name. Hamasa knew the Power was at hand. He could hear the mysterious music and the sound of kites swooshing by was getting stronger. Real food was going to be delivered; he could sense it.

Chapter 16

Sky

"The story of life is quicker than the blink of an eye.
The story of love is hello and goodbye...until we meet again."
Jimi Hendrix

"Nayanna, I'm exhausted. If you're OK, I'm gonna' join my eyes in closing down," Sky said, his head already tilting and leaning against the headrest of his seat. "And, please don't wake me for food and drinks."

"That's alright, hon. I understand. I'll be with you in my dreams shortly, but I think I'll do some writing in my journal first. You know how it always takes me a while to calm this mind of mine down."

Nayanna could feel the quick pounding of her heart from the day's rush to catch the plane. Taking some deep breaths, she tried to calm herself for the take-off. Words were already sprouting on the page of her journal, 'exhausted' was right there on the tip of her pen, as if Sky had read the page before it was written. Exhausted, exhilarated, existentialism, extraordinaire, exploits, expired... What was it going to take this time to get her mind stilled? Frantically scribbling away, she was finally forced to stop, as tears of who knows what or why were washing away her cute little drawings and words. As Sky's sleepy head fell on her shoulder, Nayanna's mind blasted over all the events that had led to this moment of flying into a sky of new possibilities.

She reflected on a time with her dad. She had known it was coming; she had been hiding, listening for weeks, waiting for him to say something, but he hadn't. In desperation, she had confronted him as he put the phone down on his latest conversation with her aunt.

"Dad, I've heard you talking to aunty – to your friends – about this arranged marriage thing that's going on. Only it's about me, Dad." Her father's face was set, his mouth a thin, angry line. But she couldn't stop, she had to get this out in the open. "When are you going to talk to me about it?" She tasted blood and knew she had bitten her lip. Her palms were sticky with sweat and her long, thick, hair stuck to them each time she dragged her fingers through it.

Finally, he spoke. "Nayanna, please don't snoop on my phone calls," he said dismissively. "Focus on your studies and still your anxieties with the meditations I taught you." He headed to his taxi with her in tow. "I'll be back to go over your homework later. Sweet child, have faith." He bowed his head to her, folded his hands in prayer and, climbing into the car, drove off.

This left Nayanna with only one option. There was only one way for her to escape the certain fatality her dad planned for her. Nayanna rushed to get ready. As red spread across her lips, like a snake shedding its skin, she shook off her fears and jumped into the new skin of a raging hormonal teenager.

This was all Hamasa's fault, she told herself. He was the one who had awakened her inner demons and womanly needs. But it seemed Hamasa had been coming around only to fulfill his needs, and lately, not coming around at all. Nayanna shrugged. His loss and she certainly wasn't going to continue hopelessly pining over him when Sky, the cute waiter from Mary's restaurant was subliminally dancing with her soul and she was dying to spend every waking moment she could with him.

Sky spotted her the moment she walked through the door of the restaurant. He broke off speaking to James, one of the other waiters and hurried over. "Nayanna, I'm so glad you could make it here again." He led her to a table for two, tucked away in a corner of the room, waiting for her to sit before lowering himself onto the chair opposite. "I've so much I'm dying to share with you."

His hair, usually confined to a ponytail, was loose today. Nayanna watched him tuck it behind his ears, as if to make sure she got the full impact of his startling baby-blue eyes. "It's official," he said, excitement vibrating in his voice, I'm selling everything and going to India."

She could tell from the question marks in his eyes that there was more he wanted from her.

"I want to get initiated into the mysteries of the beyond and into the T-N-S-S-U-T-M movement."

Nayanna stared at him. "The what movement?"

"'The New Spiritual Scientific Universal Truth Movement'. It's headed up by a living Saint, a Perfect Master," he told her earnestly. "He can bring us to God in this lifetime.

"Initiation provides definitive proof God exists, that we have a soul, and that a living Perfect Master makes all these spiritual experiences, the journey back to God and all of created life possible."

Nayanna frowned. "My father says there are no true living Masters anymore. The ones proclaiming themselves to be are only out for status, family security, power, fame and money. Sikhs believe their scriptures are the embodiment of truth and hold the key to enlightenment and thus salvation of the soul. Arjan Dev, the fifth Sikh guru, compiled the verses which make up the Sikh scriptures. They contain the poetry of Guru Nanak, as well as six other Sikh gurus, and Sufis, and Hindu Holy men. Gobind Singh, the tenth guru, declared the scripture of the Granth to be his eternal Successor and the Guru of the Sikhs for all time. Therefore, Guru Granth is last in the lineage of the Sikh gurus, and can never be replaced, making a living Master obsolete."

"Come with me, Nayanna," Sky pleaded. "Let's go to India together. What if it's all true and this is the greatest purpose on Earth to have? We can find out first hand. We can meet the living Master and see for ourselves. What if everything they're saying is true? This could be the smartest move we ever make. What a mind bender, but we'll experience it together. You've been coming to all my shows, watching me play music. I go to your games to watch you win at sports. This is something we can do together, for each other. I'm willing to sacrifice all my years in music for this." Noting Nayanna's silence, Sky gripped her hand. "Say something, will you!"

Trying to avoid Sky's eyes, Nayanna finally whispered, "What if it is all a lie? I mean, I've seen it in my own temple, the way people state things as fact when it's clear to everyone they only read it somewhere and never experienced truth from the source, from God."

"Come on, Nayanna, nobody could be that evil they would lie about being God and mislead millions of people with that lie. In this day and age of science, no one could get away with doing that, could they? Besides, he has written books and claims everything is proven scientifically, so it must be right! Please, come away with me."

"Excuse me a moment." Nayanna shot to her feet and dashed to the washroom. "What am I supposed to do, run away from home?" she groaned. Nevertheless, by the time she made her way back to the table, she had come to a decision.

They had planned for months and saved every penny they could manage. As per the requirements for initiation, they had to prove at least three months prior vegetarianism and chastity. To be allowed to travel as a couple and stay together at the ashram, they had to be married.

Her father did not even notice the change in her diet. As long as he got his meat, and as long as she was mostly home when he was, he was happy.

By selling most everything they owned, they had more than enough money to make it for at least a year; they planned the trip to be three months at the least. Everything was going well… mostly.

Sky was certainly doing things right, even under the pressure of having to keep everything secret and the obstacles that they faced. He thought he was protecting her from her family but what Nayanna hadn't told him was he was also protecting her from Hamasa, as only she knew he was spying on them. Therefore, it worked out great that big events like the wedding were being planned for elsewhere. She had complete faith in his course of action after his past successes with the engagement and organizing his life around her now. But she was getting ahead of herself.

Sky's friend had property on Salt Spring Island and Sky had taken her there one weekend. After two ferry rides they hitched up to Long Harbour, where his friend's property was.

The gravel road was cedar lined and the sun was warm. They strolled along, holding hands, smelling the salt air and listening to the distant sound of the sea. After forty minutes or so, they found themselves on a narrow path winding along cliffs that overlooked the ocean. The pounding waves that crashed below them were exhilarating.

Just as they reached a corner, Sky stopped suddenly. "Stay here," he said, a big grin breaking out all over his face.

"What? Why?" Nayanna asked, a little anxious.

Sky brushed her lips with his. "I'll be right back. I promise," he said laughing, backing away. "Don't…don't move." And he was gone.

Nayanna stood nervously chewing at her lip. The minutes dragged by and just as she decided enough was enough and she was going to find out where Sky had gone, he reappeared. He brought her around a corner and Nayanna could see, at a short distance, a tree house lit up like it was Christmas Eve. "Oh!" she gasped. "It's so pretty!" Grabbing hold of Sky, she hugged him hard. "I can't wait until night fall to see all those diamond lights glistening against the ocean. You did all this for me?"

Inside, around a big bed, there were candles burning, shedding their mellow light onto the soft, clean sheets. The wall facing the water rolled up to give the perfect view out over the ocean. It was so close, it almost seemed as if you could jump off the tree house and safely land in the waves below. For most, it would be exciting but for Nayanna to hear the waves crashing so close was frightening, but she wasn't going to reveal that to Sky. The house was high up on the edge of the cliff, affording them complete privacy.

Taking off their hiking boots, Sky lifted her onto the bed. His kiss started slow, gentle, rapidly turning into a searing, passionate meeting of mouths that went on and on.

"Wow, Sky," Nayanna breathed, "that was wonderful." She smiled. "You're on fire…and this place is incredible."

"This is all for you, babe." Sky smiled. "We're the first to enter this celestial abode. I just did the finishing touches last weekend, and…with the help of friends, voilà."

He left her kneeling on the bed and returned from the fridge with a bottle of chilled alcohol-free champagne and two wine glasses.

Looking into the one he handed to her, she could see a small, wrapped box in it. Sky got down on one knee. "Oh my God! Oh my God!" Nayanna sobbed, tears rolling down her cheeks.

"Nayanna," Sky Bill Sydney Adamson's voice was very serious, "will you marry me?"

Nayanna Grayson didn't so much as hesitate. "Yes! Yes, yes, yes!" Wrapped in each other's arms, their tender kisses turned into tender lovemaking.

Subsequently, while proclaiming to ocean creature witnesses in fits of laughter and tears, their love for each other, and their vow of marriage, they popped the cork on the now un-chilled bottle of champagne. Nayanna opened the carefully wrapped present that was still in her wine glass and put the diamond ring on her finger. "It fits perfectly! Oh, Sky, I love you so much!" Filling their glasses to the brim, they toasted their engagement and continued kissing passionately.

"Nayanna, where are you going?" Nayanna turned around, gave Sky a devious, sexy look and wiggled her body seductively. She ran over, grabbed Sky's hand, and dragged him to his feet. Nayanna tore down the steps and started running to the cliffs.

"Nayanna, we're in our baby suits not our bathing suits! I thought you hated to be in the water."

"Hey, lover boy, this will be a swim you'll never forget. Hurry up, will ya'. And who said I would be going in the water?"

"Here, at least put on your boots, that's a long, steep path to the beach. You look amazing!" He kissed and fondled her.

"OK, but how am I gonna' put them on with you humping away on me?"

"Just keep them on when we hit the water, there are rocks and barnacles."

"Aren't you gonna' dive in?" Nayanna asked as she froze, ankle deep in water. "I can't believe I can be near water like this, but I want to try my best so this can be a great memory for us."

"Oh my God, look at your perky nipples," Sky yelled as his splashing soaked her completely.

"It's not from the cold – it's from my fear of water. Oh my, where did your thing go?" Nayanna shot back. "It's so cold it's hiding in that mound of whatever. Remind me to shave that thing."

"It's so cold!" they both shouted out after Sky took a last dive into the frigid Pacific and held onto Nayanna. They ran back to their warm bed.

"Hey, my nipples aren't the only thing that's cold, Ham..." Nayanna almost said Hamasa's name aloud as she responded to Sky's intense sucking and lovemaking. Bad habits die-hard she thought to herself as she wondered what triggered her to do that.

"So how many orgasms have we had today?" Sky asked as he came up for air. At least the chastity period for married couples isn't strictly enforced."

"Oh really? Well, lover boy, I'm sure we can have a few more blowouts then," Nayanna said, relieved he hadn't noticed her slip of tongue.

"Yeah, it's only two weeks of chastity before initiation for married couples," Sky said as he came up for air again.

"Stay focused, would ya', you almost had me off again."

"Haha, I love you, babe," Sky screamed. "I love eating your mango, too!"

"Mango? Where did that come from?" Nayanna asked as they played on through the night.

The next morning Sky showed Nayanna the bikes that he bought for them and they rode home. Nayanna was so excited for all the fun, adventurous things Sky would always plan for them to do together.

Time flew, lost in a spin of planning, preparation and lovemaking. On the surface, everything was fine, but Nayanna fretted. Nothing more had been mentioned about their wedding and the date for leaving edged ever closer.

"Sky, it's almost the time for us to go to India and meet God." Nayanna fiddled with her hair. They were sitting on the bed in Sky's sparsely furnished basement apartment. With no couch, the bed was where everything, except lovemaking, as they were suffering through their required chastity period, took place. She had two blankets wrapped around her to fight off the damp cold. "Are you sure you love me? I mean, we hardly know each other. They say it takes two years to know someone and to test a relationship. And here we are, it's only been a few months, and we're already engaged, planning marriage and surrendering our lives to a Master we've never met." She tugged at her hair again. "Are we still planning to get married? When and how will it happen?"

She wasn't going to let Sky spiritualize her out of her dreams of a traditional wedding. She was going to make sure all their time wasn't spent in meditation.

Sky looked thoughtful. "I still think we need to sell the car before we go. So why don't we elope to the mountains…just you and me, in the car." He ran his thumb down her cheek and along her jaw line. "And, yes, I love you madly, Nayanna. And I love the life we both want to have, serving God and the Master. Going to India will be a magical, mystical way to start our marriage. We'll find a Justice of the Peace somewhere…how about in the Nelson area? There are mountains, the lake and it's a beautiful, spiritual place."

"Plus we'll get high just breathing in that fresh, mountain pot air, ha-ha." She cocked an eye at him. "It's the marijuana capital of Canada, right?"

Sky grinned. "That's OK, it'll add to the ambiance. When we get back, we'll sell the car and off we go to India."

Nayanna nodded happily. "I just found out that Dad will be going back there, too, to attend a funeral, so I'll only have to work around my auntie. What about your mom and sister? Won't you want them to be at our wedding?"

"Mom will be happy to help us with what she can, but no, she won't be there. Sis will just be happy for us. Sky took her hand, squeezed it gently. "This will be our time, Nayanna. I'm more concerned about your dad. But if he'll be in India, that might be the perfect time and place to tell him about us…and everything. We could invite him to the Master's ashram, maybe he'll be inspired to see everything from a spiritual perspective and accept and bless our union."

"My dad, my dad, how will I tell my dad? When will I tell him? I feel so torn." Nayanna brushed away tears. "But I know I have to be true to myself and take the consequences. I surrendered my life to God, so He'll have to work this one out, as His will be done. I'll tell Dad when he gets to India that I'm already married, and that we're there to see our Master, and that he can join us. Yes, I think that'll be the best way."

Sky kissed her palm. "Sounds good, why don't you hang out at Mary's while I work for a few hours and we can talk more about our plans. It'll be dead there today, and you can make a to-do list. We'll take the bikes so we can go for a nice ride afterwards."

Nayanna enjoyed spending the morning at Mary's, sitting with her latte, writing her lists and dreaming. Sky was as good as his word, the place was quiet and once he was done working, they went to get their bikes from the back: they were gone. They stared at each other in shock; the bikes had been safely locked to the back fence.

Sky sighed, shaking his head. "I suppose if thieves are determined enough, a bike lock isn't going to stop them." He drew a shaky Nayanna into his arms, kissing the top of her head. "Worse things happen – nobody died."

"Well, they will if I get hold of them!" Nayanna wailed.

With no alternative, they headed for the bus home. As they neared the stop, they could see their bikes, mangled and destroyed at the side of the road.

"Who would waste two perfectly good, expensive bikes like this and leave them out for everyone to see. I'm calling the cops!" Sky fumed.

"No! Hold on, Sky." Nayanna chewed at her bottom lip, nervous about the dangerous secrets she kept and her past with Hamasa. "That could bring a lot of attention to us, and they might want to question us at our homes. I don't want Dad to find out about everything this way. Besides, they're never going to find out who did this."

"Well," Sky said reluctantly, "maybe I'll talk to Mom and see if she can claim them on her home insurance, and I'll just say they were stolen from her garage."

The wedding took place on a beautiful sunny day. It was a bit windy on the shores of Kootenay Lake, but that didn't stop Nayanna from making a break to the water.

"Where are you going? We have to get our pictures taken now."

Nayanna turned to Sky with a devilish, seductive look, grabbed his hand and dragged him towards the water.

"I want this to be a moment we will never forget," Nayanna yelled.

"Oh no, no, no, we're not getting into our baby birthday suits now, not in front of the justice of the peace and the cameraman."

Before Sky could say another word, he hit the deep end and went under the water hard: hair, clothes and all. Nayanna, of course, was frozen ankle deep in the water.

"Your dress, your beautiful dress!" Sky shouted, gasping for air as he splashed 'til she too was soaked.

"He better be getting this on film!" Nayanna said as she jumped into Sky's arms. They collapsed on the beach, kissing wildly. The cameraman made the most of it, while the justice of the peace had retreated to his car.

Their wedding was amazing and driving around in Sky's 1996 cherry-red, T-Bird convertible with the top down was certainly the cherriest cherry of all. It was all 'Heaven', Nayanna told Sky, repeatedly.

"I can't believe we have to sell this beauty," Nayanna said as they drove back to reality.

"It's the only way we can get to India, and I want to take advantage of its worth. Who knows what more time on the road will do to her. It will set us up after we come back from India. Maybe we can start a business or go back to school with the money."

"Yes, but it'll be a heart break."

"Once we have the money in our hands it'll be easier to let go."

The next day, Sky got up early to drive it to a potential buyer. The phone rang.

"I'm going with you – Dad's gone to India now. Pick me up outside the Caribbean restaurant." Nayanna's voice sparkled in his ear.

"For sure…I love you!"

When the engine wouldn't turn over Sky phoned her right back.

"Where are you now?"

"Home, why?"

"Can you talk? Is your auntie there?"

What's up? Yes, yes, I mean no…Auntie is not here. Yes, yes… it's safe to talk. What's up?

"Just stay there – the car won't start."

"What! Really! Did you open the hood?" Nayanna asked.

"No, I'm gonna' meditate, connect this to God, find out why He's doing this to us. I know the guy was gonna' buy it. What does this mean?"

"For God's sake, just look under the hood! Do you smell gas? Maybe you flooded it. Do that thing with the engine when that happens."

"Yeah, Yeah – hold on........effin hell! Eff! Eff!"

"Sky…what's happening? I've never heard you swear like that before. Talk to me. Sky…"

"Holy shit! Someone's gone and cut hoses and torn stuff out of here, it's a mess. The effin' engine is a mess. What am I gonna' do? Fuck, someone's smashed my car. I didn't even see…

"Stay there, Sky! I'm taking a taxi over. Oh my God, Sky, I'm so sorry. I'm so sorry…"

They were able to get the car fixed up and sold, but they couldn't find original parts, so instead of getting thirty thousand they settled for a lot less. It would still take them to India and more.

"I'm so sorry, Sky."

"Why do you keep saying sorry? It's not your fault, babe. I'm so happy we were able to get what we got and we can still go together."

Although she said nothing to Sky, she worried that the weird things happening were more than random coincidences. She could not rid herself of the idea Hamasa was behind it all. She had not seen Hamasa in months and as far as she knew, he was out of town doing research for his doctorate. But was he, she thought. However, she reasoned, in two nights they would be safely on their way and Hamasa could no longer be a threat.

The day before leaving, at Sky's apartment, going over some last minute preparations, Sky crumpled one more list in his fist and threw it into the waste sack. "Done!" he said, getting to his feet and stretching his hands toward the ceiling.

At that moment there was a loud bang and the sound of glass shattering. The noise had come from the bedroom. Sky shot out the room, Nayanna close on his heels. Sky looked at the broken window. "Kids!" He whirled around and ran outside, looking for the culprit. Nayanna stared at the hole in the wall. Glancing around her, there was no sign of a rock or missile of any kind. Bending down, she peered closely at the dent in the plaster, drawing in a sharp breath as she caught the glint of something imbedded there. Sky was still outside, hunting for the nonexistent child he suspected of breaking the window. Quickly, she bent down and scraped out the bullet that was lodged there. From that angle, she could see the shot must have come from the tall clump of trees across the street or perhaps from the roof of the building just a little further down. She closed her fingers around the slug as Sky appeared in the doorway.

He grimaced, shaking his head. "Nothing," he said irritably. "This place is like the land of the three monkeys – nobody saw anything, nobody heard anything and nobody has anything to say."

Was she doing the right thing – keeping her suspicions from

Sky and the police, Nayanna worried. Her mind went back to a night a few years back. She had been teasing Hamasa about his underwear and started pulling his boxers from his dresser drawer and throwing them at him. Suddenly, she had frozen at the touch and sight of a pistol. Hamasa had shown her the gun and demonstrated how it fired without making a sound. At the time, she had thought it must be a toy. Now that she knew him better, she realized how real and dangerous it was in the wrong hands.

Her father always said if the milk were given away free, then no one would be willing or need to buy and take care of the cow. How romantic! Nevertheless, she had screwed Hamasa for the last time months ago. Without a hint he would someday marry her and with the years rushing by, she was through. Of course, if everything worked out, her life would be thrown at the feet of the Perfect Master, for Him to protect her and sort it all out. She, after all, was only human. At least her relationship with Sky was completely spiritual. Sure, they had consummated their marriage, but from that day on and until three months after visiting the Master, they had vowed celibacy.

Sky talked to Nayanna a lot about his past, and didn't keep any secrets. He had grown up in a small town in the interior of British Columbia. In many ways, he was the opposite of Hamasa. He was not as tall, standing only five feet, nine inches; Hamasa was six feet, two inches tall. Sky's hair was blond, not dirty blond or sandy blond, but almost a white blond. He kept it long, and usually wore a ponytail. Hamasa kept his black hair military short. Sky usually wore a goatee to toughen his baby face good looks. Hamasa was genetically engineered to be big boned and muscular. Sky had to work his buns off to get any muscle, which he rarely had time to do, but he was still slim and well-toned and looked awesome in sandals, tight, faded blue jeans and a muscle shirt, at least to Nayanna's eyes.

An airplane crash had killed Sky's father when he was only

a month old. Bill Sydney Adamson, was the pilot of a Canadian air force test flight. They were testing new anti-radar devices by flying as low to the ground as they could in B-52 Mitchell bombers. The crew bailed out in time when the plane caught fire. Sky's hero father stayed at the controls so he could keep the plane from crashing into the village below. That was the story in the newspaper clipping that Sky's mom had kept.

Bill's sister, Betty, told a different story that Sky heard years later. The plane's cockpit door latch was not working properly and it had jammed. Bill died from smoke and fire inhalation while trying to get the door open. His parachute and the open door to safety were only a few feet away, on the other side of the locked door. But his escape route was blocked by a faulty part that the air force had been aware of for years but never bothered to correct because of budget cuts and corruption.

Sky's mom suffered post-traumatic stress syndrome for the rest of her life. She was a good, strong woman and managed to raise her two children, clinging to whatever security she could.

Sky had one sister, Cathy, or so he thought, until there was a knock on his door years after he had left home for university.

"Hello, I'll be right there!" Sky shouted. Opening the door, Sky came face to face with a neatly attired, young, attractive woman. "Can I help you with anything?" he asked politely.

"Are you Sky Bill Sydney Adamson?"

Sky smiled. "Yes, ma'am, I am."

The woman gave him a long look. "I think you're my brother."

Sky's jaw dropped open, his mind refusing to take on board what she was saying.

"Look," she said, "I know this must be a shock, but...I need to talk to you. Could...could I come in?"

"Yes, certainly," Sky was on automatic, "but I'm sure you must have the wrong place, the wrong person."

As they settled into the living room, getting comfortable on the couches, the woman spread pictures out on the coffee table. Then she looked at Sky with her bright-blue eyes. "I'm Wendy," she said, introducing herself.

"Is your mother Margaret Anne Sydney Adamson? Is this her? Reddish brown hair, bangs, very attractive…?" She pointed at one of the photographs.

Sky raked his fingers through his hair. The numbness was fading, replaced by disbelief. "What are you saying here? This is so surreal. This can't be happening. What are you saying here?"

"Your mother had two children with Luke that they gave up for adoption – me and your half-brother, Peter. You can phone Luke right now and verify everything I'm telling you. I contacted your mother but she doesn't want anything to do with me – denies it all outright and ordered me not to contact you or your sister." For a moment, Wendy's face was swamped by sadness. She said quietly, "I haven't contacted your sister yet or found your half-brother, we weren't adopted together. I still don't know where my brother is, but I have a detective working on that."

"A detective? Is that how you found me?" Sky was beside himself with surprise, mixed with sadness and curiosity.

"Yes, he was able to find your step-dad and Mother and that led me to you."

"I can't believe this." Sky shook his head. "It's so surreal. I'm sorry, I don't know what to say. Is–is there anything I can do to help you? What got you going on all this? Do you need help finding your brother, my half-brother?"

"Thank you, Sky," Wendy said gratefully. "Well, first of all, it's going to help a lot if I can find out what our medical history is. I'm sure you probably know, but a lot of what or who we are comes from our genetics, certainly a lot of our physical and medical conditions. So it's important for me to know more about that, I have a baby and plan to have more, they may be affected by what I find out. I was adopted into a Mormon family and

I'm also a believer. Family is tremendously important to us. We believe when we die we'll be granted a planet the whole family will live on, together, forever. And we will no longer have to wear this magic underwear! See...? They protect us from evil spirits! We do special ceremonies where even dead family members can be baptized and given a chance to be reunited on this planet."

Sky nodded slowly. "OK, I see, well that's great. So, where do we go from here? Do you want me to phone my sister and tell her?"

"No, actually I'd prefer to do that, and I'll tell Mom I contacted you. All we have to do is keep in touch and be a family together, if you like."

"Well certainly, yes of course!" Sky grinned broadly. "I'm going to call Luke right away," Sky replied, holding back his confused emotions.

Wendy gathered up her pictures and got to her feet. "OK, but do it after I'm gone. I need to get back to the hotel. My husband's waiting for me and he's probably worrying. He's not used to dealing with people outside the faith or with me meeting strangers on my own."

"Well, this is a defining moment for all of us," Sky said thoughtfully. "I mean, this is huge. My mom went through so much and now there's this, too."

He didn't put down the phone for what seemed like a whole week, talking to his mom, Luke, sister and now his new sister. He was paying close attention to how everyone was dealing with the news. Sky was a pretty good listener. He had learned to be from listening to his mother. The traumas she had been through would play repeatedly in her mind and be so real to her that she felt as if they were happening in the present moment. She vented her feelings out to Sky, but sometimes she struck out, too. Growing up, Sky had tried his best to ease her pain.

It took a while, but finally Sky persuaded his mom to visit. Inevitably, the small talk soon turned to questions. "Mom,"

Sky asked, keeping his voice gentle as they settled in to a pot of morning tea in the kitchen. "Why did you deny that you had two babies that you gave up for adoption?" That was all it took for Margaret to slam her teacup down and storm off to the living room.

"I'm not here to be interrogated!" she threw the words over her shoulder. "No one will ever understand what I had to go through. The bastard government promised my identity would be kept secret."

Sky sighed, picking up the mugs of tea and following his mother into the other room. "Governments change, and laws change, Mom. No one's blaming you. I just need to understand, and figure out what we do for the best now."

"A promise is a promise," Margaret said stubbornly. "They should honor their promise, that's what should be done," she huffed. "Now I'll have to suffer for their mistakes. I'm exposed and now there'll be nothing but criticism for what I had to do."

"Mom, don't say that," Sky pleaded. "We all love you and understand what you went through. You could have aborted, and it couldn't have been easy, but you suffered through...to give life! What's to criticize?"

"Women couldn't even vote until the twenties," Margaret rambled on. "Men had all the privilege. Sure, they offered their lives for it and many died. But what could I do after your dad died and left me alone to raise you and your sister? All the insurance money went to your dad's parents, your grandparents, they took everything for themselves. I had nothing. I met Luke and got pregnant before we even knew if we were right for each other, never mind marriage."

"So you never married Luke, like you told us?" Sky ran his hand across his face. After a moment he said, "I don't even remember you being pregnant. I've no idea how you pulled that off. I must've been lost in never-never kid's land."

"All I had back then was your dad's pension," his mother

said, "and if I'd remarried, the government would've taken that away from me. They don't do that anymore, but back then they sure as hell did."

Confessing all this was too much for Margaret, and she stormed back into the kitchen.

Sky went after his mom and tried to give her a hug, but she turned away and started doing the dishes. Her hands were always busy doing something.

"Mom, you're gonna' break the glasses! I'll do them later. Let's sit down and talk this over. I want to know how I can support you while you go through all this. Mom, listen, no one is criticizing you or judging you. The government never cared how vulnerable women were, if the husband was abusive, if he deserted, or in your case, died. You did what you had to do to protect yourself… and us. Mom, you have to calm down," Sky insisted, guiding her to a chair. "This will just make your anxiety worse."

Back in the day, they didn't recognize post-traumatic stress syndrome or even have a name for it. Sky frowned; even now they still didn't really know how to treat it. His mother would have been the perfect poster child for having all the symptoms: anxiety, paranoia, hallucinations, agitation and anger were but a few. Her brain was constantly sending out fight or flight messages that kept her hormones pumping adrenalin; not a good situation for someone trying to stay calm raising kids, never mind just trying to stay healthy.

She had once told him her ex-boyfriend, Luke, was the devil and had created the whole Universe just to get at her and make her life miserable. All Sky could do was to hold her in his arms and tell her he was there for her and he wouldn't let anything bad happen to her. One time, her sickness got so bad she had even attacked him. He accidently stepped onto her newly cleaned, polished, kitchen floor. She flew at him, yelling at him, calling him every name in the dirty-word book, while trying to scratch his eyes right out of their sockets. He left soon after that.

It wasn't her fault, and he knew she did the best she could, but it was unbearable.

It was his mother who had seen the big ad in the paper: 'Transcendental Meditation: Cure the mind from anxiety and worry; live stress free.' That weekend, Sky, his mom and sister were on the road to Calgary, Alberta, the big cow town, where they went every year to see the Calgary Stampede. The Beatles had met the Maharaji, so it seemed to them like a cool idea to meet him, too. Sky was only nine at the time but it had a huge effect on his spiritual journey. His mother told him it was very expensive, so he had better pay attention and get the most out of it. It was a seed that was planted, that she hoped would one day lead him to God. It opened his mind and heart to yoga, breathing, mantras, Mahatma Gandhi, 'The Prophet' by Kahlil Gibran and many other exotic, strange and interesting ideas from the Far East.

Sky's best friend's father was the church minister where they attended. When the church heard the false rumor that they had gone to India and learned levitating, they threatened excommunication if the practice was not immediately discarded. "It was the devil's work," they had told them. Sky's mom complied but Sky stopped talking to his friend, who kept teasing him that he would turn into Yogi Bear if he meditated again.

At University, he finally found some comfort studying psychology, which helped him understand and empathize more with what his mother was dealing with. They began to get along better and Sky found himself supporting her more and more. If only, he often wished, he could have found that magic pill that would cure her.

Music consumed Sky. By the time he turned thirteen, he played in a band for school dances. By the time he was fourteen, he traveled around to all the nearby towns playing weekend gigs. That was how he met his first love, Cindy. She was their lead singer. Sky played piano, flute and rhythm guitar. He was sixteen and Cindy was a vivacious twenty-two year old with a baby: a feisty beauty. 'Opposites attract', seemed to sum up a lot in their relationship. They kept their affair a secret for six months.

Sky's first love came to a heart crushing halt when he awoke one night to strange noises. The band was playing at a hotel tavern up in the Rocky Mountains near Radium Hot Springs. Cindy's room was joined to the room the lead guitarist was in by a shared bathroom, while Sky's room was separate and a little further down the hall. As prearranged, Sky snuck into Cindy's room for a bedtime cuddle but, worn out, fell asleep. He woke in the middle of the night to strange noises coming from the bathroom. The bed beside him was empty. There they were, Cindy and the guitar player naked, just a splishing and a splashing away in the tub. Water and soap bubbles covered the entire room.

Disgusted and heartbroken, Sky grabbed a bottle of tequila and ended up passed out under a big semi-truck, oblivious to the fact that the band members had to stay up the rest of the night in order to make sure the trucker didn't show up and drive over him.

Apparently, Cindy's father had found out about them and forced her to promise she would break it off. She followed her dad's orders the best way she could: running off naked with another man. It took Sky over two years to get her off his mind and for the pain to subside. Not even music could soothe him through that. Like a tattoo, she would always be there as his first love, he had confessed to Nayanna.

Maybe some confessions are better left with God. Obviously, Nayanna was less than happy to hear this. But, she reasoned, it was better out in the open than hiding in the background. Besides, now that they were married, she was certain she could evict his painful memories and fill his heart with new better ones as he was doing for her.

Chapter 17

Interrogation Continued

"I used to live in a room full of mirrors; all I could see was me. I take my spirit and I crash my mirrors, now the whole world is here for me to see."
Jimi Hendrix

Hamasa continued talking into the tape recorder as though Harold remained in the room. Behind the glass, eyes were still watching him. He thought about picking up the table and throwing it, and the satisfaction of watching the smooth, polished surface shatter. But that was just wishful thinking, the glass would withstand a bullet. Besides, there would have to be at least something to be gained, entertainment perhaps or release or to create some attention for his starving guts, otherwise he was just wasting energy. No need for showy behavior he told himself, things would change soon; he could feel it. The Power was coming. All he needed to do was to stay calm, be patient and finish his story.

"I was brain washed, like most kids, to believe that God existed, God was love, He loved us unconditionally, He was our divine Father and was the Creator of everything. It was the devil and the people the devil inspired who were the enemies and the creators of all the evil on Earth. I was taught God would soon destroy the devil and evil forever. I was told there would be an eternal paradise in Heaven, and a Heaven on Earth that would last forever. After reading the documents I stole from Guiardo, I realized what I was taught might not be the truth and I could be mistaken about my faith in God. All my beliefs were turned upside down. Now that my eyes had been opened, I could see even the Bible gave clues to alternative interpretations I just hadn't understood or, perhaps, had ignored before.

"In First Samuel, 2:6, it says, 'The lord killeth and maketh alive. The lord maketh poor and maketh rich.'

"You see? It wasn't the devil doing all the bad things. Why is it that every leader of every company or country wants it his way or the highway? It's because that's the way God is. It's God's way or we go to hell."

"In St. Matthew, 7:21, 'Not everyone...shall enter the kingdom of heaven, but he who does the will of my Father.'

"Why do people kill? Is it because God's killing someone, somewhere, every second of the day and night, in a million horrible different ways? God is the Father and the example that everyone is taught to mirror and emulate. Talk about grand hypocrisy!

St. John, 1:3, 'All things were made by Him; and without Him was not anything made that was made.'

"Neither people nor the devil created evil, lust, greed, attachments, anger and ego. God created all these forces of nature or of the mind and He forced them upon us. Yet people continue blaming one another and punishing each other for things we have no responsibility for. God kills, is full of desires, creates endless amounts of evil and yet He is not affected in any way, stays happy and full of bliss, yet tells us not to do these things. The minute a human does any of those things they are sent to prison by other humans or to hell by God. People do not choose to be here. We are here, but we have no way of knowing how we got here or why. Yet we are held accountable to discover all of God's laws on our own and to obey them, as well as all human laws or suffer the consequences.

"Jesus said in St. Matthew, 5:48, 'Be ye therefore perfect, even as your Father which is in heaven is perfect.' St. Matthew 7:13/14, 'wide is the gate and broad is the way that leadeth to destruction but strait is the gate and narrow is the way which leadeth unto life and few there be that find it.'

"Jesus is known for his love and forgiveness, 'love thy neighbor' but we overlook the fact that the idea of an eternal hell of suffering was first taught by Jesus.

St. Matthew 25:46, 'the evil doers, these will go away into eternal punishment...And if your hand or your foot causes you to stumble, cut it off and throw it from you; it is better for you to enter life crippled or lame, than having two hands or two feet, to be cast into the eternal fire.' (Matt. 18:8).

"God says to love unconditionally but His love is conditional; if we don't obey his commandments and love Him, we are doomed to suffer the consequences for all eternity. We're supposed to be truthful, but God doesn't tell us the truth about anything. In the Bible, it says that God has many secrets and keeps many things hidden.

"The reason everybody wants to rule the world and be obeyed is because God is that way. They use power to fulfill all their desires, no matter who is hurt or what is destroyed. Why? Because maybe God is that way. He is the example that we all follow.

"Then we have all the natural disasters, things like hurricanes and diseases that God creates, which make people suffer even more.

"It's obvious that when people invented a revengeful, power-hungry, jealous and good/evil God, who is sadistic enough to send the souls He created to eternal damnation, that they themselves would be emboldened to behave that way, too. If humans invented God, as some of the documents suggest, then they could have at least invented a loving God, who's forgiving and who educates people on how to cooperate to create a paradise on Earth for everyone. The barbarians of the dark ages created a God that was barbaric, like them, and we are still worshiping and emulating Him."

Hamasa stopped; craning his head around he saw a group gathering outside the iron gates.

"Why are you here?" he yelled. "The Power has not yet arrived! Brothers and sisters, the hour is at hand, the minutes fly by, but you will know when the time has come."

Most of them had their hands folded in a prayerful way and some were on their knees. All wore the absent, glassy-eyed, fixed expressions of people in a trance. Like sunbathing lemurs, they had come to bask in the rays of energy that were piercing their cores. Hamasa knew the Power was at hand, but only the recipients clustered on the other side of the bars knew of the secret ambrosia that poured from his eyes as his gaze rested on them.

"We believe the Power has already arrived! We can feel it, Hamasa! We see it in your eyes. It's even in the air – a magic force," a voice from the crowd yelled back.

Forgetting they were guards escorting prisoners, custodians, cooks, agents, psychologists or the flotsam and jetsam of society, they sojourned together to drink every drop of the nectar, wandering off once their vessels reached their fill. Hamasa carried on speaking into the recorder, as he knew it was the sound and not the words that captivated them.

"In my hands, the documents inspired a whole new reality for the necessity of terrorism. This time it would be terror against God. I realized that God was the first and true terrorist, and that the only way to fight back was by using the same methods. I wanted to go after God and the people who say they are God on Earth. I knew I would have to keep that secret from the recruits that I needed. So I got a hold of 'The Bomb'. We were always in touch anyway and often worked together on assignments through the years. Together we organized a group of past associates and decided to go after those who proclaimed themselves to be God but were not Muslim. From 'The Bomb's perspective, anyone who wasn't promoting Allah was fair game and he and the others were eager to take them out. What better way than to hit the leaders first. I kept them in the dark as to what my true plan was – to change God's will. My biggest concern was keeping them from getting trigger-happy and killing people before I completed what I had to do. They were all eager to put their training into practice and get to the 72 virgins as quick as possible. They couldn't wait to start killing the non-believers. I had to stress the importance of taking the leaders as prisoners first, so that we could get the necessary intelligence to inform our strategic planning and to enable us to get to the masses. As far as the group was concerned, we were going after the leaders so that we could draw all the followers together in one place and blow them all up at one time.

"My parents thought I had gone insane and were definitely not going to have anything to do with it and warned me to stick to the script given by my superiors. That fell on deaf ears and they were sorry for introducing me to the project in the first place. As far as I knew, they were paid off handsomely for my well-executed mission and were off to their secret haven. They always dreamed of such a retirement. They said I wouldn't be able to reach them, but in time they would contact me. They never did, but I never imagined they could have been killed. So eventually, Harold, you'll have to explain to me everything you know about their assumed deaths. Since you're not here while all this is being recorded, I'll ask you again, in person.

"OK, well, to carry on, we dug deep and found there were living Masters. All religions and spiritual movements seem to center around a Master who would appear to know and speak the will of God. Our research told us these Masters were still alive and spreading what they believed to be God's will. However, all the scriptures warn there are many false teachers, so one must be aware and know what to look for.

'Beware of false prophets…Ye shall know them by the fruit they bear. A good tree cannot bring forth evil fruit; neither can a corrupt tree bring forth good fruit.' St. Matthew 7:15

"It was evident that we must find the Master who performed

good deeds, or at least had the best appearance or reputation of doing so.

"Of course, there were many documents to go through, some with clearly conflicting beliefs. As I said earlier, one short document stated God and religions were all man made in an attempt by the wealthy to control and rule over the masses. I didn't pay much attention to that document because, at the time, I believed it was obvious that a great power had to have created everything. Only a Creator could have initiated the big bang and have it end up with life on Earth the way it is today. No mortal human created the Universe, and even if we did evolve from bacteria, ocean creatures and monkeys, I believed that there must have been a powerful Creator behind the process, albeit that Creator could be indifferent or evil.

To be fair, I'll recite that document first and then I'll go on to the others."

Chapter 18

The Ashram

> "Majority rule only works if you're also considering individual rights; because you can't have five wolves and one sheep voting on what to have for supper."
> *Larry Flynt*

Leaving the airport in India, Nayanna and Sky were about to encounter culture shock. In addition, not having lived their entire lives in a sauna, there was nothing that prepared them for the hot, humid air that weighed heavily on their bodies, even heavier on their brains, and there was no escaping it.

A mad hatter on a three-wheeled tricycle whisked them away, escorting who he must have believed was Alice and friend, through a new urban wonderland. Nayanna and Sky shared disbelieving, slightly unnerved looks as, one minute they were on one side of the road, then the other, then swerving up onto the sidewalk to avoid a cyclist. Next, they were swerving into oncoming traffic to avoid crashing into a sacred cow as it ate mangoes off the horse drawn carriages meandering down the middle of the highway. Nayanna clung to Sky for dear life, not wanting to see what was coming at them, while Sky twisted his head about, not wanting to miss a thing.

They passed by streets of tires – everything was tires: tires hanging, tires to sleep on, tires made into shoes, tires as billboards and tires to burn for cooking. There were streets and streets of clothing stores with sarees hanging everywhere. Clothes were billboards with cloth lettering, clothes were stacked up to sleep on, clothes were made into tents to sleep under, and it seemed as if clothes were chasing the kids into the streets where their rainbow colors were displayed in order to be sold to the passing vehicles. Clothes were stacked ten feet high onto carts pulled by cows, horses or even humans. There were streets for electronics, streets for eyeglasses and yet others for pharmacies.

Finally, they reached the street of the ashram. People were sleeping on top of their cars, resting on their motor bikes or huddled by fires just outside the gates. It was late at night but kids were still up, peeing by the side of the road where the sewer system, an open ditch of water, tried to flow. Friendly strangers greeted and took them to their private room, one without doors or windows. Sky wondered where the toilet was and, as if reading his mind, the host pointed to a drain and a tap jutting out of the wall across from the bed: no toilet paper to be seen anywhere. Their enthusiastic guide even squatted down and gave a demonstration on how to use it as a toilet: too much information, Sky thought. They were told not to sleep, as the Master knew of their arrival and would summon them shortly. They arrived at 11:00 p.m. and were called to see the Master at 3:00 a.m. Morning meditation started at 4:00 a.m.

The Master was serving mango ice cream to a small group of westerners when they entered his home. As the sweet, creamy freeze melted in their mouths, it also instantly melted away all the fatigue, all the sweat and all their nervousness. Nayanna, dressed as an ashram angel in a white Panjabi suit, with a pastel scarf covering her hair, boldly spoke out, "I can hear the most wonderful music, it's been playing from the moment we entered the ashram. Is it being created live or is it from a radio or TV?"

She had been looking around for the source of it for quite some time.

"Can you describe the music you are hearing please?" the Master asked.

Nayanna answered, excited to get the Master's attention, "It keeps changing," Nayanna said slowly, "but it sounds like symphonies from all the different countries in the world. I can hear harps, flutes and trumpets. It's very loud. Can't you hear it?

Why isn't anyone talking about it or gathering to watch it being played? It's so beautiful!"

The Master replied with a chuckle, "It is a gift from God. You are hearing the music of God, the 'music of the spheres', as described by Plato and Aristotle."

Sky whispered to her that he certainly did not hear anything.

"It can't be from God – I can hear it as plain as day through my ears!" Nayanna said, bewilderment written all over her face.

The Master laughed loudly. Getting up from his chair, he took Nayanna by the hand to help her up. "Well, my dear," he said kindly, "let us go and find this symphony of players, this music of music." He called out to the crowd that had gathered and was sitting in his suite, "Does anybody hear the loud music being played?"

The room became full of chatter and laughter and a thin, elderly, English woman stood up and said, "My dear, we do not have musicians playing. Only you can hear this music! At this ashram we haven't had electricity for many days now and radios and TVs are not even allowed here. If you still hear the music tomorrow, then I'll personally accompany you around the ashram 'til we find the source."

"We have arrived at the hour of meditation," the Master told them, "and if you go now to the hall where the devotees are meditating, you can focus on this music with the right ear, and as it comes into your right ear it will bring your soul back to God. Please do not listen to any sounds coming from the left ear as that is created by the negative power and will surely lead you astray."

The Master sat back down and Nayanna and Sky followed the group to the mediation hall. They were told people would sit or lie in meditation here for days, blissed out on the inner planes. They sat and immediately tumbled over on the hard floor, asleep.

Sky awoke hours later, in bed, with Nayanna on top of him,

ripping away his clothes.

"Let's make love! I need you inside me so badly. Do you love me, Sky? Is all this love I'm feeling really happening to me?"

It took Sky a minute to adjust to the heavy, heated air and frenzied thrusts pressing on his body and mind. He rapidly came to his senses with the realization the naked girl on top of him, moaning through an orgasm, was his wife and not a fantasy. Nayanna was having a cathartic orgasm in a room with no doors or windows, in the middle of a holy ashram, with the Perfect Master a few houses away.

The realization made him quickly jump up, knocking Nayanna to the floor. This seemed to be the catalyst for her to choose this perfect moment to have a complete emotional breakdown. All her pain and insecurities from the moment her mother died came pouring out as tears streamed down her cheeks.

"You don't love me, do you? You don't want me here with you! You're going to leave me here, aren't you? You want me to leave. You want to be left alone! That's it, isn't it? You would rather be left alone here, right?"

"Nayanna, I'm sorry. I didn't realize the bed was so narrow and that you'd fall off. How did we get back here, anyway? Where's all this coming from? Of course I love you! I thought coming here was what you wanted, too. We've already had our honeymoon and this is spiritual. Remember the vows…?"

Just then, as the two were scrambling to get dressed, a young, clean cut American walked into the room.

"Listen you guys, we don't think what's going on here with you two arguing and everything else is very appropriate for the ashram. The Master told me to come to get you. He'll speak to you right away."

Sky walked out of the doorway into a blistering hot sun and there was the Master storming past him going into their room. He came out holding Nayanna's hand and as they walked past Sky he said, "Never hurt someone." Sky followed them, dumbfounded by the turn of events. In the meditation hall, the Master pointed at a couple of chairs across from where He sat Himself down. "Sit, please. These upsets come up as a result of past karma," the Master continued. "The only remedy is constant deep meditation, with full faith in the Master Power that is doing everything to help in your journey homeward to God. Please close your eyes and look into the middle of the darkness in front of you without straining. Look into the center of the light that comes up and it will give way to lead you higher. Repeat the Holy charged names slowly, with intervals of silence between each one. Please do not move for the next twenty minutes, until I say to come out."

The Master got out of his wicker chair and placed his thumb on Sky's forehead, who had decided to sit on a pillow on the floor. Immediately, he saw a movie playing in his mind's eye that showed a young, tall, thin man hovering over a woman, continually beating her. The movie faded away into bits of light floating around in bubbles of different colors, until it all went to darkness as Sky once again tumbled over, asleep in the meditation hall.

Sky woke up to the voice of Master saying, "Leave off, open your eyes."

"Master," Sky called out, "I saw a movie of a man hitting a woman. Was that me in a past life and is that why you told me to never ever hurt somebody?"

"Yes, the husband may look at another woman but can never sleep with another woman. However, if a woman is too clutching and jealous towards the man, then the man will feel suffocated and will want to leave."

It was all extremely confusing at that moment, but Sky assured himself that at a future date it might make sense and have some relevancy.

As they were walking back to their room, still feeling guilty for creating a scene at the ashram, Nayanna and Sky ran into a group of westerners arguing. As they approached, a married couple broke away from the group. They were visibly upset.

"Hi, we're new here, from Canada. I'm not prying, but if there's anything we can do to help, please let us know," Sky offered.

"Under different circumstances we'd love to get to know you, but we're out of here. I'm not going to get into it with you, but we were involved in the accounting end of things. We found many discrepancies that the Master can't or won't even explain to us, so we're outta' here for good. We're leaving the path," explained the husband. "We gave the best years of our lives to this spiritual movement, and for it to end like this is devastating for us. Words can't describe how we feel. It seems as if the whole thing is a fraud we were sucked into. The Master has become extremely rich and His kids go to the best schools in the world. They've started businesses, too. Where do you think all the money comes from? We slaved here for free all the while this was going on. The last straw was when we had to raise money to buy ancient documents that supposedly linked the present living Master to the Masters of the past and even Jesus. We'd always been taught Jesus wasn't a true Perfect Master, so we couldn't figure out why or how to justify spending precious dollars buying them. Not only that, but the documents were in the hands of the mafia, and that's who we'd have had to deal with. Anyway, all the best to you, but we have a flight to catch."

Sky and Nayanna exchanged puzzled glances as they watched the couple walk swiftly away.

Later they found out the husband and wife had been long time initiates in charge of many important jobs to do with running the ashram. One of their jobs was to look after the accounting and ensure that the books were in order. Other initiates told Sky they had probably tired of ashram life and were looking for an excuse to get out. They were also told it would be better not to have so many questions, to focus themselves on their spiritual development instead, and not to get involved with gossip.

The ashram buzzed with a plethora of devoted, joyful, selfless workers and those they served, who had come from all over the world to taste the sweetness of ashram life. There were many large gatherings where thousands would attend. Huge outdoor tents were set up that dwarfed the sandstone, two-story buildings that were scattered throughout the sparsely treed landscape. A few wondering cows and goats became trapped amongst all the people.

Sky's favorite gatherings were the small ones, when only a few seekers would be gathered at the feet of the Master. One time, the Master asked Sky to get his flute, so he scrambled off the roof, raced through the tranquil courtyard, trying not to disrupt the meditators and re-assembled almost too out of breath to play. The Master's wife was an accomplished East Indian musician. Sky was embarrassed to play, but with everyone's love and encouragement, he joined in. With the Master gazing into his eyes, he was transported to another world. They were high up on a rooftop, a full moon illuminating them with a radiant glow. Sky's flute seemed to play on its own and somehow he managed to keep up with the different Indian scales and ragas. Master's wife played the harmonium while others played the tablas and sitars. Master's wife kept watching Sky who was staring at Master. She observed Master staring back at Sky. It kind of threw Sky off his game plan a bit but he stayed focused, more on the Master than the music. He was sure Master's wife, by now, was accustomed to not receiving any attention when the Master was around. As everyone stood up and dispersed, Master's wife approached Sky. "Very nice tone you have, sir. Thank you for playing so nicely with us."

"The compliment has to go to you and your group," Sky responded.

"You are so lucky to have the freedom to study music," she continued. "It should have been my life, but I was never allowed to study or play. That is until recently, after years of complaining, I am now finally allowed to play – but for these spiritual occasions only," she moaned.

Sky was so shocked by her statements that he did not have a response. He merely thanked her again and told her to continue making her spiritual music tapes and that he would be sure to buy them.

What a glorious event it was for him, being able to play for the Master. It touched him deeply and he later wrote a song about the experience. However, on that day, a poem erupted from the depths of his soul.

"Man,
The indestructible force in nature?
Mangles, rips, procreates and dies.
Yet Meditates,
On the first flowers of spring
Oh love,
Bring me closer to the indestructible force within man."

In the days that followed, Nayanna could still hear the music playing at times.

"Does it sound anything like the Indian music from that full moon night with the Master and His wife?" Sky asked.

Nayanna shook her head. "No, it was more like a symphony playing."

Sky told her what the Master's wife had said to him.

"That's so strange, for a perfect soul to say something like that," she stated.

"What do you mean, perfect? Only the Master's perfect, not his wife or anyone else in this whole world. There's only one Master alive on Earth at any one time, except when the Master transfers his power to the Successor. But even then, the Successor has to wait until after the death before he can take His place."

Nayanna frowned. "No, of course she's perfect. She has to be perfect, too. It wouldn't be fair otherwise. I'll personally ask Master about this." So the next time they were in the presence of the Master, Nayanna marched right up to Him and asked, "Your wife has to be perfect, too, right?"

"We are all on a journey and she, too, is on a journey back to God, just like you. No, my dear child, she is not perfect. God in his great wisdom has only allowed the Master to be perfect. In our great history, there were women who were regarded as Masters though if that makes you feel any better. Cheer up, daughter, every saint has a past and every sinner has a future. Maybe you can be the next Master?" His bellowed laughter was in complete sympathy, Nayanna hoped, as she struggled to accept that knowledge.

Sky never did hear the music she heard, but when he stared at the Master with full attention and devotion, he would notice His form would become lucent and change into other forms, just as he was told would happen. He could appear as different Masters. Sky clearly saw Him change into past Masters he had seen pictures of, such as Kabir, Guru Arjan, Guru Nanak, and many others. He was sure he saw Jesus, too. It was truly remarkable and he couldn't wait to progress spiritually and experience God directly. By coming to the feet of the Perfect Master and obeying His commands, they were promised they would be able to see and talk to God in their very lifetime and in death they would become one with God, eternally.

Master was always sweet, patient and loving, so it came as a shock to Sky to see Him jump out of his chair and yell at an elderly woman who sat on the ground directly in front of Him. Unfortunately, He was talking to a small group of Indians in their language. Sky asked someone what the person had done or said to make the Master react like that. He certainly did not want to ever make the same mistake. Again, he was told to mind his own business and not to get involved in gossip or questioning the Master's conduct or teachings.

Finally, the day of Initiation arrived.

"Wow, this is so intense," Sky murmured, overcome by the importance of what was taking place. "How are things going for you, dear?" Sky asked Nayanna. "This is going to go on all day. Thank God we got a break. My legs were falling asleep and killing me but I was too afraid to move and disturb someone. So," he asked again, "how was your experience? Did you see anything? What happened?"

"Hey, that's not fair. You know we aren't allowed to tell our experiences. How can you be asking me that?"

"Come on, that music you keep hearing that no one else can hear must be taking you to Heaven by now. I want to know what it's like. Come on, tell me, please," Sky begged. He held Nayanna's hand but she pulled it away.

"I'm still so embarrassed for what we got caught doing when we first got here, we'd better not show any physical connection in public."

"Yeah, OK. Well, I didn't see God or speak internally with the Master as others reported. But I did see light and I heard a bell ring. When I got here, before you arrived, I heard a loud bell ringing." He grinned. I half thought it was the dinner bell calling us to eat. It was the most beautiful, mysterious sound. I asked the people around me if they could hear it, too. They all said they'd heard nothing. I heard the bell again, loud and clear. Again, I asked the crowd beside me if any of them could hear it ringing out. They all said no." Sky shot Nayanna an excited look. "It's like the music you can hear and no one else can. I heard the bell ringing but no one else did. I haven't heard it since though, unfortunately. I wonder what would've happened if I'd been meditating when I heard it. Maybe it would've transported me to the higher planes and to God – it was that powerful and real." He searched Nayanna's face. "Is it like that for you, too?"

Nayanna only nodded.

When the dinner bell did sound, they were both more than ready for it. The food was generally good and they made sure to mix it up for Westerners. That day it was pizza on a chapatti with chickpeas: a new one for them.

In the late afternoon, Master summoned them to the courtyard for a special treat. The courtyard was a sparsely decorated area at the back of his house, with a huge ten-foot wall around it. There was a group of about twenty foreigners lined up along one wall. The Master came down from His house, attired completely in white. His long, black, curly hair, which had never been cut since birth, was freed from the traditional turban He usually wore and hung like an ebony blanket to his waist. His beard was also free of the traditional knots that cropped it to His chin. It tangled with His hair somewhere around His belly. It was a wondrous sight for an ex-hippie musician like Sky to see. He felt camaraderie and bonding as never before. Sky likened it to a newborn colt seeing its mother for the first time. Looking at her, the colt would also be seeing itself for the first time. The Master walked by each disciple and gave out precious Parshad. Parshad is anything the Master blesses, but he usually gave out little sugar balls. The disciples, out of respect and humility, obediently would gather it up into their outstretched, open palms, then closing their hands around the gift, touch it to their bowed heads. After giving the Parshad to Sky, the Master asked if he was doing well. Sky put on a brave smile and said he was doing great and thanked the Master for having him and for the initiation.

In truth, he was feeling anything but well. All afternoon he had been experiencing crippling stomach pains, leaving him weak and light-headed, and they were steadily getting worse. As the Master began to move on to the next person, everything went black and Sky collapsed to the floor. Master rushed to him and picked him up. The most miraculous thing happened. As soon as the Master touched Sky, all the pain released and he no longer felt as if he was going to have diarrhea or die. He realized the Master was talking to him, telling him he was not to keep any of his problems or pains secret from Him.

"I am here," Master said, "to take on every initiate's karma, so you can all rush home to God." He smiled kindly. "Please let me know immediately if you have any further problems. I am always here to help."

Nayanna, moved by what had happened, bowed down and touched the Master's feet.

Sky knew what had happened had definitely deepened their faith. He only wished the Master had warned him to stay away from the most delicious treat he ever tasted: rich mango ice cream, made with fresh cow's milk and probably lots of sugar. Every chance he had, he would rush out of the ashram to the nearby ice cream heaven. It ended abruptly. Weeks later, he was still mostly confined to bed and the drains with a case of monsoon revenge. After only two months into their planned three month stay, the Master said he should go home, so that he could recuperate before it was too late, and also to comfort his mom, who, He said, missed him dearly.

He turned to Nayanna, who was hovering solicitously by Sky's bed. "It is your karma, my dear, to make sure this young man makes it home safely."

Chapter 19

The Way to Freedom

"There is no slavery but ignorance."
Robert Ingersoll

Hamasa began to recite into the tape recorder the secret document that he had acquired; in the hope it would exonerate him.

Introduction to the 'Great Plan' by the 'Seekers of Freedom':

This plan has been handed down from human to human, slave to slave, since humans first walked the Earth with a brain capable of self-consciousness. From the beginning, it has been a game of survival of the fittest human or tribe, which is modeled by the rest of the natural world seen and experienced around them.

Humans have always been shackled with lust, greed, ego, attachments, anger and animal instincts, but also have an innate desire to question their place in the Universe. Gods were created to explain all the mysteries of life.

With so many external and internal forces working against them, it is easy to see how humans are vulnerable to coercion and manipulation. Even though each person wants control and wishes to have everything their way or no way, it has been evidently clear to most that the chances for survival were increased by the safety of numbers, by living within a community. This led to the need to have strong leaders, but those wanting to be leaders were always in competition with or at war against each other. Many left to start their own tribes and eventually were at war with other tribes fighting for limited resources. Over time, strategies were continually refined and improved, until great god like Kings were created, attracting huge numbers of people and tribes together. They were able to take advantage of people's beliefs and need for their gods that gave meaning and reasons for everything. Empire building grew, along with the advances in agriculture and architecture. It became extremely difficult for newly forged tribes to flourish. People were trapped, needing the kingdom and the King to survive. Yet they were held prisoner by them, and forced to surrender their lives to the service of the King. Kingships passed down through descent and lineage and the common person had no chance of advancement within the system. The sons had to kill the King if they wanted to be King: ordinary men would never have that chance.

This is a plan for a way out that can be adopted by anyone, even a slave who has the courage and conviction to see the plan through to eternity. There can never be a second of doubt or delay in implementing and executing this plan. As most humans toil for daily survival, mystified and petrified by the external and internal forces plotting against their very success, the person with 'The Plan' can unite the masses and either blend with the existing tribe or strike out on their own. The person with 'The Plan' will have all the benefits of all the other Kings, such as slaves to do all the hard, nasty work, but will not be subject to the pitfalls of being killed off or always engaged in war.

The Plan: the Way to Freedom.

The Plan involves creating a god greater than any god previously created. This god will have to be invisible so it cannot be destroyed and so no one else can replace it. This god will be the epitome of everything every human would love to be: eternal, omnipresent, omniscient, all powerful, yet full of bliss and love. All the other gods had small roles to play; they were in the sky like the sun and moon gods, or like the Greek gods who were too human, except they didn't die off like the kings. This god must empower and overpower them all. He must rule by fear but reward with love and an eternal, blissful life. The person using this Plan will become 'The Teacher' or 'Messiah' and shall be exalted because he will be the sole entity who can communicate with the one true God and no one will wish to see him destroyed. He will have a secure, bright future and survive as the new fittest of the fit. He will be able to secure a great empire that will benefit his family and friends for all future generations. Follow these simple steps for guaranteed success. Remember that you can never be found guilty of fabricating anything because it will never be possible to prove the whole thing is a lie. Humans cannot prove that God exists, nor can anyone prove God does not exist. No one can prove that you cannot communicate or become one with the one God created. So even thousands of years from now people will still be worshiping and praising the Messiah, who God sent to save the world.

Make sure to introduce the big miracles that the Messiah supposedly did in front of the masses, after the Messiah has died: for the obvious reason that by then no one will be able to disprove the miracles occurred. With the loyal few, make sure they are proclaiming the Messiah's greatness and declaring many miracles. Be as liberal as need be with abundant stories of the greatest God, while providing plenty of intimidation and fear within the teachings so the message spreads and holds with the masses. The following is a list that needs to be implemented to guarantee success in creating a great empire:

- Conjure up great tales of miracles that can be neither proven nor disproved such as: the Messiah had a virgin birth. (The Kings of Egypt used that one and it really impresses the ignorant masses). The Messiah can heal the sick and raise the dead. (Begin small with these, using a few loyal disciples; over time this can be greatly exaggerated).
- Write a great book, with many details emphasizing how great and unique God and the tribe that is being converted

is. (People are easily swayed by enticing their egos). You may have to bribe some of the priestly caste to share some of their great wisdom: stories of the cosmos and of the Earthly medicines to make the great book impressive. Fill the book full of practical wisdom as well, so it has at least some usefulness to the ignorant masses, but be sure to give good excuses for not divulging very much of the great wisdom and secrets of the mysteries of the Universe. Make up a story as to why there is not much information about the beyond: God is mysterious, God has many secrets and people are too ignorant and not ready to hear the truth, etc.

- The priests and teachers possess ancient secrets and potions that will cause people to hallucinate spiritual visions they will swear are real. Learn these secrets and get people to see light and hear sounds and to see the Messiah's form even after he has died. All their hallucinations can be said to be signs from God.
- Create all the major events of the new religion to coincide with traditions already in place, such as harvest, the start of seasons and other important time encoded events that are depicted by the movements of the sun, moon and stars, like December 25th.
- Manipulate people's weakness for attachment by making family attachments central, but only after demanding and assuring their attachment to God, the Messiah and the Church is paramount and comes before all.
- If necessary, you can create a dark and evil force likened to the Devil and place blame for everything bad upon him. People will relate to this as the forces of the night or the moon that can cover the light of the all-powerful sun for a short time, until the great sun returns and wipes out the darkness.
- In the past, God has been seen as the sun; make countless

references to God as being as powerful and bright as the sun.

- They must give ten percent of their time and money to the Messiah. (Once the number of disciples grows, you will soon see this will be the greatest law of all for creating a great empire to benefit the Messiah and the loyal few).
- If the Messiah wishes to remain within the kingdom, he should proclaim to be a servant of God and the people. If he wishes to break free and create a new kingdom then he can proclaim himself the Son of God, the new King or Messiah. This will make him one with God and for all intents and purposes the Messiah will be God and rule over the people.
- Remember, you will need many healthy, long living slaves that are indoctrinated to live in an organized, productive society. People are born with no sense of right or wrong, other than what is ingrained in their biology as survival instincts. Therefore, this must be instilled at a young age.
- Teach them to hate and shame anyone who questions the teachings.
- They must be taught that self-sacrifice for the sake of the Messiah and society is good and natural. People will instinctively prefer to do their own bidding and to enjoy vast amounts of free time to indulge in sex, day dreaming, hallucinating from drug use, carrying out sporting activities and their artistic expressions, as well as indulging in their main passion and activity, which is ego boosting by socializing with family and friends. All this will be a huge drain on empire building. These activities lead to injuries and diseases that cost dearly in time and money. Therefore, maintain strict control over the masses. Threaten them with eternal hell and damnation if they transgress any of the laws. If caught, punish them publicly to keep the masses in a constant state of fear.

The following rules are imperative to keep them focused on work:

- Sex will only be allowed for procreation among married couples. They must have many children as the young will be easily converted. Religion will spread like wildfire as children are easily brainwashed.
- Sex only enhances the spreading of diseases and wastes time and energy; do away with hugging and kissing and shame those who indulge.
- There will be no stealing or coveting anything from another. Those who obey and work hard will be rewarded more and we cannot allow others to steal these incentives away. People will need to learn the way to riches and security is to submit and work hard.
- There will be no killing allowed as you will need all the slaves you can get to stay alive and work hard. However, it will be necessary for the Messiah to kill in the name of God and His church, to keep power and authority and to punish any opponents.
- There will be no adultery. (These activities cause distractions from work and spread diseases).
- They must believe in God and the Messiah or be punished with eternal hell. (For fast, easy results converting the ignorant masses use plenty of fear and intimidation. You only have to look at how the early kings used torture and murder to build their great empires).
- Do not bear false witness. Tell them to tell the truth and that way they will believe you to be truthful, too. People caught lying should be given the harshest penalties. (Remember this will never affect you because you can never be caught having lied as no one can prove you are lying).
- The slaves must work hard for the Messiah; sacrifice

everything for the church.

Fabricate other commandments you deem necessary for your particular tribe in your particular time and place in history. Build slowly but surely as not to enrage the jealous and powerful against you too early.

Remember that if done properly, most societies and governments will secretly support you – if not outright support you, because they, too, want their people to be good, healthy slaves. In their arrogance, they will seek to use you as one of their crafty tools to accomplish their goals. They may even help you to grow by making laws to protect your church and the money you make may not even be taxed, which would be the greatest boon and irony of all. In time, you will become the new society and government and have all the power over all the people and all the riches.

Remember, those with enriched pleasant lives are the easiest to convert. They will believe life is great and they are great and deserve great things and that God created all these special, great things just for them. They will be too busy being happy to care or notice all the suffering in the Universe. They have good karma so they will choose to praise God rather than opposing you and risking going to hell or losing all their wealth.

Beware of those who suffer because they will have more empathy with all the great suffering in the Universe and wonder why God does nothing about it. To win them over you must emphasize they suffer for their evil ways and they must repent or suffer in hell for eternity.

To win over the very rich, tell them money is evil and it is impossible for them to be saved unless they support the Messiah and church generously.

Nothing but great things can happen if one amongst you has the gall, charisma, leadership, ego, conviction and steadfastness to carry it through. Being a great liar with a

> stone face would be a handy asset, too. Remember, it is for the greater good that you lie: free yourself, your family, your friends and tribe members from the grip of slavery forever.
>
> Brothers for Freedom

If this document is found, it must be destroyed immediately or you will be cursed by the demon of darkness and die by the force of his sword that can strike off a thousand heads through time and space and through all the Universe if need be!

Chapter 20

The Documents

"The duty of youth is to challenge corruption."
Kurt Cobain

"Now I'll recite the other document. If any of it is true, then the human race really has something to worry about, never mind nuclear war! Hearing this will help you to understand why we did what we did: why terror was necessary."

He cleared his throat and began to speak...

The Beginning of the Light

We, the Essenes, the Brotherhood of Light, declare we are in possession of sacred documents that were handed down from past Masters: found, acquired, translated and transcribed. May God guide us to the truth, light and eternal life! May God's mercy be upon us!"

The Way of Truth

In the beginning, God was an ocean of all consciousness, Alpha and Omega. God has no beginning and no end. God is omnipotent, omnipresent, omniscient bliss and love. However, having all power, God was also full of desire to manifest all His creative powers. In the beginning was the word and the word was with God and the word was God. God first created the word or the light and sound which was the first manifestation or expression of God. All things that God created were created from the word. With a single thought, He could create whole Universes, palaces, and places of breathtaking beauty beyond imagination but He also became immensely bored with perfection as He could never escape from Himself and the ecstasy. There was no one else with which to share His marvelous creations. The pain of eternal boredom and loneliness was too much to bear and with the greatest urge and desire He ever experienced, He split Himself in two. In an instant, there were now two Gods. For thousands of years they were fulfilled and happy to keep each other entertained and boredom did not enter their consciousness. With time, slowly but surely, the two became even more bored and the pain of this boredom was now two fold. In desperation, they created a space of eternal darkness. One would leave the other to enter this darkness and all their powers would be gone. The God who stayed behind was the only one who could save the other. They would alternate who would leave and who would be the Savior. The ecstasy of being miraculously saved once again to become an eternal God with endless powers to rediscover was truly a new high never before imagined. However, in time, the ecstasy wore off; it was just too predictable. Therefore, together they came up with a plan to create the greatest game, one that would keep them from the pain of boredom forever.

The game consisted of creating many Universes, with many levels, called planes or regions.

First, there is the purest region where God resides, where everything is pure consciousness and eternal. This nameless wonder region is called Anaami, Agam the ineffable region or Alakh the inconceivable region.

Then there are the regions where God manifests Himself as light and sound and creates whichever amazing things He wishes. This includes the fifth region, called by some Sach Khand or the true home, where God manifests Himself and dwells as the Holy Spirit.

The fourth region called Bhanwar Gupha is where God created an infinite number of souls that would inhabit all the regions. In this region, the sun shines brighter and is bigger than one hundred thousand physical suns. The light and beauty of God here is colossal.

God next created a vast area of darkness called the barrier region, where no sound or light could permeate; only God possessed the power to travel through this dark region. Souls that become lost here will ultimately suffer a slow, painful death as their energy depletes, and they are eventually absorbed by the darkness.

He then created the Super Causal Plane or third region, the second region called the Causal Plane, the first region called the Astral plane and last, the Physical Plane.

All the souls were created to serve God and were forced through the Dark Barrier region into the Super-Causal region. Everything that was created below the dark barrier region was subjected to time and all the laws of the Universe, like the law of Karma or cause and effect. These regions were created to expand and evolve and eventually to dissolve back to God. The souls were given bodies and minds that are subjected to the evils of lust, greed, attachment, anger and ego. Thus, the game of good over evil began. In the higher planes, good always won, which became too predictable and boring. Therefore, God forced many souls into the physical or lowest region, where evil and good were equal forces and nobody, not even God could predict which side would prevail. He devised the rule that only from the physical region could souls find God through the living Master and win back their eternal freedom. God fashioned all the laws that everything He created is subjected to, whether or not the law is even known to the souls did not matter. Depending on their thoughts, words and deeds each soul is rewarded or punished; rewarded by going to Heaven in the Astral region or punished by going to Hell, which is also located in the Astral region. Souls are likewise forced to reincarnate into all the living organisms, plants, insects, animals and humans. The object of the game is not to get to Heaven but rather to find and become one with God through the Master and return to eternal freedom. The souls learn everything will eventually be destroyed, but are eager to be born into the physical plane, where they have a chance to meet the Master and find eternal life. Everything that happens is the will of God, forcing the souls to pray for His grace. The soul is given no free will since everything that happens is the will of God as dictated by His laws. Yet the souls in the higher regions possess more freedoms and means to fulfill their desires.

God has the power to appear anywhere in His creation, because there are now three Gods that are equal and one with each other. One is born on Earth and becomes the Son, who searches and finds the other God, who is called the Father, who is already one with the eternal God. They are able to do this with the help of the third God who stays and appears in the first to fourth regions and is called the Holy Spirit. Of course, they're all the same entity, but now they take turns who will be the Father, the Son or the Holy Spirit. They enter the darkness, completely forgetting whom they are, only to be woken up later by the Father or Holy Spirit to rediscover the glory of their exalted position; thus never again having to experience the excruciating pain of eternal boredom and loneliness.

Ever since God first manifested on Earth as a human, with all the other human souls, and set into motion all the laws, He has always remained here on Earth and will remain until all of creation is destroyed and returned to God. In the beginning souls simply manifested here from the astral plane and God bestowed them their different bodies. Some were female and others were males of all the millions of different species. Later the souls could only come to Earth after the male and female mated and at the time of conception. In this way, God populated the earth of all the plants, insects, bacteria and humans. They eventually forgot how they were originally put on Earth and they lost all connection and memory of God. Only the Master could awaken the soul to its true purpose and identity. After this, the whole game of creation begins again.

Godman is always on Earth to take on the sins of the world; otherwise it would disintegrate and disappear in a flash because of all the evil that exists. Everything is according to God's will. God decides which souls advance in the game and which do not. The object of the game is for souls to find out who the living God or Master is and go to Him to obtain eternal life. This must be done before all the regions below the great dark barrier are destroyed. God does not allow any more souls to become one with God. The few that God chooses and guides through the great dark barrier are allowed to have eternal life in the fourth and fifth regions. When the pain of boredom hits them, in desperation, they will often throw themselves into the darkness of no return and God will have to rush in and rescue them. By doing this, their pain of boredom is cured for many, many years. Sometimes God will take some of these souls with him when He is born into the physical world. They will become His helpers. This also relieves them of an eternity of boredom.

God can justify all this by thinking what is best for God is best for all He creates. All the souls are living in illusion, pain and misery, but God lives amongst them and suffers as well for all the sins and evil that He created. God comes to Earth seeking out the lost souls that He wants to take to the higher planes. Taking on the sins of the world also helps the world advance through its many stages or cycles known as the Iron Age, the Bronze Age, the Silver age, and the Golden age. All souls are encouraged to do good deeds and obey God's commandments as this lessens the amount of Karma or pain and suffering the Master has to endure, as well as allowing the souls to experience Heaven and all things good. The souls must meditate many long hours on the light and sound that emanates from God and is God. The light and sound or word of God leads the soul back to God. The souls are told to be perfect and made to believe that it is possible, but in reality, only by becoming one with God can a soul become perfect. Becoming one with God is only possible for those souls that are chosen by God to meet the perfect Master on Earth. Love and effort are required of the soul but it is also the result of God's will and grace. Mysterious are the ways of God. The special blessed souls the Master initiates into the mysteries of the beyond must keep everything very secret and are tested repeatedly for their trustworthiness to keep these secrets.

This document is written by God and passed on in secret to the first living Master, who will sign it and pass it on to the next chosen Master.

In His name, Amen.

Message from the 'Brothers of Light'.

Jesus of Nazareth was convinced that He would be the next Messiah because God led Him from within to the great Master, who lived in India. However, the living Master told Jesus that He was not yet ready to be the next Messiah. Jesus was convinced that he was already the Son of God, so He took all the sacred documents, which He felt were rightfully His. These documents contained the names of all the living Masters that had come to Earth. They also contained the living will of each of the Masters and told who their Successors would be. They revealed all the laws of God: how the souls could escape their imprisonment, all the secrets of how to tell who a real Master is and all the ways that they save the souls. For example, Masters are not allowed to charge money and must earn their own keep. The mark of the lotus flower is formed by the lines on their palms and feet. Masters do not show their powers or perform miracles openly but their close followers experience many of their powers and see many miracles they must keep secret. If Jesus had become the living Master He would have had written permission from the previous Master and He would have written who the next living Master would be. We do not know what happened to the documents. Were they buried with Jesus in the tomb and stolen by the Romans when they entered or did Jesus give them to His Successor? We, The Essenes, The Sons of Light, The Brotherhood of the Righteous, preserved and hid many sacred documents in the caves along the northwest shore of the Dead Sea. We had no time to make copies of the documents before the Romans invaded. We do not know if Jesus was the true living Master and had a Successor or if His Successor received the documents. We do not know if they were among the documents buried. The person who finds this document must realize they must keep looking for the many other documents that were hidden. There are further documents that tell the hiding places of all the riches of our people: gold, silver, doctrines and our written history. There are unwanted documents that were meant to be destroyed that say that God does not exist and was invented by people to gain control over the masses. If these documents are found they must be destroyed. They would ruin all the Holy work of all the great saints and of God since the beginning of time. We have also hidden a book that was partially translated, that declares aliens created us. We did not have time to properly study the texts to determine and punish those who wrote them, nor to destroy the evil documents, so they, too, are buried here in case we do survive this apocalypse.

Jesus never allowed anyone to see the sacred documents He had and we do not know who He gave them to or where they were hidden. During the time of Jesus, the Romans pursued, persecuted and killed the Keepers of the Light. May God have mercy on us all and may truth prevail. Amen.

Chapter 21

Search for Truth

> "To know what you prefer instead of humbly saying Amen to what the world tells you you ought to prefer, is to have kept your soul alive."
> *Robert Louis Stevenson*

Hamasa kept talking into the tape recorder hoping the truth of his story would set him free. By now, the devotees were making little shrines along the rock walls, hanging up pictures of Hamasa, placing candles and laying flowers. Most of those passing by were affected by the vibes and at least became respectful and quiet. Once a restricted area under tight security, it had now become a destination without impediment.

"After reflecting on the documents, I realized I was wasting my time being a double agent. It was causing me to lose my mind and soul. I was so good at convincing the enemy I was on their side that I forgot whose side I was on. I wanted to spend the remaining years of my life terrorizing God and the Godmen whom He supposedly sent to Earth. I wanted to find the truth and stop the insanity. Imagine, all the endless suffering from evil, death, sickness and disasters, for all the people and animals since time began, is God's will and the result of God being bored! I was horribly confused and angry after reading all the documents. Once I'd read and realized everything is a game that God created to thwart boredom, I believed maybe I could enter the game and become an active participant in it. I thought maybe I could even beat God at his own game.

"There was only one way to find out what was the truth. I thought if I kidnapped and threatened to kill the Godman then God would change the rules of the game to benefit all humans.

Instead of God forcing the souls to suffer millions of years of death, fear and humiliation, just to keep God from being bored, we would force God to free all the souls from slavery and return us all to the eternal regions. From there we, the souls would find a way to keep God and ourselves from becoming bored without having to force any souls into suffering. I mean, why doesn't God use robots instead to play His games?

"The documents state there is always a Godman on Earth, who transfers that power to a Successor. I wondered what would happen if the Master was not allowed to transfer God's power to the next Master. I thought this might force God to negotiate with us directly in some way. With most religions, their prophets or messiahs were dead. It would do no good to kidnap their current leaders, they claim only to interpret their holy books – such leaders as the Dali Lama openly admit this. Even some great Yogis and Gurus of Indian religious and spiritual movements freely admitted they knew nothing of God other than what they read about Him, like the rest of us. Ghandi was such a soul, who admitted he was but a humble seeker.

"Faqir Chand, who was known as the Honest Guru, because even after many miracles happened, where he would appear to people, cure them or use his spirit body to take them out of the path of danger, admitted he had no knowledge of this or control over it. He said a higher power he had not yet met must be doing this or it was all done by some yet unknown power of mind. He said Masters have not yet met God, never mind having all of God's power. He was told to give initiation, probably because everyone already worshiped him as a Master, but he refused to lie about it. He wouldn't accept any gifts, money, or even credit for the miracles. He didn't even want to be worshiped as a Master, but people still do.

"We already know from the documents what will happen if we allow and follow God's will. A few, special, lucky souls will be saved and will be allowed to have eternal life in the highest inner planes, while the rest of the millions of trillions of souls will be destroyed, along with the whole Universe and all the inner planes up to the Dark Barrier region.

"Jesus said, Mathew 7:13–14, 'for the gate is narrow that leads to eternal life, but those who find it are few.'

"What would happen, if in the spirit of 'The Game', I could change the rules, and change God's will? What would happen if God had no more Masters on Earth to rule over all the souls?

"Jesus said, St. John 9:5, 'As long as I am in the world I am the light of the world.'

"It appears every religion believes theirs is the only truth and the only way to salvation is through their prophet or Master. Most people inherit their beliefs from their parents and from the country they're born in, without ever knowing what the truth really is. They have a blind faith and belief they're willing to sacrifice their lives for or even kill others for. Faith is held up to be the greatest sign of a true devotee. But what is faith really? Is it just an excuse not to search for the truth, not to question? We're told to have faith but is it a clever way to shut us up? What are the consequences of faith? Will we stop evolving, searching and questioning? I thought about how faith forces us not to question authority, which is great for those with all the power and money, who have authority and wish to keep it. But what's the cost to humanity, I asked myself.

"We've always been taught everything is 'God's will', God will never change, we must accept God's will, surrender to God's will and that there is a divine reason for all evil. I believed the lie that we were given 'free will', along with the choice to do good or evil, thereby justifying that those who choose evil should go to hell, while those who choose good deserve to enter Heaven.

"I became obsessed with finding and knowing the truth. It seemed as if I was on the verge of getting the greatest questions answered.

"I also wondered if I should look at everything from a totally different perspective. What if there was no God? This was almost impossible for me to do since I was brainwashed from birth to believe there had to be a God. From the time we're born, we see a church on every street corner and it's instilled in everyone by schools and governments that there is a God. How can we not believe that there is?

"Is man's true Achilles heel our relentless need for purpose and meaning, that we will sacrifice our own life and everyone else's as well to find it? People will sacrifice their worldly interests, goals, lovers, spouses, family and eventually themselves to find this elusive great purpose and meaning. Did greedy, selfish power brokers hoodwink humanity into believing there was a great purpose – a love that was worth dying for, a God that was worth killing for? Did they discover this was man's greatest weakness and milk it for all it was worth? Is this the real, true root of all the evils and ills in the world? Thus, the ignorant, gullible and trusting were giving the rich and powerful the greatest, simplest means to ensure that their power and riches would keep increasing forever.

"After hearing Nancy talk to Nayanna about atheism, I looked into it closely, with the intent to terrorize atheists and put an end to such evil ways. So yes, I also read a lot about the atheist organizations to find their vulnerabilities. However, in light of the documents I read, I began to see how Nancy's ideas for a better, more evolved world might make sense. The more I studied atheism, the more it made sense. Playing the devil's advocate, I started to challenge all my beliefs and assumptions. Islam has a saying, 'Do your prayers and have faith, but tie up your camel'. In the west it is said, 'God helps those who help themselves'. There is always the practical side to things. We're really on our own. We have to do and figure things out and there will be no God there to help us. So to me, it made sense that atheism was based on having evidence and using the scientific method, with all its principles. I started to realize we were stuck in the dark ages of thinking and it was mostly because of our religious beliefs. We honestly can't know anything for sure unless there is evidence, and there really is no evidence for the existence of God. It's all based on blind faith."

Hamasa noticed the prison psychologist hanging around and writing down notes. He seemed to be puzzled by the scene unfolding before him as the numbers of gathering devotees grew. He seemed a friendly sort, with a Santa Claus beard and a belly to match, so Hamasa laboriously trundled his chair over to him.

"Do you believe in God?" Hamasa asked.

"Hello, Hamasa. It's nice to see you again." The doctor gave him a friendly smile. "There's been a few times when I was instructed to check up on you, but you were mostly in an unconscious state or tied up attending to other things, pun intended." He laughed loudly through his beard, losing balance as his belly rocked. "Interrogations are a nasty business, but you seem to be coming round nicely. They'll probably have me visit with you soon, once the drugs start to wear off. By the way, I'm Dr. Frederick. So what's your take on what's happening here?" Once Hamasa had pushed himself and his chair closer, the doctor whispered, "And no, I don't believe in God, why?"

Hamasa gathered his scattered thoughts. "Well, as I'm sure you're aware, I've been asked to tell my story and explain myself into that tape recorder," he nodded towards the machine, "while Harold's out for food," he added, a cackle escaping his parched throat. "I was a naughty boy and kidnapped God, well, a Master – someone who's said to be one with God. Yes, this place has been visited by a great Power, but these devotees and their shrines have little to do with me. It's the Power – it's coming. So have you heard about the documents, are the rumors going around yet?" He asked.

The doctor tugged on his ear lobe. "I heard about it, actually I read a copy of one of the documents. It would seem to pretty much agree with my view that God is a made-up construct to benefit the ruling elite. Yeah, a copy's getting passed around the offices here, an interesting read indeed." The doctor beamed at Hamasa again.

Once Hamasa had drawn close, a wonderful, sweet aroma permeated the area, giving the doctor some distraction. He couldn't find the words to describe it, finally he decided it must be a new dish the kitchen was concocting.

"So if people had not created gods or God, how do you think the world would've turned out? How would it have progressed?" Hamasa inquired.

Dr. Frederick gave a slight chuckle and drew a deep breath. "I think by now we might've developed a world where there was true equality, where people saw all life as a miracle and cherished it. There wouldn't be the hierarchy there is with God, the priestly classes and the rich and powerful on top. We could've created a world where all our resources would've been put towards making sure every individual was looked after and all knowledge and resources were shared equally. Extra time and money could've gone towards finding more truths and solutions to all the problems humanity faces. It would be a world without any hierarchies because humans would realize it was not their choice to be born. Humans do not decide what talents, DNA, environment, genetics or abilities they are born with. People wouldn't be held accountable in the same way as they are today. There would be no sin and evil, just actions done out of our collective ignorance. In all honesty, no one would know the purpose of life, so no one would impose a purpose on another. The only truths would be the ones that could be scientifically proven true for all people, for all times. We might've wasted thousands of years following false truths and leaders, kings, masters and gods who claim to know everything, when they very well might not know a single truth, like the rest of humanity. Now that we know better we must do better."

Hamasa broke in… "Yes! I see your reasoning! In our present world of 'survival of the fittest' we want to prove we're not losers but we also go to even greater lengths to prove that the other person *is* a loser, so we can gain power and steal for ourselves what they have. The truth is, we're all losers – we all die! It should be against the law to proclaim a truth that isn't scientifically verifiable. We should all be humbled by our collective ignorance, right."

"Well, I'm glad to hear you agree with some of the things I believe," Dr. Frederick added. "I also believe they wouldn't be able to hold the afterlife up as the carrot or the stick to motivate people. If religious teachers are lying or can't prove their claims, they shouldn't be allowed to preach. If they continue, it should be a crime against humanity and they should be put in a jail where they could be reformed." With his free hand, he stroked his beard, fixating on Hamasa's eyes, but he continued talking.

"The scientific method, if applied properly, uncorrupted by politics or money, could have come up with cures, fixes for all our problems, and created a whole new, better reality for humanity and all living things. We spent billions developing the atom bomb and putting a man on the moon but we haven't found a cure for addictions or other horrors of the mind and our biology. Now, when there's a disaster, people say it was destiny or that it's deserved for going against God in some way. Many superstitions come up and nothing's done to find the true causes and solutions. However, if we put all our resources into using the scientific method, we'd find the true cause of disasters and find the best solutions to be protected or cured from them for next time.

"We have to endure undue stress, humiliation, shame and abuse by trying to live up to impossible ideals that are based on lies, just so the few in power can keep us as their slaves and get richer. Those in charge of finding, shaming and prosecuting people who aren't perfect, are hypocrites and far from perfect themselves. We should be finding ways to evolve instead of believing we only need to be in touch with our souls and God or God will one day save us if we only believe and give all our money to the church. Of course, the church capitalizes on promoting that view, ignoring all the crimes committed by people of the church. We've been doing that for thousands of years and it obviously doesn't work. We act like the same barbaric animals we were when we climbed out of trees as monkeys millions of years ago. Let's be honest here, some monkeys might actually live with more empathy and harmony than some humans. By now, there should be a cure for our inhumanity towards each other. We should be hooked up to super-computers by now that could regulate our moods and behaviors so that we're good to others and to ourselves. Every day we have to fight and compete against each other for survival. We have to slay the dragon – be the hero to our family and communities. Isn't it just too much to bear? Isn't it time for a major change? There's far too much suicide, stress, sickness, pollution, war, crime and people treating themselves and others horribly badly for this to continue.

"I wrote some thoughts down years ago I still try to live by. You wanna hear?"

"Of course, I would be honored," Hamasa said respectfully.

Encouraged, the doctor began to speak, softly at first, his voice growing more powerful as he warmed to his theme.

"Love," he began, "is the perfect dream that we are soon woken up from by reality. By love, I mean divine love, the idea that God is love, by which all feelings and acts of love are measured. Love is a wild fantasy, a magical mix of mysterious matter. A potion that is rendered powerless by the savage forces of reality. Love is one idea among many that humans embrace to find purpose in a sea of, as of now, endless undiscovered meaning. Love is but one of many myths that have been handed down to us from times immemorial. Many myths have been discarded, Zeus, Apollo, Atlantis, the Earth is flat, or the Universe revolves around the

Earth. Many new ones are being created – aliens exist, Elvis lives, sasquatches freely roam the Earth, and capitalism is the best system. The myths that define us, that we kill to preserve, that we let ruin our lives and destroy the Earth for, seem to have lives of their own. Are they worth preserving? They've served a few people extraordinarily well in their fight for survival, but at what cost to the rest of humanity, to planet Earth and the Universe."

"Wow," Hamasa responded, "sounds like you've written a book on this. I believe in the Power now because I've experienced it, but trust me, there was a time I toyed with the ideas you speak of as well."

"Sounds as if there's hope for you anyway. "Thanks for the compliment about my ideas, but it's just random thoughts. So," he said, his face serious, "you feel you've actually experienced some God like power? Do you mean you actually have proof and you're not just talking about some personal hallucination? I mean, I've known for years that only in works of fiction can the laws of physics be broken: as in Superman or... Anyway, and no, he shook his head, rushing on without allowing Hamasa time to answer, "I haven't finished a book yet, but I keep working on it." He spread his arms. "You only need to look around, there's lots to write about. I see the effects of people's weird worldviews everyday here. These are incredibly violent times, when everyone is at war with each other and themselves to gain power and money or just to get a job and hang onto it. It is violence hidden within laws, economics and society's expectations. It's women against men, the old against the young, business against business, religion against religion, country against country, and of course, by default, each person against the other in a fight to the death. 'May truth prevail' is my chant, my mantra. One day the fossil records will prove much of what I'm saying – I just hope, before it's too late."

He fell silent, raking a pudgy hand through his salt-and-pepper beard. "Hey, I'd better get a move on. Maybe I've said too much or talked too loud and these good folks here," he nodded toward the small crowd on the other side of the doors, "will lynch me for my opinion. I'm not sure what you mean by the 'Power is coming', but from the looks of these people, I'd say you're the power they're searching for."

Hamasa sent him a crooked grin. "Ha-ha, no, not me, I hope the Power will be here soon though and that it hasn't abandoned me." He aimed a nod at the psychiatrist but his head just lolled about uncontrollably on his neck. "Very interesting listening to your worldview," he slurred. "I hope we meet again. My head's so messed up at the moment, I sure could use a little shrink talk. Thanks for sharing – you take care."

Hamasa stuck his hand through the iron gate. "Shake?" he offered, but Dr. Frederick just gave a big, hearty chuckle. Hamasa managed to turn himself around and push himself towards the table. He appreciated the chance to get some exercise, and he had enjoyed his little chat with the doctor.

Hamasa was back on task and hoping to avoid being handcuffed again, trying his best to convince himself that there was no one behind the glass wall to report him for his chat with the shrink. He frowned, determinedly marshalling his sluggish thoughts, picking up from where he had left off in explaining his anger and frustration and the reasons he had decided to kidnap the Master.

"All these conflicting thoughts were driving me crazy, and I had nobody I could confide in, only my research. I couldn't wait to force the truth out of someone, soon.

"I got carried away with my internal conflict, thinking this, thinking that, what was right, what was wrong, if there was a God or not. My head was a mess. But eventually I got back to the tasks at hand. First, I had to find out if there was any truth to what the documents were saying. I also needed to find out more about the Masters.

"I prepared a letter to give to them, if and when we kidnapped them. This will help you to understand what really motivated me. I didn't know who the true Master was, because they all say they're the true one, so I decided to kidnap them all! I hoped to find the true Master based on the fruits of their actions and by the other criteria I'd found during research."

Hamasa began reading the letter containing the demands he made to the Masters and God.

Demands Made to the Perfect Master and God:

- Does God really exist? Who is God and who created God if He does exist? Is God evil, good, or both?

Scientists have shown many of the spiritual experiences people and saints claimed they had could have been caused by hallucinations. By stimulating certain regions of the brain, scientists are able to reproduce many of these so-called divine experiences. Even love has been proven to be a chemical reaction in the brain. The truth needs to be revealed once and for all.

- Is love real? Is God love? Do we have an eternal soul?

Instead of getting people to spend so much money and time trying to be one with God and building and going to churches to pray to God to destroy the devil and all evil, should we instead spend the money saving people from natural disasters, disease and people's evil actions against each other. Should we spend all the money and time making this world the best that it can be for everybody. Should we find a cure for our bad thoughts and evil actions. We could use the money for research to find if God was merely fabricated for the benefit of some power hungry, greedy, manipulating, evil humans.

Some people swear aliens abducted them. Maybe the

mind created it all and there is no God or soul? Perhaps these experiences come to people in the same way doctors use the placebo effect to cure. In the same way, if we're told to see and experience miracles from God or the Masters, then maybe the mind creates them?

"If God exists, can we change God or at least pray that He will change His will? Right now, I know God loves to create evil because of what the documents claim and because God has all the power and could easily change everything if He wanted to. He could destroy the devil and evil right now if He wanted to, but He doesn't. So would it not be better to teach souls how they can change God? At the moment, God is perfectly happy with everything the way it is, because if He was not, He would change it; He has the power to do so.

However, if there is no God, then forget it, just change people.

It's a game of karma and a war of good over evil. He loves the evil He created more than the souls He created. He loves pleasing Himself first to keep from being bored. He wants to be loved and adored, even though He has created evil and suffering, and if a soul doesn't obey and love God, He sends them to hell. He will no longer be allowed to force souls to play this horrifying game of good fighting evil.

- Is the purpose of life to become one with God, to reach Heaven or to attain eternal life? However, it obviously doesn't matter if I or anyone else becomes one with God because nothing changes. He will never stop the insanity of evil and suffering. The Master became one with God and it didn't change God or stop the evil or get rid of hell. All the souls who are one with God never stopped the suffering or the evil or stopped the will of God to keep creating hell, evil and suffering. Therefore, we must stop becoming one with God and begin finding a way to stop God from creating this endless game of karma and suffering.

- How can we stop people being like God, playing their own games as God does, and creating even more suffering than there already is?
- The worst evil God created was to begin this horrible game of karma. As soon as there's a game, there has to be one winner and many losers. The game's always fun for the winner and for those who watch but for the losers it's a nightmare beyond imagination. The Romans created games, too, and as they became bored, they made the games more and more deadly. People were fed to the lions, all for the pleasure of the emperor and his chosen few subjects. They obviously learned well from how God created and played His games.
- Everything is the soul's fault or responsibility for choosing evil over good, even though it's obvious the soul did not create the Universes or lust, greed, attachment, anger, ego, the mind and body or the souls or anything that is created. Then He says everything is the fault of the devil for tempting us or it's the fault of free will. At other times He will say everything that happens is the will of God, which is the exact opposite. God says the purpose of power is to protect. If we abuse power we're sent to hell, but God has all the power and yet He does not protect anyone from anything. Instead, He uses it to send souls to hell and forces souls into illusion, suffering, evil, and does nothing to protect children or anyone.

If there is no God – hell yeah, power to the people!

- Do we have free will? God is free to kill or love, to travel to the highest or lowest regions, and never to suffer any consequences for His actions. He has total free will. It's not free will to choose to kill someone and then be forced into jail or killed only to end up in hell. God kills, yet isn't sent to hell because He has true free will. There are no consequences for a soul with free will and that soul would be able to choose eternal life in Heaven any time it wanted to. We pray that God gives every soul true free will as He has it.

If there is no God, then stop willing it into existence, will you people?

- We're told Jesus or Mohammad will return to defeat the devil and bring everlasting life. We've waited thousands of years now and the pain and misery continues. What kind of loving God keeps waiting and waiting and ignores all the cries, pleas and faithful prayers?

The Lord's Prayer

Our Father who art in Heaven,
Hallowed be thy name.
Thy kingdom come.
Thy will be done,
On Earth as it is in Heaven.
Give us this day our daily bread,
And forgive us our trespasses,
As we forgive those who trespass against us,
And lead us not into temptation,
But deliver us from evil.
Amen

"This is my version of the 'Lord's Prayer'"

The Human's Prayer

Why, Father, art thou in Heaven and not here?
Mysterious is thy name and will.
Creator of all that is good and evil,

Thy kingdom of eternal love and peace for all souls come.
Only Love's will ought to be done on Earth as it is done in Heaven.
We pray your current will be undone and evil is none.
Thank you for this day and our daily bread,
And for the miracle of life and all life's blessings.
Forgive us for our trespasses and help us forgive others who trespass against us.
Help us forgive you, too, Lord.
You forced us into this Universe of pain, suffering, death and illusion.
We incorrectly follow your example of creating evil, death, illusion, deceit and filling our lives with desire.
That we fulfill without concern for how it may bring suffering to others, as you do.
Do not lead us into your temptations.
But deliver us from your evils.
For thine is the Kingdom, the power and the glory to keep you from your boredom forever,
Forever and ever, be broken.
Amen

"If, however, there is no God, then curse and shame to those who started and perpetrated all the religions and lies. It should all come to an immediate halt."

Chapter 22

Confronting the Truth

"When mere mortals emerge from technology's womb, materialize true embodiment:

Predators, power hungry, scavengers, animals, death avoiders, addicted, afflicted, sexualized

Shamed, sued, expelled, enslaved, incarcerated

When Masters of the Universe emerge from technology's womb, materialize true embodiment:

Predators, power hungry, scavengers, animals, death avoiders, addicted, afflicted, sexualized

Exulted, triumphant, Masters of manipulation, mastering the destruction of the Universe"

John H. K. Fisher

"Sky, we have to talk." Nayanna confronted Sky while he meditated and as she paced their humble room's cement floor at the ashram. Today would be a good day to get a favorable response from Sky for the things she had forgotten to tell him, she thought. He will be agreeable, submissive, amenable, compliant, yielding, complaisant… She kept repeating the litany of words to herself, hoping he would subliminally reflect their command: no response.

She tried again. "Sky, I'm sorry but this can't wait!"

"I thought if I just ignored you, you'd think I must be in Heaven with the Masters and go away," Sky responded, unsuccessfully trying to be funny.

Nayanna raked her fingers through her hair. "I'm never going away," she said, her voice strained. "Your life's ruined now because of me and there is no escape. Besides hiding my insecurity, as you've been finding out lately, I'm also wickedly jealous. I'm capable of whipping the thorny roses you might give me for Valentines across your bleeding face if I think you looked at another girl, or taking an ax to your music instruments if you're ignoring me while you play on them. I am capable..."

Sky stared at her. "What, so you've done these things before?" he interrupted, afraid of the answer.

"I truly believe the world should revolve around me, what's the word for that...nas, nar...?"

"Narcissistic," Sky replied: getting the sense this was going to be another very scary day. "Listen, Nayanna, no one's perfect in this world. We start out young and beautiful and as we get old and ugly we develop inner beauty that makes us truly lovable, but it takes time, we just have to have patience."

"Not only am I afraid of the water, but bugs, too, spiders, heights, going fast in a car, I freak out, I sometimes pass out... I'm talking hysterics. I was run over as a little girl and I have steel pins in my knee, see! Oh, I almost forgot – if you need a real good blow job I just have to remove these teeth, see!"

"OK, Nayanna, you don't have to show me with that banana, I get the idea and please put your teeth in. The big difference here is I told you everything about me before we got married and I trusted that you did the same, but no, you decided to wait 'til after. But like I said before, nobody's perfect. I might get hit by a bus tomorrow and you'll be pushing me in a wheel chair the rest of your life. So is there anything else?"

She kept repeating the words in her head, it seemed to be working: compliant, easy going, submissive, understanding, agreeable, amenable...

"Nayanna Grayson isn't my real name! I just thought it sounded nice and someone told me it's a good numerology name and it'll bring me better prosperity, with seven's for being a good scholar and nine's for being spiritual. My real name's Chitralekha, which here in Canada sounds like 'shit-reeks, eh' or at least that's what people called me when I first got here. It means 'celestial maiden', I guess my family used to want me to stay a virgin. My dad was OK with Nayanna, but didn't know about the Grayson part. But there's more!" Nayanna paused, covering her face with her hands for a moment before meeting Sky's gaze.

"I have an ex-boyfriend! I think he's a terrorist! He has a gun! He tried to kill us. He doesn't know I think he's a terrorist, but he might know that I know he's controlling, jealous, a narcissist, possessive and he loves me insanely. He's always away on trips. I think he spies on me. I think he knows about you. I think he'll kill us or you, probably not us, just you. You're a dead man!

"My dad's coming to visit us here. He's immensely upset! I told him we were married. I think he's coming to kill us or you, probably not us, just you. You're a dead man!"

"Wow, Nayanna, is there anything else you can conceivably think of before it's too late and I'm dead before you can make all your confessions? I wouldn't want you to feel guilty for not telling me everything before my demise!"

...Compliant, amenable, nice, lovable, self-sacrificing... She recited her silent mantra, increasing the intensity and frequency. "Maybe we should go to the Master with all this?" Nayanna offered. "I'm sure my ex is the one who wrecked our bikes and your car."

"Why didn't you say anything?" Sky asked, astonished. "Are you protecting him? What if he's still out to make trouble for us? The first thing we have to agree on is, at the first sign of trouble we've got to contact the police," Sky emphasized.

Leaning into the windowless window, a beaming face tells them, "Your dad, Mr. Singh is here, Nayanna. He's actually been with the Master for the past few hours, but now we're all having a very blissful time in the langar, pigging out on treats, tea, and of course, Parshad. Don't take too long thinking about it, just hurry and come."

"Now! He's here now?" Sky groaned. "Of course he is." His eyes bored into Nayanna. "That's why you told me all this isn't it?"

Nayanna nodded meekly, her gaze on the floor.

Sky sighed. "Well, we'd better not keep them." They hurried out the door, Nayanna just managing to grab a scarf off the back of a chair to put over her head.

"Father, what an honor!" Nayanna folded her hands in prayer, bowed before him and then touched his feet under the grand canopy of the langar tent. She did the same as Master stopped to give them a blessing before tactfully leaving them to their privacy.

Nayanna's father drew her to her feet, touching her cheek gently before saying, "I flew in this morning from the Punjab, my daughter." He laughed. "But I didn't expect to arrive in Nirvana." He shook his head, a bemused expression softening the hard lines of his face. "The Master let me see my past lives right before my very own eyes," he whispered. "This is my destiny from God, my way has been shown to me through you, my dear one. 'The child will lead the man.' I am so overwhelmed! I believe I need to lie down somewhere. Do you have a bed I can borrow until they are able to show me my quarters." He wiped a shaking hand across his brow and again gently touched Nayanna's cheek, a chuckle escaping him at her startled expression. "Sadly, I have to leave in a few days, to undo your big wedding into a notably VIP family. They are going to kill me. The Master says I must do it in person, and so I must." He took hold of Nayanna's hand, patting it. "I'd like to stay longer," he gazed around himself as if in a daze, "in this wonderful place."

He made a visible effort to collect himself. "You must be Sky?" he asked as he finally took his attention off Nayanna and looked Sky directly in the eyes, something Sikhs are not allowed to do, and chuckled again. "I came here to definitely kill you, definitely, without question, definitely, with my bare hands!"

"I've been hearing that a lot today," Sky offered. "I think I might get the Master to tweak my future instead of showing me my past. Anyway, as I appear to be safe, at least for the moment, let's make our way back to our room so that you can have a nap."

They settled Mr. Singh down, still muttering about the Master showing him the light as he drifted off to sleep, or perhaps it was back into a blissful meditation.

There was nowhere to sit so Sky and Nayanna left him sleeping and went to look for a place to grab a drink. Nayanna's thoughts took to rhyming:

Comply, try and question why –
Apply, sigh and then decry –
Imply, wry and got so high –
Deny, lie and said good-bye –
Nearby pie and drank some chai…"

Her mind was playing with words; she was nervous.

Compliant, agreeable, persuadable, acquiescent, resigned…

The words were furiously erupting from her mind. She was in a mess: clinging to Sky, desperate, frenzied, and hazardous… unlovable.

A jubilant wedding throng danced by as they stood outside under the shade of the ashram banyan tree. Sky put his arms around her, pulling her against him. He had brought her mango ice cream, her default comfort food. None of it worked to cheer her.

Finally he spoke, "My dearest Nayanna."

"Ha-ha, are you trying to sound like my father or the Master?" she quickly shot back.

"Ha-ha, excuse me while I go find a monkey to cheer you up," Sky joked.

However, not funny at all, in the 130 degree, Old Delhi heat of late April, even under the shade of the banyan tree, licking mango ice cream, she was feeling decidedly light headed.

"Sky, I forgot to tell you, I also pass out in the—"

When she awoke, she was being dumped off a stretcher onto a strange bed, in a strange room at the ashram. As water was splashed at her, spilling into her mouth, she gargled, "Don't kill him! Don't kill him!"

If meditation and Master can't emancipate us, then mercy materialize and minimize misfortune, her final thought as sleep saved the day.

Every now and then she would surface enough to be aware of meticulous nurses fussing around her, checking her vital signs to make sure that there were no lingering effects from her dehydration.

Nayanna had no idea where Sky slept but as soon as she was fit to get out of bed, a compassionate woman caregiver helped her to where her father still lay.

"Have you seen Sky, Dad?"

"Yes, yes," her father nodded. "He was by your side the whole time, he just shortly came to check on me. He is probably on his way over to where you were. Just wait here for him. Sit here on the bed while I get ready."

The nightmare of Hamasa cutting Sky's head off with a machete was still vivid in her mind and frightening. It was all she could do to force herself to stay put and when Sky walked in, she was so relieved that for a moment she thought she was about to pass out again. She clung to him, trembling, as he did his best to reassure her.

"I think your nightmare scared everyone more than you passing out," he told her. "Yes," he said, smiling at her embarrassment, "everyone's talking about you screaming, 'Don't kill him'." He glanced around. "Where's your dad?"

Nayanna pointed to the washroom and Sky nodded and gave her a long, comforting hug.

Nayanna rested her head against his chest, letting some of the tension ease out of her. "I still have to tell Hamasa about us – that we're married, so I guess it's weighing on my conscience." Nayanna paused. "I'm going to do that the first chance I get." Managing a small smile, she said, "You've been so fantastic about all this, Sky. I was so scared of what you'd do—"

Nayanna was interrupted by her dad bustling back into the room. He had fallen asleep with his turban on but now he busied himself taking it off so he could put it back on to appear well turned out and respectful.

"You are my only true family, Nayanna," he said, "and I want you to know I am so proud of you. When I heard you married a Canadian, I imagined the typical beer-drinking, hockey obsessed, tattooed, swearing, but polite, bushman I drive around in my taxi all day." He turned to Sky. "To my astonishment, you are a Master loving, meditating, vegetarian who doesn't drink beer. Go figure, 'eh'. I am so proud of you, too, Sky. The Master has used you to bring us back to the fold. In our past lives, as the Master pointed out to me, Nayanna and I always served the Perfect Master personally, and he promises this is our last time on the wheel of karma, we will not have to come back to this land of tears any more. We have been promised eternal life in the higher planes of existence, through initiation by the Master."

"Look, this is so good," Nayanna cut in. "Maybe we could eat first, before we meditate? Are you both feeling OK this morning? Sky, how's your stomach? Let's see if we can bring the food here, so we can keep bonding and not be interrupted. I wish we could move here and never have to go back. I feel like we're all so safe here and no harm can come to any of us, if we only stay here."

She knew there was no way to fight fate and the karma waiting for them, but she had to say it anyway. It was so easy to be spiritual and feel fulfilled at the ashram, but she knew the second they stepped out it would be a struggle to keep the soul alive. They were rising above their karma here instead of being beaten to the bottom by it. What evil awaited them, she did not want to imagine. She kept on repeating: compliant, agreeable, persuadable, acquiescent, resigned. Maybe her new mantras were working after all, for the moment anyway.

Chapter 23

'The Bomb'

"A hero is someone who has given his or her life to something bigger than oneself."
Joseph Campbell

Hamasa knew Nayanna thought he was her worst karma, a nice, perfect dream that became twisted, turned freaky, and decomposed into her worst nightmare. He felt bad he was never around to work things out: there was no longer any communication. He knew she had no way to contact him, and with his parents gone as well, there was no way to find him. She had slowly got on with her life, without realizing he was fully aware of her every move.

Hamasa relocated when his parents moved on and sold the house. They didn't want any loose ends holding them back or connecting them to where they were hiding. They had also left him with a large bank account, which greatly helped him to be flexible and hard to locate, a necessity in his line of work. He had no fixed address and moved around, often staying out of the country for extended periods.

His involvement in tracking down documents and the ever present spectra of the mafia carried him all over the world. Now he was in the middle of planning the absurdist terrorist attack the world had ever seen, against God Himself, and the God-men that represented Him on Earth. He had put together the best team and the best plan he could. They were waiting for the perfect moment to strike.

'The Bomb', Hamasa's terrorist friend, was in his second week of settling in and preparing. They were hiding out in the suburbs of West Chicago.

"Now that I'm here in the evil USA, it's so different than what I imagined. Even if we didn't kill all these infidels, their lifestyles will. After seeing all the American ads and movies, I thought all the women here would be thin and beautiful. Most are all blown up like balloons and too ugly to rape."

Hamasa chuckled. "And you can add downright mean and nasty to that list. Some aren't afraid to whip your ass, so be careful."

"Yeah, nowadays, you just look at a woman here and you can end up in jail. Damn feminists, just another play for money and power. So when do I meet your little lady, a Paki right, better be a Muslim, right? Ooh, so you thought you'd keep that a secret did you?" The Bomb smirked at Hamasa's shock. Stoking his long beard and rubbing his shiny, bald head while flexing his Arnold Schwarzenegger biceps he continued. "I like to use my intelligence training for extracurricular activities, too. You wouldn't believe how fun it can be finding out what neighbors and friends are really up to."

"So you probably think Canada is just a few miles from here, along with the Pacific Ocean and the Rocky Mountains?" Hamasa teased. "No, she's a long way from here, and speaking of rocky, well that just about sums it up. Gotta keep my mind on business. I don't know how you manage being married, with kids, and still being able to keep your head in the game. She kept nagging me for marriage and kids, but I couldn't even begin to think of it with all this going on. I think I've lost her now, to another guy, and if not him, then her father's got her set up with an arranged marriage back in India. So I'm screwed. I did some homegrown espionage on her, too. I went away – it was her big test to see if she could hold us together and she eff'd it up big time."

"Let's see the intel," Bomb's voice was sympathetic. "Any pics? When I run into the guy at the hotel, I'll take him out for you." He laughed loudly. "Allah have mercy, there you go again, shittin' your pants. Don't look so surprised. You're gettin' sloppy,

Hamasa. You've got Nayanna and Sky written on your calendar over there, landing in Chicago two days before that Master guy gives his talk. You don't think I can put two and two together?"

"Hey, you just stay out of my business," Hamasa snarled, "you got that. You don't go near them. Come on – let's get back to work here. We've got a lot of stuff to get through." He stormed over to a large pile of unopened boxes stacked up in the living room. Furnishings were sparse but even the couches were pushed out of the way to make room. "What the hell are these?" He pulled one down and opened it, his jaw dropping at the contents. "What the hell are you thinking?"

"Hey, don't take your failed relationship out on me," The Bomb snapped. "I had nothing to do with you being away all the time. You're the one who said no outside communications 'til this is over." He nodded toward the box. "And that's an effing bomb. What the hell does it look like? You said we needed some diversion and distraction for the cops, well there it is – '9/11' seems like a long time ago. Mr. Bin Laden would be proud to know someone's shaking up the USA again." He bared his teeth in an approximation of a smile. "Don't worry, the other boxes are all medical equipment and supplies. If anything goes wrong, we'll end up here for treatment."

Hamasa dry washed his face. "Shit, you're right, I can't get her off my mind – she's the only woman I can imagine being with, the only mother for my children." He stared at the box. "This'll take out a city block! It's all blowing up in my face now," he muttered. "I might as well go out with these explosives."

"Hey, don't make yourself a liability here," The Bomb grated. "You're a warrior, stay focused. You did everything you could. Sometimes it's just the way it's meant to be. Let it go, Mas."

"How'd you know that was my nick name? No one's called me Mas since I was a teen."

"OK, so you're really that out of it? The picture in your wallet – of you in the corvette, it says, 'Hey, Mas, get out of my car'. I mean, that was a big hint, right?"

"Wow, you really don't have any sense of boundaries, or decency, do ya'."

"Ha-ha, listen to you! A terrorist's gotta' know who he's workin' with whatever way he can, right? Besides, I needed a few bucks to get a coffee – you owed me one, right?"

"OK, I'll get the past out of my mind if you can just stay the hell out of my personal life, agreed? You were never like this before, on the other jobs." Hamasa walked across to the low coffee table and dropped onto the edge of the black leather La-Z-Boy recliner. "Let's go over some of the details, shall we? We can't afford any mistakes. You with me?" Hamasa asked.

He couldn't let his friend get under his skin. He proceeded to spread out the plans he had drawn up and that he hoped would rock the world.

"So I'll bring the old man back here. We'll have medical personal at the ready in case anything goes wrong. You can take the young one to your secret location and meet your crew there. Once the coast's clear, you know where to find me. I just need two men with me at all times," Hamasa stated. "Remember, none of us are captured alive – take these cyanide capsules. Take enough for everyone who's in on the deal, and one for the Successor fellow you'll be handling. We don't want any loose ends now, do we?"

The Bomb nodded. "Agreed."

Hamasa stuffed a few of the capsules into his own jacket pocket and left to pick the others up. The bullet had left the gun.

Chapter 24

Chicago

"Seek the darkness; it holds the secrets of light."
John H. K. Fisher

Back home in Vancouver, Nayanna and Sky rented an apartment while they looked for a suitable house for themselves. Most things were still in boxes, piled up in the bedroom, though many months had flown by. That's why Nayanna spent much of her time at her dad's place. The apartment was the cheapest they could find, but as long as they had each other it didn't matter they were sleeping in the living room. They were having a rare, special moment hanging out in their own space.

"Nayanna, guess what?" Sky teased.

"What now, my boy wonder?" Nayanna teased back.

"OK, I'll get right to the punch. I can't take the suspense any longer." Sky laughed. "We're going to see the Master in the windy city. 'New York, New York'", he hummed. "Oops, that's the wrong Frankie tune, it's actually… 'Chicago, Chicago that toddling town'."

"What! We're going to Chicago?" screamed Nayanna, as she jumped into Sky's arms and wrapped her legs around his waist. He ended up on the floor while she stood over him.

"Can we bring Dad? Chicago, Chicago, that toddling town," Nayanna tried to pick up the tune while dancing around in her underwear.

"Woo, I think we better learn the tune first," Sky fired back as he picked himself off the floor. "Apparently the Master's going straight from India to Chicago to introduce His Successor. Although He lives and has His ashram in New York City they've decided to have everyone meet in Chicago. I guess, now that he's getting older, he wants everyone to know who will carry on God's work here on Earth. I've read that the Master has to transfer his God given power to his Successor through the eyes. That's how the new Master acquires all his capabilities. Yeah, so I wonder if that's taking place there as well. Sounds kinda like Earth shattering stuff, kinda spooky, too," Sky told her, laughing. "I'm actually working on a song I hope I'm allowed to sing for the Master. I'll play it for you later…'God is love and love is God and the way back to God is love'". Sky sang to her.

"Sky, it sounds fantastic! I can't wait to hear the whole thing! So you already bought the tickets?"

"You betcha I did, and we're staying right at the hotel where the Master's giving all the talks."

They had decided to arrive in Chicago a couple of days early, so they could look around. The hotel was nothing fancy, but it boasted a pool, and it was more than they'd expected for the price. Three nights at the feet of the Master and then Sky was going to take Nayanna to see Niagara Falls. That's where they would really splurge and treat themselves.

"I can't believe you got this room overlooking the pool! You know how the sight of water makes me feel!" Nayanna complained as she settled into their suite, head drooping and shuffling slowly about.

"But we're three floors up, and look, there are trees that come up right outside the balcony so we can hardly even see the pool. I thought it would be romantic to have this view. On the other side there are no views. As we saw coming here, the hotel's in the middle of an industrial complex, out near the airport, on the outskirts of Chicago. Even on the top floors there's nothing to see, no views of the city. Remember how romantic our engagement was and our wedding was…by the water? You survived that!"

"Romantic! Romance is the last thing you should think about when you're around the Master," Nayanna stormed. "I hope you aren't planning to knock me off the bed and onto the floor again! Romance! Then why are there two beds in this room, huh? Listen, we still have time before the Master arrives for the big formal event. I think I'll take a walk around and maybe I can inquire at the front desk about changing rooms."

Sky closed his eyes. His head was pounding, his stomach churned and to top it all, he had totally forgotten about Nayanna's fear of water and how it brought up memories of her mother's death: not a good start to things. Somewhere in the back of his head he had hoped that after all the time she had spent meditating, she would have transcended the problem by now.

Sky loved the water. He frowned; he supposed he had better tell Nayanna about their surprise trip to Niagara Falls as soon as she came back. He took out his guitar, at least he could do some more work on his new song. But he wasn't feeling at all well and after only a few minutes he put the instrument aside and lay down. In an instant, he had dosed off.

Nayanna's return woke him up and it was with some relief that he saw she looked a little happier.

"We might be able to change rooms later," she informed him, "when the front desk manager comes back on shift. So let's check out Chicago, if you're up to it. Actually, you don't look too good."

"You got that right! Let's head out tomorrow. It's too late now anyway. We can use room service, cuddle in front of the television and make plans. For sure I want to check out a blues joint tomorrow. How about you?"

"You know…what we talked about…a nice dinner overlooking a pretty view. Hey, I thought you booked a tour."

"Yes, I did, so the day's all planned. I'm not gettin' outta' this bed, so you might as well climb in with me." Sky chuckled.

Even though he wasn't feeling well, the next day they had a wonderful time and ended up staying late at the blues club. After sleeping in, he thought it best they spend time in meditation to re-focus their minds back on the reason they were there. Sky fell asleep as usual and when he woke up, Nayanna had already dolled up for the big event and went to secure good seats. Sky hopped in the shower, hoping it would help to revive him before the Master began his talk. The shower helped, but he was still feeling sick. If it was the flu, he hoped he wouldn't be throwing up during the event. He decided he could always make it back to the room if he had to, so he headed for the ballroom. By the time he reached the ground floor the pain in his gut had increased, he squatted down, his back against the wall, facing the elevator. The elevator door opened and the Master's Successor poured out with a large entourage. To Sky's amazement, He came right over to him and helped him stand up. The moment He touched Sky, all his pain and flu symptoms disappeared.

"You should let the Master know when you are having troubles," he told him gently. "The Master will always help in any way He can."

"Th–thank you!" Sky stuttered, blown away by having the same thing happen to him here as in India with the Master.

The Successor smiled. "You know, the Master really likes your music and the special song you have written for Him."

A flood of emotions swept over Sky and he fell back to the floor, crying and thanking the Successor and the Master for everything. With a big grin, the Successor carried on to the ballroom, leaving Sky in utter bewilderment at how He had known who he was and that he had written a special song for the Master.

The evening was pure magic for both Sky and Nayanna. There were wonderful performances by incredible musicians and the talk the Master gave was soul inspiring. As Sky listened to the Master, he experienced the Master changing forms, as he had seen previously in India. This time he saw him change into the Successor as well. Nayanna also continued having the experience of hearing incredible symphonies, which, she told Sky, she was starting to realize were emanating from within her own mind or perhaps from her soul or were a beckoning from God.

After the talk, the Master quickly left, but His Successor had a private pizza party just for the initiates in his huge suite on the top floor.

As the hour grew late, the Successor clapped his hands for silence. "Tomorrow," he said, "I want you all to come to the main ballroom one hour before the Master is to arrive." His glance travelled around the room. "I will be there, and I will personally help each one of you with any questions or problems you may wish to discuss." He smiled. "We will also meditate with the help of a special treat of Parshad," he added.

The group was to meet after lunch, at two o'clock. The Master would arrive at three to give a special talk to all the children and their parents. All were welcome to the afternoon talks. Then they would share a meal with the Master before that evening's formal talk, during which the Master would perform a special ceremony to pass His power over to His Successor.

The gathering went on late into the night as the group was plied with treat after treat, as well as spiritual stories of all the Masters throughout history and the mystical, miraculous, mysterious myths that surrounded them. Many of the initiates that were there shared a special poem or song for the Master. Everyone sang along to the songs they knew.

"I myself," the Successor told them, "have been a successful software developer, working for a company in the US. I have a wife and three children." He smiled kindly, opening his arms. "So, you can see that a person does not have to leave the world to be spiritual.

"My Father, who is the Master, has always worked in the world. He can predict future events and when the things he sees are bad, he never spares himself in trying to help others. Once, he even became sick trying to save others from the cold."

Finding himself deluged by questions about the afterlife and God's purpose, he laughingly replied they should stop asking so many complicated questions about the deep mysteries of God and instead enjoy the moment together in laughter and song.

"I believe that now is the perfect time for Sky here," as He pointed to him, "to sing a special song he wrote for the Master."

Nayanna sent out a shrill and everyone clapped in anticipation.

"Only if everyone sings along," Sky replied as he was handed a guitar to play.

"God is Love and Love is God and the way back to God is love.
God is Love and Love is God and the way back to God is love
Master our Lord; rejoice for he has come.
Eyes that beam the way, His face outshines the sun.
He comes to join us with God's love
He comes to join us with God's love."

Everyone joined in, including the Successor. When they were finished, the Master gave the greatest compliment by asking for the last verse to be sung again. He went on to give a talk based on the words Sky had written. Sky had the greatest spiritual day of his life and was so proud to have shared it with Nayanna.

The late night had turned to early morning by the time they got back to their room. They slept like babies and didn't even wake in time for lunch, never mind breakfast. By the time they had washed and dressed, it was almost time for the afternoon meetings. Nayanna hurriedly disappeared back into the bathroom to apply her makeup. They had missed morning meditation so Sky thought he could squeeze in a few minutes of bliss while Nayanna got herself ready. He had learned early on in the relationship that it was best to let her have the washroom all to herself when she was getting her face on, ready to go out. Today was different; she was ready more quickly than usual and was out the door on a mission to see if they could change rooms away from the pool. They had completely forgotten to inquire about it before, so she let Sky meditate alone.

Absorbed in meditation, or maybe sleep, Sky became aware of an insistent pounding.

"Sky, Sky, open the door, I forgot my key. Sky, please, this is urgent, hurry!"

The terror in Nayanna's voice instantly brought Sky out of the deep zone. Panicked, thinking he might have meditated too long and missed the meetings, he sprang into action. "What is it, babe?" he asked, pulling open the door.

Nayanna stared at him, wide eyed and trembling. "It's Hamasa! I'm sure I saw him dressed up in a bellman's outfit. He walked through the lobby on his way to the ballroom." She cradled her face in her hands. "Oh, Sky! I'm sure it was him! Anyway, I thought, screw it, I'm going to settle this now. I ran after him but he disappeared. I asked at the front desk if they knew anyone by the name of Hamasa working here and they said no – maybe he used a false name."

Sky drew her into his arms. "OK, baby, it's gonna' be OK." He planted a kiss on her forehead. "I've had it with this guy. We made a promise to each other, so now we're gonna' call the police and give them all the info we have." He frowned. "Too bad we don't have a photo of him. Is there anything on the internet, anything that would have his picture? We could show it around and see if anyone recognizes him.

"What time is it? Has the event started, what's going on out there?"

Nayanna made a visible effort to pull herself together. "There are a lot of people here already but they're mostly just milling around because they announced the 2:00 p.m. meeting with the Successor was canceled."

"OK," Sky said, trying for calm and not quite hitting it, "you phone the police and I'm going to get security. I'll be right back."

"No! Please don't leave me!"

"I have to let them know what's happening, Nayanna. Look, I'll be as quick as I can and when I come back I'll say Chicago, Chicago, OK? That way you can lock everything up tight and you'll know it's me."

Sky was out the door and running for security. What the hell was Hamasa doing here? Was he just a harmless snake or were their lives in danger, he worried?

Back in their room, the seconds seemed like hours. Nayanna struggled to control her shaking enough to dial 911.

"Hello, I need the police – someone's going to attack me and my husband."

"Please stay calm, miss. Has anyone been attacked yet?" asked the dispatcher.

"No, but I need the police here right away."

"Miss, are you in a safe place?"

"Yes, we are at a hotel, but my husband is out of the room looking for security and he could be attacked."

"Has anybody been attacked, has your husband been attacked?"

"No, but..."

"Miss, you need to phone the local police and file a complaint."

"What, you're not going to help?"

"Miss, stay calm! Call us if someone is attacked."

"What, I can't call if someone is about to be attacked? This can't be happening! So call when someone's dead but don't call if I need help preventing someone's death: 'catch 22', I guess. Please, just send the police. I don't have time for your freakin' protocols or to look up the number."

Sitting on the edge of the bed, Nayanna stared at her mobile, her mind racing; her heart was thumping so hard she could hear it in her ears. For some reason, something compelled her to throw down the phone and bolt out to the balcony. Looking down she saw Sky topple into the pool. A scream tore from her throat but no one seemed to hear. People were stampeding past the front lobby area like wild buffalo. No one seemed to be aware of what had happened to Sky. Without a thought for her safety, with the instincts of a monkey, Nayanna thought she would leap from the balcony onto one of the trees outside and scurry down. It wasn't until she reached the elevator that she realized she took the long, safe way. The seconds waiting were beyond bearing and she ran, looking for the stairs. It wasn't until she heard the ding of the elevator and the door opened that she realized she didn't find the door to the stairs and that she must have taken the elevator. Reaching the pool, she stopped, terror washing over her. She *had* to do this, she told herself, there was no one else. She had to overcome her fear of water or Sky would drown. She rushed down the steps to the shallow end and pulling in a deep breath, she dived into the water. Sky was at the bottom of the pool. Around him the water was rapidly turning red. Nayanna slid her hands under his armpits, struggling to lift him. With precious seconds at stake, arms reached down to her, dragging her and Sky to the surface. Nayanna's head broke water and she gasped in another spluttering breath. "Help me! Please! Help me – my husband's been shot!"

"Do you know CPR?" asked the man who dragged them from the water.

"No, please help!" Nayanna pleaded.

As the man performed CPR, Nayanna ripped off her jacket and tried to cover the hole where blood was pouring out. She wanted to scream at the people gathering for what she overheard.

"He's a goner, look at all the blood," said one stranger.

"If he's one of the kidnappers, then let him die," said another.

"Kidnapper? What happened here? Who was kidnapped?" asked yet another onlooker.

"Help, call the police, call an ambulance!" Nayanna screamed.

"Yes, I have called, please be calm, everything will be OK," a woman responded.

"The Master was kidnapped, right in front of the hotel, very shocking. And the Successor is also missing and nowhere to be found." The voices around Nayanna kept bombarding her mind.

"They will need all the evidence they can get from here. They're actually contaminating the crime scene," another onlooker commented.

"Go away! Get the fuck out of here if you won't help! Go!" Nayanna screamed, looking straight into the eyes of the strangers, not able to take it any longer.

Nayanna would not let go of Sky, even while the paramedics loaded him into the ambulance. 'Hamasa did this! Hamasa did this! What took you guys so long?"

"Miss, you'll have to come with us. We'll take you to the hospital. What is your relationship to the gentleman?" the police officer asked.

"He... he's my husband! Promise he'll be OK!"

Chapter 25

The Big Plan

"Oh murderous life!
How dare you ask that we be calm and compliant!
If we rebel against your reckless ways, it's only that we wish not to add to your indifference."
John H. K. Fisher

Hamasa was exhausted, he was also very hungry and wondered when Harold and the food would arrive, but the 'liquid truth' surging through his brain urged him to carry on.

"The documents have a lot in common with all the main world religions, but with some obvious differences. One problem is there are many different branches within each religion, all proclaiming different truths. This makes the search for God and truth very difficult because a person can never know for certain where the truth lies. Also, there are the many conflicting translations and interpretations of all the words within the scriptures. I was always inspired by the words of Jesus, '…seek and ye shall find.' St. Matthew 7:7

"These words kept me strong in my search for truth. All religions preach of the significance of a Master and I really began to recognize how fortunate those souls were that met the living Son of God while He was on Earth. Jesus said to his disciples, 'for verily I say unto you that many prophets and righteous men have desired to see those things which ye see and have not seen them and to hear those things which ye hear and have not heard them.' St. Matthew 13:17. The Buddha supposedly said if you want enlightenment then go to one who is enlightened.

"Jesus said, '…and no man knoweth the Son but the Father, neither knoweth any man the Father save the Son and he to whomsoever the Son will reveal Him.' St. Matthew 11:27.

"Kabir and Nanak of the Sikh religion stated very clearly that only through the Master could a soul find God. At the time, it made sense to me, because in all spheres of life there is always at least one genius who surpasses all others. There is always a musical genius, a scientific genius, a genius inventor or a genius at some sport. Therefore, it made sense that there might be a spiritual genius. If God and spirit existed, it seemed possible that a man might have reached that lofty level of oneness with God. Obviously, if God is a fabricated fantasy then there can't be anybody who is one with Him, including all the past Masters such as Jesus. They would then be geniuses at deception, delusion and salesmanship. It became very clear that I had at least to try to find out if there was a living Master or Son of God that I could apprehend. I knew I'd have to go to the cradle of spirituality to complete my research. I'd have to go to India and travel as either a seeker or perhaps an initiate. I would have to investigate the places where the Masters lived.

"I came across a spiritual path that really seemed to have a lot in common with the ideas revealed in the documents. They were based out of India and called themselves: 'The New Spiritual Scientific Universal Truth Movement.' We focused many of our tactics towards this group in the hope their teacher or prophet was a true living Master. However, they were splintered into competing groups, and within each cluster there were those who proclaimed to be the Master. Each had followers who would sacrifice their lives to prove they had the one truth and the true Master. I attended a talk in the United States given by one of these Masters and it was like finding the mother lode. Astonishingly, it was as if the Guru was reading from one of the documents itself. He said that God wanted to play a game but wanted to make sure He or goodness was not favored in any way to win. He said that God could end the game at any time but preferred to keep the game going, for fun. He compared it to watching a sports match.

'It's boring,' he said, 'when a really great team opposes a really bad team and the great team always wins. There's no contest. People gain more enjoyment and don't get bored when teams are equally matched or when they take turns winning. This presents some unpredictability in the outcome, there's some suspense when you can only guess who might win. If God had the upper hand and could always wipe out evil, Kal or the devil's team, then what would be the fun?'

"I couldn't believe what I was hearing; it clarified exactly what the documents were trying to express – how God will do anything to keep from getting bored. I made sure this Master was on our hit list. This kind of thinking is how psychopaths justify their evilness. No wonder the world is so screwed up and divided against itself. In Canada, the police caught a psychopath filming himself killing people. He said the killing was necessary to make the movie that he was shooting better and more realistic. Pretty much the same justification this Master used for why God has to kill everyone. Nevertheless, it was exactly how some of the documents described God.

"We were able to narrow the list down to five contenders that we would kidnap. The police and the intelligence agencies were completely caught off guard and didn't give us any concern. Who's going to spend money protecting Gurus? The main problem was the followers who were always hanging on the Master's shirttail. The local police would be the first to be notified, so we created diversions. Most of the kidnappings would happen in broad daylight, right in front of many observers. The escape routes were paramount and meticulously planned.

"After a year of preparation, I felt we were ready. We had closely monitored the targets, studying their every move. The signal was given for each cell of the terror network to spring into action.

"I took on the Master from Toronto, Canada. I tell you, it's quite remarkable that these so-called Godmen can run around doing their thing, building huge followings, raising funds and building empires, all with impunity. I mean, there's only one true Master according to the documents, yet all these others are committing fraud, probably raking in millions, yet governments around the world allow it to happen. We don't even know for sure if God exists and yet they allow religions and so called Masters to build these huge empires. The Pope's even allowed to have his own country to rule from and collects roughly one trillion dollars a year.

"I discovered immediately that I didn't have the Perfect Master. The Guru I'd kidnapped broke down and admitted right away that he was a fake and was only in it for the fame and money. Those who had the real power and controlled the followers and money had coerced him into it. He told me they wanted to keep the followers united, happy and continuing to constantly donate money. He showed me documents that described secret signs that can verify a true Master. A true Master will have the symbol of the lotus flower formed from the lines of his hands and feet. He showed me his hands and feet had no such lines. I asked him how he could live with himself, deceiving all the people? He merely replied that everyone in society was doing the same and if he hadn't agreed, someone else would have. That it was tradition after all. How else would he get such a great life and be taken care of in old age?

"I asked him, 'Do you think God or any of the tales of God or Masters are true?'

"He explained it was what the people wanted and what the people were willing to pay for. He said people needed to believe in a God whether it was true or not. How else could they face death, disease and the inhumanity of man towards his fellow man? Believing in God and His punishment was the only way people could get revenge on all the wrongdoers who got away with their crimes. They needed to believe that God would be the final judge and send them to eternal hell and suffering. But he admitted that from all his years of experience, he had found no proof of the existence of God or of a 'Perfect' Master, but that supporting the idea made a great business."

"Do you have a wife and children?" Hamasa asked.

"Yes," he said, "certainly, a Master may lead a normal life to show that it is possible for everyone. Is that your point?

"Well," Hamasa said, "you clearly must know that you are not the Perfect Master. So what have you told your wife and children? How were you able to keep it a secret from them?"

"Oh," he said, "I see what you're getting at. Well, yes, of course. The mafia boss doesn't go home and tell his loving family how many people he had to steal from or kill that day. The politician doesn't go home and tell his family about all the lies he has to tell to the people he governs to keep them from rebelling. The doctor doesn't go home and tell the wife and kids about the organs he removed that day or if mistakes were made that led to a patient's death. A person does what a person has to do to survive. The deceptions and lies start right from birth and are well documented by therapists and the courts. By puberty, the effects are life shattering as the male will lie and do anything to spread his seed to as many egg bearing beauties as possible, while women will do anything and lie to obtain security, their nest and offspring. A man will say many things to 'hook up' but none of them will come close to the truth. If men and women were honest with each other, they'd go without sex or go broke paying for it. They'd never mate and the human race would cease to exist. Lies are what keep us alive."

"I had a laugh at that. The stories poured out of him like water from a faucet and I just let him ramble on and listened."

"Look at all the conspiracies throughout history," he babbled, "and all the lies that were kept secret. For many years the governments have been spying on all their citizens and on other countries by recording their phone calls, which is illegal. Yet it was kept a secret, until one day, Russ Tice, in 2005, poor soul, revealed the truth. However, look how many said nothing and for how many years. That proves that conspiracies do happen and that many people exercise their power over others to keep them secret – 9/11 was probably an inside job."

Hamasa continued speaking into the recorder. "Anyway, he was told to destroy the documents, but he hadn't. He told me that the One who was called the real Master was in New York City, but was dying of old age. So right away, I regrouped and made contact with the cell that had kidnapped that Master. I had, of course, already set up the emergency procedures."

"So what's that you're saying, Hamasa?" Harold inquired as he re-entered the room with some food. "'Emergency procedures'?"

"What else do you want from me? I'm telling you everything that happened!" Hamasa pleaded.

Harold set down a plate of sandwiches and a flask of coffee on the table, in plain view of Hamasa. "Well, if you want to earn your food, you'll need to be a little more forthcoming. How did you find out about the Master in India? Was it from spying on Nayanna? We have the bullet that was fired into the apartment in Vancouver and I can't wait to see if it was fired from your gun." Harold shook his head. "There's so much evidence stacked against you, Hamasa. Shall I tell you what I think happened? I think you followed her to India and that's how you found out about the Master. You weren't interested in getting to the truth by kidnapping him. You were only interested in getting revenge on Sky by going after his Master. It's obvious! You're a terrorist who had no interest in Masters until Nayanna had one. Isn't that right? Are you sure you kidnapped the Guru in Toronto? Wasn't it you that kidnapped the Master from New York, while He was in Chicago? Are you sure you're telling us everything? Tell us what you know about Sky, Nayanna's husband?"

Hamasa lifted his head and his eyes cleared for a moment.

"How long you been spying on me from behind that glass wall? Wait! We don't have time to go into all this mess. I'm here to help Nayanna and save the world. Those are my only goals now and if I have to go down for shooting Sky, then so be it, but it'll only happen after Nayanna's safely home and by the will of God. But I had nothing to do with Sky's murder! Now," Hamasa fastened his attention on the food, "can I have something to eat?" Harold made no move toward making that happen.

Hamasa allowed himself a tight smile. "I won't be any good to you if I pass out from hunger."

Slowly, Harold handed over the sandwiches and poured some coffee, standing back as Hamasa wolfed it down.

He was sure Hamasa still had no idea that Nayanna wasn't and never had been a prisoner. In fact, Nayanna was the reason Hamasa had been caught.

"How did you know Sky was shot if you weren't there?" Harold asked, his patience frayed by the long hours of questioning and waiting. "How do you know how Sky was murdered? If you weren't the one who murdered him, then who is? We can cover your butt for a lot of things, but not the murder of an innocent civilian. The Americans want answers. They want justice. They're not going to drop this until they vindicate themselves and provide a suspect. They're not going to be the ones looking stupid on this one – not to mention the broad daylight kidnapping of spiritual leaders. How do you explain that as part of your job?" Harold buried his face in his hands as he realized he had had enough.

"Hold on a minute here!" Hamasa shot back in desperation. "Do you know who you're threatening here? Our government sent me into hell on 9/11. Did you think I'd take that to my grave or that I wouldn't use that as collateral to save my ass in a situation like this? I have everything documented. You think the world wouldn't like to know how the Israelis were involved with 9/11? If anything happens to me then the cat is out of the bag. Israel will be screwed in front of the whole world. They'd have to start their secret 'One World Government' operation the next day. World War III would follow! You want that on your head, Harold?"

"I have no idea what you're talking about!" screamed Harold. "I don't believe a word you're saying! You're just stalling; the Israelis had nothing to do with 9/11, and you know it! There is no secret operation! Now, you either answer my questions here and now or I'm finished! I've had enough of this bullshit. I'll throw you back to your two good friends to work it out of you."

As Harold got up to leave, he noticed the crowd had started to gather again outside the cell gate.

"OK, people, the party's over. Get back to your jobs or I'll have you all court-martialed for deserting your posts. Take all your ridiculous idol worshipping stuff with you…now!"

He whirled around to Hamasa. "Can you explain any of this to me? What's going on here?"

Hamasa grinned from ear to ear. "The Power, Harold! The Power is coming, you'll see. It has nothing to do with me. You'll know what it is … soon."

Chapter 26

Interrogation of the Master

"This life we live is a strange dream, and I don't believe at all any account men give of it."
Henry David Thoreau

Hamasa sighed, the coffee and sandwiches demolished, Harold was already pushing him for more answers, more information.

"The kidnappings went smoothly, with no major setbacks," he told his impatient interrogator. "The different cells with their hostages were able to make it to their pre-planned destinations." Hamasa paused, images vividly unrolling before his mind's eye. All the events that led up to meeting the Master were still so clear, carved into his very being for an eternity.

"I got back to the house and entered the room where the Master was being held and I could immediately see that something unusual had the medics in a twitch.

"I remember," Hamasa's voice was hesitant, his eyes growing distant, "His voice was very gentle, calm and candid for a man who was surrounded by a group of armed terrorists and medical personnel, and who had just been kidnapped at gun point."

"Ha...It's a good thing you people travel with doctors," the Master said jovially, "my heart stopped beating about a week ago." He glanced toward the medical equipment and chuckled. "Your doctor, with his machines, has been unable to measure or detect the spirit, the love that runs in my veins, keeping me alive. God's love has many mysteries and I'm sure you're about to be shocked and awed." The Master laughed again, the sound filled with unadulterated joy.

Hamasa shot a questioning look at the doctor, who shook his

head, bewildered.

"This man has no pulse, he's flat lining the machine."

"Well, if it's OK with our guest, and if you think he's fine, then maybe we could be left alone for a while," Hamasa said, excitement beating a thready tattoo through his veins.

The Master beamed. "Yes, yes, that is fine, but we actually don't have as much time as you might hope."

Hamasa glanced suspiciously at the Master. "OK, I admit I hoped for a bit more control over the situation but this isn't a very typical hostage situation now is it? Anyway, I hope you've had a chance to review the documents and letter that explains why you're here. And I hope you're ready to do some serious negotiating for the benefit of all humanity. My only goal is to end death, pain, war, evil and suffering for all souls, including the animals and plants. Some animals will have to be changed or modified though, like mosquitoes – we just don't want them in the 'New World'. Predators will no longer be allowed to kill to survive. All creatures will be modified to abide on delicious inanimate cuisine, and to get along with each other without having to tear each other apart for food."

Hamasa gave the Master a long, searching look. "Are you willing to cooperate with us?" he asked. "You must have read our manifesto by now and our letter of demands. Let's go through each condition, each question that we demand an honest answer to."

Hamasa pulled out the document and spread it before the Master and together they went through each point. Hamasa was still studying the Master intently. "I don't want to aid God in any way," he said. "I'm not going to help God force souls into this physical world of death, pain and suffering. I also don't want God to force me to be here. I'd prefer not to exist in body, mind or soul. If I were God, I'd free all souls and grant them eternal life and love. Then I'd create the most amazing robots that could explore the physical Universe and report to all the souls and to

God on how amazing the whole of creation is.

"Oh, and by the way, I was told my parents were killed, and I was wondering if you could make sure that they're OK, and please don't send them to hell. You have to understand they lived through extraordinary times that surely forced them to do what they did.

"I'm sorry for going on and on, but I read your books, and you said the greatest moment in a person's life is when they start to question why they're born, whether there is a God, and what happens to us after we die. You say in your books that, 'seeing is believing.' So I guess I'm getting a little carried away with my questions, but it comes from the promise 'if we seek we shall find'. So, is there really a God who created the Universe, or did it all happen by some cosmic fluke and we only evolved through natural selection? What created life or the big bang in the first place? There could be a million explanations that don't involve God or a creator – especially a loving God. An evil God – now that's something that might make sense to me!"

Now that he had started, the questions flooded out of him, hardly giving him pause for breath. He went through all the demands that were written down and then some. All the while the Master sat unperturbed, radiating an aura of peace and love, a love that reached out to Hamasa in a visceral fashion, threatening his own composure. "I understand we interrupted a very important ceremony," Hamasa continued, "where you were supposed to pass your duties and Power onto your Successor. Will what we've done stop God from forcing souls into this misery of death and war?"

For some reason Hamasa felt himself to be standing on the edge of an abyss, as if one more step would see him spiraling into nothingness, into some space where the laws of the Universe were outside of his comprehension. The idea both thrilled and terrified him. "I'm...completely committed to getting to the truth, and as I'm sure you know, we have your son, your Successor, so if you don't want to see him tortured and eventually killed, you'd better start talking!"

The Master's eyes twinkled. "Well there, young man! Now that was a mouthful. I think we'll have to back up a bit on this one. It's a little more complicated than that, as you're about to find out."

The Master treated Hamasa to another unconcerned smile. "The job of being Master is not as easy as you might think. I know you're not up to the task, but you've left me little choice in the matter."

It was at that point that Hamasa realized he was not in control of anything that was happening. The Master looked intently into his eyes as he was drawn into a state of exquisite surrender. Pictures flashed across his vision and he saw the Master morph into different people that he somehow knew were other past Masters: Kabir, Nanak, Jesus, Buddha, Rumi, and many others. Finally, he recognized him changing into the future Successor. Even though the Master was only ten feet in front of Hamasa, he saw Him disappear into a blaze of light as a gust of air swirled around him. The Master floated upwards, surrounded by light and Hamasa watched with bated breath as a huge, golden throne revealed itself, surrounded by all the Masters that had lived and died on Earth since the beginning of time. Pillars of gold shot up from the ground and many angels or beings of light stood around the throne, but everyone was looking at the Master ascend it. The angels placed a huge jeweled crown on His head and the light of many suns seemed to pour forth from the crown. The Master stepped down; the crown was removed and placed on the Successor, who then also ascended the throne. The same light of many suns again emanated from the crown. The Master lay down and appeared to die. Everyone rushed to His side and the Successor held Him in His arms. The whole time the amazing sounds of bells ringing and angels singing could be heard. Hamasa recalled the stories he had read in the Bible describing similar scenes. Revelation 4:1, 2: 'and immediately I was in the spirit and behold a throne was set in heaven and one sat on the throne.' Moreover, 1:10: 'I was in the spirit on the Lords' day and heard behind me a great voice as of a trumpet.' Hamasa knew he was in the presence of a great Power.

He found himself on his knees, tears streaming down his face as the experience rocked every cell in his body. He wanted to scream or to jump into the scene and grasp the Master or any of the other beings so he could experience the total reality of it all. Abruptly, the whole thing ended and the Master was back before his eyes, still gazing intently into them. Hamasa, exhausted from the uncontrollable outburst of emotions, cringed from that intensity. He tried to turn away but could not. He closed his eyes, but there was a bright light instead of the usual darkness and the Master was still there looking intently at him. His whole life began to parade before his eyes, and he remembered a line in the Bible from St Matthew, chapter 6: 22: 'the light of the body is the eye: if therefore thine eye be single, thy whole body shall be full of light.' He had always wondered what that meant and had made it his business to enquire of many priests and scholars, but to no avail. Now, it clearly made sense. He could see with his mind's eye the Master standing before him and simultaneously, he could look into the vast distance. Everything was lit as brightly as though it was daytime, but there was no sun emitting that light; it was all viewed by the one eye of his mind.

Suddenly, he was flying in a sky full of glittering stars, wondering where he was and what was happening to him, but also overcome with an incredible feeling of eternal love. All the people he had ever met came to mind and he hugged them mentally and loved them unconditionally. The love he experienced kept expanding until it engulfed the whole Universe and he soared into greater and greater depths of love as he ascended through space. He was drawn into a huge, thousand-fold sun that he burst through, landing on a mountaintop overlooking the most beautiful city of lights that words could not describe. Words could never express what he felt or the state of his mind: the freedom, power and unbounded love: a love that could embrace the whole of creation. Looking up to a bright, full moon, he quickly realized that it had turned into the face of the Master and that he was trying to engage Hamasa in conversation. He began to wonder where he was and whether he was dreaming. If he was, he never wanted to wake up and leave this profound experience of fulfillment and love. Automatically, he found himself on his knees, gazing into the eyes of a beautiful, benevolent being of light. Beside the Master, equally as radiant, was the Successor.

"Where are we, what's happening to me? Is this real?" he bellowed!

"On Earth, the Master is subject to the same laws of nature as everyone else," the Master replied, smiling, while he helped Hamasa stand back up. "Here, in the astral plane, we can manifest God's mysteries more clearly. Yes, Hamasa," the Master was suddenly very serious, "this is very real. This is the astral plane and that is the city of Amritsar. That is where people's souls go when they die on Earth. This plane is where Heaven and hell exist. From here the souls that are ready can start their spiritual journey back to God."

Hamasa stared around himself incredulously. "Just how many people live here, in this city, and what jobs do they have to do?" he asked, before rushing on. "It looks like the kind of city that The Venus Project would like to build on Earth. Are you familiar with the great work and vision of Jacque Fresco and Roxanne Meadows? They'd like to build a city and a world where no one has to work, where people can follow their passions. A world where there's no need for money, no need for corruption and competition. Unlimited energy from the sun, air, water and wind – all free. Everything a person needs given to them freely. Everything automated – machines and robots giving humans an ideal life. Is that how things are done here?"

The Master ignored Hamasa's questions. "You've separated the Successor physically from me at a crucial time. Therefore, I transferred the duties and power of God that the Master is blessed with to you. Now you'll have to transfer them to the Successor. You see, the power of God is transferred from one Godman to the next through the eyes. You looked into my eyes and I have brought you here, this is as far as we need to go. You have been given power up to the Astral plane. Since you've interrupted and prevented me from transferring my power to my son, I've decided to make you responsible for completing the task." The Master chuckled. "Of course, you won't be given the full power of God to transfer, but enough to get the process started. This mission must be carried out as soon as possible. The Master endures a great amount of suffering every day to keep the physical Universe from destroying itself. It's a long, complicated story that can be summed up as karma. You would never survive even the tiniest amount of this pain and life on Earth would be destroyed within a few months.

"Let me give you a glimpse of a couple of scenarios that could happen once my body dies. Are you seeing the movie?" The Master's voice was sharp.

Hamasa gasped as a crushing pain beat down on him. At the same time, a series of images flashed across his mind: the planet plunging into world war: asteroids falling to Earth: tsunamis, hurricanes and Earthquakes battering the planet one after another in rapid succession: all life becoming extinct: the Earth plunging into a deep freeze until the end of time. Then, finally, the whole Universe brought back into oneness with the ocean of God's consciousness.

"When it comes to anything regarding God or all the mysteries of life, they can only be understood through direct experience. You've experienced a small taste of the power of love and what happens to people when they die. Do you think you would have believed me if I'd simply *told* you about these things?" The Master scratched at his beard, letting another chuckle escape him. "There's a bit more to life than you thought, isn't there, Son? You've done many things against the law of love. You've got a chance now to change your life around and to benefit many souls who would sacrifice everything they could to be in your shoes now.

"Actually, it was Nayanna's karma that brought you to this place. Her connection to the Master runs deep into many past lives. She was greatly tempted by the influences of modern life, but she's returned to being faithful. You now know things that many would give their lives to know, you're privy to many secrets that others will never know. You shall have to transfer that power to the Successor so that He will be able to carry on the mission of the Masters to take on the sins of the world.

"If the living Master is able to transfer the power of God to the Successor then many disasters are prevented and souls have a way to find peace and love, and ultimately to become one with God. The Master suffers every day so that the world prospers and can eventually enter a new golden age, when peace and love will flourish for many, many years. You, too, would be able to live a fulfilling life, raising your children with Nayanna."

"If I wasn't here, experiencing all these things first hand, I'd never be able to believe any of it," Hamasa forced the words out of his mouth. "I'm truly humbled." He looked squarely at the Master. "How will I ever restore my life knowing what I've done? You say Nayanna and our children. Nayanna will have nothing to do with me now that she knows I was a terrorist. I wish I could go back – to before I became the man I am now. I have so many questions. What about all the people I killed? And now there's a chance that Nayanna will believe I killed her husband. How can all that be forgiven? How can I go on to marry Nayanna and have a family with her? Nothing makes sense!" he said, anguished. "How will it happen? Nothing about God ever made sense to me and that hasn't changed – except now I'm actually experiencing this incredible bliss and fulfillment that I couldn't even imagine being possible." Hamasa paused. "I did taste this once, many years ago, when I was 15 years old...I'd completely forgotten!" Hamasa ran a shaky hand through his hair. "How could I forget such a wonderful thing?" He stared at the Master. "I never want to lose this love I'm experiencing! Is it possible to keep it – to always have it?

"Who were all those beings of light that I saw you with? Were they the past Masters who had come to Earth? Isn't that the Successor beside you now? Why can't you just zap him? He's already here!"

The Master shook his head. "Whoa, young man! There you go again, with so many questions. God is the author of all that happens, so you can forget about feelings of guilt. Guilt is a trick of the mind to keep the soul trapped in the physical world. Everything happens according to God's will through the laws He created. Just live in the present moment with your newfound consciousness and let God take care of the rest. Don't think you're going to tell anyone about this either – it's against the spiritual laws for humans to know these mysteries. Besides, anyone you told would think you were crazy. By the time this is all over, most of what you will go through with me will have been erased from your memory or seem like a distant dream you can't quite remember. Humans are just not spiritually advanced enough to accept or understand the truth about God. Even though I'm revealing much to you, it's still very little of the great mystery of God.

"Yes, you were in the presence of all the past Masters. Yes, the Successor is here with us too, but only in spirit, which he is not fully conscious of yet as a human, that is, until you're able to find him and 'zap' him as you put it.

"Only a true Master can unite all the Masters. There are many false Masters, but they cannot take on the karma of the Universe and of all the souls, and they cannot literally guide and escort a soul back to God. You discovered some documents that led you to hate God's will and you felt that you could, in some way, influence or change God." His gaze was compassionate. "Ultimately, that would be completely impossible, for in truth, we are all God. You are God and everything is God, expressing His laws and will. You found a paltry piece of a puzzle that made you puke and you attempted to pluck it out, but you didn't apprehend that the puzzle needs each puny piece to be perfected." He chuckled at his 'Peter Piper' type alliterations. "Remember this!" His eyes were now stern. "Death, pain and suffering are temporary but God's love is forever. God is the author of everything. He writes the stories for every soul throughout all creation and throughout all the ages. You could kill all the Masters and blow up the Earth and even destroy the physical Universe, and in God's world it would mean nothing. In the blink of an eye, He could have all the souls brought home to eternal life. You want to understand God with your mind and ego intact but they will have to die before you can even begin the journey to God and to understanding Him. You want to hear His reasons for creating evil and suffering. Do you want Him to justify the Heavens, bliss and love, too? For every second of pain there is a thousand years of bliss, for every war a million years of bliss. To humanity, there is no justification for evil, but the human being is not a human being – the human being is God. You will have to become one with the Divine to know all these mysteries about Him. Only by becoming one with God and rising to His level will you ever understand and know Him. No matter what the gossip, words don't give the vaguest glimpse into the Absolute. You have so many questions to ask but you can only ask them of God when you go inside and see Him for yourself. Life's a gamble. Are you going to gamble your life on worldly pursuits or are you going to gamble your life on God, eternal life and the Master who makes all that very possible?

God has given us a test to see which way we will turn, and if humans don't turn to God and find eternal life, they will continue to suffer. Nevertheless, they need the living Master to do it – don't forget that." The laughter lines at the corners of the Master's eyes crinkled. "Just for the record, there is no life on other planets. God is happy with His creation and will never change it, so human beings had better get it together and wear the thick boots of meditation to walk on the hot coals of their lives of suffering so they don't suffer as much. God plans to keep this creation going for another million years or so. By coming to the Master, your future family for many generations will be saved, as well as your past generations. This is just one of the many benefits. By giving all your money to the Master many of your diseases will be taken away or diminished and you will receive rewards tenfold."

"But I thought you were God," exclaimed Hamasa! "Why do I have to go within and ask God when you're right here to ask? If this is so important and true then why can't you give humanity at least some proof that God exists?" As the questions flooded his mind, Hamasa was torn from his feelings of bliss and entered his torturing doubts.

"You teach that the soul travels back to God by emerging into the light and sound of God, which comes from God and is the word or first vibration of God. Yet you claim that before a soul can get to God, there's a great barrier of darkness that no light or sound can get through. It's very confusing and contradictory. How can God create a beam of light and sound that emanates from Him and creates and sustains the whole Universe, but that light and sound is unable to penetrate the great, dark barrier region which divides God from what He created? How can a broken beam of light sustain the Universe?" Hamasa stared at the Master in frustration. "Then, you say, 'God is love', and the criteria to know God is through love, but go on to say He creates evil and look at all the suffering. What's that all about?

"You said that people must meditate to see and talk to God and all your advertising states that 'seeing is believing', but then you later said that God would never allow people to know the truth, to talk to Him or see Him. So why do we have to waste all our time in meditation, and again, why all the contradictions?

"The recent Masters started out as poor Indians, but now their kids go to the best schools and you have businesses worth millions and properties all over the world. If there really were a God, people would live as if it were real. Now, nobody does. People live as if religion is all made up and use it if and when they feel it's beneficial or convenient for them. They use religion and spirituality to gain power, money, status and security.

"If all of creation were the result of God being bored, then that would never justify all the ignorance and suffering that souls have to go through! Never! Never! Never!" Hamasa punctuated each 'never' by smacking his fist into his other, open, palm. "Surely, a perfect God can't get bored?

"I haven't even begun to question you on all the ways your teachings go against the scientifically proven facts of evolution. I can't wait to hear how you explain that away. You say God put humans on Earth, but it's been proven beyond a reasonable doubt we evolved from ocean creatures, reptiles, mammals, and eventually an ape like creature. If a perfect God created us then why are we so imperfect? All manner of creatures have better systems for seeing, and breathing.

"Why all the contradictions, all the lies and secrets? Why should I let you off easy without any logical explanation, without any proof of what you say? I mean, we need real, scientific proof – proof that can be scientifically verified by everyone. Right now I'm filled with all this love and bliss, and awe for what I just went through, but my mind still wants answers. I still have so many questions, sorry.

"Right now, I feel like I'm in a weird fantasy. Is this just a dream I'm having? Maybe this is a flash back, a hallucination thing, like from when I was fifteen and forced to take acid. Now that was a trip, too! When I was on drugs, my mind could hallucinate whatever it wanted, and it seemed as real as this or any experience. How do I know that this isn't all a hallucination? Maybe parts of my brain are being stimulated somehow, causing this to happen. Prove to me this is real, that it's not just a hallucination! If you're really the all-knowing, all-powerful, and omnipotent God, then how did you end up in this mess – kidnapped and the Successor's life in danger – and all the evil that's happening to you now?"

The Master tugged at his beard again. "I guess I need to repeat what I said before. God is about being – whether He's being an ant, an angel, a Universe, a human or being Himself as God – He is always being," the Master continued, ignoring Hamasa's questions.

As the Master continued talking, Hamasa realized they were now back to the reality of Earth, back to the house in Chicago, and the Master now appeared as a regular human.

"Right now we're being tardy," the Master said, "and we really need to get a move on. Rather – you have to get a move on, as I'm going to lay myself down right here and die. I, too, have had enough of this place and have many things to do in other Universes. When Jesus said 'in my Father's house are many mansions', it was a huge understatement. Don't worry," he added, seeing Hamasa's frown, "my spirit body will be with you until we see this thing through. I've given you powers up to the astral plane, they'll come in very handy, you'll be able to read people's thoughts and you'll have some idea of the future and the past. But don't get carried away with them, walking through walls and flying can only be done in the strictest secrecy and only in life and death situations. Although I must admit, some powers would just spontaneously erupt from me from time to time and I did bring a few souls back from the dead. It was a very exciting event for those involved, I must say." He studied

Hamasa sternly. "You, however, will behave implicitly or I'll personally give you a huge migraine. Got that! Oh! And don't worry about Nayanna. As she connects to her divinity, she'll be filled with forgiveness and the ability to live in the present with amazing love – even enough love to live with the man she once thought killed her husband."

Having said what he'd needed to, the Master lay down and died right before Hamasa's disbelieving gaze. Hamasa held the Master in his arms, drenching him with the tears that poured down his cheeks.

"Doctor! I need the doctor in here, fast!" he yelled. Within moments, Master's body was on an operating table, the medical team doing all they could, but there was no bringing him back.

Hamasa made his way to his room, driven by the need to give in to his overwhelming grief.

However, miraculously, as Paul on the road to Damascus saw the resurrected Jesus, he, too, saw and spoke to the resurrected Master. First, there was something in the way the air circled him and danced on his skin, then an intoxicating aroma, and He appeared as gentle and natural as a blooming flower.

"So it was true that Jesus resurrected and appeared to His disciples?" Hamasa asked through his tears.

"Yes, certainly." The Master gave his, by now, familiar chuckle. "Death is but a change from one type of consciousness to another," he said. "Like a snake shedding its skin, we leave behind one body and enter another."

Hamasa still had questions to ask about the documents and God getting bored and creating evil, and how the Master could appear to him, but just then, he became aware of the sound of a helicopter, quickly followed by the noise of warning sirens. The police had found them!

The Master's voice reached him from beyond the veil, "Do not resist arrest. Cooperate fully as they'll be our greatest allies through everything we need to do. And for God's sake throw away those cyanide capsules!"

"How did you know? Ah…OK, OK," Hamasa sighed. "You'd better not desert me. You'd better be there when I need you. You'd better not be sending me into hell for all I've done."

Chapter 27

Interrogation Continued

"The hero is one who kindles a great light in the world, who sets up blazing torches in the dark streets of life for men to see by."
Felix Adler

This time Harold was having a hard time chasing away the devotees. He found himself being caught up in the mesmerizing vibes. He struggled to shake off the effects of looking into Hamasa's eyes.

Hamasa, for his part, was in a heightened state of otherness. He knew the moment of truth had come upon them.

"Well, that's my story, Harold, that's how I ended up here. I don't know how you uncovered where we were hiding out," Hamasa stated. "Who's the inside man that snitched on me? Listen, Harold, I know you don't believe much of what I'm saying, but we've really got to get a move on here. We don't have much time. Just forget about all the insignificant details. Once you understand the magnitude of what I'm now involved with, I'm sure you'll have to agree. We're dealing with God here – the Creator of the whole Universe. If He says I'm free to go, then I'm free to go. If He says I'm going to save the world, then I'm going to save the world, with or without your help."

Harold got to his feet and stood looking down at Hamasa. "We found the gun that was used right where we found you," he told him. "If the bullets match, it's just a matter of time before we can pin this murder on you. We'll get a match for your DNA from the bellman's outfit you wore that day, too. Are you sure you don't want to make a confession? That's why you're here. We also have a witness; I won't mention a name to protect their identity, but do you really want to drag this out in court? Think about the media revealing your sick life to the world. Sky was a complete innocent. His only crime was being there for Nayanna when you couldn't be. Isn't that right, Hamasa?" Hamasa said nothing, gazing silently at Harold.

"OK," Harold snapped, losing the last of his patience, "if you refuse to talk, then I'll just go and get caught up with outside duties and leave you here with a couple of guys who are dying to continue making you talk."

"No, you can't go!" Hamasa ordered. "As I've already stated many times, this is very urgent and we have to get a move on. Please, I know where we have to go and only you can get this done in time, but only if we leave now! Actually, the Master's asked you to stay calm. He's going to appear to you right here in this room. There just isn't any time to waste."

Suddenly the air seemed to shimmer, the kites were swooping down, and the next instant the Master stood before a surprised, awe-struck Harold.

"Dear Harold," he said very gently, "these are very desperate times and it seems as if everybody's willing to take great risks to find their fulfillment. Now, even God seems to be doing desperate things," he said, smiling. "I come to you with God's blessings and through the karma started with your grandfather. You know he once met a great past Master in Jerusalem, at a religious conference that even the Pope attended." Harold was nodding his head and rubbing his eyes in disbelief at the same time. "You still have a picture of that meeting hanging on your dining room wall. I know you're very familiar with the good deeds of your grandfather. That brief meeting changed his destiny forever and helped him in his afterlife. Now your grandfather is also urging you to help us out."

From out of nowhere, Harold's grandfather appeared and started to tell Harold of all the wonderful things to come and of the urgency to follow the Master's instructions. Harold started to warm up to the encounters.

"What Hamasa has been telling you is true," The Master insisted. "However, he wasn't able to convince you to find and save my son, the Successor. Hopefully our appearing to you will succeed where he failed," continued the Master. "I've entrusted him with a great mission to ultimately save the world, as well as the Universe, and you, too, have a great role to play in this with many great rewards awaiting you in the beyond. Go with love and justice in your heart and you will not only save yourself and your loved ones but also God's chosen one, my son, the Successor. He's in a dark place, waiting for you to rescue him. So please leave right away."

Harold, too, found himself on his knees, crying at the holy presence of the Master.

He nodded through his tears. "Yes, Master, we'll leave right away!" he sobbed. Turning to Hamasa, he quickly untied his leg bonds. "Let's go!" he ordered.

The door swung open, the Master and Harold's grandfather disappeared, and the shrill scream of sirens started to blare. Harold was on his phone as they ran down a corridor, giving orders for a helicopter to take them to the military airport, Joint Base McGuire-Dix-Lakehurst, N.J., where a jet would rocket them to Chicago. Within the hour, they were off the ground. Before they left, Hamasa made Harold promise that if anything happened to him, Nayanna would be looked after and kept safe. He had faith God would work everything out between them, and for now, he could only deal with the present situation and the dark forces he knew he was about to encounter.

He was back working with the Israeli government. Although they hadn't legally freed him yet or dropped the charges against him, he had a newfound strength and hope. He felt free as a kite, soaring to new heights. He now carried himself as a man who knew everything would work out for the best.

Chapter 28

The Power

"When the power of love overcomes the love of power, the world will know peace."
Jimi Hendrix

"Hamasa, what are you doing? Just stay inside the helicopter," Harold screamed over the roar of the rotary blades whirling inches above his super cerebellum as he nudged him back onto his seat.

The military jet had made the New York to Chicago trip in under an hour, compared to the usual two-hour domestic flight. They had transferred to helicopters and whizzed to the south side of Chicago. Here, it was the law of the jungle, as gangs openly walked around displaying their muscle: not the kind attached to an arm either. It must have taken some negotiating, Harold mused, to guarantee them neighborhood safety and free passage. He would've liked to be a fly on the wall when that went down – a group of white, Arab Jihadists, transporting a group of turban wearing East Indians through the black streets of south Chicago must have been quite an operation. So much for any element of surprise: The Bomb and his group must have marched right in and let it be known what their business was.

Harold and his elite team of soldiers didn't need the element of surprise; they were not there to arrest any of the residents. Hopefully, this didn't have to turn into a war. Nevertheless, if trouble did erupt, he knew it was his team that should be in the thick of it and not Hamasa. If only he could get him to realize that. At the moment his persuasion was having little effect.

"I'm the one who got us into this mess," Hamasa argued. You don't have a choice, Harold. I'm the only one who knows the code, and the lingo. I'm the only one they'll respond to. One false move and they'll blow themselves and everything around here, including us, up. And if the Successor dies, then so does humanity." Hamasa lay down his trump card. "So," he said, knowing he'd won, "what's it going to be, boss?"

"OK, I'll give you ten minutes." Looking at Hamasa's response, Harold changed his offer. "OK I'll give you twenty minutes, twenty minutes, Hamasa. If you're not out by then, we're coming in, bombs or no bombs. You got that?" Harold rolled up his sleeve revealing his liberty tattoo to show Hamasa his watch.

Hamasa nodded. "She'll be smiling at us, that lady of liberty. Yes, sir! Twenty minutes, sir!"

Hamasa jumped out of the chopper, ran weaponless to the door of the warehouse and disappeared inside shouting, "Ali Akbar, Shahada."

"That's far enough!" The voice echoed around the darkened room. "Why aren't you dead, Hamasa? Why didn't you take your cyanide pill? What are they holding over your head? I had a feeling you'd turn out to be a liability. They've got your lady love don't they? I should've taken her out when I had the chance. Well, I guess you've brought them all here to be with you when we all go up to Allah. You're ready for the glory, Hamasa? Or do you have a black hole where your faith was? You got something going on you don't want Allah to know about? You can't face your God today, Hamasa? Poor Hamasa, you won't be a martyr. You won't be getting 72 virgins, will you, Hamasa? You sold us out didn't you? You freakin' idiot! I'll see you dead first."

Hamasa knew he had to act fast. The man behind the voice was ready to pull the plug, ready to blow himself up, taking the whole warehouse, everyone in it, including the Successor and maybe even the whole block with him. He had recognized the voice immediately. He wasn't surprised that 'The Bomb' was sticking to the plan. He had no time to explain why things had to change or to talk him into surrendering. He had to act fast, but distract him long enough to engage. There was a faint light from an upper floor window near the back of the warehouse, but with no one in sight, he knew he had to make a move.

"Hey, my friend," he yelled, but there was no answer. "Let me explain, please." Hamasa's thoughts were remarkably calm and ordered, given the situation. The Master had bequeathed him special powers for use in life and death situations like this, and, although he wished he'd had the chance to try them out, he was just going to have to take a leap of faith. Launching himself into the air, Hamasa found himself flying across the warehouse like a great albatross, defying gravity, sailing over a hail of AK-47 bullets. Below him, in the dark, The Bomb never even knew what hit him. Hamasa got him with his feet. The Bomb was out cold; Hamasa would never use his powers to kill unless there was no other choice, but he had no such reservations about using them to silence a man and to prevent destruction. Picking up Bomb's AK-47, he patted him down for a few more rounds of ammunition.

He had to find the Successor quickly. Gunfire erupted outside. The chopper! Harold! Hamasa glanced out a window and saw six, shiny, armored, black pimpmobiles pulling up in a hail of bullets. The vehicles stopped and a tall, finely dressed, black man in a white shirt, bow tie and dark suit jumped out with a rocket propelled, grenade launcher pointed at the chopper. Harold and his men scattered and ran towards the warehouse, sprinting through the door, almost knocking Hamasa over as the chopper exploded into flames. Harold was on his walkie-talkie, calling for back up, and within minutes it was the pimpmobiles exploding into a fiery cloud of fragments.

"I guess we won't be getting introduced to any of those folks," Harold, grated, breathing heavily. "But now we'll have the whole Chicago police force breathing down our backs. We'd better get a move on. Where are they holding this man of yours?"

"I'll take care of that," Hamasa yelled as he ran off through the warehouse. At the back there were stairs leading to second story offices – the manager's loft, where they could look out the windows to monitor the workers below. He heard a window smash and felt the burn of a bullet smashing through his ribcage and tearing through his heart, but he continued flying up the stairs, passing through a wall and then a locked door and suddenly appearing from out of nowhere to the bewilderment of those still in the room. He let off a few rounds from the machine gun up into the ceiling.

"It's over! Put your weapons down! You don't have to die for this. We've got amnesty. We gotta' go before the cops get here."

"OK, Hamasa, you're the man. Hafiz had his radio on when he was talking to you and it didn't sound too good down there. What happened to him?" inquired a voice from behind a large filing cabinet.

"You mean Bomb? We'll get him on our way out. He's fine. Where's the Indian?"

There were three Jihadists in the room and they pointed to a cabinet. Hamasa's grandfather was one of them!

With frozen horror written on his face from recognizing his grandfather, Hamasa asked, "What the hell are you doing here? You're alive! The man with nine lives."

"I'm here to finish the job you weren't able to do. What, you think I want to miss out on all the fun here! You better pull your friend out from the cabinet there."

Bound, gagged and scrunched up like a pretzel, the Successor lit up when Hamasa looked in.

"We've changed his diapers a few times. He doesn't react well to surprises or violence," one of the other jihadists said. "You better check him down there again before we leave, ha-ha." The man broke off, his expression growing serious as he stared at Hamasa. "Man – you're bleeding real bad."

Hamasa looked down at his wound. Putting his attention on

it was all it took for it to heal. The bullet had gone right through him and now there was no trace of the entry hole or the exit hole. There were some excellent benefits to having some of the Master's powers, Hamasa decided.

"It's nothing serious. You're a lousy shot. I'll deal with it later. OK guys, we're surrendering to Israeli intelligence, his name is Harold. He's on his way up. This is the only way up to the roof, so let's get going," Hamasa ordered as he put down his gun and dragged the Successor out of the cupboard. The Successor had a long, black beard and his hair was in a bun, ready to be covered by the turban that lay on the floor. He couldn't be more than thirty, Hamasa thought. For going through such an ordeal, he was still in good health and sprang to his feet, even though his hands were bound. Hamasa looked into the same intense, bottomless, brown eyes as the Master's.

"Sorry about all this," Hamasa apologized. "Your father, the Master, has a message for you He asked me to deliver. But it'll have to wait till we reach a safe place."

"Safe place, you think I'm going to surrender, let you get to a safe place? There's some pretty weird shit going on here. I saw you fly, walk through that wall, you're a devil creature! I'll send you back to hell where you came from!" Hamasa's grandfather shouted as he emptied his gun into Hamasa. Harold burst through the door and within seconds three jihadists were on the floor riddled with bullets.

"Jesus, Harold, you didn't have to kill them! That one's my grandfather," Hamasa screamed over the silence.

"I heard shots; I thought you and Akhee were dead. Thank God you're both safe. Let's get the hell out of here!" Harold replied as Hamasa was secretly healing himself.

Harold and his men carrying Hafiz, 'The Bomb', were right behind Hamasa as they burst through the roof door out to a waiting chopper. As they flew off they saw the swarm of cops, like wasps with stingers flaring surround the warehouse.

"Perfect timing! Chicago's finest can deal with the press down there," Harold announced. "I'll gladly let them take the credit for getting rid of the gang members."

"The Successor has an ashram in New York City. Can we be dropped off there?" Hamasa inquired. He suddenly realized he could read Harold's mind and commented, "Oh, I guess not."

"We've a nice place picked out, where the two of you can do your song and dance. It's been your home away from home lately."

They were headed back to the converted mine, back to the hell-hole of no escape. What about the promised freedom? The Successor's freedom and civil rights would have to be honored. Was everything going to be kept a secret, buried in a mine so the public would never hear the truth? Worry ate into Hamasa as the chopper began to descend.

Back at the mine, Hamasa was finally allowed to be alone with the Successor. The two men stood silent, Hamasa wondering what to do next. Should he explain or did the Successor already know everything and just needed him to get on with it? Then he felt it – a thickening of the air, followed by a shimmer, as if a curtain had been disturbed by the wind, the same air turbulence he mistook for kites flying, again the intoxicating aroma and the Master appeared.

The Master gazed at his son. "I'm sorry you had to go through all this, my son. Karma had to be played out, but I'm glad I'm the first one to tell you this – I've left the body and have returned to our eternal spiritual home. You'll have the chance to grieve my death later. For now, Hamasa's here to take you into the astral plane. From there, you and I will be taking the journey home together. So, as far as you're concerned right now, I'm still very much alive. Stay calm, stay strong! This will be the pinnacle experience of your life. Don't ask questions now. Look into Hamasa's eyes while he repeats the sacred chants and absorb the power of God you see there."

As requested, the Successor stared, without blinking, deep into Hamasa's eyes, echoing the chants. Soon, Hamasa realized his job was completed. He got up and left the room, leaving the Successor alone, absorbed in a deep meditation. He could only speculate on the wonders the Successor would be going through on his journey to God.

Chapter 29

Freedom Found

"The great enemy of the truth is very often not the lie: deliberate, contrived, and dishonest; but the myth: persistent, persuasive, and unrealistic. Belief in myths allows the comfort of opinion without the discomfort of thought."
John F. Kennedy

Hamasa was back where he started: at the facility where Harold had interrogated him. After his demands to be allowed to meet with the Successor again failed, Hamasa was handcuffed and brought to a tiny cell with a steel door. Left alone, he called out but there was no answer. Glancing around, Hamasa saw there was a bed, a toilet and a sink. Wearily, he freshened up before collapsing onto the bed and assessing his situation. He went over the facts. First, he was still a prisoner. Second, all his plans to save the world by forcing the Master to change God's will had crumbled: the Successor was now the Master and the world hadn't changed. Third, he was still separated from Nayanna and hadn't heard from her. That was as far as he got before falling into a deep blackout. When he woke up, it felt as if he had slept for days, not hours.

The guards brought Hamasa back to the interrogation room where Harold was already seated.

"How are you, Hamasa? I hope you had a good rest," Harold said, looking casual in his tennis outfit. "Excuse the unprofessional look, but I'm just on my way to a match."

"Jesus, Harold, why are we still here? Why am I still a prisoner led around in handcuffs? Our mission's just started. We've got more important things to do than play tennis. By uniting the Master with the Successor we saved the Universe from being destroyed, but now we have to save humanity. With the Successor here, behind bars, maybe there's still a way to make Him change God's laws. Now that we know the truth, we have to do something. We can't let this opportunity slip past us," Hamasa begged.

Harold ignored him. "Good news for you, Hamasa!" he announced. "The Successor's cleared you in the murder of Sky. He says you were holding him captive at the exact time Sky was murdered. We also found your gun didn't fire the bullet that killed him. I believe you'll soon be a free man as the Successor isn't pressing charges. He says he went with you voluntarily. As far as your employment with the agency goes, well, anything's possible at this stage. This whole messy case can finally get settled."

As Harold removed his sophisticated persona from the chair and signaled the guards to open the big iron gates of the chamber, Hamasa burst out… "Where are you going? We have many things to go over! Let's do it now!"

Harold stood in the open doorway. "Hamasa, calm down! You've been through a lot. I'm going to have you checked out right away here. There's a doctor coming to pay you a visit. The drugs wore off a long time ago but you're still going on with your hallucinations. I'm worried about you. That's why we have you in handcuffs – for your own safety. We need you of sound mind to make a statement about everything that's happened in the last few days."

Hamasa's voice filled with emotion. "Sound mind? What are you talking about? You were there with me when the Master appeared out of nowhere…from the dead, and your grandfather too, ordering us to save the Successor so the Master could transfer his power. It wasn't a hallucination, Harold!"

"I've no idea what you're talking about. The agency made the decision to bring in the witness, the Successor as you call Him, and they took a big gamble involving you. But it worked out and the witness has just cleared your name," Harold told him.

"My God, Harold! You forgot everything? That's exactly what the Master said would happen," Hamasa uttered, bewildered, as he pounded his right fist into his left palm. "I wonder why I didn't lose my memory…? I'll have to check if I still have powers. But what about the other witnesses? Who was behind the glass wall when the Master appeared? They must have a video recording. I know everything was being recorded. There must be some evidence. What about 'The Bomb'? He saw me fly through the air. Did you get his statement yet?"

"Listen, Hamasa," Harold continued as he took the handcuffs off him. "We've debriefed everyone, we went through everything, but not a single thing has come up that verifies your outlandish claims. Hafiz, 'The Bomb', as you call him, said that as you were distracting him someone knocked him out. So, no, he didn't say anything about you flying through the air."

"And I guess you killed off the other witnesses and my grandfather, so how about the Successor, what is he saying?" Hamasa asked, looking dejected.

"The Successor says He's just a man, like everyone else, and doesn't have the powers you talk of. By the way, His name's Akhee. He said it means, 'in the blink of an eye'. Anyway, He says God has all the power but is only interested in love and changing the world through the love that comes from each person. He says He can be killed or die and the Universe will continue without Him. I told him to seek salvation from Jesus, halleluiah, and you should too! He's the only Savior, I told him, but he just laughed. So anyway, I don't know where you're getting all these fantasy ideas from, but I'll be right back with the doc, hold tight."

"Where's Nayanna?" Hamasa beseeched. "Can you find a way for us to communicate with each other?"

Harold nodded. "Yes, I'll see what I can do. I'm sure she'll be relieved to hear of your innocence. She'd told us she saw you murder Sky or at least she saw you there that day, so you'll have to understand she might want to take her time in contacting you until she's had a chance to digest the new information. She also feels guilty for turning you in. Yes, because of her we were able to trace the phone call you made to her."

"Harold, please, just hear me out. We've got to get through to the Master and get him to change God's will and to have mercy on humanity. At least have the Successor agree to demonstrate the power of God to everyone. If you want a one-world government, you'll need all the religions to come together as one. You can't have Muslims and Christians killing each other and expect a one-world government to work. If the Master agrees to overcome the burden of proof, all religions will unite under Him. Maybe you'll have to try a bit of waterboarding as you did with me."

"You know that would never happen. Akhee, the new Master, gave his statement and he's been released. Let's see if we can get you there, too. It's in all the newspapers – how thousands of His followers waited at His ashram for His return," Harold responded. "So why don't you do it yourself? You're the one who can survive a bullet to the heart, fly through the air and pass through walls. Show the people your miracles and they'll follow your truth, I'm sure."

Hamasa reflected for a moment. "So that's it then. I'm on my own. Well, to tell you the truth, I'd take my followers and I'd start a new world…one without a God. If this is the best God will do for us, then who needs Him. He's just looking out for His own interests and trying not to get bored. He won't save us from ourselves, His laws, and He won't give us any evidence of His existence, so screw Him! I'll take my followers to The Venus Project movement, and we'll maximize happiness for everyone. Everyone'll have autonomy to create competence in whatever they love to do and they'll have a feeling of belonging and purpose. This is our only life and our only world and we'll make it the greatest for everyone. I'll use my powers to prove that God betrayed us, and I'll use them to prove that there's hope for all humanity and that humans can create a Heaven on Earth."

Hamasa's voice carried to every corner of the underground prison and people left whatever they were doing and came to the source. The sounds also carried above ground and attracted all those who were near.

Hamasa's thoughts focused on the new powers he had experienced. What a great feeling it was to defy gravity: to actually fly like a bird through the air and pass through walls. He wondered what other powers the Master had given him. He could fly, survive bullets and was able to read people's thoughts. It would be nice, he thought, if he could also defy aging, avoid accidents, diseases and breathe under water, but most importantly, save others from death. But he wondered if he still had any of them.

"Now I realize the joy I got from flying kites as a youngster wasn't true freedom, but was of power and control. Science has proven we're hard wired through our DNA to be cooperative and helpful to each other within the family when we're first born – just as each cell in our body cooperates with each other cell to keep the body alive. Trouble is, soon after, we're programmed by society to be competitive, to always win in the game of 'survival of the fittest'. We're taught at an early age to hate." Hamasa's voice was animated and on fire. He was no longer talking to Harold but to the multitudes gathering, and, to the world.

"Kite flying was always about who pulled the stings, making the kite follow the flier's orders, proving who the best flier was and who could destroy the other's kite. But true freedom is when everyone is flying their kite for the sake of each other and for the sake of the kite as well. When all humans work together to give every person a dignified life, creating a safe place to breath, drink, eat and live. Then and only then will we be flying the kites of true freedom. However, that's unlikely as no one will ever find true freedom. We'll always be under the dictatorship of nature who says, if we don't breathe, we'll die, if we don't drink water we'll die, and if we don't eat we'll die. If we use up all of the Earth's resources, we'll also all die. But by following The Venus Project movement, which advocates for a resource based economy, we can fly as free as a kite, or as free as possible. Follow me and together we'll challenge the laws of nature – with me all things are possible. We'll achieve fulfilment in all things."

As Hamasa poured out his heart, the crowd got bigger and bigger inside and outside of the interrogation room. Agents came out from behind the mirrored glass wall to join Harold. Guards, cleaning staff, nurses and even the cooking staff started to assemble outside the chamber, all mesmerized by Hamasa's voice and presence. No one said anything against the congregating worshippers. As if giving blessings, Hamasa would look intently into each person's eyes. Love and power beamed out of him, piercing souls, leaving them in a love-trance state. Guards were releasing prisoners so they, too, could also be cleansed and washed clean by the Power. Over a hundred people had gathered in this vast, expansive chamber of love.

"I have a newfound purpose and strength. I'll support and hold only truth, love, human dignity and human rights above corporate profits, greed, lust, ego, anger, ignorance, attachments, governments and religious agendas or biases. The world cannot go on believing the individual can be sacrificed for the benefit of the system. However," Hamasa held up a finger, "the whole of society should not have to suffer because of a single individual. It's clear, now more than ever, that a few greedy people are ruining all life on the planet. The majority of people are facing incredible hardships and fear because of them, and these few ruthless, ignorant, greedy persons are destroying the planet itself. However, the worst problem is the poor would rather befriend the rich than go to war against them. I will stand up to them and I will live to see the world changed.

"It's impossible not to be completely embarrassed to be part of the human race at this time. I can only hope that there'll be a brighter future for humankind after I've shown and proved all the powers that I have.

"Some people, I believe, would like to create a world that had more cooperation, equality and love. A world with no need for militant feminists or militant anything. A world where everyone enjoys clean air, clean, abundant water, healthy food, effective, proper education, efficient shelter, health care and time to enjoy all the great things life has to offer. Once everyone experiences the benefits, they will all agree it's the best way to go, but it might also take changing people's brains to function better. We'll leave that to the scientists.

"The new code or constitution for the world could be: 'create the greatest good for everyone, at all times, in all situations, based on available resources, equality and freedom for all.' How could it be any other way?"

By now, Harold and all those gathering were soaking in every word Hamasa spoke. Quietly at first, but steadily increasing in volume, they began to chant. "Yes, create the greatest good for everyone, at all times, in all situations, based on available resources, yes, yes, yes."

Yesses echoed all around as people cheered and clapped for the new constitution they all agreed to live by.

"Yes, it's true that there's no scientific way to prove what's right or wrong," Hamasa continued. "There's no way to prove what the meaning of life is. So people continue to do what they think is best only for their own selves. That's how 'survival of the fittest' came to be, or 'an eye for an eye'. That's how and why people came up with the idea of being a Christian or a Muslim or Jew or any other label you care to stick on a bunch of people. These labels brought people together to fight for a common benefit and belief. Unfortunately, we're mostly operating out of ignorance in creating ways to live. The slave owners would never have thought to ask their slaves if it was right to make them slaves. The cannibals never bothered to ask the people they were eating if it was OK to eat them or to sacrifice them. Just as the rich today never care to ask if plundering the Earth's resources and creating pollution, forced education, forced wars, forced employment, poverty, taxes, or forced punishments and rules for every thought, word and deed is OK for all the people who have no other choice but to obey. Look around and there's ample proof of this in the way the rich keep getting richer and richer, hoarding trillions in offshore banks and avoiding taxes, while the poor get poorer and have less say."

Although hundreds of people were gathering at the gate, his eyes were able to penetrate each soul. Each person felt they were alone with him, witnessing the birth of a new power and a new world. As the sound of Hamasa's voice penetrated all around, even the animals began to make the pilgrimage to sacredness.

"They are amassing unimaginable wealth and one day they will reveal themselves and their true intentions to the world. They already own all means of production and natural resources, the banks, the armies, atom bombs – they have all the money and power. "We have to act fast. Only humankind can save humankind and I promise to be there leading the charge. Using the best advances made by science and the triumphant nature of the human spirit, humanity will succeed. I'll unite all the people! Whoever follows will help create the new world with me. People in the new world will no longer be divided by their religious beliefs, their ideologies or patriotic principles. Science has already proven we are all connected and that we all have the same basic needs. The power that I will show and prove will allow people to actually live up to these truths and live harmoniously with each other. I *will* live to see this happen. I was unsure of my power – if it was real, when I was allowed to use it, and who controlled it, but now that God has deserted us, I know He's willed it to be mine, to use as I deem necessary. Only scientific and verifiable evidence of my love and power will save humanity."

Harold had the foresight to notify Nayanna. He thought she might be needed to help in Hamasa's journey back to reality. By the time Hamasa had got this far in his soliloquy, Nayanna was already one of the many who had gathered to hear the Oracle. Standing by the water that ran down the far wall, she still had no trouble hearing his speech. He was roaring out to the masses that came to witness his power, see his miracles, and hopefully, hear and respond to his message.

"You know you can't change the world, Hamasa," Harold yelled from amongst the crowd that had gathered as he walked over to stand with Nayanna. "The world will change but very slowly, through the usual ways of millions of people suffering and dying in wars and natural disasters. When these catastrophes break down egos, people will finally look for better ways to think and act. Or maybe it'll take a time in the future, when all people will be hooked up to computers that'll regulate and control their every thought, emotion, hormones and actions, so that each person is optimized to be the best they can be, without hurting another. Then there'd be enough happiness and bliss to go around for everyone, and one person's riches and happiness won't have to come from making another person a slave, poor, unhappy or by killing them."

"Hamasa, we need proof of what you're saying!" The doctor, who had come to check up on Hamasa's mental condition, shouted out. "We've heard all this a million times before but no one's changed the world for the better. People will never change."

Moving away from Harold and towards Hamasa, Nayanna spoke her truth. "People, we have to give Hamasa a chance here. He's telling us something that we really need to hear and understand. It must be from his own experience, it's that powerful. Please, just listen!"

Hamasa rose to the challenge of being told he could never

change the world and was spurred on by Nayanna's faith in him. Nayanna was wearing glasses he had never seen before but he thought she looked as beautiful as the last time he saw her. His heart started melting. With his chest swelling, he said, "But people see the current conditions of poverty, suffering, climate change, natural disasters and wars as definitive proof of the validity of their scriptures, which they say prophesize such events – the apocalypse cometh! Consciously and unconsciously, they're creating these events as self-fulfilling prophecies. They don't realize scriptures were written by barbaric, first century, scientifically unknowledgeable people, who were desperate victims of the brutal Roman Empire. The motives for their writings are questionable, to say the least. And now, what they've written is completely misunderstood and misinterpreted. People will never change until I show them the truth and offer them proof. Truth is, and always will be, the most important element for human survival, as well as prosperity for the whole Universe. I am the eagle, I am the owl that created the fire that burns for the light of truth. I am the sheep of sacrifice. I will do what no Master before me would do. I will free every human being so they can live in peace, love, and dignity. I will free every human being from the chains that the laws of nature have given us. I will free God from God. Yes! I will free everyone from God and then I will free God from God! First, I'll prove it to you, and together we will change the world. Are you with me?"

"Yes, we're with you," the crowd roared.

"This is why I was spared from death and why the Master gave me all the power. He took a vow never to reveal the truth of His power to the world, but that vow made him weak and a liar. Finding ways to thwart boredom has thrown Him into trouble. The Master gave me the Power without making me take the same vow. He thought He could control me but I have the Power to make sure that doesn't happen. God wants it this way. This is the fulfillment, the rapture. We don't need the apocalypse. God has shown His mercy and is allowing me to save humanity. Saving the world can only happen through the scientific method – there has to be evidence that can be verified by everyone, including you, Doctor. Science has created and discovered all the greatest things on Earth and it will be through science that I'll save the world." His eyes searched for and found Nayanna's. "You'll see, Nayanna," he promised. "You'll all believe once you see. We know nothing of ourselves and the world we live in except what science has revealed to us. From now on, we'll all proclaim our ignorance in humility and seek to educate ourselves through science. This will be humanities greatest purpose and it will unite everyone."

Hamasa had everyone in the palm of his hand. By beaming his love and power through his eyes to everyone's conscience, the love and hope within each person was bursting forth and basking them in their own ecstasy. Guards with machine guns were in tears, agents with the power of nuclearized governments behind them were on their knees, praying and chanting Hamasa's name.

Hamasa, emboldened, yelled out, "Who is brave enough to put a bullet through me? I'll prove my power here and now. The world will be changed, now!"

The doctor rushed over to Hamasa yelling, "This nonsense talk must stop now. It's gone too far. I won't sit by and watch you be killed here today." He glared at Harold. "Harold, you have to help me stop this lunacy!"

"Yes – Hamasa, this has gone too far," Harold pleaded. "The situation's dangerous for everyone here. We'll take you by force if you don't come with us – now! I should have left you in handcuffs."

Suddenly, from across the room, Nayanna spoke out and there was silence. "Wait, Harold, Doctor, Please! Hamasa, there's a letter that came for you. Please read it first. I was waiting for the right time to give it to you, but you need to read it. It's addressed to Hamasa Abdul Baghrani." She handed the cross-engraved, delicate envelope which was hand written in small, clear letters, over to Harold who handed it to Hamasa.

Hamasa held it in his hands, turning it over a few times, fascinated by the engraved, ornamental designs. With everyone crowded around, Hamasa carefully opened it.

Pictures fell out that Harold was able to snatch up and tuck in his jacket pocket, as he said, "Let's not get distracted. We should read the letter first."

"Dear Hamasa," Hamasa began aloud.

"You do not know me, but I am your brother's wife, Betty Anne Keating. Your brother, Mullah Abdul Massoud Baghrani was a good man, a great man. I never took his last name for many reasons that I will share with you in time, if you so wish. The reason for this letter is to share with you a true story of how one man sacrificed his life for others, and for you, too, Hamasa, even though they were total strangers.

"A Russian KGB secret service agent relayed this story to me. He was able to show pictures and video footage to prove what he said. He came to me because he lost his partner and best friend in a street battle as he was uncovering intelligence in the days following, so he will never rest until he finds the killer. The killer would have his partner's gun and he believes you may be able to help him find the answers he is looking for. He also confirmed suspicions that Massoud had warned me about for years and that I completely ignored concerning my daughters. I might have been able to save Massoud, and will never forgive myself. The KGB kept our home and village under surveillance for many years. The agent was able to produce pictures and video to support this claim as well.

I could let this letter become a long story, but I would rather it be a short introduction to further meetings and dialogue in person. So I will stay on topic and relay the Russian's story.

The KGB had followed Massoud from Siberia to Afghanistan. While he waited at the airport to meet you, Hamasa, the agents received word that there might be a planned terrorist attack on the airport: specifically targeting the passengers. They were undercover and had no authority to arrest Massoud. They introduced themselves and asked him to leave with them so they could talk in private, away from the public area. Massoud refused and said he would not go anywhere without first seeing his brother, who he was there to meet. He explained how this would be your first meeting. The agents were hoping he was there to meet a high-ranking spy or uncover some other secret operation that they could be privy to. Under the circumstance, they felt it necessary to tell Massoud about the possible terrorist attack. Instead of worrying about his own safety and getting out of there, he immediately responded by getting closer to where the passengers were entering the airport to gather up their baggage.

Massoud was determined to warn you. Just then, he noticed a baggage handler riding an electric cart right up behind you as you were walking up a ramp to the terminal building. The agents saw it too, the baggage handlers' coat had come open, revealing a strapped on bomb. They ran to warn the authorities while Massoud jumped the security barrier yelling, "Run!" as he leapt at the man on the cart. The cart, with the two of them, rolled back down the ramp out of harm's way. As the terrorist opened fire and the bomb went off, Massoud was running to save you. He took the bullet and the shrapnel that would certainly have ended your life. The agent told me Massoud died a hero, saving many lives that day as the bomb would have killed most of the passengers that had just got off the plane with you. Massoud died saving your life, Hamasa: a brother he had never met. I know he would love you to get to know his life story, and I would be honored to relay it to you.

Years ago, your brother could have saved my daughter and myself from so much pain and suffering at the hands of the Master of the Jesus Followers: if I had only listened to him then! I am listening now and my children and I are now free human beings, safe here in the USA.

Please find enclosed a few pictures of your two nieces, one nephew and me: Elizabeth Ameera Sydney Baghrani, (Liz for short), Mehria Ameera Sydney Baghrani, (Ria for short) and Massoud Junior Ameer Sydney Baghrani, (Massi for short).

We are all so happy and thrilled at the news of your return to Canada. When we meet, may it be within a timely fashion so that you will still recognize us from the pictures. The years are not kind to us woman folk, so get well soon and we shall meet: please, while I can still walk and have a mind that remembers. My deceased brother's wife, Margaret, also lives near you, in the interior of British Columbia, and would like to visit you, too. I believe her daughter is already there in Vancouver, studying at the University. Her son, Sky, was recently murdered, but that is another story for another time. I will be up that way shortly to reconnect with long lost family members. I hope you are free by then and can stand some visitors.

Please convey my love and best regards to your mom and dad. We have never met but have been in touch. They will be glad to fill you in on the many facets of our exchanges.

Yours truly,

Your sister in-law, Betty

"People, this is what it's all about – family," Hamasa shouted. Family is all about looking out for each other and loving each other. We're all family here today."

Harold pulled out the pictures and handed them to Hamasa, who passed them around, soaked in his tears, to the devotees. There was a quiet awe, as if they were gazing at a newborn. The pictures of the people written about in the letter told many more stories and raised many more questions.

The silence was broken when Hamasa asked, "This must be the face of my brother? This one when he was ten-ish and this one taken just before he passed. His name is written on the back or I would never have guessed. Has anyone found a picture of Sky?"

Was murdered Sky a cousin-in-law, he pondered? He thought the coincidence too great, but it brought his deepest emotions to the surface and he brushed up against the pain that Nayanna must have gone through.

Looking into her eyes, he could see the love, forgiveness and respect that he hoped would create a beautiful family someday. He could only hope that they would be able to raise their children in a new world of cooperation and respect between all people. In Nayanna's eyes, he could see a reflection of all he believed was worth living for; the complex, intriguing, mystical beauty of being human was more than enough to live or die for.

"I will not let my brother's death, or my cousin in-law, Sky's death be in vain. Now more than ever I have to show my power and prove to you and the world that I am the new, humble leader that will take us from slavery to freedom. Who will put a bullet through me? Is there no one brave enough? It's the proof we all need – to see for ourselves."

"Don't start that again, Hamasa! Come with us, to safety!" Harold said firmly as he and the doctor took hold of Hamasa. "We're not going to stand by and allow you to be killed today."

Nayanna's voice rose above the turmoil. "Fly for us, Hamasa! Fly free as a kite! We love you, Hamasa! We believe in you, Hamasa."

The crowd swarmed around Hamasa and someone started to chant, the rest of the people taking up the cry. "Fly, Hamasa fly! Fly, Hamasa fly!"

Harold and the doctor struggled against the push of the crowd but, inexorably, they were driven back.

Freed, Hamasa flew over to Nayanna and hovering over her, he held her outstretched hand. "Nayanna, my love. You're my family." Grabbing ahold of both her hands, he hoisted her above the elated crowd. "People," he cried, "this is all about family and we're all family. I love you all. The Power will heal all of you – and the world! Your presence here is a precious, great gift. I feel all your love and love all of you. I'm a free man, so come and be free with me! I'll wait for you – Nayanna and all of you that are here today. You're all here to witness my true Power and love. You may all join me in creating a new world. I wait for you all in the new world! How about it doctor? And you, too, Harold, are you with me, will I see you on the outside?"

"Yes, yes, certainly, Hamasa," Harold shouted.

"That's all we ever needed or asked for, a little proof, and you've given more than I could've ever imagined, so yes, I'll be there, too," the doctor yelled.

Hamasa flew above the ecstatic crowd with Nayanna wrapped up in his arms, her tears streaming down. As they managed a passionate kiss, the worshippers cried out in exhilaration. High into the celestial ceiling of the chamber they floated. By the time they slowly descended and Hamasa had returned Nayanna safely to the concrete, prison floor, the people, including Harold and the doctor, were transcended believers. Hamasa calmly walked towards the mirrored glass wall and disappeared into his reflection.

Chapter 30

A New Perspective

"A rare moment in the Universe's thirteen billion years is uniquely human, when the truth can be whatever one wants it to be."
John H. K. Fisher

"Nayanna, it's me, Hamasa," he yelled over the crashing waves of the Pacific Ocean. "I knew I'd find you here. I'm coming up." Hamasa entered the tree house Sky had built for Nayanna.

"WTF, Hamasa? Where have you been? How…how did you know I was here? How could you leave us like that?" Nayanna had jumped to her feet and was pacing the floor. "Everyone's waiting for you – Harold, the doctor, everyone! Jesus Christ, Hamasa! They're still there…camped out…calling your name! They left their jobs…to change the world with you. They're being arrested, probably as we speak! How can you let that happen? I escaped…" She glared at him, "Without your help! What the hell are you doing here?" She stopped pacing and looked carefully at Hamasa, seeing a rarely visible, vulnerable boy. Swamped by emotions, Nayanna buried her tears in his chest, sobbing brokenly.

"I'm so sorry, Nayanna," Hamasa whispered. "I got scared. I don't know who I am any more or what I'm supposed to do. I've been wondering around Vancouver and going to all our favorite places – remember? We were together longer than you and Sky were together, remember?"

"I…I came to spread some of Sky's ashes… here," Nayanna choked out between sobs. She stepped away from him. "I still hold you responsible. You're the one who brought 'The Bomb' into your little plot to kidnap God, right!"

"Yes, yes, I know… There are no words to express how sorry I am. I can't imagine what you are going through. But I've missed you so much," Hamasa said quietly. You're the only one I want to talk to…who truly believes in me. You've got to help me figure it all out." A sudden thought struck him. "Is that why you were crying when I held you, when I kissed you as we flew above the crowd – you were thinking of Sky?"

"It's complicated… But me…help you? What can I possibly do?" Nayanna asked, evading his questions about Sky.

Hamasa could see the truth in her eyes, in the way she looked at him.

Nayanna met Hamasa's gaze for a brief moment, blinking suddenly, she was struck by their charge. Grabbing a corner of his shirt, she wiped her face as she got her emotions back under control. She tried to find salvation in his piercing gaze again but only black holes peered back at her. When he closed his lids, the world went dark for her.

Hamasa sighed. "If God gave me these powers, then why isn't He here with me, guiding me? I'm so lost, Nayanna. I don't know what to do. I know, I know, I promised to go forth without Him, or in spite of Him, but I'm afraid. When I close my eyes… the light's gone. I can't burst through the moon and stars to where He is…like I could before. How am I supposed to take on the world, all the evil? I went to the living Master for help but He refused to see me. He put a restraining order against me. His ashram's crawling with FBI and even the army. Who knows what traps they're planting for me. I don't understand any of it. I don't know what powers I have…I've no control over any of it. That's why I haven't found my parents yet. I haven't even got around to proving they're still alive – what if I bring danger to them, too! But yes, we will go back. Nayanna, will you help me to go back and explain to the others?" Hamasa walked to the edge of the tree house floor where Nayanna and Sky had become engaged and flung himself into the ocean. After a moment of swimming against the ocean waves, he flew back up the way he had come. "I just needed to cool down a bit. Did you want to try that with me?"

"Ha-ha, show off, and you should know better than to ask me that…water right…?" She gave a sarcastic look.

"With me you can conquer all your fears." Hamasa lifted her above his head. Lowering her, he held her in his arms.

"You're soaking wet, let me go!" Nayanna squealed. "Oh, so you're getting your confidence back?" She stroked her hands through his un-kempt, shaggy, wet hair. "It was a thrill to fly with you, but what if I fell? Would you be able to bring me back to life?" she asked as Hamasa gently put her on the bed and sat beside her. "You look good with your hair a bit longer. I just need to style it now." She turned serious. "Actually I had a feeling you were near. It's your aroma, some magical essence. But that swim should've erased it." Nayanna breathed in deeply. "I can't get over how good you smell."

"Hey, you keep changing the topic," Hamasa said. "We were talking about if I could bring you back to life!" He shook his head. "I just don't know. How do I test that out? What if I put you or the group in danger, and I'm not able to heal your wounds or bring you back to life if you're killed. Being with me could be dangerous. I saved myself but I have no idea if I can save others. Nayanna," he said gently, tilting her chin up and meeting her troubled eyes. "Don't you see why I'm so afraid? Once I've addressed the world, the world may want to destroy me, and those who stand with me. If I can convince 99 percent of the people, then the elite, the one percent of humanity who have all the money and power and control everything, will have to surrender. But they're the ones who'll say I'm the devil, insane, the Anti-Christ – anything to make the people turn against me. What if they use their weapons of mass destruction against us? How will we survive that? If people only knew their biggest enemies are the systems themselves – of course the corporations, but also the economic systems, the government institutions, the institutions of education, even the institutions of science have been corrupted. They're the true terrorists – working against all life. I have to go up against all of them." Hamasa smiled grimly. "The first thing I'll have to do is take out all their nuclear weapons – they aren't going to like that. We'll need to take their corrupt money and put it towards saving the world before we become extinct. Next, we'll find a way to enhance everyone's brain so their behaviors and thoughts reflect empathy and compassion and follow scientifically proven realities and principles. But we need to have a home base to work from."

"Let's find some land and bring everyone together and draw up some plans," Nayanna said enthusiastically.

"I've been thinking about talking with First Nation's people. Their land's right on the border with the USA and it'll be hard for anyone to arrest us there," Hamasa responded. "Their chief will be on his morning ride by the time we get there. I observed his movements while I was in Vancouver. That's where I got this harness that's going to secure you to me."

"OK," Nayanna leapt to her feet, "let's go then! So we're going to fly?"

This time Hamasa's smile held more conviction. "It's cloudy enough to get away with a flight, but it's over the ocean. Will you be OK?"

"Do I have a choice?" Nayanna asked as she climbed on Hamasa's back. She let out a nervous laugh. "Good thing you came prepared," she quipped, donning the safety harness Hamasa had improvised from an old mountain rescue harness he had found in a store on the reservation. "Oh my God, what am I doing?" Nayanna shouted, her eyes shut tight, holding on for dear life as they flew off into the clouds.

"How do you know what's ahead – how do you avoid smashing into anything?" Nayanna asked, finally remembering to breathe as they stepped onto solid ground.

"I don't understand the mechanics of anything I can do, but I get clear readings in my mind of what's up ahead and which way to go. Like when I can read other's thoughts – I've no idea how I do it, it's just there for me to know."

"Take me to your chief. He's probably got a legend or prophecy that explains everything," Nayanna said, as she spotted whom she felt must be him in the distance.

"You're probably right. He's been watching us. His horse is freaking out more than he is at the sight of us," Hamasa said.

The Chief had been riding along the Pacific beach when his horse had startled. Dismounting, he looked up in time to see Xelas descend from the clouds. His eyes peered from rounded cheeks. He moved slowly, his hands, like sponges that soaked up the salted seas, grasped at the reins preventing his horse from stampeding as Hamasa and Nayanna approached after landing.

"Xelas," he shouted to Hamasa, "our people haven't seen you for over a thousand years. My horse thought you were Cheni, the evil one come for our children, but my heart saw the truth of who you are and spoke to me. You've brought our people's Mother back with you." He bowed down with outstretched arms. "Come, I will let all the people know you've arrived. The crisis is so severe, you couldn't have waited another minute without it being already too late. All the world leaders are corrupt. The smell of evil is everywhere. There's so much that needs to be changed. Far more than you can imagine since the last time you visited. It's interesting and clever you're disguised as a white man, but that's probably the only way they will hear your voice.

"First, please bless the totem we carved for you to honor the great things you did for our people. When the white man came and stole our lands, my people thought it was Earth's last days. But you did not come as promised. They prayed day and night for you to appear, but when you didn't, they knew life in the bowels of the whale would continue for many years. This, now, must be the end times my people talk of – for here you are, among us now. We've seen you in our vision quests and sweat lodges but never in the flesh like this. Our people are at your service. What bird did you transform from?"

"We need land where hundreds of us can meet in secret and safety," Hamasa stated, wondering what transforming into a bird would be like.

The chief brought them to the totem pole and a quick ceremony was performed. Hamasa did the blessing as instructed.

"Also, we'll need to have an abundant source of clean drinking water and food," Nayanna added as they continued to reflect on the totem.

The chief gave a dry chuckle. "You won't find any reserves with those essentials. The colonizers made sure of that. They made sure we stay in a constant state of surrender from the day we were first brought to our knees." He glanced from Hamasa to Nayanna. "Perhaps if you stay state side."

"No," Hamasa said, determined, "we'll stay here. First, we'll take Vancouver, then the Island. Canada will soon be ours – eventually the world!"

"Whoa there pony!" The chief was caught off guard by his frisky horse. "I think," the chief said, laughing as he gently patted the animal's neck, "my pony's up for that ride."

"You're sitting on great wealth you stole from this land and people. You will no longer be one of the corrupt leaders you talk against. We'll be back in three days. Gather all your people here – distribute that wealth equally to all and to those who were forced to leave through economic hardship. Hook up the water lines as you've been promising to do for years now and prepare a feast. Your rewards will be tenfold," Hamasa promised.

The chief fell to his knees, covering his face with his hands.

"How did you know…I'm so sorry…I'm so sorry. What else could I do? They stole from us first. They took our servants, our way of life, our language, our culture! I was going to leave it all to our people when I died. I'll show you my last will and testament.

I needed the money and power to hang on to the little they did leave us. They built a highway through our sacred lands for goodness sakes! Millions in my hands gives me real power! If the money was shared among all of us, it would give only thousands and then we would be left divided and conquered as always. How else can we persevere with the constant hostilities they wage on us? How do we endure, rebuild? This is our tradition, I am from a high lineage and it is expected I will have the markings of wealth and power so the people will follow my orders…my, err, wisdom. All was stolen from me, so, yes, I grabbed it back when I could. Our people are so damaged the money would've been wasted on booze, on gambling, anything to cover the pain. Don't you see? Before we can give up our old ways, our traditions, we need to re-own them. We need our culture and our languages back before we can give them up as gifts for the sake of our future. But yes, yes, I will do as you command with love, hope and wisdom from the four directions." He got up and led them to his home where he would honor his guests before they left.

Three days later, Hamasa, Harold, the Doctor, and hundreds of followers were back as promised. He had brought them out from jails, using all his powers and the cover of night: the government in hot pursuit had no idea what or how it happened.

The chief kept his end of the bargain by bringing in state of the art water filters, digging more wells, laying pipes to connect with the city's water supply system and having a fleet of semis, packed with food, at the ready. Tents were erected to house everyone, Hamasa only grateful that it was June and not February.

A large dais had been prepared for him and taking the microphone in his hands, he addressed the crowd.

"Good afternoon everyone!" Hamasa looked intently into the eyes of everyone present. He found Nayanna in the crowd and motioned for her to come on stage, but she shook her head and stayed put. "Thank you for making this perilous journey with me. Many of you left good jobs and family to be here. Many of you are here because you heard rumors of great things that are going to happen from here. Well, I'll make sure you hear and see things directly from the source, which happens to be me." He smiled at the crowd disarmingly. "So who am I? Well, for those of you who do not know me and are new to the movement and have only heard the rumors, let me explain. First of all, I'm just an ordinary person. I'm up here in my blue jeans and flannel shirt with my sleeves rolled up, ready to get to work like the rest of you. My name's Hamasa. The chief of this land calls me Xelas, the Transformer, a great spirit from their legends." The crowd let out a thunderous wail and applause, full of approval and appreciation.

"Thank you, thank you." Hamasa waited for the crowd to be silent, motioning for silence with his hands. "I assure you, I'm here as your friend and servant and a savior of the world. I'd like to be the guardian angel you've always dreamed of having." Again, the crowd went wild, clapping, and chanting his name. Hamasa paused and then continued. "However, I make no promises until I can be certain they can be kept. We'll take it one day at a time and one miracle at a time. There will be complete transparency, accountability and communication between us at all times. There's a tent set up as the main communication hub and each of the other tents will house the teams that will be organized to take care of the tasks that need to be done. But, before I get ahead of myself, there is one promise I can make with absolute certainty. I promise to use my powers for all of our good, and the good of the Universe. This is all happening so fast I haven't had a chance to do an inventory of all my powers yet, but flying, walking through walls, healing my death wounds and reading minds have all been tested."

Again, the crowd let loose, chanting his name and clapping. Hamasa grinned. "OK, OK, Hallelujah to that. Who among you has a gun and the faith, based on direct experience of my powers, to put a bullet through my heart? This time Harold won't try to stop anyone. Isn't that right?" Hamasa asked as he looked lovingly at Harold. He looked back to the crowd. "This is Harold everyone, he'll be in charge of security. Come up here, Harold – greet the people you'll be protecting." Hamasa greeted him with a big hug and pat on the back.

Those gathered gasped as some among them pulled out their guns and fired at Hamasa. Blood splattered everywhere, but just as quickly as the bullets went through him, Hamasa was able to heal each of the wounds. Harold, however, was still completely thrown and ran off the stage to find the doctor.

"OK, OK, that's enough, haha, or I'll need a blood transfusion soon," Hamasa joked. "Remember, you've all promised to keep all of this a secret for now. Soon, we'll address the world, but not until we're completely ready."

Hamasa flew high into the sky, then descended slowly to the ground, into the midst of the crowd, greeting each person individually. Some had fainted with excitement and the emotions released, while others wanted to check over his healed wounds.

Weeks went by as everyone got organized. Speeches and even performances highlighting various talents were presented. Top leaders from other organizations attended and also gave speeches and offered help. Priorities had to be agreed on and the best approaches to reach goals had to be planned out.

They set themselves up as a not for profit church and the donations started pouring in.

Hamasa wasn't going to wait for criminals to start getting generous, so he flew off to help himself to whatever loot he could get his hands on of theirs. As he gathered up the profits of crime from around the world, he also withdrew billions from illegal offshore accounts the rich had set up as well as appropriating the illegal money stashed in their safety deposit boxes. No one could hide their ill-gotten gains from Hamasa – no one was spared, from the richest people, to corporations, religious organizations and dictators. A corrupt system had allowed trillions of dollars to be hidden away and now Hamasa was going to give it back to humanity. He also discovered he had a knack for winning at every gambling joint he attended and every lottery he bet on. Eventually, he was banned from most of these establishments.

Hamasa and his people needed billions of dollars to buy land, build a city, run their 'church', and feed everyone. All were promised a living wage. They bought huge stretches of land north and west of Calgary. They also bought land in the Rocky Mountains, in case they had to build bomb shelters.

They wanted to show the world how a modern city could be built that would provide shelter for millions of people, be completely self-sustaining and pollution free. They would build vertical greenhouses for all their food production. Everything would be built to last, using the best materials available. Recycling would be taken to the next level, as even all human waste would be re-used. Robots would build and sustain the city, as well as allowing automation of all tasks needed to sustain life. One goal was to eliminate friction such as trains on tracks, thereby doing away with the creation of dust; therefore all transportation would move on cushions of air. The city would be completely interconnected indoors, with lots of outdoor spaces also available. The Venus Project had already supplied the blueprints and the city would be built quickly.

Hamasa's followers from the US applied for refugee status in Canada and others came from all over the world to join the movement. People got into their routines and everyone seemed happy to be making their dreams come true and saving the planet.

"So when are you going to show the world who you are, Hamasa?" Nayanna asked. She had been busy helping in any way she could and wasn't feeling close to Hamasa in the way that she had when they first got re-acquainted. Part of the problem was he could read her every thought, and that made her nervous. Their time apart was giving her the space to deal with Sky's death and to go through all the coping and grieving stages.

"Yes, I can read your thoughts, but it doesn't happen spontaneously, at least not so far. I have to really focus on the person and it seems to help if I can see their eyes. So much seems to happen through the eyes. If it makes you uncomfortable, I can consciously choose not to know your thoughts," Hamasa explained.

"Really!" Nayanna responded. "That would be great for now. Sky found out things about me that I wish he'd never known. It kinda ruined the romance, for me, anyway, in some ways. Sorry for bringing his name up all the time…but…"

"It's OK, Nayanna, I'm just so grateful we have this chance to build a relationship again, whatever that turns out to be. With everything we're going through, it's a one day at a time approach, for me anyway. I've changed so much, and I'm moving on with my life. The things I have to get done…there's just so much. You're still grieving anyway." His expression softened and he gave her a shy smile. "Time will tell, right? If you could have my powers, then maybe you would understand me."

"Yeah, no pressure's best for both of us," Nayanna agreed as they gave high five's. They were spending the final days of preparation visiting the reservation and the chief.

"You can feel the time's right, too, can't you? Hamasa asked. "Well, I'll leave shortly and do what I have to do, but they're going to be all over us after I reveal myself. That's why I want us to be completely off the chief's land before I go public."

Hamasa and Nayanna said their last farewells to the good people of the reservation. Hamasa distributed money tenfold as promised and prophesized a great future for all First Nation People.

He circled the globe rendering all nuclear weapons of mass destruction useless. While the masses rejoiced, world leaders prepared for war against an invisible enemy. Of course, everyone blamed the other and complete chaos ensued.

While the world was reacting to the chaos, Hamasa was secretly meeting with Canadian leaders and the press. Canada held a referendum and an overwhelming majority agreed with the Prime Minister that a complete surrender to Hamasa and his ideals would be in the best interest of the whole planet as well as the Universe. They knew with Hamasa's godly abilities and talent for gathering money, they were lucky to be the first invited. Vancouver would always be Hamasa's favorite city, so he chose it to have his coming out party. He invited all the news networks to a conference where he promised to reveal himself as the culprit rendering countries less harmful.

"People of Canada, planet Earth, it is with great honour and humility that I introduce myself. Many of you may have seen videos of me displaying my abilities. My name is Hamasa. I am your guardian angel. My plan is to facilitate the rule of love, introduce a resource based economy, equality, fairness, and great joy in the world for everyone. First we destroy all weapons of mass destruction, divide power, money and resources equally and finally to compassionately, scientifically change the human brain, so it is never again able to create evil and harm to others. Without a brain-changer people will never stop finding ways to hurt others. However, there are those who would oppose everything I hope to do. People are manipulated into perceiving the world with their animalistic instincts and their reptilian brains. They will see everything we do as a threat. I have taken away their money – sorry, but anyone who got rich while others starved or the planet suffered was not the best for humanity, even though the system allowed it. I have taken away their weapons of mass destruction. Nevertheless, we are still vulnerable to their cunning ways. They will do whatever they can to preserve their worldview and their power. They will see any attempt to reason with them or change them as a threat to the survival of their egos and identities and their very survival as people. They will strike out. We must be vigilant. However, we will prevail if we stand together with our human values of love and equality. It is not enough to love yourself, your family, or your tribe – we must love everyone and take care of our home – planet Earth. To that end, I propose to pay everyone who joins our movement a universal income, until such time it is no longer necessary. Sign up and offer to help in whatever way your talents and interests dictate. Our ultimate goal is to change the world and people completely by doing away with all governments, all systems of currency, exchange, or trade. We will automate everything, and supply each family their needs based on available resources. Scientists will find a way to optimize our brains. We have started a model city here in Canada, and hope to emulate its success all over the world. Details can be found on our web site, www.freedom-now.com. May love prevail!"

As he exited the stage, Hamasa noticed someone he had met through The Venus Project movement who was there to speak and give support.

"I'm so glad you could be here to help answer questions," Hamasa said, shaking hands. "So, Reg, thanks again."

"Yes, yes, of course, anything I can do to help. It's a very complicated topic, so it needs to be explained very carefully," Reg said. "People's first reaction, based on the brainwashing techniques and propaganda of the elite, is to freak out believing we are implementing communism or socialism, which is totally unfounded. This is building systems and dealing with reality and the finite resources of our planet. I am here on my own, and in no way representing The Venus Project, but I am always glad to help wherever I can. I never believed I would see this day come in my lifetime. However, thanks to you, Hamasa, there's hope for everyone. Supporters around the globe are at your service."

"Do you know experts who could deal with the backlash we'll be getting soon?" Hamasa asked, concerned. "What really worries me is there might even be a chemical weapons attack. Very soon now," he continued, "we'll know who our enemies are and we must have a way to neutralize them. If armies don't surrender or won't allow people to join our movement, then I'll have to take out the leaders myself and move them to an isolated place," Hamasa pondered.

Reg nodded. "Good idea, maybe to Antarctica, but after removing one, another'll take their place. It could be a long time and many arrests before people stop resisting. We could house them on a cruise ship for now, until we get the chance to build housing for them somewhere. They can fight over who'll be the ruler of the ship or have to scrub the floors," he said. "By the looks of it, we might need a few cruise ships to hold everyone in the short term."

"Can you get that set up while I go out and grab a few of these dictators?" Hamasa asked. "It's one thing if the people of a country vote to stay where they are, but if they aren't even allowed the choice, then I have to do something about that."

"Would you kill in self-defence?" Reg bravely asked.

Hamasa was silent for a moment, then, "I hope I never have to face that situation, but yes, certainly. It would have to be a direct threat and if there were no other way...it would be for the good of everyone, right?"

"Canada's come to their senses and joined in but if you go around abducting world leaders without even the United Nations giving you the OK, you might be going against international law and be subject to arrest yourself. So we'll put the cruise ship in Hudson's Bay. That way it won't be a sitting duck, or, for that matter, a sitting Canada goose," Reg joked, "sitting in international waters. Canada will give you all the protection it can for now, I'm sure. Hopefully, other countries will soon sign on. In the meantime, I'll definitely be moving here with as many like-minded associates possible."

"Well, can you find a way to deal with that, too? I know you have the connections," Hamasa pleaded.

Reg smiled. "Sure, we'll compile a list of everything that needs to be taken care of while you're away." He clapped Hamasa on the shoulder. "I'm here to help in any way I can. One thing that's really puzzling me though – if you don't mind me asking?"

Hamasa nodded consent.

"You saw God, then?" Reg continued. "I've read all the documents and gone through all your public statements, but what makes you so sure you saw God? Thing is," he said, shooting Hamasa an openly curious look, "the word 'God' must have some benevolent significance to it, don't you think? And so far as I can see, there isn't any benevolence going on in this world." He paused, eyeing Hamasa again. "Anyway, I was wondering if you'd be interested in being part of a scientific investigation into this whole phenomenon...your phenomenon, I mean." He shook his head, laughing quietly. "My journey to truth has taken many twists and turns, like yours. But as soon as I think I know the answers, it usually turns out to be just another fork in the road. You know what I'm sayin' here? I'm not trying to question your take on things, but there could be other explanations for what you have been through and I'd like to make a thorough investigation. I don't doubt the powers you have, I've seen them with my own eyes, really, but let's try to find the true source of them. It shouldn't take much of your time, but it would be good to get started before you leave. There are great facilities here in Vancouver we could go to while you're here."

Hamasa said nothing, his eyes staring blankly ahead, then, "Do you have a working hypothesis you'd care to share?" he asked.

Reg pushed his windblown hair back off his forehead before meeting Hamasa's gaze. "Let's just say, based on intensive research over many years, you may've had a 'close encounter of the fifth kind'".

"A close encounter of the what-who kind?"

"Hey," Reg spread his arms wide, "we just have to get you into an MRI. Researchers...neuroscientists, would love to see what's going on in your brain when you do your miracles... probably when you do anything!"

Hamasa turned the idea over in his mind, admitting it held some appeal. "My first stop was going to be North Korea," he said. The people haven't been allowed to hear about me. And it's a matter of priority to free them from those hideous haircuts," he joked. Then more seriously, "But it can wait. Most countries are declaring martial law and trying to hold onto power. If I wait a few days, I'll know how my message to the world has been received by the people, and what other countries are keeping their people from hearing what I have to say." He smiled tightly. "OK – let's get it done."

"We have to get the US on board here right away," Reg mused. "That's got to be our first priority anyway."

Hamasa nodded. "I totally agree. I'll focus on the US first. In the meantime, we'll start your research but I'd prefer to do it in Alberta, where my new home is. I'm sure they've got good MRI facilities there, too. Then you can study the results with whomever and wherever you choose."

"Sounds good to me," Reg acknowledged.

"Nayanna, I missed you so much. When can I have you always by my side?" Hamasa proclaimed, hoping to get a favorable response. He had just flown back to the Calgary area, where millions were gathering to help build the new world, and had gone straight to her.

"I'm so excited to be part of everything that's happening," Nayanna said, smiling widely. "We've so much to focus on that's more important than...well..." She treated Hamasa to a long look. "You could have anyone you want. Heaven knows, I'm not perfect…I'm not even sure any more if I want kids with what's going on now. And you never call when you go away! You must think I have telepathy too?" Nayanna sighed, raking her fingers through her long hair. "I'm so confused! And I'm still mourning Sky, and Master. My dad," she paused, pulling in a deep breath, "Dad's going to Akhee's ashram in New York – wants me to go with him. He wants to spread the rest of Sky's ashes there." She could see Hamasa's head tilt down and the tight lines his lips made and felt his pain. She changed the topic. "Bottom line, Hamasa, I'm here for you. What can I do? I'm sorry, but I just can't believe there's now a good chance we can change the world for the better." She met his gaze. "In my lifetime!"

"I accept the past that we can't run from, but why New York, why Akhee? He deserted us, I reached out to him… If he interferes with anything, so help me, I won't put up with it!"

Hamasa reined in his anger, saying more gently, "Hey, on a more positive note, we've started paying universal income to everyone – and I can't believe the cooperation we're getting. It's great to know people have faith in us and our ability to meet all their needs. We've started manufacturing the robots that'll build and run the world. Speaking of the world, I have to meet with all the leaders at the UN tomorrow. Well, at least it's great to come home and have you here. I don't know if it's a link to my past life or a natural healthy desire for good things to come, but I can't get you off my mind. Stay safe, Nayanna. Be mindful. Things are going well so far but these are turbulent times and not everyone's happy with the plans. I'll feel safer once the US comes on board." He pulled Nayanna into his arms, pressing her close in a long hug. Letting go of her, he headed to bed, alone. Turning back to where Nayanna stood, tears spilling onto her face, he said, "I'll respect whatever you decide to do, Nayanna. We've got things covered on this end. Just take your time, do what you feel you have to do. Just don't go anywhere until we know it's safe, OK."

Nayanna nodded, swiping at tears that wouldn't stop, refusing to voice the fact Hamasa's single-minded attention for his missions and the time apart was a big divide and hard for her to live with.

Chapter 31

Transformations

"When time heals, heal the times."
John H. K. Fisher

Addressing the world leaders at the UN convinced Hamasa he had a long way to go to convince countries to give up their military and their monetary systems voluntarily. Most surrendered, but what could followers do if their countries declared martial law, brought out the military and didn't allow anyone to leave? It was a tense standoff. Some countries were taking advantage of the power shifts in the world and were marching into neighboring countries to take them over. Some religious leaders refused to give up power and declared the antichrist was now amongst them and the end times were at hand. The US, with fundamentalist right wing Christians in power, was preparing for, in no particular order: World War 3, war with Muslims, Armageddon and the return of Jesus. They were freaking out at the thought of not being the strongest bully without their atomic bombs. At the moment it was hard to tell how the country or the world would react or cope.

It all spelled danger ahead. Hamasa knew he had to find out if he could protect his followers, and soon. Without raising the dead, he worried how he would be able to maintain his leadership.

In the meantime, he stayed focused on the most important tasks. With millions of people focused on building a new, high-tech, sustainable city, Hamasa was hoping it could be done by year's end. Top leaders in the field were on-site with ready-made plans in hand, created by 'The Venus Project'.

"This is the perfect place to start a new city," their

spokesperson told Hamasa. "Millions of skilled people already live in the area and there's a bounty of natural resources – water, sunlight, minerals and building materials."

"But if we can't get the US on board, we'll be like sitting ducks when they invade," Hamasa stated.

"Well, you better go do your thing, appeal to the people and show them it's in their interest, or squash their leaders if need be. But we've got this here covered. Your new home will be up and running in no time now that the robots are in charge."

"Robots in charge?" Hamasa reiterated.

"Well, you know what I mean. No AI, no city. You also talked about changing the human brain to function with empathy and fairness, well AI may be just what we've been waiting for to do that for us. In the meantime, we're sure AI will come up with a good defense system so you can sleep well and conserve your energy. We're so honored you incorporated The Venus Project manifesto. They are the true founders in all this."

"The honor is truly all mine," Hamasa said. "Jacques Fresco's energy and focus is amazing for almost being a centenarian and Roxanne Meadows is such a talented artist, doing all the technical renditions to help build this new city and world. She's dedicated to the vision and getting the word out." He smiled. "You're lucky you've had the chance to work with them," he threw over his shoulder as he hurried away. He was off to deal with the US, get a brain scan, and imprison a few dictators until a cure for bad behavior was developed.

He went to say goodbye to Nayanna, to promise her he would keep in touch better. Instead, he discovered, without notifying anyone, she had gone to New York to see Akhee. In a panic, he flew off into the starry night. A full moon reflected off his threatened eyes as he scorched by.

He descended on the ashram too late. The house he searched first had crime scene tape all around and over the doors; it was empty of humans. Furniture was overturned and blood was everywhere he looked. Hamasa ran through the next building and found Akhee, alone, meditating. Giving him a good shake opened his eyes.

"What's going on here? Where's Nayanna?" Hamasa demanded, staring scornfully at Akhee.

"The police have just left, Hamasa," the Master answered quietly. "She's been taken. They killed two of my disciples and hurt a few others that tried to save her." He paused, his eyes on Hamasa. "I don't know, she might've been injured, too. She put up quite a fight I was told. The others could do nothing. Her father is safe, but hasn't been informed yet. Maybe that's something you could handle when he wakes."

"You were told! Where were you the whole time it was happening? What are you doing here?" Hamasa screamed, not expecting an answer. "What kind of God are you? What if it was your wife…you just gonna' sit there?"

"I know you don't have all the powers you were hoping for," Akhee said, staying calm. "Sit here; focus your whole attention on the memory of Nayanna's eyes. I'll be repeating some words. Write down what you see," he added, handing Hamasa a pen and a notebook. He walked over to a digitally locked, steel door, punched in the code and entered an office. Hamasa stealthily snuck over to see the Master open a safe and pull out a large, ancient manuscript he carefully placed on a desk podium. Gently thumbing through a few pages, he started reading. Hamasa ran back to his place and sat down again just as the Master locked the door behind him and continued chanting. "Omri monasay podamay ommmmmatay, omri monasay podamay ommmmmatay."

Hamasa listened intently, eyes closed in meditation, as Akhee repeated the words over and over. The chanting ceased and Hamasa grabbed the pen and started writing.

"I've got it! I saw where they took her! Fly with me, we can't lose any more time."

The Master was unperturbed. "This is a matter for the police. I'm not going anywhere with you." Picking up the phone, the Master dialed the number the detective had left with him. Reaching across, he took the notebook from Hamasa and read out the directions. "Yes, yes, a boat called '*The Protector*.' Yes, Lower Bay, just past the Narrows Bridge, Staten Island. No, no, we didn't see her go there personally, but we were—"

The phone line went dead. As Akhee tried to redial, he was thrown flat on his back by a bullet that penetrated the window, smashing through his rib cage, just missing its mark. Tear gas began to fill the room as a man in a gas mask rammed open the door, shooting at Hamasa with a tranquilizer gun. Hamasa charged the man, who had thrown down his weapon and drawn a knife. He got one good strike into Hamasa's heart before his arm was ripped out from his shoulder. The assailant went down on his knees coughing as Hamasa removed his gas mask. Snapping his neck, Hamasa left him dead on the floor. Rushing across to the Master, he picked him up and brought him to the steel door.

"Open it, quick! More will be coming!"

Akhee was weakly coughing up blood, but he was able to punch in the code. Safe inside the room, Hamasa focused on his wounds and stared wild eyed as they healed in seconds. He turned his attention to Akhee.

"Nothing's happening!" he cried moments later. "I can't save you! Do something!"

Pointing a trembling hand at the safe, the Master spat out a series of numbers and letters. "7-13-92-Florentia-24-3-Aliens-200K-B-C, two left one right," before collapsing.

Hamasa ran to the safe. "OK, to the left 7, to the left 13, now to the right 92." Hamasa muttered, desperately hoping he was correct. "To the left F and then L or just F? OK, just F, then 24 left, now right three. A left...what! There is no 200, OK, OK, 2 left then 100 right, or would it be 100 X two, no, no, that wouldn't work."

He armed sweat from his forehead and carried on, still muttering to himself. "OK, K and B left and C right…and it should open! "Hor-ray!" Hamasa yelled, overcome with relief when it did. He could hear the police sirens getting closer. He had no idea where to look in a thousand page ancient manuscript.

"Akhee," he said, while turning pages, "don't die on me! Can you hear me? What page am I looking for?"

Akhee's fingers slowly started to shift with his index finger touching his thumb to make a zero; it left three fingers.

"Thirty?" Hamasa murmured. He watched Akhee's left hand fingers make a four as his thumb disappeared under his palm. "Thirty-four!" Frantically, he thumbed to the page.

"Om, nar, nar, tar, ti, anom," Hamasa chanted the words that were written on the page, looking worriedly into Akhee's face. Suddenly the Master's eyes opened and Hamasa continued with full concentration, starring into his eyes. "Om, nar, nar, tar, ti, anom."

"Yes…yes, Hamasa, it's all about the eyes! The eyes receive the code, the energy. Please keep going! You're saving my life."

The police were banging on the door. Hamasa sighed. "I'd better deal with them before they break in here," he said. A couch leaned against one wall and Hamasa snatched up a pillow to cover his eyes and nose before opening the door. "We're fine!" he told the masked officers, holding up one hand in a gesture of surrender while handing over his ID. "We'll come out as soon as you clear out the tear gas." The officer verified the ID and let Hamasa retreat back into the room.

He closed the door and tore into Akhee. "What the hell's going on? Who the hell are you? Tell me what this book's all about? If I don't start getting some answers, I swear I'm going to let you die here, I promise! If that's what it's going to take to get your dad back here, to get God to finally reveal Himself, then so be it!"

Akhee tried to take the book from Hamasa but he fended him

off.

"The book's useless without me alive...and you'll be useless, too," Akhee rasped.

"You're the one who seems useless. Where's all your God given powers that I thought your dad gave to you? He has given me more than he gave to you it seems. You're a fraud. Hey, sit down," Hamasa ordered. "You aren't getting anywhere near this book until I get some answers. Why the hell aren't you flying out of here?" he shouted, losing patience. "The miracles I can do, you must be able to do better and more, right? Come on, what's going on? I gotta' go and make sure Nayanna's OK, but I'm taking this book with me."

"No! I can't let you do that! The police won't let us leave. You don't know what you have there. You could ruin everything."

Akhee charged at Hamasa who sent him sprawling on the floor with one swipe.

"Well, well," Hamasa drawled, as Akhee slowly picked himself up. "We're finally getting somewhere. So, when did it become all about the book? I thought we got rid of the books and were going for the real deal, the source of all the energy, of all creation – God and finding Him through meditation not some book. So now, what's the deal with the book?"

The police were banging on the door again. Book in arms, Hamasa called, "Yes, officer, is it safe to come out yet?" He opened the door and looked as the officer stood there, holding a raw, meaty looking stump of an arm. Hamasa's gaze traveled downwards to the hand, the fingers and, finally, the knife. "Where's the body?"

"We were hoping you could tell us something about that?" the officer told him. "Hello, Akhee," he said, looking past Hamasa. "We meet again, so soon. I'm afraid, too soon – for the wrong reasons." He brought his attention back to Hamasa. "I'm Detective Bowers by the way," he added, offering his hand. Hamasa and Akhee shook the officer's hand. "Any idea who could've done this or why? What the hell was going on in here?" he asked, glancing around himself, his eyes skimming over their blood stained clothing. "We'll need a full statement. It's late and I know you've both been through a lot already, but we'll keep it brief for now and we'll pick it up in a few days. Seems like there was fighting going on in here, is everything OK?"

"Well," Hamasa ventured, "there were shots—"

"Hold on, hold on," Bowers interrupted, "we'll take statements separately for now, thanks. I'll stay with Akhee and you can go with Lieutenant Greeves over there, Hamasa."

"Officer, he has my book!" Akhee screamed as he again tried to wrestle it from Hamasa. The officers separated and restrained them both.

"OK, who owns the book?" Bowers asked, looking intently at Hamasa. "Hey, aren't you the guy on TV the other day, changing the world?"

Hamasa nodded.

"Alright, alright, well I guess you get to keep the book. I sure as hell aren't taking it from you." Bowers laughed. "Well let's go have that chat then, this should be interesting, probably mind-blowing!"

After giving his statement, Hamasa had some questions of his own. "Have you heard from the police you sent to save Nayanna?" adding impatiently, "I've got to get out of here right away. I have to make sure she's safe." He frowned. "Am I free to leave?"

Without waiting for an answer, Hamasa ran through a wall and flew off into the night with the book carefully wrapped and tucked into his backpack and an officer too shocked to react.

He arrived just as negotiations with the kidnappers failed; police were storming the boat. Hamasa wasted no time; he flew straight into the room where Nayanna was being wrapped up in saran. Her kidnappers had a water barrel, partially full of metal beads that would take her to her Atlantic Ocean grave, alive: well, at least for a few minutes. Instead, Hamasa managed to stuff all three startled, rogue sailors into it. He sealed it tight before carrying Nayanna out onto the upper deck where he unraveled her from the saran wrap. Bullets were flying everywhere. Hamasa hesitated, deciding he would have a better chance jumping into the water unnoticed than flying off into the sky. He told Nayanna as much.

"No! Not the water, Hamasa! My God, what are you thinking?"

Ignoring her, he carefully wrapped the book with the saran, put it back into his waterproof backpack and grabbing hold of Nayanna, he grated, "You want to stay here and die or come with me and live?"

Nayanna screamed as they went into free fall like the ride of doom. "Don't let go of me, Hamasa!"

The best part for him was giving Nayanna mouth to mouth so they could stay under the water for the mile it took to clear the reach of any bullets searching for them. "That didn't take long," the Master said, unmoved by Hamasa's grand entrance through the wall. "Where's Nayanna?" he asked just as the sound of someone gently knocking on the door came to his ears. "Yes. Yes, Nayanna, come in. He can bring material things with him through walls, like my book," he muttered as Nayanna stepped into the room, "but I guess he was afraid to try that with living cells. He should know if he can bring himself through, then he'll also be able to bring you, too." He glanced at Hamasa, who was busy embracing Nayanna as if they hadn't seen each other in months. "Don't worry, we'll have a chat about that. OK, you two, I think we have some business to take care of here." He directed another disgusted look at Hamasa. "I want my book back now, please, or I'll call the police back here."

Hamasa ignored him completely, his attention solely on Nayanna. "Where are you injured? I know they shot you with a tranquilizer, but why did you have blood on you?" Hamasa asked, remembering how he had checked her over carefully at the boat.

Nayanna snorted. "That's some fool's blood. He thought he could mess with me. Keep looking, you might find an eye or two."

"You're OK then?" Hamasa asked

Nayanna laughed, her face flushed. "I feel wonderful! I've had an oxygen transfusion, I've overcome my fear of water and my love life's bouncing back! What more can I say? Oh, and it smells great in here," she said, looking dreamily at Hamasa.

"I need my book back," the Master interrupted as they fell into each other's arms again, kissing.

Reluctantly, Hamasa released Nayanna. "OK, so where did we leave off?" Hamasa addressed Akhee. Spotting a comfy couch, he steered Nayanna over towards it. Sitting down, he pulled out the book. "So," he said, eying the Master speculatively, "I think you were just about to die unless you start explaining what this book's about. It's in a language I've never seen before."

"Go to page 862. Repeat the words there while looking into my eyes," Akhee said, unruffled. "The letters may start to have some meaning for you," he added. "Then you can ask me what you like."

Hamasa thumbed through the first few pages of the book, suddenly able to understand every word. "What!" he blurted. "Computer game! There's that idea again, that life's just a game. Aliens! Extraterrestrials!" he yelled as he read further. "What's going on here, Akhee? With the turn of a page, you've gone from God to Alien! You're telling me you're from Florentia?"

"Is that in this galaxy?" Nayanna asked, getting excited by the unfolding revelations, but also becoming anxious at the thought of her father finding out his beloved Master was an alien. She was cuddled up close to Hamasa on the couch, looking over the book, her pouty, Elvis lips at the ready.

Master sat in the chair across, "Yes, yes." He nodded his

head slowly. "But you must promise to keep this all top secret. I mean this is all news to me, too. My father kept all this secret from me. He was my God and savior. I had no idea about any of this. That's why the book is so important to me – it holds all the answers, the history and all the knowledge. I need the book to develop all my Powers.

"Apparently, our planet was dying, being sucked into a black hole along with our suns. They had to leave everything, all they'd accomplished. After many thousands of years of evolving, they had finally been able to build a super computer, and they were just starting to make contact with the creators of this Universe, of this simulation. Instead, they had to head out in a mother ship to find a new world to inhabit."

"Simulation?" Nayanna frowned. "Is this a weird dream I'm having? So what's real then? What will I tell my dad?"

"What's the truth? Is that what you're asking, Nayanna?" Hamasa stared at her perplexed. "So what is the truth, Akhee?" he asked, brushing the hair from Nayanna's eyes and looking impatiently at the Master. "Did your people…make contact? How would they know?"

"Well," Akhee hesitated. "My ancestors developed greater powers and with the super computer tapped into energy they had no explanation for, things would appear out of nowhere, defying all the laws of physics. Then a voice contacted them through the super computer and told them who they were, that they were required to do many things throughout the Universe before being allowed to return. The new energy would propel them forward, they were told. Once they were onboard their ship, they found themselves teleported to different places in the Universe – against their will."

Hamasa was still browsing through the book. "What? A simple cure for cancer! You've been hiding instructions on how to rid the world of cancer?" Anger blazed from him. He raked his hand through his hair. "I think I'll just smack you so hard it'll send you back to your mother of a ship."

"Please, let me explain, and remember I was kept in the dark about all this, too," Akhee begged. "Yes, I think they got close to finding the truth, but then..." He stroked his beard. "Every time they got it together, they would end up in some battle with each other. Finally, they learned to control and conquer their inner demons. Then, when victory finally came and everyone was working together, when there was peace and progress and hope for eternal life, they were challenged by forces out of their control."

"Like that damn, big, black hole that would have sucked them all into who knows what hell!" Nayanna stated.

Akhee sighed. "Yes, or like the volcanos and ice age that nearly wiped us out here," he elaborated.

"You've been here that long?" Hamasa asked.

"Well, my people have, or what we transformed into. A small craft was sent out from the mother ship to explore earth, but it crashed and lost all communication. Those on board expected to be rescued at any moment, but that never happened. Eventually, they realized the mother ship must've been teleported somewhere else. On top of that, they weren't adjusting too well to the environment and knew before long they would die, possibly before they could reproduce, as some were already doing. Desperate, they tried mating with animals to see if that would help their offspring adapt better – mostly using artificial insemination. But when that proved largely unsuccessful, some of them transplanted their brains into them instead, well largely into the monkeys, and that proved to be a lot more promising – it created the human race. Then the volcanos and ice age hit. The rest is history, as they say."

"History, what history? History didn't start for another two or three hundred thousand years for us, maybe a million if you came that long ago," Hamasa said.

"You want all the details?" The Master asked mildly. "Then

you will have to read the whole book like I just did."

Hamasa snorted. "Well, just what's necessary to get out of this mess, alive!" He shook his head, anger boiling up in him again. "Why d'you let the world burn and not do anything? Why don't you use your power...should be greater than mine?" He looked over to Nayanna who looked as if she had questions of her own.

"This looks like the Sanskrit language," she said slowly. "My father showed me books with this kind of writing."

"Yes, that's the language they brought to Earth." The Master glanced fondly at Nayanna. "There are many secrets...ummm?" He looked back to Hamasa. "We need to preserve our energy. From what I am reading, if I use my power in this world, then I lose connection with the world or the super computer they were able to create in the Master's mind, which is in my mind now. That's just how the creators of the Universe programmed things. Of course, they never say what the rules of the game are, but through trial and error, my ancestors figured out a lot. It seems as if they want large numbers of people working together solving tasks. And that's the hardest thing to make happen. Our race had to make a choice back in Florentia, and then again here on Earth, to work together. Although they were able to get some people cooperating, they still couldn't find the right materials or a conducive place to build a super computer here on Earth, so they built it in the Master's mind. He had to sacrifice his life to get the job done but by following certain laws, his successor was able to receive the super computer into his mind and upload the Master's brain to the computer and in that way they were closer to finding eternal life when they died. One person is always able to carry this work forward to a new generation. That will be where I will go when I die. Yes, to a simulation within a simulation. When I die, my mind will be uploaded to the new Master's mind, my Successor, who will have received the super computer by way of transferring all the software and instructions through the eyes. That's the process Dad made you a part of when he got you to look into my eyes. In the past everyone died, body and mind, until they were able to start building the machine, the super computer. We need to try to connect with the programmers – the ones who created this Universe and discover the truth, and find eternity, and now it's possible." Akhee fell silent for a moment. "But it's all just a big game to them," he added softly, "and who knows how they want it to end. They seem to keep changing the parameters and the rules. Who would've believed they would let you loose on the world with the powers they gave you?"

"So these...programmers, they're the ones controlling everything that's happening...not the Masters?" Hamasa asked.

"But now you're the creators of your own worlds?" Nayanna asked.

"You're Gods there, creating everything you desire," Hamasa added.

"Yes, yes," Akhee admitted. "Yes...much more interesting than anything going on in this Universe, where we have no control. But the programmers, yes, they control it all, we only control the mind world we are creating. We can use our powers in the inner mind world and we create things that are as interesting as we like," the Master replied.

"Oh, so the document that states God gets bored easily, is kind of true then?" Nayanna asked.

"So they, and you aliens as accomplices, created this crazy game, where it's like karma on steroids, so they can keep themselves amused," Hamasa piped in, ready to explode.

"It might appear to be that way to you, but believe me it has nothing to do with us, other than the bad effects we create by trying to survive, by hiding the truth while we try to find the truth, if that makes sense at all," the Master replied with a chuckle.

"We kept track of the lineage, until the natural disasters struck and destroyed records and scattered everyone throughout the planet. The spaceship got swallowed by a volcano and we lost all our technology. Things would've worked out a lot differently if we hadn't had to amalgamate with apes and other animals. Fortunately, the first Florentians were able to live long enough to make sure the new births were successful. After many failed attempts, they even managed a successful birth of their own. The baby was able to quickly evolve and adapted well to the new climate. He lived for thousands of years helping us evolve. With his help, my ancestors created many great civilizations around the world in order to avoid disasters that could've wiped out everyone. He sacrificed himself, he gave his life and mind so we could have everlasting life, much like the choice you'll have to make, Hamasa. The creators will give you all the power, if you choose to save the world, but you'll have to sacrifice your life. That first pure-born infant was the one who was able to create a super computer within his own mind using technology brought in the ship. It was lucky to be done before the ship was lost. Anyway, he transferred it to his Successor's mind, who then passed it on to the next Master. From there, many Masters and their followers have populated that mind world. He created the first true Master from the alien/monkey mix and the lineage has been unbroken since. Otherwise, we would've become extinct. We started religions and handed down sacred writings to keep the truth secret. Our dream is to find our creators and eternal life, while we're still alive."

"OK, so how does it end?" Nayanna asked. "And why do you bother getting people to meditate and to be peaceful and follow you?"

"The meditation helps balance negative forces so we don't have to use our powers to stay alive," Akhee replied, looking lovingly at Nayanna. "Meditation is also the only way to test who carries the best software in their brains. In addition, we need to populate our mind world. By the time the meditators die, their brains are ready and programmed to enter or be uploaded to the world we created in the Master's mind. Again, we need large numbers of people willing to work together to get the job done. Atomic weapons were a game changer. We all could've died – that's where you came in handy." Akhee smirked. "I still get to Heaven and you stopped the idiots. Now we can stay focused on finishing building the super computer, which is now in my mind, and getting in touch with the aliens who created us. You see, we need each other!"

"Well we aren't home free yet, there's still climate change, AI that can go rogue, pollution causing species extinction, over population and many other disasters," Hamasa pleaded.

"That's where you save the day and me again and again," Akhee responded.

"What did you guys look like before you mated with monkeys and became the human race – wow, I guess that's me?" Nayanna asked.

"Well, first of all, we didn't have our sex organs as part of a sewage system like you do. Ours were at the end of our tails. But sex was purely a mental activity." Akhee stroked his unbound beard. "I'll leave the rest to your imagination.

"We had no hair. We didn't breath through the same passage where food passes. Anyway, you can't imagine how horrible it was for them to start the mating process with animals. The results were some pretty strange creatures running into the jungles and oceans, from what I read." Master chuckled. "After the disasters, many of my ancestors died out and our race almost became extinct. That was when the ancestors realized the importance of writing everything down. They spread these records around, in case of another disaster."

"So I'm half monkey and half alien?" Hamasa was just starting to come to grips with all the facts he was having a hard time accepting. "More importantly, do I have the power to bring others back from the grave now, like I did with you? I want to make sure I can protect everyone. I want to find my parents, and make sure I can keep them safe."

"Yes, yes, Hamasa." Akhee nodded vigorously. "It's all in the book. It explains everything. How the game's played and how it affects everyone. Like I said, we figured out a lot from trial and error. You can't imagine all the secrets discovered using the super computer. The brain's an organic computer with lots of different software components. It's all in the sounds, the codes. That's what stimulates the software programs and gets them up and running. That's why people are so different, too. It all depends on the programming...the words or sounds they get at birth, and what programs managed to survive the birth – that's what determines so much of the brain's development. At just the right stage in a baby's development, certain sounds had to be inputted into their brain. My people carried out certain rituals for each stage. The many disasters separated a great number from these rituals. That's when it became the wild west, the law of the jungle. It's all in the books that were hidden in our pyramids, where the rituals were performed. I've been studying and learning all this history from the moment I was released, after Dad transferred everything to me. I didn't grow up knowing all this. Soon I will get all my information from within my mind, from Father. You wouldn't believe the shock I had to go through when I first got the keys to this place and found the book. Every turn of the page gave me the promise of powers beyond my wildest dreams but also revealed the truth that had been hidden from me. It also revealed the decision I had to make – never to use the powers on Earth. It was mind-blowing and very emotional, as I had to piece my whole life back together to account for these new revelations. In time, by studying the book and doing all the rituals, I will be able to fully access the super-computer Father uploaded to my mind. But to answer your question, yes, you'll be able to bring people back from death, especially since you are willing to sacrifice your life to this world."

"Oh, so I won't be able to join your world and have eternal

life because I want to save this world. That is a disgusting choice to have to make. So is that why your dad was so interested in the documents the mafia had. He thought they'd found one of your books. OK, I think I've heard enough of this craziness. Just tell me how I put a stop to it all?" Hamasa asked as Akhee shook his head. "So I assume you plan to keep your T-S-S-U-T-M movement going then? You'll try to keep everything a secret even though we don't want your eternity. We want Heaven on Earth now!"

"What do you mean, stop everything?" Akhee, still shaking his head, responded defiantly. "There's no stopping anything, Hamasa. It's all beyond anyone's control, even the Master's. Remember, this simulation is being controlled by who knows whom from who knows where – it's still a great mystery. The only hope is to find a way to access the first computer, the one that started everything and obtain everlasting life. Then we sit back and watch the game unfold as humans blow themselves into extinction or not. Just read the book, it explains everything in great detail. And, yes, Hamasa, we have to keep the game going – religions, and the illusion of there being a God."

"So I guess that means I won't be joining you any time soon, as I plan to save this world from extinction and from all the psychos out there who rule it. I'm going to bring us into the golden age of peace and love and I don't care how boring that may be to all the deranged out there, or to you. So no, we'll not be keeping the game going – it won't be business as usual with me here. It's as if you found a zoo and handed out money, power and guns freely to every creature. The insane asylum is being run by the insane. Well that's got to stop!"

Hamasa got to his feet. "Well, Akhee, it's been very enlightening. I was always looking for the truth. Past explanations didn't quite make sense in the context of this evil world, but now it's starting to. In some weird way, I guess I have to thank you for this extraordinary experience, though trillions of life forms have suffered and died so you could keep your secrets. Your book holds the key to reprogramming everyone's brain to make them actually work properly. For thousands of years people have been shamed, imprisoned and killed to force them into behaviors that fulfil the changing needs of the ruling elite – to work jobs and join armies in order to avoid poverty and death, and the whole time – you had a cure! Wow, that's some twisted sadism going on there. You need some deep therapy. Maybe it's time you had to face the consequences of your actions? The end goals just don't justify the means in all this human misery. No human was ever responsible for anything that happened."

"Hold on a minute!" Ahkee jumped in. "I'm not responsible either! In our own way, Masters have been trying to save as many as we can. By keeping the secret going, we might be saving millions. It's all the fault of the algorithms. The programmers are the ones responsible. You can hold them to account once we find them. As soon as we connect to the main frame, we'll pull everyone into eternity with us. Who knows, maybe that'll be you and Nayanna, too. I know we're close," he professed. "You have to promise to keep all this a secret. We're in this together now. Your powers, coming from the programmers, are the only way we're going to make this work."

"OK, Akhee, I'll hold you to your promise and I'll keep mine, we have no other options. Save us if you're ever able to," Hamasa beseeched.

He had some further questions for Akhee. He wanted to know how his father was able to trick him, and so many, even Harold, into believing he was God. Once he had finished, Hamasa and Nayanna headed back to their city of dreams.

"Hold on there, before you leave, I need my book back like you promised!" Akhee shouted.

"What promise? Yes, I understand now how it's all about the book. But I also know you can't do a damn thing about it if I decide to keep it. You can't risk using your powers and losing connection with the inner world, where your dad lives. I think I'll just hang on to this book and you'll just have to come visit when you need it. I've a hunch there's more powers and secrets I need to learn about." Taking Nayanna by the hand he whispered to her, "Come on, Nayanna, we're outta here." Turning back he said, "If I were you, Akhee, I'd live up to the meaning of your name and move closer to where your book will be residing."

As they flew over the US, from New York back to their home in Canada, news spread and people came out of their homes to cheer them on. Hamasa knew it was only a matter of days before Americans joined the fight for freedom, joy, love, and peace.

"So who would've believed we'd be flying around free as a kite?" Nayanna laughed delightedly. "Your boyhood dreams are coming true in ways you could never have imagined, Hamasa. I'm so proud of you. I love you so much. I want you to know, I'm here for you, willing to give my life, as you are, for the sake of humanity. Your parent's are going to freak to see you flying around. So by the way, how soon can you make the President of the United States cooperate with what we are trying to do?" Nayanna asked as she and Hamasa had one last smooch as they flew over their favorite city of Vancouver; yes, they took the long way home.

"I think we'll have a referendum." Hamasa looked deep into her eyes. "And I'm pretty sure the good people of America will agree it would be in everyone's best interest if their President was playing miniature golf on the cruise ship we've prepared for people who refuse to do what's best for humanity.

"With him out of the picture there'll be renewed hope that we can save the world from the apocalyptic effects of climate change, too. Once we solve that problem, then we can get back to tweaking the software that operates all of us, then everyone can safely run free again."

"OK, sounds fair." Nayanna smiled. "You'll be free to spend

more time with me then!" she stated, as they landed on Grouse Mountain to take in the view of the Frazer Valley and the city of Vancouver they loved so much.

Hamasa kissed the tip of her nose. "Yes and we'll have more of this romance," he said. "So how many kids are we planning on having, and when do you think we can start getting to work on that project?" He chuckled.

"Ha-ha, give me a kiss."

Hamasa happily obliged.

"Wow," Nayanna said, coming up for air, "look at this beautiful world we live in. The stars are so amazing. Gets me thinking…umm…so if aliens with super computers created this Universe, then who created the aliens?" Nayanna pondered.

"Now you're using good scientific reasoning," Hamasa replied. "We'll just have to leave that for the scientists to find out. They'll never stop looking until they find the truth – that I'm sure of."

For the moment, together, they had peace. Their families would be brought back together in truth. As Hamasa breathed in the light perfume of Nayanna's hair and Nayanna breathed the special sweet ambrosia Hamasa emitted, they each knew that whatever they had to face in the future, they had found Heaven on Earth: embraced in the eternal here and now.

FANTASY, SCI-FI, HORROR & PARANORMAL

If you prefer to spend your nights with Vampires and Werewolves rather than the mundane then we publish the books for you. If your preference is for Dragons and Faeries or Angels and Demons – we should be your first stop. Perhaps your perfect partner has artificial skin or comes from another planet – step right this way. If your passion is Fantasy (including magical realism and spiritual fantasy), Metaphysical Cosmology, Horror or Science Fiction (including Steampunk), Cosmic Egg books will feed your hunger. Our curiosity shop contains treasures you will enjoy unearthing. If you have enjoyed this book, why not tell other readers by posting a review on your preferred book site.

Recent bestsellers from Cosmic Egg Books are:

The Zombie Rule Book

A Zombie Apocalypse Survival Guide

Tony Newton

The book the living-dead don't want you to have!

Paperback: 978-1-78279-334-2 ebook: 978-1-78279-333-5

Cryptogram

Because the Past is Never Past

Michael Tobert

Welcome to the dystopian world of 2050, where three lovers are haunted by echoes from eight-hundred years ago.

Paperback: 978-1-78279-681-7 ebook: 978-1-78279-680-0

Purefinder

Ben Gwalchmai

London, 1858. A child is dead; a man is blamed and dragged through hell in this Dantean tale of loss, mystery and fraternity.

Paperback: 978-1-78279-098-3 ebook: 978-1-78279-097-6

600ppm

A Novel of Climate Change

Clarke W. Owens

Nature is collapsing. The government doesn't want you to know why. Welcome to 2051 and 600ppm.

Paperback: 978-1-78279-992-4 ebook: 978-1-78279-993-1

Creations

William Mitchell

Earth 2040 is on the brink of disaster. Can Max Lowrie stop the self-replicating machines before it's too late?

Paperback: 978-1-78279-186-7 ebook: 978-1-78279-161-4

The Gawain Legacy

Jon Mackley

If you try to control every secret, secrets may end up controlling you.

Paperback: 978-1-78279-485-1 ebook: 978-1-78279-484-4

Printed and bound by PG in the USA